DESE

The only way Corey could get herself on to Fraser Mallory's expedition into the Kalahari Desert was to disguise herself as a man—but she really couldn't expect her disguise to remain undetected for long; nor was it. But the subsequent problem that faced her was quite different from the ones she had expected!

Books you will enjoy
by ROSEMARY CARTER

KELLY'S MAN

It was Kelly's fiancé's fault, not hers, that George Anderson had been injured—but it was Kelly who was doing her best to make amends, helping George's wife to go on running their hotel in the Drakensberg mountains. How galling, then, after all her efforts, that Nicholas Van Mijden should persist in thinking of her as just a spoiled rich girl!

MAN IN THE SHADOWS

Stacy knew that the mysterious 'Brett', whom she had encountered on a lonely part of the Natal coast, was in fact her husband Greg, who had lost his memory. Should she tell him who he really was—when it also meant telling him what a disaster their marriage had been from first to last?

MY DARLING SPITFIRE

When Siane decided to join her fiancé on the South African game reserve where he worked, she thought it would be a pleasant surprise for him. But she hadn't realised just how remote Crocodile View was—and she hadn't bargained for the fact that the only way she could get there was in the company of that *maddening* André Connors!

RETURN TO DEVIL'S VIEW

To please her fiancé, Jana had come to Cape Town, to Devil's View, to try and find some vital information. But she could only succeed in her search if she took the job of secretary to the enigmatic Clint Dubois. It was clear that Clint suspected her motives—but was that the only reason she found him so disturbing?

DESERT DREAM

BY

ROSEMARY CARTER

MILLS & BOON LIMITED

15–16 BROOK'S MEWS

LONDON W1Y 1LF

First published 1980
Australian copyright 1980
Philippine copyright 1980
This edition 1980

ISBN 0 263 73342 4

Set in Linotype Baskerville 11 on 13 pt.

Made and printed in Great Britain by
Richard Clay (The Chaucer Press), Ltd., Bungay, Suffolk

CHAPTER ONE

IT was raining as Corey parked her car in the carport and hurried towards the house on the wooded slopes of Table Mountain. The mist which covered the summit and crept down the slopes was thick and white and swirling, and the distant sea was a churning mass of grey. The weather was as bleak as her mood, Corey thought, as she fumbled in her bag for her keys. She was glad to be home.

In the kitchen the kettle was boiling, and the tray was set for tea, a sign that her father—in retirement, but still as active as possible in the face of increasing frailness—was already home.

Running a hand through rain-wet hair, Corey entered the living-room. 'Been home long, Dad?' she asked.

His eyes were on a magazine which lay on his lap. 'Half an hour.'

'Just as well. The mist is coming down fast. I had a few nasty moments.'

'Uh-huh,' John Latimer murmured, still without lifting his head.

Normally he awaited Corey's return with eager impatience. His behaviour today was decidedly odd. Curiously Corey looked at her father. It was a long time since she had seen him quite so absorbed. 'Interesting article?' she asked.

'Yes.' For the first time he looked up, and she saw that his expression was wistful. 'Fraser Mallory is leading an expedition into the desert.'

'The Kalahari?'

'A little to one side of it. Look, Corey, there's a map....'

She went to his chair and looked over his shoulder. The map was small but concise. It showed a piece of land in the south-western part of Africa, a vast and lonely tract of land almost entirely devoid of names. This was the Kalahari Desert. John Latimer's finger was on a narrow shaded portion which adjoined it.

Gently Corey put a hand on her father's shoulder. The map was one which would mean little to the average person, but Corey had been raised on tales of the desert. All her life she had heard of paintings on rock, and long thirsty marches, and solitude coupled with the excitement of discovery. She understood what this article meant to her father.

'You knew about this expedition?' she asked softly.

'No.' His tone was sad rather than bitter. 'I'm past the age of being invited to join in this kind of thing.'

Usually he did not mind. John Latimer's life had been a full one. The expeditions he had taken part in were numerous. His discoveries, coupled with the articles he had written about them, had brought him a certain amount of acclaim. Yet Corey knew he had one regret.

'You're thinking of the frieze,' she said softly.

'Yes.' He turned to her. 'It's there, Corey. It's right there, in that strip of desert bordering on the Kalahari.'

She was silent a few moments, studying the weather-worn face alight now with an enthusiasm which she remembered from her childhood. 'You're so certain, Dad?'

'As certain as a man can be of anything which he hasn't actually seen with his own eyes,' he said abruptly.

'And you'd like a record. Photos. . . .'

'It would round off my book.' He paused. When he went on his tone had become musing. 'It's what I've needed all this time, Corey. The animal frieze would be the final touch to all my research. The manuscript has been ready for months now, and yet I've held back. It's almost as if I'd been waiting, as if somehow I knew. . . .'

'That Fraser Mallory would be making a trip into the desert,' Corey finished for him.

A wry glance. 'Absurd, isn't it?'

'No,' Corey said cautiously. 'Think there's a way you could turn this expedition to good purpose?'

'Not a chance.' Her father's lips tightened. 'Even if my age were not against me, I'm the last man Fraser would want in his team.'

So the old animosity was still alive. Corey reflected on all she had heard of the expedition in which her father and Fraser Mallory had been partners. It had taken place at least ten years ago, when she had been a child of no more than twelve, and she no longer remembered the details of the incident as told to her by her father. There had been an argument, she recalled. It had had to do with the frieze. Even then it had been her father's overriding ambition to study and record it.

They had been on the verge of finding the painting—or so her father had thought—when the weather had begun to turn, and Fraser Mallory had insisted on starting the trek out of the desert. Her father had protested, he had even tried various tactics in an attempt to stall for time. But Fraser had been adamant. The ensuing disagreement—one which Fraser had won—had been violent. Even more violent than she had understood at the time, Corey now realised.

'Suppose I join the expedition?' She said the words tentatively, unthinkingly almost, without proper consideration.

'You?' Her father looked at her, his expression startled. After a moment he relaxed and gave a short laugh. 'Sorry, love, for a moment I didn't realise you were joking. Even if it weren't impossible, you'd have no more of a chance with Fraser than I would.'

She looked at him disbelievingly. 'Because I'm your daughter?'

'That too. But mainly because you're a woman.'

'He doesn't like women?' she asked curiously.

'Oh, he gets his fun when he wants it. And he can be a charmer where women are concerned,' her father said grimly. 'But Fraser has little respect for the female sex in itself. His mother was a fragile butterfly of a person, pretty enough, but entirely unable to cope with the demands of her family. She left Fraser to his father when he was very young, and married a man who could afford to indulge her every whim.'

'And he's condemned all other women ever since?' Corey was incredulous.

'Something like that.' John Latimer was looking at the map once more, and his voice had become vague. 'My God, love, I know that frieze is there. It's just waiting to be found. I'd give everything I have for a decent set of photos for my book.'

Corey left him poring over the article and went to the kitchen. As she began to make supper all thoughts of the animal frieze and the trip into the desert left her. It was late and she was hungry, and she had problems of her own to sort out in her mind. As yet she had not told her father about the confrontation with Eric Hogan. She needed to think things out before she did so.

Normally the supper hour was filled with talk as Corey and John discussed the day both had spent, but for once the meal was silent. Father and daughter were each occupied with thoughts of their own.

John went to bed early. Corey's smile as she

kissed him goodnight hid her pain. It worried her to see her father grow visibly older. His face was thinner than it had ever been, and he had little of the energy he had once possessed in such measure. She did not need a doctor to tell her that her father no longer had the stamina to withstand the rigours of a desert expedition.

When she had finished in the kitchen Corey settled herself in front of the television. It was weeks since she had watched a programme of any kind. So much of her time had been spent with Eric Hogan that what spare evenings there had been she had used to catch up on neglected chores. There were tasks now that needed doing, but she was in no mood for them.

She watched ballet until she found her concentration waning. *Swan Lake* was beautiful, but it was fantasy. Her own problems were very real. She could not hope that they would vanish merely because she tried to focus on something else.

The six weeks with Eric Hogan had been exciting. Eric was handsome, attentive, fun to be with. Corey, a rising model in the Cape Town fashion industry, had never been short of men who wanted to take her out, but Eric had been unlike the other men she had known. He was a film producer, and the sparkle which was part of his work was also part of his personality.

Corey never knew what to expect when she was with him, but she did know that she would have a good time. Eric took her to the restaurants and the night-clubs where the well-known congregated, and she never ceased to be astonished that he was recognised and fussed over wherever he went. People asked for his autograph. Women ignored the fact that he was not alone and flirted with him shamelessly.

Once the flare of a flash-bulb exploded before her eyes. A few days later a picture appeared in one of the local papers. It showed Eric and Corey at a table. In front of them was a bottle of champagne and two glasses and their two heads were close together. Corey's smile held a special quality that might have been taken for rapture.

She remembered the moment at which the picture had been taken. Eric had been telling her an anecdote; it was noisy in the nightclub and she had leaned towards him in an effort to catch his words. The photograph suggested a different mood altogether. The average reader would see only two people who were utterly absorbed in each other—the girl being even more caught up than the man. The caption which accompanied the photo read, 'A lasting romance for playboy Eric?' It went on to give Corey's name and a few words about her career.

While resenting the intrusion into her personal life Corey had not been unduly worried by the photograph. Eric Hogan was well known enough to be a newsworthy target, and gossip items were frequently unkind in their choice of words. She did not mind that her name was linked with his, for she was more than half the way to falling in love with him, and with each day that passed she became more certain that her feelings were reciprocated.

When he asked her to spend a week with him on the yacht of a friend she was in a dilemma. Part of her wanted to accept. The thought of being alone with him for so long was sweetly tempting. Till now their physical contact had been limited to kisses—expert kisses which she had enjoyed—but the invitation implied a change in their relationship, and there was a part of Corey, a strongly moral part instilled in her by her parents, which was not ready for such a change without marriage.

As gently as she could, she declined. Eric was astonished. It was as if he had never imagined it possible that a girl could resist him. He recovered himself quickly, and was more gallant than before. But there was a moment, just before his good manners took over, when Corey saw derision naked in his eyes.

He still took her out, but their dates became less frequent. He was busy, he told Corey; a film was nearing a point of crisis. She wanted to believe him, and so she did. It was only today that she had discovered the truth. It was told to her baldly, by another model, without any thought for her feelings. Eric was seeing an actress, and the girl had spent the week with him on the yacht.

The lunch date had been planned a few days earlier, and Corey's first instinct was to put it off. She was dialling Eric's number when she thought better of it. She could not let him be condemned by someone else; he must tell her the facts himself.

For once the charm of the restaurant, with its view over False Bay, was lost on her. As they sipped their cocktails and Eric entertained her with an outrageous incident which had happened on the set that morning, Corey forced herself to relax. It was only when they began their meal that she told him, as calmly as she was able, what she had learned.

'What did you expect?' he countered after a long moment. His glance moved away from eyes which were wide and violet and steady despite the pain in their depths. 'I'm not celibate, Corey. What you seem to treasure so highly other women can't wait to give.'

'You could have told me.' Her voice was very low.

'Why?' This time he made no attempt to hide the derision she had seen once before. 'I owe you nothing. I made no commitments. I'm not that kind of man, Corey.'

She didn't answer. There was a dryness in her throat which would have prevented speech even if she had been able to think of the words. All she wanted was to leave the restaurant. Blindly she put down her fork and knife and was about to bend for her bag, but a hand checked her movement. To an onlooker the touch might have seemed playful, but

Corey felt the cruelty of the grip.

'Stop being a fool.' His voice was low, meant only for her ears. 'We're being watched. You can't walk out on me.'

And let his public know what one woman thought of him? Eric did not deserve her co-operation. But she wanted a scene as little as he did. Somehow Corey summoned the will-power to take up her knife and fork once more. After a few moments Eric began to talk again, show business talk, bright and brittle, just as if nothing had happened between them, but her numbed mind took in nothing that he said.

Lunch ended, it was back to the bright lights and poised smile of a fashion model's world. By the end of the afternoon Corey felt as if each facial muscle was stretched to breaking-point.

Now, alone, in the snug dimness of the living-room, she was able to relive all that had happened. She was able to think. She switched off the television and curled up on the sofa. Closing her eyes, she rubbed her hands lightly across tired lids. The particular movement was one which a model learned not to make for fear of stretching sensitive skin. But oh, what relief it gave!

It was strange how one thought led to another. She would not see Eric again, that much was obvious. But it came to Corey that more changes were needed in her life. She knew, quite suddenly, that she no longer wanted to be a model. Subconsciously she must have known it for some time, but perhaps the weeks with Eric had obscured what must have been a growing disenchantment with her career.

It was only now, as her thinking broke down barriers in her mind, that Corey could admit to herself that she did not have the dedication of a true model, that she was bored with the long hours and the discipline and the monotony. She knew too that more and more she found herself wondering what life would be like on the other side of the lights. Photography had been her hobby for so many years that somehow she had never considered making it a career. Was it too late to enter a new field?

Go slowly, she thought, go slowly. Before giving up one career only to plunge into another which might be wrong for her too, she must be certain that she knew what she was doing. She needed a break, a break from work, from the people she knew. A break from surroundings where there were too many things to remind her of her shattered romance. A break from everything which would prejudice her decision. She had had some leave due to her for weeks, but because of Eric she had not taken it. What better time to make use of it than now? Where could she go? she wondered. Dozens of places came to mind; the Cape and its lovely surroundings were a haven for tourists. Yet it seemed important she go somewhere she had never been before.

Restlessly she sat up, and her eyes fell on the magazine which her father had left on his chair.

Almost without thinking she reached for it and turned the pages till she came to the article he had been reading.

The article was illustrated. There were photos of rock strata and one of ruins. There was a picture of a bushman painting, a conventional scene which Corey glanced at only briefly.

There was also a photograph of Fraser Mallory, and Corey studied it thoughtfully a few moments before turning to the article itself.

The gist of it she knew already. Fraser Mallory planned to lead an expedition into the desert. Besides being a farmer, he was also a geologist, and he had been commissioned to research the rock strata of certain desert regions. The expedition was still in the planning stages. The men who would make up the team had not all been chosen. Scientists were needed, and experts in certain fields. A photographer was needed, one who would work closely with the leader, and who would record the findings of the team on film.

A photographer.... With a strange sense of excitement, of anticipation almost, she re-read the paragraph.

Then her gaze was drawn once more to the picture of Fraser Mallory. The face that seemed to stare up at her was lean and tanned and stern-featured. The eyes were dark and intelligent, the mouth was firm above a broad chin. It was not a handsome face in the way that Eric was handsome, but it was an arresting face with an impact uniquely its own.

Corey had always known that Fraser Mallory was younger than her father. Now she saw that the difference in their ages was even greater than she had imagined. Judging by the picture the man was in his mid-thirties. He could have been no more than twenty-five when her father had known him. He must have been more exceptional than she had realised to have led a team at that age. An exceptional person in more ways than one, it seemed from the article, this man who could inspire respect in men and who had no respect for women.

Putting down the magazine, she went to the window. It was too dark to see the sprawl of houses against the mountain and the sea that lay beyond. It was still raining, and the smell of moist air was strong. It was a smell she liked; it would be rare in the desert.

'Perhaps I could join the expedition,' she had said to her father, and he had treated the words as a joke. Had she been joking when she had said them? Yes ... and no. For at the back of her mind there might have been already the desire to leave Cape Town and to steep herself in entirely different surroundings for a while.

What better place than the desert? In the vastness and the solitude of that strange land she might eventually come to terms with herself. By joining the expedition she would be achieving another purpose also. If the animal frieze existed, and her father was so certain that it did, then she would make it her business to find it and record it so that it could be included in the book which was so near completion.

She thought of her father, his face lined and his hair grey, and was swept by a wave of tenderness. John Latimer was a shadow of the man who once had explored the lonely places of Africa with a zest which had led to important discoveries. Most of his life had been devoted to learning more about the origins of the ancient people who had inhabited the continent. All that he had found and learned and recorded was reflected in his book.

Corey, who had typed most of the manuscript, thought sometimes that its very fabric was part of the man who had written it. Each photograph, each carefully pencilled sketch, was a loving and painstaking memento of a man who had made his career his life.

For some time now it had been as good as completed, and still her father had hesitated to regard it as such. It was as if he had been convinced that somewhere, somehow, he would still come across the one record which would make everything else fall into place.

Would she take part in the expedition? Yes! said something deep inside her. She had known about it only a few hours, but already she knew that she wanted to go on this trip more than she had ever wanted anything in her life. *Could* she take part?

That was another matter altogether.

No chance, her father had said—on two counts. She was Corey Latimer, and the name Latimer was anathema to Fraser Mallory. And she was a woman, and women had no part in the leader's scheme of things.

Corey left the window and took up the magazine once more. The strong stern-featured face looked at her from the flatness of the page, and it seemed to her that a challenge was in the eyes.

'I *will* go,' she said aloud.

She laughed, quite suddenly, the sound light and lovely in the empty room. Then she went to her room and began to make her plans. It was a long time before Corey fell asleep that night, but by the time she did she knew what she would do.

Next morning she woke with a sense of purpose. The impulsive decision of the night before did not seem fanciful in the light of day. If anything, she was more determined than ever to put her plan into action.

Tomorrow or the next day she would drive to Fraser Mallory's sheep-farm and apply for the job of field photographer. But first there were things she must do. She could not approach him as Corey Latimer; he would reject her outright if she did. The face in the picture showed a man who would be unmoved by pleas or tears or any other ploys of a feminine nature.

She would approach him as Colin Larson. She

would take with her a portfolio of her finest photographs, and they would discuss the matter on a man-to-man basis.

It was fortunate that she was tall, Corey reflected, as she studied herself in the mirror. A halter-necked sun-dress showed her very feminine curves to perfection, but with it she was slim. With the right clothes and a few careful tricks she would easily pass for a man.

Twenty-four hours later she studied her appearance again. She was satisfied with what she saw. The trousers, which she had had to shorten just a little, were well tailored and smart. The striped shirt fitted her snugly, yet was just loose enough to hide the evidence that she was a woman. The long dark hair of the model had been cut, not too short, but in a length which many men favoured. Square no-nonsense glasses covered eyes that were almost violet, and a moustache, as authentic as any she had ever seen, was pasted carefully over her upper lip. 'Colin Larson,' she said to the reflection, 'you are a fine-looking man, and woe to anyone who dares to say differently!'

John Latimer had already left for the city when the slim figure, flat portfolio under one arm, slipped out of the house and into the car-port. Corey had timed her departure with as much care as she had chosen her costume. Until the job was hers her father would know nothing of her plans.

She drove slowly down the steep winding mountain bends, quickening her speed as she came at last to the national road leading into the interior. Soon the city was left far behind, and after a while even Table Mountain, with its great cloth of white mist, faded from sight.

She tried to relax as she drove. It would take time to reach the farm, which was situated more than a hundred miles north of the city. Before leaving she had made two phone calls. One had been to the agency where she worked, to say that she would not be in that day; with no important assignments lined up she had known there would be no objections. The other call had been to Fraser Mallory, a precaution to ensure that she would not be driving this distance only to find that he was away.

The further she travelled from Cape Town, the better she understood why the man she was going to see could adjust so easily to desert conditions. The Cape Peninsula, that narrow strip at the southern most part of Africa, was bordered by sea. It was a place of green and purple; a land of forests and vineyards and long golden beaches whose loveliness attracted tourists from far and wide.

As Corey travelled north she began to see another part of the Cape, a region of wide open spaces, a land that was dry and hot and ideal for sheep-farming. Almost a semi-desert this, Corey thought, and understood why the people who farmed here were often a tougher breed than those who lived in the city.

She had been on the road quite some time when she began to look for the turning to Mooifontein—fountain of beauty in English. A dusty side-road led to a pair of big iron gates. Corey got out of the car to open them, drove through and closed them before continuing on her way. As she took the wheel once more her hands shook just a little.

On that first day at Mooifontein Corey was too keyed up to take in much of the lands through which she drove. Dimly she was aware of a vastness which seemed unlimited, of short-scrubbed veld where sheep grazed in their thousands. But the sheer magnitude of the place did not impress her as it might otherwise have done, for the conscious areas of her mind were tense with anticipation, taut with the sense of challenge.

The farmhouse itself was two miles from the gates. She came upon it quite suddenly, nestling in a copse of willows beside a small stream. The house was big, much bigger than she had expected, built with a classic Cape Dutch beauty which took her by surprise. She had not expected the home of the stern-faced adventurer to be quite so lovely.

If she was surprised, she was shaken too. Perhaps the man was more of an enigma than she had expected. Now that she was here her confidence was ebbing and she wondered if she was mad to think she could get away with what Fraser Mallory would regard as a cheap feminine trick.

For a moment she was tempted to get into her car

and drive back the way she had come. Her hand was on the ignition, about to turn the key, when quite involuntarily her mind went to her father. She could see him in his chair by the fire, his eyes wistful and tired but hopeful still. The hand left the key, slim shoulders squared, and Corey opened the door of the car and walked towards the house.

The interview took place in the study. Fraser Mallory sat at a big stinkwood desk. He was writing. He did not lift his head immediately as a servant showed Corey into the room, and she saw that he was absorbed in his work.

At length he looked up at the slim figure just a few feet inside the room. He stood up and walked around the desk. 'Mr Larson,' he said pleasantly.

Corey stood quite still as he came towards her. An odd paralysis had attacked her limbs, so that for a moment she could only stare in shock at the man who towered above her.

'Mr Larson?' he repeated.

Corey swallowed hard. She saw the curious expression in the dark eyes, and the hand that was held out to shake hers. As her head cleared she knew she must get a grip on herself, quickly. She put out her own hand, and in her deepest voice she said the words she had rehearsed. 'Mr Mallory. Good of you to see me.'

The hand took hers. The grip was strong, solid, a man shaking hands with another man. There was no reason why the touch should produce a tingling sensation which shot through her palm and up her arm. No reason at all. She made her own grip as forceful as she could, then withdrew her hand.

She followed him to the desk, glad to sit so that she could compose her trembling limbs, glad also to have the reassuring width of the desk between them. The moment when she had been unable to speak had unnerved her badly. Her reaction had been totally unexpected. Admittedly, she had been a little scared of the meeting. Normally one would not trifle with the man in the picture. But she knew that her reaction had not stemmed from fear. Appallingly, Corey recognised that what she had felt was a response to an encounter with the most compellingly attractive man she had ever seen.

'You'll have something to drink?' she heard him ask.

Her throat was so dry that she would have welcomed a long cool orange juice, but that would arouse his suspicions immediately. A man who had driven so far would want a beer, and Corey had never acquired the particular taste. 'Thanks, but no,' she smiled.

'Right. In that case, shall we talk.' It was a statement, not a question. Fraser spread his hands on the desk in front of him. They were long and tanned and well shaped, Corey noticed, much like the rest of him. 'You want to join my expedition.'

'As a photographer.'

'You've brought some of your work with you?'

'Yes.' It was easier to handle the conversation now that it had become more businesslike. She handed the cover across the desk.

With his head bent over her work, it was safe to study him. She wondered how she could have been quite so shocked a few moments ago. She had seen his photograph after all, and had known what to expect. He did resemble his photograph—the shape of the mouth, the slant of the dark eyes, even the thrust of the head above the strong column of the tanned throat. But the photograph, for all its accuracy, was a thing of paper; it did not reveal the virile maleness which this man seemed to possess in such measure. Nor did it do justice to the air of power and authority and the ruthlessness which she sensed existed beneath the surface veneer of politeness.

Her father had spoken often of Fraser Mallory. He had mentioned all the qualities which it had taken his daughter just a few minutes to see. But he had been a man describing another man, and too late Corey understood that in a woman's eyes there was a difference. If she could still withdraw her application, she would do so—not from fear that she could not do the job justice, or that she would not be able to cope with her subterfuge; there was fear, yes, but of something much deeper, more complicated. A fear which Corey recognised yet was reluctant to analyse too deeply.

Fraser Mallory put down the photographs. When

he looked up Corey was ready for him, her face carefully expressionless. 'These look fine to me,' he said.

'I'm glad.'

'How much do you know about the technical side of things?'

'Quite a bit, Mr Mallory.'

They spent several minutes discussing the practical aspects of photography. Corey was glad that she could talk intelligently about light meters and the precautions to be taken in areas where the sand provoked an intense glare: that she knew about developing and printing and which lenses would be necessary. Not for nothing had she accompanied her father on some of his less arduous expeditions. And not for nothing was she thinking of leaving the modelling world to become a professional photographer.

She was beginning to relax when, with an abrupt change of subject, Fraser asked, 'Do you think you can cope with desert conditions?'

There was an inflection in his tone which made her look at him quickly. 'Yes.' She could have left it at that, but something drove her to add, 'Why do you ask, Mr Mallory?'

The grey eyes that studied her face were dark and perceptive. Too perceptive? Corey wondered. Her heart hammered inside her, and she was glad that the glasses hid her eyes. Without them her feelings of panic would be only too easy to read.

'You don't appear very—robust.'

It was an effort to retain an outward appearance of calm. Somehow she managed to meet the steady gaze with a matching steadiness of her own. 'Appearances are sometimes deceptive,' she said lightly, remembering to keep her voice low. 'I can look after myself, Mr Mallory.'

'That's important.' His voice was dry. 'The desert is one place where we all have to look after ourselves.'

Corey took a breath, her fingers curling in her palms. 'Do I have the job, Mr Mallory?'

'Fraser.' He grinned suddenly, the warmth that lit his eyes making him all at once more human. 'If you want it, Colin, it's yours. We leave here in three weeks.'

CHAPTER TWO

THEY assembled at Mooifontein exactly three weeks later. There were ten men in the team. There was an air of informality as Fraser made the introductions. Some of the men had met before, on other expeditions, or at conventions relating to their work. This was not surprising, Corey reflected, for scientists and engineers and geologists all moved in the orbit of their own fields.

During an early lunch and the conversation that

followed Corey was quiet, answering when spoken to but not initiating any conversation of her own. She would have to be very careful, she knew, if nobody was to see through her act. In the circumstances, the less attention she drew to herself the better.

One of the scientists came up and spoke to her. Their conversation was casual, touching only lightly on the trip ahead. His name was Mark. He was soft-spoken, with a gentle, rather preoccupied expression, and Corey found him appealing. In other circumstances she felt that here was a man she would have liked to know better, but glad as she was to be on conversational terms with at least one person, she held herself back. She did not yet dare to be friendly.

She had been only a short time at Mooifontein and in the company of the men with whom she would be living for almost a month, and already she knew that she must be ceaselessly alert. There could be no thoughtless banter, no easy laughter. When she opened her mouth to speak she must remember to keep her voice low. When she moved it must be loosely, like a man.

In her dealings with Fraser Mallory she must be doubly careful.

She had noticed already the air of perceptive watchfulness which seemed to be with him at all times. One false move, one remark that was carelessly feminine, and his suspicions would be aroused. Thus far she had seen only one side of the man. His manner until now had been matter-of-fact yet friendly. Nonetheless Corey knew instinctively that Fraser Mallory would be no easy man to cross. Even had she not learned from her father that he was stubborn and autocratic, her own impressions had been formed at their first meeting. Looking at him now, those impressions were reinforced.

Mark was still talking as Corey glanced at Fraser. He was in the centre of a group. One of the men asked a question, and Corey saw the attentiveness with which they all listened as Fraser answered. She could not hear his words, but his voice came to her, casual yet crisp, friendly yet informative.

It seemed to her that he was even taller than she had remembered him, taller than the other men. Many in the team were good-looking, they had the air of men who were alert and well thought of in their fields. Some were tanned and muscular, indicating that they spent much of their time out of doors. But of them all Fraser was the most distinguished. Corey thought that a stranger, coming by chance upon the group, would have no hesitation in picking him out as the leader. For some reason that thought gave her an inexplicable feeling of pride.

A light aeroplane was to take them on the first lap of their journey. It stood on a private airstrip at Mooifontein, and it was Fraser himself who was the pilot. Corey studied the back of the dark head with new respect as the plane smoothly left the ground.

Apparently Fraser Mallory had even more skills than she had given him credit for. The broad shoulders and the strong thrust of the tanned throat above the collar of the fawn safari jacket indicated the easy confidence of an expert.

Corey had a window seat. As the plane set a steady course northwards, she tore her gaze from the man who was beginning to fascinate her more and more, and looked instead at the land far below, vast and arid and dotted with sheep. She wondered if they were still over Mooifontein, or whether they had already crossed its boundaries.

Mark was in the seat beside her. Once, just after take-off, he had said a few words to her, but the noise of the plane did not make for easy conversation, and after a while he opened a technical magazine and began to read. Most of the men were similarly occupied. Corey herself was in no mood to read. She enjoyed flying; it was something she had always enjoyed. She glanced again at the man who sat at the controls. He would enjoy this too, she thought. Speed and power and the sense of oneness with sky and space would appeal to him.

It came to her that it was strange that she was thinking so much about Fraser Mallory when her mind should be on the days that lay ahead, and on the importance of maintaining her charade. The charade was all-important. If Fraser were to discover her identity his anger would be a terrible thing to witness. The other men would be angry too, resenting the intrusion on their all-male domain. Even her father would not have understood. She grimaced a little wryly.

She had not discussed her plans with her father—he would have tried to stop her. All he knew was that she wanted to be alone for a while after the break-up with Eric Hogan. The relationship between Corey and her father was warm and loving, but it was also loose enough for both parties to be able to go their own ways without a feeling of obligation or guilt. John Latimer assumed that his daughter had decided to take an extended holiday and he would be happy to see her when she returned, but as long as she was away he would not worry. When she returned with records of the animal frieze—if the frieze did in fact exist—his pleasure and excitement would be such that he would soon get over his annoyance at learning the truth.

Below her the scenery was beginning to change. It seemed, from this height, that there was less farmland, more treeless ground. The earth had a look of redness; it glowed in the reflected light of the sun. If they were not already over the desert they could no longer be far away. Corey felt a tautening of the muscles of her stomach. A quick involuntary look at the man who piloted the plane, then she turned her eyes once more to the window.

They landed not long after. No airport this, Corey saw, as she walked with the others from the plane along the narrow airstrip to a small shed with white clay walls and a corrugated-iron roof, just a tiny outpost on the edge of a vast and largely uninhabited land. Manned by a skeleton staff, the strip was a useful junction point for the sheep-farmers and for mining companies whose operations lay in the area.

Beyond the shed three Land-Rovers waited. Fraser Mallory had gone on ahead. Corey saw him talking to a wiry man with faded eyes and a face like beaten leather. She took it that the man was in charge of the airstrip, and that Fraser had been in touch with him about the expedition. Whatever his instructions had been, from the cordial tone of the conversation it appeared that he was satisfied with the way they had been carried out.

Would it ever occur to one of his associates to act contrary to his orders? Corey wondered. Somehow she could not see it happening. If there were natural leaders of men then Fraser was one of them. People would take for granted that they should do as he asked, just as he would see their compliance as being part of the natural order of things.

What of women? Did they too run to do his bidding? Yes, if Corey was to believe her father. And much good it did them. It had certainly not gained them Fraser's respect.

The Land-Rovers were already loaded. Fraser would lead the way in the first vehicle, and Corey was glad when he told her to take her place in the second. For the next few weeks she would see a lot of the man. He did not know that she was a girl, and treated her with the same ease he accorded the other men. Nevertheless she was aware of her own tension when she was near him. A tension, she reflected unhappily, which seemed to have vibrations of its own. If Fraser was to remain unaware of it, the more distance she could put between them the better.

The disturbing awareness of the man was the one thing she had not bargained on, Corey realised, as the Land-Rovers pulled away from the airstrip and began to make their way through a land of scrub and dust and heat. He was so different from all the men she had known until now. She thought of Eric, with his elegant clothes and dapper manner, and she thought of the actors and producers and photographers with whom she normally associated, and whose company she had until so very recently enjoyed. Fraser's inherent toughness, his hard and uncompromising maleness, would make him an unacceptable outsider in the circles in which she moved. She herself did not find him acceptable as a person with whom she could have any other relationship than the one which existed now—which made her awareness of him all the more difficult to understand.

Deliberately she turned her eyes from the vehicle some distance ahead, and stared instead into the silent desert. Had she been very foolish to undertake this venture? shc wondered unhappily. True, her father's heart was in the frieze, but he had never seen it. All his facts regarding its location were based on the words of a tracker whom he had respected. If she came back with the photos of the frieze he would be delighted. Even if she did not, his book could still be finished. Only a dream, a strange premonition that somewhere, somehow, the records would find their way into his hands, had kept a stubborn man from finishing a lifelong work.

Now, when it was too late to turn back, Corey reproached herself for allowing her unhappiness to drive her into joining an expedition under false pretences. Sooner or later she would have got over Eric's disloyalty; there would have been other dates, other men, other relationships. As for her disenchantment with modelling, it would have been easy enough to plan a new career in surroundings more comfortable than the desert.

Impulse had always been an inherent part of her nature, but this time it had led her too far. In her need to break with a life she had grown to dislike, she had not thought enough about the life which would be hers for the next few weeks. She had been so proud of her disguise—who would think that the bespectacled moustachioed photographer might be a young girl?—that she had failed to take into account the practicalities of the situation.

There was more to being a man than a moustache and a pair of tinted spectacles. There would be nights in a shared tent. She would be sleeping in close quarters with men who would not think of turning their backs while they undressed, or of moderating the tone of their all-male discussions. She would have to find ways to dress and undress, to bathe, to take care of details of hygiene that were purely feminine. Could she really hope to live in proximity with so many men and keep hidden the fact that she was not one of them?

Yes! The sudden resolve brought a sparkle to eyes which had made themselves famous in the fashion-world of the Cape for the way in which the changing light and feeling enhanced the beauty of a gamine face. She *could* do it. If there was no turning back, there were also no alternatives. She would do it, and she would get away with it.

By the time the leading Land-Rover drew to a halt, Corey's confidence had been restored to the point where she could take part in a group conversation without fearing that at any moment her disguise would be uncovered.

They had stopped beside a pan, a low depression in the earth which was filled with water. A copse of hardly-looking trees stood to one side, affording some shelter from the heat. More important, it would also give protection from the cold. In the desert, Corey knew from her father, the earth lost heat quickly with the setting of the sun, and the nights could be freezing.

Already the sun was beginning to set. Huge and round, it was a flaming ball of fire hovering over the horizon. Accustomed as she was to the loveliness of an African sunset, Corey had nevertheless only rarely seen anything quite so spectacular. Absorbed in the sheer magnificence of the sky, she did not notice that the men were putting up tents.

'Quite something, isn't it?' A vibrant voice sounded just behind her.

Corey spun round. As she looked up at the man who towered above her like some ancient statue, his granite-like face warmed by the rays of the setting sun, she felt a trembling seize her body. Her throat was suddenly very dry, a dryness that owed little to the dust and heat of her surroundings. Dimly she was aware that he had spoken, that it was necessary for her to answer lest she arouse his suspicions. Swallowing hard, she said, 'It certainly is.'

Something of her difficulty must have got through to him. She saw his eyes narrow, but his voice was casual. 'Anything wrong, Colin?'

She made herself stand very still, so that he would not notice the trembling that was hard to control. She squared her shoulders and made her voice even lower. 'Nothing at all. I was just thinking what a picture it would make.'

'More suited to oils perhaps than to the camera. We have to hurry with the tents, Colin. Once the sun disappears it gets dark fast.'

'Of course.'

As she joined the group of men at the Land-Rovers Corey realised that she had made her first slip. Such a simple slip too. In the life she had left behind it was the men who put up the tents while the women attended to the cooking. Without thinking, she had stood back now.

She would have to be constantly on the alert, she resolved, as she went to the nearest group and put a hand to the canvas. Men's work was her work. If she had never put up a tent, she had been on enough camping trips to know how it was done. For the rest, it was just a question of unobtrusive watching. She would observe how the men did things, and then do the same.

'Shirking already?' a nasal voice drawled.

Corey kept her eyes down for a long moment. She did not need to look up to recognise the speaker as Boyd. Boyd was a weather-man. Almost as tall as Fraser, he was crude and rather rough-looking. She had sensed contempt in his manner earlier that day, at Mooifontein, when the introductions had been made. Then she had tried to dismiss the impression, telling herself that apprehension had heightened her imagination. This time there was no mistaking the derision in his tone.

'Well, little fellow?' The drawl had deepened. Corey understood men well enough to know that this one would enjoy provoking a fight.

'I'm not aware of shirking,' she said levelly. Her voice was low, her shoulders squared.

'Looking at sunsets.' This time the jeer was accompanied by a rough nudge. 'I know your sort,

Larson. You won't last long in the desert.'

He took a step nearer. She could feel his aggression. The quality was as tangible as the hard broadness of his shoulders so close to her own. The man was a bully.

'How did you get into this team anyway?' His breath was hot on her cheek. 'Photographers scarce right now or something?'

It was one thing to dress up as a man, quite another to don the essence of a male personality. How would a real man react to Boyd's baiting? Corey wondered with a flash of despair. Would he wither him with a few well-chosen words? Or was that only a woman's way of dealing with the situation? Perhaps he would punch him very hard in the face. Even if he lost the fight which would follow, he would have proved that he was unafraid. It was an option which was not open to her.

Carefully she said, 'Why don't you talk to Fraser? He'll tell you why he took me on.'

'My God, what a jerk!' Boyd spat in disgust.

A drop of spittle touched Corey's cheek. She drew a deep breath of anger. In that moment she forgot who she was, and the image that had to be hers. Blind to potential consequences, she had lifted a hand to strike Boyd's face when a moderating voice said, 'Leave the kid alone.'

It was Mark. Corey had not seen him approach, she had been too angry to be aware of anything but the loathsome face so close to hers. Through a clearing blur she saw her lifted hand. She stared at it aghast, then dropped it very slowly, trying to hide a sudden trembling as reality flooded back.

Woman-like, she had been about to slap Boyd's face. He would have taken her for a man, and there would have been a fight. In just a few seconds she would have been exposed as a girl.

'Keep out of this!' Boyd had turned to Mark, his tone threatening.

'No.' Corey was surprised to see the gentle scientist stand his ground. 'It's our first day out, man. Don't you know what a fight would do for the general morale?'

Boyd's hands were clenched. 'The kid's a jerk—hooked on a sunset when we're doing all the work! We don't need him.'

'Fraser chose him.' Mark was unafraid. 'Give him a break, Boyd. He's very young, he'll learn.'

Slowly the big fists unclenched. Boyd looked back at Corey, who had remained silent through the interchange. 'Just stay out of my way, jerk!'

'And that, I'd say, is sage advice,' was Mark's wry comment when Boyd was out of earshot. 'Keep out of his way. The man knows his work, that's why he's here, but he's a trouble-maker.'

'Why does he pick on me?' It was hard to keep her voice low when she was trembling.

'Because a pal of his wanted the job and you got in first. But your build is against you too.' Brown eyes flicked her assessingly. 'You're slight for an adult, the type school bullies latch on to, and Boyd is your typical bully.'

'One good karate chop would put him right,' Corey observed with a bravado she was far from feeling. 'But I guess you're right, Mark—I'll keep out of his way.'

CHAPTER THREE

It was almost dark by the time the camp was ready for the night. A fire had been lit. Even after the cooking was done, it would be kept going all night as a deterrent to the wild beasts of the desert.

Seated beside the flickering flames, Corey was able to relax properly for the first time that day. Through the air wafted the aromas of roasting food, and over the buzzing of the night insects the juices of the meat hissed as they dripped into the fire. On the glowing grids lay all the traditional foods of the braaivleis. There were boerewors, the spicy sausage which was its most delicious when cooked over coals; and mealies, long and golden on the cob, and potatoes baking in a covering of silver foil, yet how different this was from any other braaivleis she had ever attended.

A mischievous smile curved Corey's lips as she wondered what her colleagues would think if they could see her now, crouched on the sand in a masculine safari suit, with a bottle of beer at her side and a plate that was piled so high as to make any self-respecting model cringe.

Tonight's supper was special. It was the first camp and the food had been kept in cool boxes until now. Soon they would be on expedition rations—no less satisfying, perhaps, but very different. Corey had seen Fraser's supplies—crates of dehydrated foods that were light and took up little space; stores of water, more precious than gold in a land where fresh drinking water was a rarity.

Around her was the hum of voices. It was a composite sound, deep and masculine. It occurred to Corey that she had never been quite alone in an all-male group, or if she had, it had been consciously, as a woman, a pretty girl who merited flattery and attention. This was different. The men around her were relaxed, at ease. There was no compulsion to be on guard with their language or their jokes. She wondered at their reaction if they were to know that a female invaded their privacy.

Mark was beside her. He was deep in conversation with a geologist. His voice came to her, low and controlled and intelligent. She was glad that he was her friend.

Boyd was a little way away. He was telling a joke, his language deliberately crude, his laughter hearty. Corey's lips tightened. She could only hope that their functions were so different that they would not need to have much contact.

As much as her encounter with the weather-man had upset her, it was Fraser Mallory whose presence she was most conscious of. She watched him move from one group to another, exchanging a few words with each man on his team. She saw the friendliness with which all responded. Even Boyd's manner to his leader was tempered with respect.

Then it was her own turn. As the long lean body squatted beside her Corey tensed, her relaxation instantly gone.

'Heard you had a spot of bother with Boyd.' The comment was quietly spoken. Not even Mark could have heard it.

'I did,' she admitted.

'He's rough, but he's a good man. Try to get on with him, Colin.'

'I will,' she murmured, and wondered if he heard the unsteadiness in her tone. If he did, perhaps he would put it down to the nervousness of an uncertain young boy.

He could not know that his nearness had set her pulses beating uncomfortably faster, or that she was filled with an irrational urge to move closer to him. What was this madness which had taken hold of her? she wondered wildly, especially now when she could least afford it. One of her reasons for coming on this trip was to get away from a man and all he represented. She needed time to be alone, to think, to regain control of herself. The last thing she had anticipated was that she would meet someone whose impact was more devastating than anything she had ever known.

Fraser was still talking. He was telling her a little about the different members of the expedition. His voice was low and friendly, his sole purpose to put her at ease, so that she could function smoothly as one of the team.

Corey's awareness of him was so acute that she took in almost nothing he said. It was too dark to make out the separate features of his face, but it came to her with a sense of shock that she knew them already almost as well as she knew her own mirror image. He was leaning back, his long legs stretched out in front of him, his elbows supporting his weight on the ground. His attitude was one of relaxation, yet even now the aura of power and strength was still with him. It was as much a part of him, Corey realised, as the virile maleness which had made such an unexpected assault on her senses.

Was it irony, she wondered wryly, that the one man who was different from anyone she had ever known should think of her as a moustachioed boy? The thought led to another. Would he have been interested in her if he had met her as Corey Latimer, a girl with shoulder-length dark hair and eyes that could change from deepest light to dark violet depending upon her mood, and a mouth that many a man had wanted to kiss? Would he have felt anything of the attraction that Corey was experiencing now? Would he have guessed that she longed to move a little closer, so that her shoulder could touch his and her head could rest against his chest?

Heavens! she pulled herself up sharply. She could not let herself go on thinking this way. Not only must she remain constantly alert, she could not let herself be drawn into a one-sided emotional involvement which could only lead to unhappiness. Her father's words came back to her. Fraser Mallory had no respect for women, though he was not averse to taking his fun where he could find it. It would not be hard for him to find. Women would always be drawn to this hard attractive man.

Perhaps if they had met under normal circumstances there might indeed have been the possibility of a relationship—but it would have been a relationship based on physical attraction only. It would have had no future. She was a model, and John Latimer's daughter, and Fraser would have despised her even more than the other women he knew.

Despite the warmth of the flames Corey shivered. She was glad when Fraser stood up and moved on. A little bleakly she stared into the darkness.

When the fire began to die, somebody threw on more coal. On this first night in the desert the camp was filled with a sense of excitement. In time the life would become routine, but tonight there was a party feeling. The cloudless sky was ablaze with the light of a million stars, and the air, much cooler now than it had been during the day, rang with the sound of crickets. The fire crackled and hissed, and now and then a red tongue of flame leaped and died. Once, in the distance, there was a low trumpeting sound. Elephants? For a few seconds silence reigned around the fire. It was as if the men were sobered by the reality of the wildness in which they found themselves.

They were talking again when Corey left them. As unobtrusively as she could she walked away from the fire and to the tent which had been allotted to her. Four sleeping-bags were stretched out on camp-beds. She could not have requested a tent for herself; to have done so would have invited suspicion. Only Fraser as the leader of the expedition slept alone.

There was only one way to handle the problem of dressing and undressing. She must get to know the habits of her tent-mates so that she would be sure of privacy when she needed it. Going to bed a little earlier than the others was an obvious solution.

Corey was still awake when the party around the fire broke up and the men came to the tents. Lying very still, she made her breathing slow and regular. Boyd was one of her tent-mates—a pity, that—but short of asking Fraser if she could be moved there was nothing she could do about it. Mark was in the tent too, and Corey was glad. She liked most of the team, but Mark, with his easy gentle manner, made it easy to be friends.

'The pipsqueak needs his beauty sleep.' Corey

recognised Boyd's jeering voice. At the same time someone bumped, very hard, into her camp-bed. Corey did not need to open her eyes to guess who it was.

'Leave him alone.' Mark was firmer than she had heard him thus far. 'Fraser's noticed you picking on him.'

'Why did he need to choose the little squirt?'

'Fraser usually has his reasons.' There was an edge to Mark's tone. 'We've just set out, Boyd. The trip won't be easy. It'll be hellish if there's friction.'

'Little squirt better watch it,' Boyd muttered. There was another jerk of the camp bed and Corey held her breath. Then she heard the man move away.

It was strange to listen as the men prepared for bed. Corey was uneasy, wondering once more how they would feel about the intrusion on their privacy. She could only hope that they never found out. As she listened to the swish of clothes and the thud of dropping shoes, she kept her eyes closed. She had done some strange things in her life, she reflected, but this surely must be the strangest.

Soon the sound of slow steady breathing filled the tent, but it was a long while before Corey slept. Tired as she was, she was also excited and a little overwrought. In the darkness she relived the curious day she had spent—the parting with her father, and the arrival at Mooifontein; the strain of maintaining an image; the flight to the desert and the unpleasantness with Boyd. One memory gave way to another. Last of all she thought of a tall lean man with a tanned face and stern features, whose physical magnetism made her wish very much that he knew she was a woman.

They had been three days in the desert, and Corey was more relaxed now than she had been at the start. Three days of living in camp, of using cameras and enjoying the work. Three days of male companionship. The friendship with Mark had deepened. Boyd was as obstreperous as ever, but Corey had learned to avoid him as much as she could.

Only with Fraser was she tense. Nothing had changed in so far as the leader was concerned. Corey had hoped that she would become accustomed to the sensual maleness of the man, but if anything she was even more aware of him now than she had been at their first meeting. Her reactions to him were quite instinctive. It seemed there was nothing she could do about them except to maintain a bland exterior and a non-committal tone.

In the main the charade she was playing was easier than she had expected. On the first night, when she had gone to bed earlier than the others, she had set the pattern for the nights to follow. In the mornings she pretended to sleep late, getting dressed only when her companions had left the tent. Washing was a problem—there were no baths—but it was a problem with which she coped. She learned to juggle time and chance, and because she was quiet and unobtrusive nobody seemed to observe what she did.

They had not done much travelling. The first campsite had been carefully chosen. It was situated near a pile of rock which had some relevance to Fraser's research. Corey had not imagined that she would get quite so caught up in the work. From her father's studies she had picked up information relating to geology, and as she photographed rock speciments she found herself eager to know more about their origins.

The team worked hard. After three days research one the first site was complete, and today they were moving on. This time Fraser was in the last of the Land-Rovers, Corey was in the middle one, and Boyd was driving in the lead.

She was actually beginning to enjoy herself, Corey reflected, watching the red desert sand make shifting patterns by the roadside. It was satisfying to do work that was different from anything she had ever done before. It was exciting to be in all-male company. These men behaved quite differently from the people with whom she associated in the modelling world. They were more basic, more direct. Pretence and sham and pseudo-charm were missing here. It was as if the absence of females, together with the stringent demands of the desert, had stripped the men of anything that was not genuine, revealing to the full their characters and their personalities. To Corey, securely incognito behind her thick-lensed glasses and the trim moustache, it was a revelation to watch these men go about their work without any artifice whatsoever.

The desert too was a revelation. She had expected limitless heat and sand. The heat was there, and the sand too, a red sand which seemed to take its colour from the flames of the sun.

But there was far more to the desert than sand. There were pans, where stunted trees grew at the shallow water's edge. There were vast tracts of bush, a special desert scrub, resilient and hardy in a land where rain was scarce and where plant life had to draw upon its own resources.

They came to a river where the water reeds grew tall and thick. Corey shivered when she saw the first crocodile, grey and hideous, stretched out in seeming slumber on the hot surface of a sandbank. Mark, seeing her shock, told her that crocodiles lurked here in great numbers, and warned her not to put a hand or a foot into the muddy stream.

In the plains beside the river there was game. At night sometimes Corey had heard the trumpeting of elephants, but she had not realised the size of their herds, nor did she know that the bush teemed with leopards and lions who fed on the buck and zebra when they approached the river to drink. Once the Land-Rovers passed a herd of gemsbok. They stood quite still, horns all pointed the same way, as the vehicles passed.

So far she had seen little of the human life of the desert. From her father she knew that it existed. Sometimes around the nightly campfire the talk turned with a strange reverence to the Bushmen. They were a unique people, Corey knew, tiny in build and yellowish in colour, with a capacity, like the plants and the animals who inhabited this strange world, of husbanding their water resources so that there would always be enough in times of need.

Nor had Corey seen any rock paintings, the basis of her father's research. Yet after only three days she could understand his obsession with this vast and brooding land where the sun burnt down with flames of fire, and where only the strongest forms of life could survive.

In growing fascination she watched the scene beyond the Land-Rover. She did not know how much further they would be travelling that day. It was hot in the vehicle, but she was growing accustomed to the heat, and her interest in all she saw made her oblivious to any discomfort.

The Land-Rover jerked to a sudden halt and a moment later Corey heard a shrill keening wail. Startled, she glanced at the driver, then she leaped out of the vehicle to join the men who were already forming a group at the side of the road.

A little boy knelt in the dust and beside him a goat was stretched out grotesquely. It took only a moment for Corey to take in what had happened.

The little boy had been herding a small flock of goats. One of them had darted into the road just as the convoy was passing, and it had been run over.

Boyd, the driver of the vehicle, tried to jerk the child up. His colour was high as he told the child in no uncertain terms that he should have taken better care of his charges. The effect of his tirade was to make the little boy cry even more bitterly.

Fraser came from the third Land-Rover. Nudging Boyd aside, he took charge of the situation. He bent down and ran a hand over the broken body, and after a moment he stood up. It was evident from his expression that the animal was in fact dead. Gesturing to one of the other men to help him, he pulled the goat out of the road, then he turned his attention to the child.

The little boy's grief was enormous. The keening which Corey had heard from the car was a sound that rent the air. One or twice he beat his head against the ground.

The men stood by uneasily, uncertain what to do. Fraser spoke to the child. He tried English and Afrikaans, and then two African dialects, but his words had no effect, and the keening continued.

'Playing for sympathy!' Boyd's face still burned with colour, and his expression was petulant. 'He wants money.'

Corey spun round. 'Don't you have any feelings?' The words were blurted out before she had time to think.

'Keep out of this, pipsqueak.' There was truculence in the man's voice, even the hint of a threat.

'It was an accident.' Fraser was impatient. Corey saw him delve in the pocket of his safari jacket, then he took the child's hand and put some notes into it.

The little boy raised his face. Save where the tears made a rivulet from the eyes to the corners of the nose it was muddy and dust-stained. A more pathetic sight Corey had never seen. He glanced at the money, then balled his fists and went on crying.

'I'm sorry this happened, but I've given him more than enough to replace the animal.' Fraser sounded troubled.

'Stop thinking about it, chief. The kid will go on crying till he bleeds us dry.' Boyd had lost any shame he might have felt at the start. Corey thought she had never disliked a man so much.

'Perhaps.' Fraser pressed one more note into the dusty hand. 'We do have to get on. Back to the vehicles, everybody.'

'No!' Corey's voice was high and indignant. There was a buzzing in her head as she swept the faces of the watching group with a contemptuous look. 'We can't leave the child in this state!'

She did not think as she bent to the little boy and cradled him against her. She did not think of the dirt that stained her clothes. She did not even stop to think of the effect her behaviour might have on her companions. She knew only that a defenceless child was in distress, that he needed comfort and reassurance.

Holding him against her chest, she fondled the curly head with one hand while she crooned soft words of comfort. No matter that he did not understand what she said, her tone and her manner would communicate themselves to him.

Gradually the little body ceased its shivering, and the distraught crying faded to a whimper. The child was no more than a baby, Corey thought compassionately, a baby who had seen the object he loved torn from him with a finality that was crushing. Money could replace the goat, but only time and love could heal the wound its death had made in a little boy's heart.

When the child was still Corey straightened. They could go back to the Land-Rovers now and continue the journey.

She looked up. The group was silent—a strange silence, shocked and waiting. Glancing from one face to another, Corey began to tremble. The men were eyeing her intently, a wariness in their faces which she had not seen there before. Boyd's lips were twisted in a leer that was frightening and Mark looked uneasy. Fraser's expression was tight and grim. It was Fraser's face which frightened her more than anything else.

Unsteadily she stood up. 'We can go now.' Her throat was very dry. It was an effort to speak at all, yet she had to remember to keep her voice low.

Nobody answered, nobody moved. A little hammer began to pound in Corey's head. She struggled to keep her shoulders squared, her expression unconcerned. 'We can go now,' she repeated.

'In a moment.' Fraser's tone was harsh. 'Come with me.'

Corey shot an appealing glance at Mark, who was still watching her with an expression that was both wary and thoughtful. He did not speak, but she saw the imperceptible shake of the head. 'You're on your own,' it seemed to say.

She had no alternative but to follow Fraser. Suddenly she was very frightened. Yet even through her fear she knew that it was important that the group should not guess her feelings. Lifting her chin, she followed Fraser. She did not need to look back to know that the rest of the men were watching. They would stay where they were. Casual and friendly Fraser might be when he chose, but he was their leader, and such was their respect for him that they would not presume to disturb him when he expected to be left alone.

They sat side by side in the Land-Rover. Corey darted one quick look at the granite-faced man behind the wheel, then looked away. As always she was acutely aware of him. He had never been quite so close to her as he was now; the potent smell of maleness seemed overpowering in the confines of the vehicle, and she wondered if it was just a product of her heightened senses that made her feel that she could reach out and touch the vibrations of aggression and virility and sheer masculinity that enveloped him. Was she crazy, she thought wildly, that even while she feared the coming confrontation she could not help wondering what it would be like to be made love to by this man?

Fraser was the first to speak. 'Well, Colin Larson?' He enunciated each syllable clearly, deliberately.

Corey forced herself to meet his gaze, grateful for the glasses which hid the fear in her eyes. 'Well?' she murmured.

'I think you have some explaining to do.' His voice was soft and smooth and dangerous.

'Because I held up the journey?' she asked flippantly. Perhaps it was not too late to bluff her way out of what looked like an explosive situation. 'The child was upset.'

He nodded. 'Yes.'

'I didn't hold us up very long....' She faltered. It was not easy to speak when eyes like flint studied her with an unnerving perception. 'Besides, the child was distraught.'

'That's not what we're discussing, and well you know it.'

Helplessly Corey looked at Fraser, then at the door. Escape. Only it would not be escape, for there was no place where she could hide.

'Well, Colin'—again the deliberate emphasis on the name—'are you going to tell me the truth, or am I going to force it out of you?'

There was a hardness in his eyes which made her

catch her breath. 'You don't understand,' she said, a little desperately.

'There's a lot I don't understand, you're damn right about that!' Mobile lips curved into a mirthless smile. 'But this much I do understand.' A hand reached for her face and pulled off the moustache with one swift movement.

With a trembling finger Corey touched the skin above her lips. It felt vulnerable and a little raw. 'Fraser....' she began, her voice shaking, then she stopped, unable to think of a single thing to say.

'And now for the rest of the get-up.' The dangerous voice was still without expression. 'Are *you* going to take off the glasses, or shall I?'

She could not bear to have him reach for her again in that mercilessly clinical way. 'I will,' she managed to get out, and removed the glasses.

'So.' Insolently, deliberately, the hard masculine gaze ravaged her face, taking in violet eyes that were shining with unshed tears, soft pink lips that trembled despite all attempts to keep them steady, the little pulse beating too quickly in the hollow of a slender throat. 'Very pretty. Very pretty indeed.' His voice roughened. 'And quite out of place on my expedition. What the hell did you think you were doing, Colin....' He paused, and a strange look entered his face. 'It isn't Colin, of course. What is it—Carla?'

CHAPTER FOUR

'COREY,' she whispered.

'Last name?' He was sparing her nothing.

'Latimer,' she managed.

Something came and went in the dark eyes. She thought she saw him tense, as if in shock, then he relaxed and smiled, and with it became even more dangerous.

'John Latimer's daughter.' It was a statement, not a question. 'So your father put you up to this. Strange, that. I remember him as a stubborn old devil, but I didn't think he was unscruplous.'

'He isn't,' Corey flared.

'No?' very politely. 'Then what do you call this ... this charade?' The last word was spat out with contempt. 'It was meant to deceive.'

'Yes.' Corey curled her fingers into her palms to control her trembling. Fraser was so angry, even angrier than she had expected. 'But you're wrong about Dad.'

'He didn't put you up to it?' The vibrant voice was thick with disbelief.

'No.' She put a hand on his arm, and felt it grow rigid under the touch. For a moment it seemed to Corey that neither she nor Fraser breathed, then

Fraser shook her hand away, negligently, effortlessly, and Corey knew that she had imagined the heightened suspense. Any loss of breath had been solely on her part. As calmly as she could, she said, 'It was my idea.'

'Your father wants a record of the animal frieze—the damned frieze which he doesn't even know for certain exists.'

His perception was razor-sharp. It had not taken him more than a few seconds to understand her purpose in joining the expedition.

'Yes,' Corey acknowledged.

'Then why didn't he come himself?'

'Because you wouldn't have taken him.' A tightening of lips confirmed the truth of the statement. For some reason that gave Corey courage. 'That *is* so, isn't it?'

'Perhaps, perhaps not,' was the non-committal answer. 'He could have tried.'

'No.' She was able to speak with more confidence now. 'Dad isn't well. He's no longer able to rough it.'

If she had expected sympathy it was not forthcoming. In the same hard tone Fraser Mallory said, 'So he decided that you should take his place.'

'No! I told you the decision was mine.'

'One with which he concurred.'

The crispness of his voice, the terseness of his words, brought Corey's head up proudly. 'On the contrary, Dad has no idea where I am.'

There was a moment of silence. Dark eyes were narrowed and hooded as Fraser once more studied the small flushed face just a few feet away from him. Corey was unaware that her eyes were sparkling and had deepened in colour, or that her lips, just slightly trembling, were invitingly kissable. She knew only that the stern-featured man at her side held her fate in the palms of his arrogant hands, and from the look in his face it was evident that he did not believe a word she had said.

'There is so little contact between you and your father,' Fraser said at last, evenly, 'that you can disappear from the scene without letting him know where you're going?'

Corey flinched at the attack. 'I'd heard you were a hard man, that you were arrogant and hard-headed.' Her voice was low. 'I didn't think that you were also petty.'

Well-shaped lips curled. 'Petty?'

'What else do you call your insinuations? My relationship with my father is very loving, very close. But do you think he's the kind of man to let me join an expedition like this one?' She met the hard gaze slowly. 'As far as Dad is concerned, he thinks I'm on holiday on the Garden Route. He also knows that I won't be back for a few weeks.'

'He didn't think that was strange?'

The question brought back the memory of her last meeting with Eric, and the unhappiness that had accompanied it. Something hardened inside her. Turning away from Fraser, she said, 'Dad understood that I wanted to be alone.'

Let me go, she pleaded silently, as she gazed out of the window out at the sun-scorched red sand. Stop this interrogation and let me go. I can't take much more of it. And the thought occurred to her that even more than his questioning, it was the overpowering physical closeness of the man which made her so uncomfortable.

She did not see the hand that reached for her. When long fingers touched her chin, drawing her around to face him, she all but jumped from the seat. Her heart thudded painfully against her ribcage as he forced her to look at him.

'You went to great lengths to join my team.' There was a new inflection in his tone, one which she did not quite understand. 'Was it so important to you?'

She tried to twist from his grasp, and found that she could not. There was a tingling in her cheeks and along her throat which was unnerving and at the same time wildly exciting. Fraser was watching her, his expression a taunt, his eyes mocking her silent appeal. Did he know the effect he was having on her? Yes! He knew. And it amused him.

Her throat was dry, but she managed to clear it. When she spoke it was with dignity and no suggestion of apology. 'You know about Dad's research. He's written a book on the ancient peoples of Africa.

He's been wanting a record of the frieze for a long time.

'He has other photos.' Fraser withdrew his hand from her chin.

'That's true,' she acknowledged quietly, and was aware that her reaction to his withdrawal was not solely one of relief. 'But he has his heart set on this particular one.'

'Stubborn old bastard!' There was a new note in Fraser's tone, not quite anger, not quite censure. Or perhaps a mixture of both coupled with a reluctant admiration, Corey thought disbelievingly.

'That's how you choose to see him.' Violet eyes, wide and troubled, sought grey ones in an effort to find understanding. 'Dad has dreamed of this frieze for years. He knows it's there, he believes in it. If he were a stronger man he would have made his own way into the desert long ago, but he couldn't do it —that's why I had to do it for him. If you had a dream, Fraser, wouldn't you....'

She broke off, realising that she was getting too carried away by emotion. In her mind was the image of a frail elderly man with a dream that kept him alive. In the flesh beside her was a young man who should have understood that dream but didn't. Her impassioned speech had not softened him; rather, the glitter in his eyes warned her that she could not get through to him. With every word she was only making the situation worse.

'You don't understand, do you?' she said through

clenched teeth. 'Or is it just that you don't want to?'

Something flickered in his eyes, and the ghost of a smile touched his lips. 'I understand,' he said quietly. 'I just can't help thinking that John Latimer would have been better served with a son instead of a daughter.'

'So it's true what Dad says,' she tossed at him recklessly. 'You despise women. You hate us!'

'Hate?' A short laugh. 'My dear Corey, I don't hate women. There are times when I enjoy them immensely.' He paused, letting his gaze move very deliberately over her figure, from her breasts down to her hips, sending a flame of colour flooding her face. 'As for despising, let's just say that I haven't met the woman yet who could earn my respect.'

Corey stared at him for a moment without speaking. Looking at the chiselled features in the lean tanned face, she was swept by an overwhelming desire to prove him wrong. Aloud she said, 'So it's true you wouldn't have taken me on if you'd known I was a woman.'

'Of course,' came the cool rejoinder. 'That was why you tried to pass for a man.'

She drew a deep breath. There was no getting the better of this man. Any accusations she might make, however justified, were met with the same cool self-assurance. 'You think women have no purpose,' she accused.

'I didn't say that.'

She heard him chuckle, the sound low and so

sensuous that it set the blood racing faster in her veins. His words could have only one meaning, and at that moment she could think of no adequate answer. Her one thought was to get out of the Land-Rover and back to the company of the others.

She tried to open the door, but he moved quicker than she did. She tried to wrench away from the hands that gripped her shoulders and pulled her to him, but his strength was greater than hers. As his mouth crushed down on hers his hands left her shoulders and moved down her back. His lips were demanding, cruel, possessive. She had been kissed before, but never like this. There was a brutality in his possession which left her breathless. She tried to fight him, but his lips forced hers apart and held her pinned against him. His hands moved over her, moulding themselves to her hips, and despite her resistance she could feel a surge of wild response surging through her.

As he released her, pushing her from him with an abrupt suddenness, she lashed out at his cheek with a stinging slap of her hand. Dimly she knew that her action stemmed only in part from her outrage at the manner in which he had treated her: in the main she was punishing herself for being quite so excited.

'Don't ever do that again.' The mildness of his words were belied by the anger in his eyes.

'How dare you!' She shouted the words at him, oblivious of whether the men some distance away could hear what was said.

'I dare what I like, and you'd do well to remember it.' His voice was like ice. 'Now you know the only purpose women have in my life.'

Corey felt a wave of nausea rising inside her. Somehow she fought it down. She had to get away from here, away from this man who was more devastating in his inflicting of hurt than Eric had ever been. For a moment she even forgot the reason for her journey. Had she been able to think rationally she would still have wanted to leave the desert. If there was no other way to get a picture of the frieze then her father must resign himself to doing without it. But at this moment all such thought was absent; her sole desire was to get away.

'How do I go back?' she asked dully, when she could speak.

'It's a bit late to ask that.' His tone was dry.

'Late?' She stared at him, the blood pounding in her ears as she realised what he meant. 'But surely ... I mean ... well, in the circumstances you'll have to let me go back.'

'I'm afraid that's impossible. We've gone too far to turn back now.' He grimaced wryly. 'If there was an airstrip nearby I'd send you packing on the next plane.'

'The strip where we landed....' Her voice was unsteady.

'Too far away. Every day of the expedition is accounted for.' He looked at her with distaste. 'I expect that's something your feminine mind can't comprehend. There's much that has to be done before the weather turns against us, Corey. The last thing that can be allowed to get in our way is a woman's whims.'

'You mean....' She had to bite back a sob before she could continue. 'You mean you want me to go on?'

'Want?' His lips twisted derisively. 'I don't want it at all. But at this point I no longer have a choice.'

'No!' She threw out the word wildly. 'I refuse to go on.'

'You have no choice either.'

Contempt was etched in every line of the strong-featured face—contempt and an arrogant amusement. Fraser Mallory liked the situation no more than Corey did, but it afforded him a certain amount of satisfaction to see a woman forced to remain in a situation against her will. In that moment Corey hated him as she had never hated anyone in her life before.

'I won't come with you.' Her voice was very low. 'I'd rather walk back the way we've come. I'd get to the airstrip in time.'

His eyebrows lifted sardonically. 'Without water? Because, my dear Corey, if you think I'd give you one drop of our rations you're very much mistaken. Suit yourself, however. If you want to walk, then you're welcome to it.'

She would not last more than a few hours in this

hot thirsty land, Corey knew. Either she would become dehydrated or wild animals would attack her. One way or another, she would not survive.

'And if I stay?' she asked dully. 'What would I do?'

'Photography,' he said crisply. 'That was what I hired you for.'

'Then you do think I can use a camera?' she asked, feeling as if she understood him less all the time.

'Of course.' The hint of a smile touched his mouth. 'If the portfolio you showed me was really your own, you have a good hand with a camera.'

She looked at him tightly. 'In that case, I wonder what all the fuss is about?'

'Sex.'

Just the one word, but in his eyes was a gleam which made her feel all at once very vulnerable, and even younger than her twenty-two years.

'If you're talking about what happened just now. . . .' She shook her head violently, as if to negate the excitement which had coursed through her veins. 'You'll never touch me again.'

'I'll touch you any time I like.'

She stared at him incredulously. 'You don't even like me!'

'Who mentioned liking? You're a woman, Corey Latimer. That's what the game is all about.'

'Oh, no! You don't need me!' Why was she so

breathless? 'According to Dad you can have any woman you want.'

Humour glimmered briefly in the dark eyes. 'So John Latimer has been telling stories. You still don't understand, Corey. We're talking about sex. It just so happens that there are no other females in the team.'

The statement was provocative, calculatedly so, Corey knew that. Which was why it should not have the power to hurt quite so much.

'You don't trust yourself, then?' she asked very quietly, with an outward show of composure.

The look he gave her was enigmatic. 'Did I say that?'

'You implied it.' She bit her lip. Somehow she had let him put her in the wrong again. 'I'm the only girl around here. You don't know if you can handle the situation.'

His laugh was harsh, bringing a chill to a fevered nerve-stream. 'My dear Corey, my emotions are under perfect control. What happened just now had nothing to do with passion, it was quite deliberate.' And, when he had allowed that to sink in, 'The question is—can *you* handle the situation?'

Her earlier uncertainty was replaced by searing anger at Fraser's audacity. She glared at him, eyes blazing, cheeks burning. Was there no end to his sarcasm? 'If you were the last man on earth I wouldn't sleep with you!'

'I wonder. Your body spoke a different tale when

I kissed you.' His tone was soft, malicious. She was still wondering how she could possibly respond, when he went on, 'But you flatter yourself, Corey Latimer, if you think I want to sleep with you. Your father's gossip was true. Thus far my choice of sleeping partners has been my own. No, I was thinking of the others in the team. They realise by now that you're a woman. How do you think they feel about it?'

'I can handle myself,' said Corey, with a confidence she was all at once far from feeling. 'And the men are gentlemen. They wouldn't harm me.'

'What about Boyd?' The question was lightly put.

'He's crude and a bully and he doesn't like me. At least he didn't when he thought I was a boy.'

'And you think his manner will change now that he knows you're a girl?'

'Of course,' Corey said firmly. 'He was antagonistic because he saw me as unmasculine. He'll be glad to know he was right.'

'I wonder,' Fraser Mallory said smoothly, 'if you're quite as naïve as you pretend. I advise you to be very careful of Boyd.'

'You mean you're concerned about me?' Corey asked tartly.

'On the contrary, anything you get you've asked for. My sole concern is with my men.' The eyes that rested on her were chips of ice. 'I have my reasons for not allowing women on male expeditions.' He paused, as if for emphasis. 'You'll be treated just as before. Don't expect your femininity to entitle you to any special privileges.'

'I never did expect it.'

Deciding that there was nothing further to be said, Corey began to open the door.

A long arm reached across her, grasping the hand that held the handle. The movement brought the arm up hard against her breasts, and Corey caught her breath. She sat very still, waiting for the shock which shot through her system to subside. Dimly, through the buzzing in her ears, she heard Fraser say, 'And leave my men alone. Any trouble-making from you—and by trouble-making I mean the usual female ploys—and you'll get a hiding from me.'

Corey turned blazing eyes. 'You'd enjoy that,' she accused bitterly. 'Just as you enjoyed your strong-man stunt a few minutes ago.'

'Precisely,' came the smooth rejoinder. 'I'm glad that we understand each other.'

There was a new atmosphere around the campfire that night. Corey had noticed the difference from the moment she had left the Land-Rover after her talk with Fraser. There had been a new look in the eyes of the men, a different tone to their voices. Corey reflected that if they had taken her for a woman from the start their attitude might have been more accepting. The sudden unmasking seemed to have thrown them.

She was saddened by the change, but philosophical about it too. At most it would not last more than a few hours, she thought. By the time the sun had set and the meat was cooking on the flames the novelty would have worn off.

She was mistaken. If anything the strangeness had deepened. Outwardly the men were calm and friendly, but there was a reserve in their manner which had not been there before. Their language had changed. This was something Corey had expected; while they had thought themselves secure in their all-male domain they had felt free to use words and make jokes which they were embarrassed to voice in female company.

Corey had minded neither the language nor the jokes. Admittedly, they had been on the crude side, but she was no prim miss who felt obliged to put her hands over her ears at the least off-colour remark. Once or twice, it was true, she had flinched. Boyd in particular was given to lewd comments and seemed unable to complete a sentence without using a four-letter word. But even this she had accepted. She had been on minor expeditions with her father, and had heard the language of men under strain. She would have been surprised if this team had behaved otherwise.

Suddenly they were on their best behaviour. Not a word that could be taken as even slightly off colour was uttered. Corey was brought food that had been cooked over the fire, and was not allowed to fetch her own drink. After that she was left alone, as if the men felt she was set apart in some way. If they kept this up she would be in for a lonely time.

They would change, she tried to reassure herself. Today they were awed, a little shocked. Several, she reflected wryly, might be wondering if they had said or done something out of place. She had hoped that the few hours would have been enough to dull the novelty, but was optimistic enough to hope that by tomorrow things would be back to normal. They were still so much at the beginning of the expedition. Days of companionship, of shared living, lay ahead. Unless the men accepted her as one of themselves life would be awkward.

Only Fraser Mallory was unchanged. If the rest of the group, including even Boyd, were awed, Fraser was unconcerned. There was nothing soft or friendly in his tone when he condescended to speak to her. He had made his opinions and her position clear: he was saddled with her, and that was something he could not alter. But he would in no way give an inch because she was a woman.

She could not help thinking of what he had said about the sexual aspect of her presence in the team. Not that he had tried to be flattering or complimentary in any way, she thought wryly; he had paid no tribute to her looks or her physical appeal. That she was a top-flight model would cut no ice with this man. If sex reared its head, he had implied, it would be solely because she was the only woman in the team.

And there he surely was wrong. Corey pursed lips that were still a little bruised, as much from the rough manner in which he had snatched off the moustache as from his kisses. Not one of the men was an adolescent, all would have left wives or girlfriends at home. The mere fact that she was a girl would not be enough reason to form a relationship.

Even if one of the men did show interest in her, nothing would come of it without her own willingness—and that willingness would not be forthcoming. The parting with Eric was still raw.

Corey had joined the expedition with a view to getting away from the complexities of emotional relationships. The last thing she wanted at this moment was to get involved again. If Fraser Mallory imagined she would allow herself to be embroiled in a situation against her will, he had underestimated her. Even with Mark, much as she liked him, she was in no hurry to become involved.

Quite unbidden Fraser's image inserted itself into her mind. There was the tanned face with its chiselled features. There was the power and strength and sheer animal virility of the man. And suddenly he was not just filling her mind; it was as if he was filling her body, quickening her blood and weakening her limbs. Corey let out an exclamation of outrage. Shivering, she huddled closer to the fire.

'Cold?'

Corey turned at the sound of Mark's voice. 'A

little.' She smiled at him through the gathering darkness.

'You should have your sweater.'

'I know—I'll go and get it.'

'There's no need. Take mine.'

Before Corey could stop him Mark was putting a thick wool cardigan over her shoulders.

'That's not necessary,' she protested. 'I could easily go and get mine from the tent.'

'I want you to wear it.' There was a special softness in Mark's tone.

'I....' Corey stilled the further protest. If she had one friend in camp it was Mark. She did not want to offend him. Laughingly she said, 'Last night you wouldn't have given it to me.'

'Last night you were Colin. A very nice young boy, but a male all the same.' She heard his answering amusement. And then, his voice becoming more serious, he asked, 'Corey, is it true what Fraser's told us? That you came on this expedition to get some records for your father?'

'Yes.' She asked softly, 'Do you condemn me for it?'

'Condemn! I could never condemn you for anything.' A hand reached for one of hers and held it. 'I think you're the bravest girl I ever met.' His voice became a little gruff. 'Also one of the loveliest.'

Corey's job had given her contact with men who were polished in manner and appearance. Eric was not the first sophisticated man she had gone out with; he had just happened to touch her heart more than the others. Over the years she had received her fair share of compliments. She had been flattered by some, left cold by others. Yet she had never been quite so touched as she was by the few simple words spoken by a scientist in the darkness of an African desert.

'Why, Mark!' Her voice was soft and warm. 'What a lovely thing to say!'

'And what compliments has our Mark been dropping in the lady's ear?'

Neither of them had seen Boyd approach. As he knelt down beside them, Corey stiffened with distaste.

'Hello, Boyd,' she said lightly. And, in an effort to deflect him, 'Mark and I were talking.'

'So I heard. Quite a little tête-à-tête.' The rough voice was heavy with meaning. 'How about you and me take a little walk, honey?'

Beside her Corey heard Mark's intake of breath. 'No, thanks,' she said lightly. 'I'm feeling rather lazy.'

'Lazy, is it?' A deeper meaning now. 'I could take you to the tent.'

'Boyd!' Mark's exclamation ran out sharp and angry. 'How dare you talk to Corey like that?'

Boyd laughed crudely. 'Take it easy, feller. The girl's no Dresden china doll, she can't be, to get involved in a stunt like this. How about it, honey?'

So Boyd's awe of her, if it had in fact existed, had

worn off quickly, Corey thought. She did not believe Fraser's warning that the man was dangerous. There was no harm he could do her. But it would be as well to keep things cool and stay away from him.

A retort was on her lips, light enough not to be offensive, and yet still making it clear to Boyd that she was not interested in him, when Mark got in first. 'I'll not have you talking to a lady like that.'

'Lady? Not the kind of lady you're talking of, Mark old man. A fun-lady, yeah, who likes to share her tent with men.'

'I'm warning you.' In his anger Mark spoke loudly, the sound carrying over the hiss of the flames and the buzzing of insects. 'Leave her alone!'

'And what what will you do if I don't?'

'Mark, please....' Corey put a hand on an arm that was rigid with tension. The gentle scientist was angry enough to get into a fight, but she had no doubt that Boyd, bully by nature and therefore likely to be more agile with his fists, would be an easy and merciless victor.

'Corey!' A new voice, Fraser, cutting in before Mark could do something foolish. 'I believe Pete has some steak for you. Come and get it.'

She lifted her head and stared at him. It was too dark to see his expression, but she could make out the arrogant tilt of the head. Fraser, Corey decided, had chosen to interfere. He would have to learn that he could not do that. Brightly she said, 'Please thank Pete, but I've eaten already.'

'I see.' Now there was no mistaking the sardonic lift of the eyebrows. But Fraser did not stoop to argue the point. Instead he said, 'Boyd, a word with you, if I may.'

'Trying to break up something?' Boyd's voice was truculent.

'Not at all. Some data that needs a little clarification.' And after a moment, with a new note of authority, 'Boyd?'

'Coming, chief.' The weather-man walked off heavily.

Fraser paused a moment. 'Corey, Mark, a few of the men are starting a sing-song. Why don't you go over and join them?'

'Our chief has a way of manipulating people,' Corey remarked dryly, watching the tall figure vanish in the darkness.

'Perhaps he's right. I'm sorry this happened, Corey.' Mark sounded unhappy.

'Don't think about it,' she advised lightly.

'Boyd is uncouth. It just so happens he's a good weather-man.'

'I understand.'

'But I won't let him talk to you as if . . . as if. . . .'

'As if I were wanton.' Corey managed a laugh. 'It's all right, Mark, I can look after myself.' Before the situation could get too serious she added, 'A sing-song might be fun.'

'I'd hoped. . . .' There was a new inflection in the scientist's tone. Corey caught the hint of disappointment and hurt, then to her relief he recovered himself quickly. 'All right, then,' he agreed, 'let's do that.'

CHAPTER FIVE

ONE of the men had a guitar. As Corey and Mark joined the group on the other side of the fire he was strumming it quietly. The men acknowledged Corey's arrival with cheerful smiles, and as they moved to give her the spot closest to the glowing embers, she was glad to see that they looked a little more relaxed. It was apparent they had been discussing something, and that the conversation had come to an abrupt end with her presence, but she did not mind. After three days incognito she realised that there were certain topics which men might prefer not to discuss in mixed company.

The guitar-player started a tune, and the men began to sing. In the main they were simple songs, campfire songs which Corey knew well. A wave of contentment swept over her as she listened to the low male voices. She loved this life, she thought, far from the bustle of the city, from the artifice of the world in which she moved.

In the little camp on the edge of the great Kalahari Desert life was basic. There was the fire and the braaivleis, there was the aroma of roasting meat and burning coal. Overhead the sky was a brilliant blaze of stars. Lanterns were placed here and there, but their light was just bright enough to encompass the camp—the Land-Rovers and the tents. Beyond the limits of the light was darkness, a mysterious darkness stretching over the vast miles of the desert.

There was magic in a campfire. It was a magic which crept into the hearts and minds of men, so that those who had tasted it once yearned to experience it again and again. Corey thought of her father, alone with his books and his papers in the little house on the slopes of the mountain, and was saddened. Dad had loved this life. How he would envy her if he could see her now!

Mark sat at her side. There was something comforting in his presence and she had taken to him from the start. He had seemed to enjoy her company when she had been Colin. Now that she was Corey, he sought her out too. He could have been offended by her disguise, but he had not been. Of all the men in the group, Mark was the one Corey would have chosen to be her friend, and it was reassuring to know that their friendship was on strong ground. Looking at the firelit face she thought she liked him better than any other man in the team.

Or did she? The revelation hit her so suddenly that it shocked her. And then she thrust it firmly from her. If at first she had liked Fraser, she did *not* like him now. He had an undeniable charm when he chose to exert it. He was also arrogant and ruthless—all the qualities she most disliked in a man. No, she most definitely did *not* like Fraser Mallory.

What then, an irritating little voice in her mind persisted in asking, was the flame that had sparked a response in her when he kissed her? Was it possible, she wondered crossly, to dislike a man and yet be aware of an enormous physical attraction? 'Your body spoke its own tale when I kissed you,' he had taunted her. Unhappily she had to acknowledge that the taunt had held some truth.

It galled her to relive what had happened in the Land-Rover, for in doing so she felt again the torrent of excitement which had gripped her then. She was unable to deny to herself that she had never before felt so alive, so shaken, quite so vibrantly feminine. In the modelling world she was cosseted and made to feel special because she had a face and a figure which lent itself to showing off clothes to their best advantage, but in the seat of the Land-Rover she had been made to feel that she was a woman.

Sex, she thought wryly; Fraser Mallory had said it was something she would have to contend with. Strange that the idea had never entered her mind. In all her planning there had been only the desire to get away from Eric and from the surroundings in which she had known him, together with the anxieties of wondering whether her disguise would be believed. Sex had not been a problem. She wondered now if she had in fact been naïve.

And that thought led to another. Already the night air was growing colder, and there were signs of restlessness around the fire. Soon the men would be turning in for the night.

Until now she had managed to cope with the problems attendant on sharing a tent with three men. If they had wondered at all that she kept different hours from theirs they had made no comment.

But in the space of just a few minutes all had been changed. From the moment they had seen her cradling a weeping child on her lap they had known she was a girl. How would they feel about sharing a tent with her? She glanced at Mark and wondered if the thoughts that passed through his mind were similar to her own. And what about Boyd, and of Pete, the fourth member of the tent? What were their feelings?

It took little imagination to picture the scene when she rose and left the fire. She was tired, she would say casually. There would be a chorus of goodnights, and in some of the voices would be strain. There would be mockery too; Fraser and Boyd would see to that. Tonight she would not need to hurry as she got ready for bed; the men would give her as much time as she required. And in the morning the process would be repeated. Her tent-mates would no doubt be dressed and out of the tent long enough before breakfast to allow Corey to get dressed.

She knew she was in no personal danger, the circumstances were such that nobody, not even Boyd, would dare to touch her. But in a sense the sex aspect might still be present. Perhaps Fraser had been right about that. It would be like something tangible, a heady concept in the mind of every person in the tent.

She lingered a while longer by the fire, then she heard a yawn, quickly stifled. Clearly it was time to move.

'I think I'll turn in,' she murmured to Mark.

The body so close to hers seemed to tense. Then Mark said, 'Corey....'

She caught her breath, wondering what was coming. 'Yes?'

'Oh, nothing.'

'Mark....' Her voice was unsteady. 'Nothing has changed.'

'Corey....'

'No,' she interrupted him quickly. 'Please, Mark, please let me try to explain. As far as I'm concerned, I knew all along that I was a woman and that the rest of you were men, but I found my ways of coping. Nothing happened to offend me or ... or to shock me.' She hesitated, groping for words, sensing that somehow she was putting her case badly. 'I admit it's an unorthodox situation.'

'To say the least,' came the dry rejoinder.

The tone of the rejoinder was so foreign to the Mark Corey imagined she knew that she felt suddenly on stranger ground than before. Somehow she had to get through to him. If she did, then she could also get through to the others.

'What I'm trying to say,' she attempted after a few moments of silence, 'is that nothing has changed. We were all together for three nights, and because my identity was secret nobody gave my presence a thought. Basically nothing has changed. I'm not Colin, but I'm still me, the same person who shared a tent with you previously.'

'In other words'—the same dry tone—'you say it's all a case of mind and attitude.'

'Yes, of course,' she agreed eagerly. 'Mark, you understand, don't you?'

'I understand what you're saying, yes.' In the darkness a hand reached for her cheek, lingering there for a long moment. 'But I don't think you quite understand yourself, Corey.'

'Oh, I do!'

'I'm a man,' he interrupted her. 'And so are Boyd and Pete. And you're a woman, a very lovely woman. Surely you must know what it will do to us to be sharing our sleeping quarters with you.'

'I've been very stupid,' she said at last, slowly.

'Stupid?' He stroked her cheek. 'I said earlier that you were brave.'

'I should have gone about things differently.'

'Yes,' he said quietly, 'perhaps you should have, but you didn't. Even though my nocturnal blood-pressure will never be the same again, I'm glad you didn't.'

'You're talking nonsense, Mark.' Corey's laugh was more like a sob. 'But I hope you'll always be my friend.'

'Your friend?' The strangeness was back in his tone. 'We don't talk the same language, Corey. But yes, I'll always be your friend.'

The hand that had been on her cheek withdrew abruptly. Mark did not move his position on the sand, yet Corey was aware that in a subtle way he had withdrawn more than just his hand, and she was saddened by it.

Unhappily she gazed into the darkness beyond the fire. Some complications she had anticipated, and those she had dealt with. Now she was finding complications of an entirely new kind—had she been very foolish not to give them a thought?—and all at once she was no longer certain how to conduct herself.

Perhaps the answer was really very simple. She had already resolved to play it cool with Boyd. She would be cool with Fraser too, the man who in his arrogance thought that he could intimidate her. That he was successful in that, up to a point, he did not need to know. She would be cool with Mark too, but in a very different way. Mark was one person who must not be hurt. He did not deserve it, and she did not want it.

She glanced at him. A silence had fallen between them—not the comfortable silence which existed between friends, but a silence born of tension. Corey cast in her mind for something to say and could think of nothing.

She could only hope that by morning the strain would have passed. In the meantime, there was nothing to do but go to the tent so that the weary men could make their own way to bed after whatever they might deem a decent interval.

She stood up, making her goodnights as casual as possible, then she walked away in the direction of her tent.

'And where do you think you're going?'

The vibrant voice came to her in the darkness, and she spun round, startled. She had not noticed that Fraser had followed her from the fire.

'To bed.' Corey's voice was short.

'In the wrong direction, I think.'

He was very polite, very bland. It took Corey a full second before she understood that his very tone was ominous.

'Not at all,' she responded carefully. She gestured. 'Perhaps you've forgotten that's the tent I share with Mark and Boyd and Pete.'

'I forget nothing.' Still that politeness. A peculiar sensation began to creep along Corey's spine, she had a feeling of apprehension such as she had experienced when listening to ghost stories as a child. 'That was Colin's tent,' the voice continued. 'It's not Corey's.'

If only she could see him clearly! His mouth would be curved in a mocking smile, and his eyes would be sardonic, but his expression might conceivably tell her something of what he was leading up to. Away from the fire he was just a shape, tall and dark, with a voice that shivered its way through her system. He was trying to frighten her, that much she knew. He was also telling her something, but in a roundabout way, as if he meant to exact from her as much as he could in the way of revenge. Let him see that he was succeeding and there would be more of the same. The important thing was to retain her composure.

'You have another tent?' she asked, very calmly.

'I do.'

'Which one?'

He did not answer immediately. He was deliberately creating an atmosphere of suspense, Corey realised. She stood very still, her lips pressed firmly together. She would not break the silence by asking, in the fearful way he expected, which tent he had in mind.

And then he said, 'Mine,' and she heard the mockery in his tone.

She could not prevent the sudden weakness in her legs, nor the dryness that attacked her throat. Only with great effort did she manage to keep her voice calm. 'Thank you,' she answered with as much dignity as she could muster. 'That's very thoughtful of you.'

A low laugh, unnervingly seductive. 'You see it as thoughtful?'

'It *is* thoughtful of you to move in with the others and give up your tent.'

'My dear Corey,' the mockery was beyond anything she had ever heard, 'whatever gave you the idea I was giving it up?'

'Because ... well....' Her legs were trembling so violently now that she could hardly stand. 'Well, it's obvious. I mean, you said....'

'I said you'd be sleeping in my tent.' This time the pause was loaded with emphasis. 'I'll be there with you.'

'No!' Dignity was forgotten as she choked out the protest.

'Yes.' Through her fear she heard the authority of a man who was unaccustomed to disobedience.

'I won't!' Blindly she tried to push past him and back to the fire. Mark would understand. He would be as outraged as she was. He would stand up for her.

Steel-like fingers caught her wrist, and as she tried to wrench away she felt them bite into the softness of her skin.

'Let me go!' An unashamed plea.

'You'll come with me.'

'You can't make me.' She was furious now. Her

voice had lifted, and she was unconcerned who might hear her.

The grip tightened. 'I can make you do anything I want.'

'No!' And then, as she felt him dragging her with him, it came to her that there was only one way she could save herself. Mark would come if she screamed. Pete too, and perhaps some of the other men.

She opened her mouth, but he forestalled her, his reactions quicker than her own. His other hand clamped down hard on her mouth.

'Will you walk with me quietly?' he demanded.

She shook her head violently.

'Then there's only one way,' he observed grimly. 'And don't say later that you didn't ask for it.'

He released the grip on her mouth and her wrist. As easily as if she had been a doll he scooped her up from the ground. His arms were long and muscular, his chest broad and hard. For a full moment Corey lay still against him, dizzied by the aura of sheer virility which seemed to cnvelop her. There was a delicious melting sensation, so that for one irrational moment she wished she could remain held against him for ever. And then reality returned, and with it the full implication of what was happening.

Once more she opened her mouth to scream, and again his responses were razor-sharp. The sound stilled in her throat as his lips clamped down on hers. Through the flames of excitement surging through her nerve-stream she tried to struggle. It was a thought she did her best to remember later. Oh yes!—there had been a struggle. But it was one which she could not win. Hands pummelled and feet kicked, but to no effect. Strong arms tightened their hold, so that she was pushed up hard against the wall of his chest. The lips clamped firmer. There was nothing remotely lover-like in the embrace, it could not even be called a kiss. It was just a way of stopping her from calling out. In the circumstances it was quite ridiculous that her heart should be racing so hard that it felt as if it would burst from her rib-cage.

Once the lips relaxed briefly, and in that second sanity returned. She managed to bite him.

'Vixen!' he snarled, and then, undeterred, his mouth was back on hers, and when she swallowed she had the taste of blood.

Fraser's tent was a little aside from the others. He kicked at the entrance flap with his foot. He had to stoop to enter, and in that moment she was pulled even tighter against him; his lips were still on hers and her head was pushed into the hollow where the hardness of jawbone and throat and shoulder seemed to merge.

It was very dark in the tent, and with her head beneath his she could not have seen anyway. Briefly she closed her eyes. In later years she would wonder if what happened had been a figment of her imagination. Now there was only an exciting sensuousness which was unlike anything she had ever imagined.

There was the darkness and the hardness against her and all about her. There was the smell of maleness which was entirely different from the after-shave perfumes she had known; it was a smell that was basic and rugged and headily attractive. And there were the shock waves surging through her, so that she felt as if her body was on fire.

Her gasp of pain as he dumped her on the ground was due only in part to the behaviour that was anything but gentle. Mainly it was provoked by an irrational and very sudden feeling of loss. For a few seconds she could only stare up blankly.

'John Latimer's daughter all right.' She saw him dab a hand to his mouth. 'A fighter to the end.'

Corey laughed. 'I don't believe Dad ever bit you.'

'Not physically.' She heard the rueful note. 'But verbally—many times. And in other ways too. He didn't give up easily, even when he knew that he was wrong.'

Corey had a momentary vision of the frail figure surrounded by his books. The fight had left her father; he would no longer be a match for a man who was young and strong and virile. Somehow it made the importance of her mission greater. 'I don't give up either,' she said.

Fraser did not answer immediately. He stood quite still, a tall lean giant of a man, towering ominously above her. She could not see his face from where she lay, but she sensed the vigour and energy in the vital body, the power and the ruthlessness.

He bent all at once, reached for one of her hands, and pulled her into a standing position. Still there was nothing gentle in his movements. Through Corey's excitement she felt a flame of anger.

'Let me go!' she snapped.

'When I've made a few things clear.'

The quiet hardness of his tone indicated that he expected unquestioning acquiescence. True, she had intruded where she had no right to be, yet Corey did not feel that she had to kowtow to the man. At least not without spirited opposition. If Fraser did not like her—odd how that fact could bring a brief flash of pain—at least he would respect her.

'I mean to get my pictures,' she told him.

'You might, if you behave yourself—and if the frieze exists.'

She lifted her chin. 'It exists.'

'You've only your father's stubbornness to vouch for that. And he had nothing more than the word of a tracker.'

'A tracker he believed. The frieze exists, and I will not return home without recording it.'

'More John Latimer's daughter at every moment.' Corey wondered if she only imagined the grudging admiration in his tone. 'How old are you, Corey?'

'Twenty-two.'

'Older than I expected.'

'Then you knew about me?' He was still holding her hands. She had a desire to draw out the conversation, to restore a vestige of normalcy.

'Oh yes.' She was taken aback by the returning mockery. 'I know quite a lot about you, Corey Latimer.'

She bit her lip, uncertain all at once. The tone of his last statement had been loaded, as if with a special meaning. It seemed important to turn the subject once more.

'There was something you wanted to discuss.'

'Discuss?' A short laugh. 'No discussion, Corey, just orders. Orders that are to be obeyed.'

'You think you can treat me however you want,' she said bitterly.

'Precisely.' Quiet satisfaction. 'Listen very carefully, Corey Latimer. Because if you don't you'll be heading one way.'

'Let go of my hands!' An order of her own, in a manner that was as disdainful as she could make it.

Fraser shrugged and dropped her hands. It was as if he recognised the order as a gesture of defiance, and found it too insignificant to counter.

'You'll be treated like everybody else. No special concessions because you're a female—I told you that already. And you will keep away from my men; I told you that too. No playing upon their sympathies. Already you have Mark and Boyd as rivals for your somewhat dubious favours.'

She chose to ignore the slight. 'Is that why you

moved me out of their tent? You were concerned about my safety?'

'Don't be naïve.' This time his laugh was low and mockingly seductive. 'They could do with you what they wish and I wouldn't be concerned. A girl who joins an all-male expedition, knowing that she isn't wanted, deserves whatever she gets.'

At every moment he sought to wound her. She looked at him uncomprehendingly. 'I don't understand.... If you weren't concerned, why *did* you move me?'

'I wasn't concerned about *you*.' He waited a moment for the emphasis to sink in. 'My sole concern is for the men. How long do you think it would take for Mark and Boyd to be at each other's throats?'

'You endow every man with your own base instincts,' she tossed at him scornfully.

'You call them base? I call them male. Well, Corey, how does it feel to know that all those men out there would like to be sharing your sleeping-bag?'

Anger flamed through her. She did not need to see his face to know that his eyes would be glittering with malice and his lips would be curved in a satisfied smile. 'You're the most horrible man I ever met,' she said at last, low-toned. 'And nothing, absolutely nothing, will induce me to sleep here with you tonight.'

'I've already shown you that you'll do what I say,' he threatened dryly.

'No!'

She backed away from him, frightened, but the tall male form blocked the opening of the tent. There was no escape.

'It will be my pleasure to show you again.'

This time, when he reached for her, she was prepared. She fought like the hellcat he called her. She scratched and clawed and pummelled, but he was impervious to all of it, holding her off with an effortless strength. And through it all, perversely almost, she gloried in that strength.

'Why do you fight me?' he asked once, when she had quietened a moment. 'You know you want it.'

'No!'

'Yes,' he insisted. 'We both know it.'

'I hate you!' she ground out.

'Hate?' He laughed mockingly. 'Why must you be so dramatic all the time? Is it the model world coming out in you? I told you that hate and love have nothing to do with sex.'

'That's not true,' she whispered.

'Isn't it?' She was quieter now, as a long-fingered hand trailed tantalisingly from her chin down the column of her throat. The movement sent a tremor shuddering through her.

'Ah!' A note of satisfaction. 'Is that what you felt with Eric Hogan?'

'Eric?' Corey threw back her head. 'Who told you about Eric?'

'The Cape Town papers reach my farm. There were some rather interesting photos of you together.'

Corey swallowed on dryness. So he had seen the photographs taken in the restaurant. How secure she had thought her life then. Little had she dreamed quite how much it would change. The pressure on her throat altered. Fraser was waiting for her answer.

CHAPTER SIX

'WELL?' Fraser drawled. '*Is* this what you felt?'

'Eric is twice the man you are,' Corey flung at him recklessly.

She regretted the words the moment they were out. The statement could only be a challenge to a man like Fraser.

'How very interesting,' came the sardonic rejoinder. 'Let's see if you still think so when I've finished with you.'

A hard pair of lips choked off her sobbing protest. She had experienced his kiss twice before, both times because Fraser had wanted to prove his authority and dominance, but this kiss was different. There was still the desire to show authority, but also there was something more.

Now Fraser's touch was more provocative. His lips were deliberately tantalising, teasing and tasting and exploring. His hands moved over her with a sensual expertise which set the blood pounding in her temples. The torrent of desire shooting through her nerve-stream was more intense than it had been when he had carried her through the darkness.

Her breath jerked as a hand undid the buttons of her shirt and slid to the smooth bare skin beneath it. The hand that went from her midriff to her back was light, deliberately light, then it came forward to cup a breast with a possession that was hard and intimate. She gasped beneath his lips, and felt her body arch instinctively towards him. And then, as she heard him chuckle against her mouth, some returning sanity told her that she had to get away from him—quickly.

Somehow she managed to twist her head away from his. 'No,' she implored him. 'Stop!'

'Why?' A hand brought her back to him, cupping the smooth-cropped head in its palm. He was so close to her that she could feel the clean warm breath against her mouth.

'I . . . I don't want to.'

'You do.'

'No!'

Fraser did not answer. He lifted her, as easily as he had done before, and put her down on his camp-bed. She tried to fight him as he undid the rest of the buttons and drew the shirt from her shoulders, but the battle was hard when her limbs were like water. She gasped again when he pulled down the zip of her slacks, but he held her effortlessly as he undressed her. She tried to speak, but her throat was so dry that her words were choked and incoherent. He took no notice of them, as he lowered himself on to her.

His body was hard and heavy. Corey could feel him against her, from the tips of her toes to the top of her head, where his hands were knotted in her hair. One hand slid beneath her, moulding her to him, her soft body fitting easily against his hard lines. Corey had never been so stirred. She could feel the strong rhythmic heart against her breasts and knew that he must feel hers.

Suddenly he stood up. Eyes wide, she watched him take off his own shirt. Her eyes were accustomed to the darkness now, and she could see the outline of the strongly muscled chest. He kicked off his shoes and began to unbuckle his belt.

From somewhere Corey found the control she needed. She sat up swiftly. 'Fraser!' Her voice was ragged. 'Stop now!'

'Are you quite crazy?' he demanded.

'No.' The word emerged painfully from a parched throat. 'I'm a virgin.'

Something in her tone must have got through to him, because he lifted himself a little away from her. A lantern burned in the tent, and by its light she was able to see his face. The eyes, very dark in the dimness, were narrowed and watchful, the jaw was tight. The spare features were sterner than ever.

'I find that hard to believe,' he said after a long moment. 'A beautiful model fawned on by playboys.'

'Eric was a friend....'

'You'll tell me next that the relationship was platonic.' His tone held a taunt. 'From the way you were looking at each other in the photos you were just two inches away from bed.'

'The relationship wasn't platonic,' her voice was shaking, 'but it wasn't what you think either.' She drew a small shuddering breath. 'I thought we would get married.'

'Eric Hogan the marrying kind?' A sardonic jeer. 'Come, Corey, you're too worldly not to have recognised the type. He's no more in the marriage market than I am.'

Corey stifled the tiny and quite irrational stab of pain. 'It's what I did think, all the same,' she said very quietly.

Another pause, a longer one this time. Then Fraser asked, 'Supposing what you say is true—you were pretty cool to come on this expedition, one female among so many men.'

'I came as a man,' she pointed out. 'And if I hadn't comforted the child I'd be one still.'

'Would you?' An insolent gaze moved from her throat over breasts that were soft and round in the dim light of the lantern, and from there to the curve of slender hips. 'It would have come out sooner or later.' He moved away from her with a little sound of disgust.

Corey drew a breath. 'You believe me?'

'I didn't say that. You may be a virgin; you may also be a fine actress. Either way you don't interest me. Coy virginity, whether genuine or assumed, is not my scene.'

His words hurt, as they were meant to. If Fraser did in fact believe her, she had not earned his respect. If anything he despised her more. In the world of Fraser Mallory women were good for one thing only, which meant that she had no value whatsoever.

'Where will I sleep?' Corey asked in a small voice as Fraser began to dress. She tried to look away, but her eyes could not leave the torso gleaming in the lantern-light. As if his body was still on hers, she could feel the strength and shape of it. It was only when he looked at her that she quickly shifted her gaze.

His voice was cool and amused. 'In here.'

You're still playing with me, she thought bleakly. Aloud she said, 'Then you *will* move in with the others?'

'Not at all. I thought I'd made that clear. But you'll be quite safe.' He looked at her, one eyebrow lifted mockingly. 'For tonight anyway. But you might like to put on your shirt in case I change my mind.'

Heat flooded her face. Was it possible that she had been so carried away by emotion and fear that she had forgotten she was still undressed? She was glad that the light was too dim for Fraser to see the flush; her discomfort would have given him undeserved satisfaction.

'Look the other way,' she ordered.

'I look where I want.'

'Very well.' Her fingers shook as she sat up and reached for her shirt. Slowly, deliberately, so that he would not see her distress, she pulled the garment over her head and began to fasten it. Then she crawled between the folds of the sleeping-bag and turned her face to the wall of the tent. Later, when Fraser was sleeping, she would take off her clothes and get into her pyjamas. Until then she would stay as she was.

No more words were exchanged between them. Corey heard Fraser move around the tent, and assumed that he was also preparing for bed. All the while she kept her eyes firmly away from him—and found it unexpectedly difficult. As if drawn by an irresistible force, she found herself wanting to turn her head. In her mind she could see him—the broad shoulders, the tanned muscular chest, the long hard line of jaw and throat. She knew, with a familiarity that made no sense after such a very short acquaintance, the feel of taut thighs and arms with the strength of steel. Given the arrogant personality of the man it made even less sense that she wanted to see and touch him again.

It was obvious that in Fraser's mind there was no similar torment. He was whistling as he moved about, the sound soft and unconcerned. She wondered if he would speak before he crawled into his sleeping-bag, even just once to say goodnight. But he said nothing, and Corey's pride gave her the strength to remain silent.

In a short while the sound of slow steady breathing filled the darkness of the tent. Like a child, Corey thought, for surely only children slept quite so easily and so quickly. Yet Fraser Mallory was anything but a child.

Her own body was so taut that she wondered if she would get any sleep that night. She had known that Fraser could affect her powerfully, but she had not dreamed that his physical impact would be quite so shattering. Even more disturbing, until today she would not have believed that she was capable of a desire which was raw and basic and all-consuming, a desire which could override discretion and logic and all the moral dictums she had been taught since childhood.

Outside the tent came the sounds of the campfire breaking up. She heard voices which she was beginning to recognise. The voices grew a little louder as the men came by on their way to the tents, and then she heard Boyd above the others. She caught her name and Fraser's. She did not hear every word he said, but did not need to; the gist of his meaning was clear. There was snickering as a few men responded, then the sound was quickly stifled. But Corey had heard enough. She flinched, and lay still.

The voices died away. It was still within the tent and outside. There was only the sound of Fraser's breathing, slow and steady, and the hum of the night insects. Suddenly a roar rent the air, long and low and reverberating endlessly through the still flat land. A lion. Corey's nails bit into her palms. The roar had sounded very near; even now the lion could be pacing the sands beyond the camp. There had been a few moments when she had thought she could sleep in the Land-Rover. Now she was relieved Fraser was in the tent with her. Obnoxious he might be, arrogant and tough and domineering, but she would come to no harm while he was near. She would trust him with her life and he would look after her. How she knew this was uncertain, but know it she did, and the knowledge gave her a strange satisfaction.

Sleep came at last. When Corey opened her eyes the first light of dawn was filtering through a narrow opening of the tent. She lay quietly for a moment, her eyes orientating themselves to wakefulness. Then the events of the previous day crowded her mind and she jerked up with a start, holding the flap of her sleeping bag beneath her chin.

The tent was empty, she could see that at a glance through the fine mesh of her mosquito net. On the camp-bed next to hers a sleeping bag was neatly rolled up, and a few masculine toilet articles stood tidily on a cardboard box. Fraser must have risen some time earlier. Corey wondered if he had stood beside her bed, if he had watched her sleeping. A warm flush spread rapidly through her cheeks, and she felt her breathing quicken.

The camp was stirring when she emerged from the tent. Some of the men were shaving before mirrors perched on boxes outside their tents. All were dressed. On the previous days, thinking themselves unobserved by female eyes, they had wandered around in various degrees of unattire, and where Corey might have had reason to feel embarrassed she had turned unobtrusively away. Now the need for this was gone.

As the men called out their good-mornings, here and there eyes moved to hers and then shifted away. Wryly she guessed that there were some who were trying to remember just how much she had seen.

It seemed taken for granted that Corey would take over the preparation of meals. She did not mind. She loved cooking, and had often regretted that she did not have more time for it. The little desert kitchen, with its Primus stove and dehydrated foods, was a far cry from the chrome and electricity which were hers in Cape Town, but the appreciative comments aroused by her cooking more than compensated for the hardships.

'Nice breakfast,' Fraser commented when he had finished eating.

They were the first words he had said to her since the scene in the tent the previous night. Her pulse quickened as she looked up. He seemed to tower above her, tall and lean and alarmingly male. His face was deeply tanned, and the wide grey eyes were clear and steady. If Fraser Mallory had spent any sleepless minutes in her company, there was nothing to indicate it.

She threw him a quick smile. 'So women do have their uses?'

His answering grin was slow and insolent. Her breathing grew a little ragged as his eyes swept her face and then travelled deliberately over her body, lingering longest on breasts and hips. 'I'm the first to agree,' he drawled.

She forced herself to stand very still. 'Need you be hateful all the time?'

'Do you deny that your question was provocative?' he countered. 'Don't bother to think up a wisecrack. We both knew the answer.'

She watched him walk away, tall and supple and purposeful. As her pulse settled slowly back to normal she wished that there was a way of turning back time and reversing decisions.

Mark brought his plate and sat beside her as he ate. For a while he was silent. She saw the lines of strain around his mouth and the unhappiness in his eyes and guessed that his mood was connected in some way with her. She was searching for a means of establishing communication when he said, 'What happened last night?'

'.... Nothing.'

He looked at her, his eyes hard, his cheeks tinged with colour. 'You don't need to pretend with me, Corey. Fraser Mallory likes his fun with women.'

'The woman has to be willing,' Corey said with greater lightness than she felt.

'I wasn't implying.... I didn't mean....' Mark was embarrassed.

Corey was instantly remorseful. 'Of course you didn't,' she said gently.

'You're sure nothing happened?'

Only that her world had been wrenched apart, Corey thought. But that wouldn't concern Fraser if he knew it, and it wouldn't be fair to lay the burden of her unhappiness on Mark. Aloud she said, 'Quite sure.'

His tone altered a fraction. 'Be careful, Corey.'

They both knew what he meant. 'I will be,' she promised.

'Fraser's a good leader, but he's also a hard man. If you fall for him you'll be heading for trouble.'

Corey heard Mark's distress. Gently she put her hand on his arm. 'Don't worry about me,' she smiled, 'There's really no reason.'

'Corey!'

She spun round at the sound of the familiar voice. 'Yes?'

'I've some work lined up for you. I want to discuss it.'

'Of course.' Corey's tone was as crisp and matter-of-fact as she could make it. She had seen the frostiness in Fraser's expression. His eyes had been on the hand that touched Mark's arm, and it was clear that he had misunderstood her motive. If anything, she should be glad. A little bit of jealousy—no, not jealousy, for Fraser would never experience that in relation to herself, but a touch of masculine pique perhaps—could only do him good. She lifted her chin and said defiantly, 'Perhaps someone else could clear the dishes?'

She spent the next hour with Fraser at a kind of desert quarry. There was much he wanted recorded. Fraser took measurements and made notes and told Corey what he wanted photographed. At first she resented the terseness of his orders, but after a while, as she grew more and more interested in what she was doing, she forgot to be angry.

They were making their way back to camp when he said, 'I told you not to flirt with the men.'

Corey knew immediately to what he referred. It seemed he would always think of her as the culprit in any situation. That being the case, there was no point in telling him the truth about the scene he had witnessed.

She threw him a provocative smile from beneath

long spiky lashes. 'You're jealous of Mark?'

He was so close to her that she could hear the hiss of indrawn breath. Then a hand, like a vice of steel, gripped one of hers. 'You little tease!'

'You haven't answered the question.' She wondered if he felt the speed of her pulse beneath his fingers.

'You know the answer,' he ground out contemptuously. 'Jealous? There are many more like you in Cape Town—and better. Though I don't deny that your body'—his eyes skimmed her insolently—'has its charms.'

It was hard to remain cool in the face of his arrogance. 'You *are* jealous,' she insisted.

'My taste runs to something better than half-baked virgins.' The length of his arms was against hers, taut and hard. 'But Mark hasn't had my exposure. I can't speak for the other men.'

There was no end to his insults. 'I wish I'd never come on this trip,' Corey said, low-toned. 'I wish I'd never met you.'

'Then we have something in common.' There was a new note in his tone, one which she did not understand, yet which made her feel oddly excited even through her anger. She was pondering why this should be so, when he went on, 'That's by the way. I warn you, Corey, cause trouble among the men and I'll have no scruples in dealing with you.'

'I did nothing wrong with Mark.' All at once she felt very young, very vulnerable.

'Not in your eyes, perhaps.' His voice was chilling. 'You must know that Mark is half the way to falling in love with you.'

'That's nonsense.' Corey's denial was half-hearted. Much though she might protest the fact, she knew that what Fraser said was possibly true. 'It's only this continual intimacy that makes Mark pay attention to me.'

'Of course. But too much intimacy can be a dangerous thing, and by the time Mark realises that it could well be too late.'

The words were out before she could stop them. 'We're even more intimate, you and I.'

'But it's a situation I control.' The slow drawl was outrageous. 'I can take you or leave you any time I want.'

The sensible thing would have been to remain silent. By now Corey should have realised that there was no out-arguing Fraser Mallory. But his last words had had a provocative effect. She was so angry that she did not stop to think. 'Are you any less human than the other men?' she tossed at him.

For answer Fraser threw down his instruments and pulled her roughly against him. His lips were on hers before she knew what was happening. She tried to push him away, but as before his strength was greater than hers. His lips were hard and demanding, his hands were instruments of torture, punishing and tantalising and unbearably sweet all at the same time. Somewhere, in a far corner of her mind, Corey's anger still flamed, but while she knew that she must fight him with everything she had, it became harder and harder to do so when every nerve and fibre ached to bring her closer against him.

She was no longer thinking when her arms went up around his neck and her fingers knotted themselves in the thick dark hair. Fraser put her away from him with an abruptness that was so abrupt as to be an insult. Her legs were so weak that she almost fell. She stared up through a blur, and was shocked to see the undisguised contempt in the chiselled mask of his face.

'Why did you do that?' she whispered.

'To prove something.' His tone was without expression. 'I'm as human as the next man, Corey, but I *can* control the situation to suit myself.' He paused. When he spoke again there was mockery in his voice. 'Which is more than can be said for you.'

'You're a swine!' Corey burst out.

A dark eyebrow lifted. 'For letting you know the truth about yourself? Because you did respond, my dear, however much you might wish to deny it.'

She could not deny it. Fraser was far too experienced not to have sensed the wild stirring of her body, the involuntary manner in which she had arched towards him. But if she could not deny it there was nevertheless no need to hide her disgust.

'I did respond,' she acknowledged quietly. 'You know how to arouse a woman, Fraser, I'll give you that. And that's what makes you a swine—you arouse excitement without giving respect.'

She saw the momentary glimmer in the dark eyes. Approval? she wondered disbelievingly. And then, as a second later the eyes became hooded, she understood her mistake. There were many emotions Fraser Mallory might experience, but approval, especially as far as she was concerned, was not one of them.

Head held high, Corey turned away. She did not know that even now, in the heat and the sand of the desert, dressed in the same khaki shirt and trousers as the men wore, her slender body was graceful, her movements fleet and fluid, so that to the watching man she looked as dainty and supple as a small gazelle. She only knew that she had to get away from him, from a physical attraction which was threatening to destroy a security she had never before questioned.

She did not say a word as she walked. Even when she heard the measured, 'Keep away from Mark,' she refused to look back.

Corey was relieved when Fraser did not seek her out again that day. After lunch she worked with some of the other men, and though the work was not as interesting as the morning's work had been, she made certain that she drew out her time so that when all the necessary photographs had been taken the sun was dipping below the horizon and the camp was beginning to get ready for the night.

For once there was no magic in the desert night. There was no joy in the myriad stars, or in the sands that stretched black and endless beyond the orbit of the dancing flames; there was no thrill in the distant roar of a lion, or in the laugh of a hyena closer by; no pleasure in the smells and tastes of the braaivleis.

There was only apprehension and, if Corey was honest with herself, an excitement that tingled the senses. Soon now the fire would die and the men would go to bed, and she would be alone with Fraser Mallory in the small tent just big enough for two. Though she was resolved that this time she would not let him touch her, that she would not even talk to him, the thought of their enforced intimacy was enough to make the blood flow faster in her veins.

Did Fraser think of the approaching night? she wondered. She glanced at the tall lean figure, a sinuous silhouette against the leaping light of the flames. He was talking to Pete. She could not hear what they said, but Fraser's tone was friendly, his posture relaxed. She realised he felt no anticipation at all, and was shocked at her disappointment.

As if he felt himself being watched, Fraser lifted his head and looked at her, and for a moment they stared at each other across the fire. Only a moment, and yet there was timelessness in it, for it seemed that they two were the only persons in the desert. Corey's muscles tightened, and she felt her body grow rigid.

And then Fraser turned back to Pete, and his

tone was as friendly as ever as he responded to a remark the other man had made. There had been no perceptible break in their conversation. Corey wondered if this moment too had been no more than a product of her imagination.

Suddenly it was important that she be in her sleeping-bag before Fraser entered the tent. If only sleep would come quickly. Then she would not be affected by his nearness, by an intimacy which was intoxicating. She did not want to see the naked muscled chest or the hard arms and long legs: did not want to experience the wave of desire which was more devastating than anything she had ever known.

CHAPTER SEVEN

COREY left the campfire early. Mark, with whom she had been sitting, was disappointed. But, as if he understood a little of what was in her mind, he did not try to detain her.

Her movements were needlessly jerky as she prepared for bed. Fraser would not come to the tent yet. There was no reason to fear that he would surprise her before she was ready. And yet all her rationalising did not make her feel easier.

She lay quietly when he came. Her breathing was slow and steady, her eyes closed. Fraser paused a moment beside her camp-bed. It was hard to maintain the momentum of her breathing when her heart was racing. Was he taken in? she wondered. With his perceptiveness he might well not be.

Whether Fraser believed she was sleeping or not, the matter was evidently of little concern to him. He left her side, and she heard him start to undress.

It would be so very easy to open her eyes a fraction, just enough so that she could watch him. But she did not want to look at the hard male body, she told herself fiercely, and wondered why it was so difficult to keep her eyes firmly shut.

There was nothing assumed about the steady breathing which soon filled the tent. Fraser had spoken no more than the truth when he had said that he could control the situation. Evidently he was completely master of his mind and passions.

If only she could say as much for herself! She had succeeded in keeping her eyes closed when more than anything she had wanted to open them, but the waves of desire that rocked her body were something else altogether. She hated Fraser Mallory, she told herself with a touch of wild despair. She had to hate anyone so arrogant, so supremely confident of himself. There was no logic in the depths of her physical longing, no rational way of explaining why she yearned to feel his arms around her once more. She lay rigid in the darkness, and tried to focus her thoughts on something else. Somehow she had to find a way of loosening the hold Fraser had on her emotions. Otherwise she would be destroyed.

Next morning she rose after Fraser. When she left the tent and went towards the freshly-banked fire she positioned herself as far from him as she could. Once, involuntarily, her gaze moved sideways. He was watching her, a tall figure, erect and still, like a granite statue in the early light of dawn. Their eyes held for a long moment. If Fraser had been any other man Corey would have smiled and said good morning. But he *was* Fraser, and the mundane greeting seemed inappropriate.

In the moment before she managed to shift her gaze from his Corey saw the mocking lift of one eyebrow. She kept her eyes firmly away as she took a sip of her coffee. Outwardly her appearance might well have been poised. Only she knew that inwardly she was shaking.

She would stay out of his way, she resolved. She *must* stay out of his way, even if it meant disobeying orders. The man's arrogance was such that if he were anybody else she would complain about him to the expedition leader, and ask to have nothing more to do with him. But Fraser was the leader. If she meant to keep out of his way she could only rely on her own ingenuity.

Corey spent the morning taking photographs with a group in which Mark was a member. Now and then, when he managed a moment alone with her, they were able to exchange a few words. He asked her if she would take a walk with him later that afternoon when the day's work was finished. Disregarding Fraser's orders, Corey said she would like that. She glanced at him as he worked. The brown eyes, which lit with warmth when they smiled, were serious now; the expression in the sensitive face was preoccupied. Not for the first time Corey realised how much she liked Mark. Fraser had said the younger man was falling in love with her. That could be true, though she hoped it was not. What she did hope for was that a friendship she was beginning to enjoy more and more would continue long after they had returned from the desert.

Fraser was nowhere to be seen. Corey gathered that he had gone back to the site where she had worked with him the previous day. She was relaxed in his absence. The tension which was constantly with her whenever he was near was missing.

And yet, while she enjoyed the respite, Corey found that her thoughts turned often to the man who disturbed her so much. Angry with herself, she tried to push him from her mind. She had resolved she would avoid him as much as she could. Avoidance was not merely a physical matter, it was also a matter of mind and thought and emotion. She would *not* let herself think of Fraser. Tea-break came, and she talked to the other men with more than her usual vivaciousness. She wondered if she was the only one who heard the forced brightness in her tone.

At lunch time they went back to the camp. Fraser

came to her as she was eating. He wanted her to work with him that afternoon. As always Corey reacted to the virile maleness of the man. Even now, when his tone was detached and his words businesslike, there was a restless stirring inside her which it seemed she could do nothing to prevent.

'I'm afraid I can't.' In her effort to match his detachment her voice emerged unnaturally flat.

An eyebrow lifted. 'No?'

'I'm still busy at the other site.' If only she could slow the pace of her words! 'I can't just leave off.'

Fraser did not answer, and something drew her eyes up to meet his. He was studying her, the grey eyes sweeping her with the slow deliberation which never failed to send colour flooding her cheeks. Involuntarily a sound of protest escaped her lips.

'I'm busy,' she choked, 'don't you understand?'

'I understand.' He laughed, the sound low and sensual and infinitely disturbing. A quiver ran through Corey's nerve-stream. Fraser's words held an unmistakable double meaning. Damn the man! she thought furiously. He knew exactly what he was doing to her.

His insolence merited a stinging retort. Later the appropriate words would come to her. At the moment, however, even if she had had the presence of mind to know what to say, Corey could not trust her voice to remain steady. Concealing her eyes, she turned abruptly away.

'Corey.' His voice followed her, mocking and

seductive. 'You may have your way today because it suits me, but you can't escape being alone with me for ever.'

And Corey knew that whatever victory she had thought she had won was in fact hollow.

It was hard to concentrate on her work that afternoon. Fraser was even more of an intrusion than before. Corey fumbled with light readings and had trouble with focusing, and once she came near to dropping the camera.

'Corey.' Mark's voice came to her through a blur. 'Are you all right?'

She looked up at him. His expression was one of concern, and it came to her that concern was the one emotion she would never see in Fraser. At least not as far as she was concerned.

'Corey?'

'I'm all right.' She managed an unsteady smile. 'Really.'

He was not convinced. 'You haven't been yourself all afternoon.'

'Must be the heat that's getting to me. I'm all right, really I am.'

Mark looked at her a moment longer, then he took one of her hands and smiled back at her. 'I'll take your word for it.'

'To prove it, let's go for that walk later on.' She did not know what made her say it.

'Let's do that.' He looked so pleased that she felt suddenly guilty for no reason she could pinpoint.

They finished working earlier that day. Leaving the other men to go back to the camp, Corey and Mark walked in the other direction. Not for the first time Corey marvelled at how different the desert was from her preconceived ideas. True, there were vast tracts of sand, but there were grasslands too. This was veld in a way, veld that was similar to that of the Western Cape, and yet different too. No farm-lands here, just a wildness that was stark and arid and yet with a strange and haunting beauty of its own.

It was still hot, but now that the sun was setting the rays which scorched the desert for most of the day were gone. Above them the sky was vast and cloudless, a gold and scarlet palette of sunset colour. It was very still in the bush, a concentrated still-ness, as if all the world was suspended in a special kind of waiting in this time that separated day from night.

Corey turned her head at a rustling movement nearby. A gemsbok, motionless as a statue, stood watching them. Eyes were alert, the powerful body tensed, as if the animal was poised for instant flight. Corey thought of the roars which reverberated through the silent desert nights. The gemsbok would make a tasty morsel for a hunting lion. The alertness was justified.

Some distance away a thorn tree rose high above the fronds of dry grass. On the leafless branches were vultures. Corey had seen them before, waiting in trees as they did now, or wheeling in the sky. They were birds of prey, gaunt and hideous, present always where a kill had taken place. When the lions and cheetahs and leopards had had their fill, the vultures would swoop down to finish off what was left. Seeing them in the tree, silent and watchful, Corey shivered.

In the lovely twilight stillness it was hard to think of death and hunting. And yet in another sense it was not hard at all, for in the desert life was basic and primitive. Life was lived as it had been for thousands of years. The strong were hunters, the weak battled to survive. The law of the jungle reigned unquestioned. There was fear in a concept so remote from civilisation, and yet there was excitement too, a sense of vitality and challenge. And again, for no reason that she cared to analyse, Corey's mind went to Fraser.

She turned to Mark. 'It's exciting, isn't it?'

She did not know that her eyes were wide and very green or that her expression was aglow with eagerness. She only saw the change in the expression of the man who looked down at her. A moment ago he had been smiling, but now the smile was replaced with a look Corey had seen a few times before, in other men. It was a look which disturbed her with its intensity. That was a contradiction, she knew. If she liked Mark, and she did, she should not be disturbed by the emotions his expression suggested.

'It is exciting,' he agreed quietly.

It seemed important to go on talking. 'You love this life, don't you?'

There was an odd silence. Then Mark said, 'I did until recently.'

Corey looked at him swiftly. 'You don't any more?'

'I find it lonely.' An intensifying of the expression which had disturbed her. 'Do you think you could learn to like it, Corey?'

'I . . . I'm not sure.' Eyes that had been eager and laughing were troubled now. Corey had not reached the age of twenty-two without understanding the nuances of speech or the meanings that could lie behind simple words. In the main, she had learned how to cope with them. Most men, she had found, were not unduly offended by rejection that was made with tact and humour. But Mark was not most men. She had grown very fond of him.

She knew too that her answer had not been the truth. 'I'm not sure. . . .' A lean attractive face inserted its way into her mind once more. Yes, she *could* love this life, Corey knew—under certain circumstances. In certain company. The revelation hit her with an impact that was blinding. If she could have thrust it physically from her consciousness she would have done so; it was too shocking to accept.

'I'm not sure,' she repeated, and this time her lips were quivering. 'Mark, I'm more tired than I realised. Shall we go back?'

'Very well,' he said. Nothing in his tone indicated that he felt disappointed or rejected. Yet Corey, perhaps because the intensity of her own emotions had heightened her perceptions, knew that he was hurt.

More than one head turned when Corey and Mark returned to camp. Corey was growing accustomed to the interested glances of the men, and for the most part she took them good-naturedly. It was only natural that, as the only female in their group, she should attract attention. Neither could she fault their curiosity in regard to her relationship with Fraser. For one thing, it was no secret that they shared a tent. For another, by now it was common knowledge that she was Corey Latimer, a well-known Cape Town model who had been seeing a good deal of Eric Hogan, a man who had the reputation of a wealthy playboy.

At the beginning Corey had been surprised that the doings of the circles she normally moved in could be of concern to people whose interests were so different. She could not see these men enjoying the gossip of the social pages. Admittedly Fraser had known who she was, who Eric was too. But for some reason she had been loath to think of Fraser as a man who would spread idle gossip to the rest of his team. He had qualities she did not like—arrogance, an unbearable sense of sufficiency, a sex-appeal that was so devastating that it could leave a girl physically and emotionally vulnerable—yet the role of gossip did not seem to fit him.

It was almost with relief that she learned that it was Boyd who had recognised her name, who had once met Eric Hogan and knew of his forays in the Cape Town social set. She could imagine the relish with which he had divulged what he knew to the other men.

Corey had taken a dislike to Boyd the first day she had met him, and nothing he had done since then had changed her opinion. If anything, her dislike of the man had increased. His innuendoes regarding what went on between Fraser and herself when they were alone together enraged her, so that often she found it hard to keep her temper. She saw that his remarks made the other members of the team uneasy. Whatever their thoughts—and wryly she guessed that these were much the same as Boyd's—they had the sense and good taste to remain silent.

Although Corey had learned to accept Boyd's remarks along with the silent interest of the other men for once the turning of heads made her uncomfortable. What she had discovered about herself in the last few minutes had left her feeling overwrought.

'Got something we don't have, Mark?' Boyd's jeer came from behind them. The remark brought forth a few laughs. To Corey's frayed nerves they were loaded with meaning. At her side she felt Mark grow rigid.

At that moment Fraser appeared through the

bushes. He was walking towards Corey and Mark, and Corey felt her muscles tighten. If Fraser intended to make a sarcastic remark she meant to be ready for it. He did not say a word, but his eyes, as he passed them, were chips of ice, and his jaw had an uncompromising look of steel. The laughing stopped as suddenly as it had begun. The whole camp was hushed, expectant almost, as if something momentous was about to occur.

Corey felt anger swell hard and hot inside her. She had done nothing to merit this treatment. She could flare up and tell them, Fraser and Boyd in particular, what she thought of them, or she could behave with cold dignity. She chose the latter.

'I enjoyed the walk, Mark.' Her voice was light and clear. The poised smile of the professional model belied her true feelings. She touched his arm briefly. 'Let's do it again some time.'

She did not wait to hear his reply. As she turned away in the direction of the kitchen tent she was still smiling. Her head was held high, her walk was graceful and unhurried. But as she lifted the flap and went inside she wondered how she would endure the time that was left.

Next morning she was still brooding about the matter. It was Sunday, and there was no work that day. Some of the men were reading, some were making notes, a few played cards. Corey had no plans. In other circumstances she might have enjoyed the respite, but uncertainty and an odd unhappiness made her restless.

She had to get away from the camp and from an atmosphere that was beginning to be stifling. At the back of her mind she recalled that Fraser had warned her once not to go walking alone, but it was a warning she felt she could safely ignore. There would be no dangerous animals quite so near to the camp, and she would not walk far enough to run the risk of being attacked. That any other dangers could exist did not enter her mind.

Mark sat on a folding chair, writing in a notebook. As she passed him he lifted his head briefly and smiled, then went back to his work. She was glad that he made no attempt to follow her. Of Fraser there was no sign.

The tension began to drain from Corey as she walked. The sun had not been up long, and though it was beginning to get hot there was still enough of the night's chill in the air to make walking pleasant. Not far from the campsite was a grove of mopani trees, and in the distance a line of low hills was blue and hazy.

Here and there a baobab tree rose from the desert ground. The baobab tree was unlike any other tree Corey had ever seen. It was very thick, as thick as five normal trees, and quite hollow, so that animals could easily make it their home. At its crown were short stunted branches, with just the barest covering of leaves. The oddest-looking tree she had ever seen, Corey thought. With its prehistoric appearance it seemed a fitting ornament to the desert.

She wished she had brought her camera with her. Today she could have taken photos for her own pleasure, photos her father would like too. How he would have enjoyed being here! For John Latimer the heat and the dust and the companionship of the men would hold no strangeness.

Corey wondered when she would see the animal frieze. *If* she would see it. So far she had not seen any bushman paintings at all. She had hoped to return from the desert with the photograph her father had dreamed of. If she did not she would have destroyed her peace of mind—she knew already that nothing would ever be quite the same again—to no purpose.

She did not know at what point she became aware that she was being followed; the knowledge seemed to penetrate her consciousness very gradually. There was no sound of footsteps—these would be deadened by the thick sand underfoot—but there was the rustling of dry grass, the snap of a twig. Corey knew quite definitely that she was not alone. If she had not been quite so absorbed in her thoughts she might have realised it earlier.

An animal or a person? Corey wondered if she should look back. She had been followed thus far without incident, perhaps the very act of turning around might provoke an attack.

Every instinct urged her to run, but she forced herself to walk slowly. Each nerve and muscle was tensed, and yet, with the discipline of a model, she maintained an outward appearance of calm. She was walking further and further away from the camp. Somehow she must find a way of getting back. She *must* find a way. And it must be without turning and walking back the way she had come.

The snapping of a branch, shockingly loud in the intense stillness. Corey's heart thudded against her rib-cage and a hand flew to her lips to stifle the involuntary scream. Without thinking she turned.

Boyd was a few feet behind her. She looked at him numbly, her heart still racing. She had never imagined she would be glad to see the florid red face, but now her relief was so great that she could have flung herself into his arms.

'You!' she choked out. 'Oh, Boyd, I thought....'

He smiled. 'What did you think, Corey?'

'I thought I was being followed....' Her words trailed off uncertainly, her initial relief disappearing as she took in the not quite definable expression in the opaque eyes. 'Why did you follow me, Boyd?'

'Why do you think?'

Corey swallowed. 'It's a lovely day,' she ventured with a deliberate show of innocence. 'I suppose you felt like a walk.'

'More than a walk, my pet.' An indulgent chuckle. 'But of course you know that.'

'I don't know what you mean.' Fear was a hard ball inside her. Camp was some distance away, and the trees would muffle a scream.

Narrow eyes glittered. 'Innocence doesn't suit you, not with Eric Hogan warming your bed in Cape Town and Fraser warming it here.'

'I'm going back.' Her voice was very firm, hiding the frightened pulsing in her head.

The strong squat body became all at once a menacing obstacle, blocking off her escape.

'Let me get past, Boyd,' she ordered.

He smiled. 'Enough games.'

For a seemingly clumsy man he was surprisingly agile. As Corey tried to push past him he caught her and twisted her towards him, and Corey let out a gasp of pain as strong fingers dug cruelly into the soft flesh of her upper arms. She fought him wildly, but she was no match for him. As fleshy lips crushed down on hers, and her nostrils were filled with a smell of animal sweat and excitement, she choked back a wave of nausea.

'Might as well enjoy it,' he ground out once, when he lifted his head for breath. 'You make no bones about enjoying it with Fraser.'

Taking the opportunity the raised head afforded, Corey smashed her fist against his face. She was aiming for his eyes when Boyd moved, and the blow struck his nose instead. There was a dull thud and then a furious oath.

'You'll be sorry for this, you little tart!' No indulgence in the crude face now, only rage and an undisguised lust.

He threw her easily on to the ground. Corey was

more frightened than she had been in her life. Boyd was an unpleasant man, but she had not believed Fraser's warning that he was also dangerous. He would have no scruples in forcing his attentions on her, would rape her if she did not give in of her own will.

Thoughts raced through her head. Should she fight him? She had seen how his lust was increased after she had struck him the blow on the nose. Was it better to lie quite still, limp as a rag doll with no feelings? Would he be disgusted enough to lose interest in her?

If only she knew what to do! From deep inside her welled a silent cry. Fraser.... Fraser, come! There was no thought, no logic, just an instinct that Fraser alone could help her out of any danger.

He was at her shirt, forcing open the buttons. Still with no clear idea of what she should do, Corey tried to push him away. Boyd pushed her back down, holding her with one hand clamped over her mouth, so that she could not scream, while the other hand continued to tear at the buttons. When Corey felt him squeeze a breast, hurting her, she twisted her head and tried to bite him.

The grip on her breast grew stronger—there would be a bruise tomorrow—then the hand went to her trousers and he was ripping the belt open.

He was tearing down the zip when Corey saw his mouth open slackly. He looked up, his expression one of surprise, changing quickly to new fury.

Mark was standing above them, his hands on Boyd's hair, yanking him upwards. Even through her distress, Corey saw that Mark's face was a mask of terrible anger.

Boyd was on his feet in an instant. 'What the hell!' he snarled. 'You had your fun yesterday. You can have it again when I'm finished.'

'Shut your foul mouth!' Mark ground out, and swung a fist against Boyd's face.

They were fighting before Corey could say a word to stop them. Helplessly she watched them, wincing as she heard the thud of fist on bone. She feared for Mark, for he was slighter than Boyd, and more gentle, and she doubted he had fought often in his life.

To her surprise she soon saw they were evenly matched. Boyd had weight and brute strength on his side, but Mark's anger had given him strength of a different sort. Even then Corey felt the fight must run against him. From her position on the ground she looked around her, searching for some object —a stone, or a branch perhaps—with which to catch Boyd off his guard.

Nobody was aware of the third man's approach. With deceptive ease he pulled the two snarling men away from each other. Mark fell back, panting a little. Boyd tried to struggle loose so that he could launch himself into the fight once more, but even he was helpless in the vice-like grip of the man who held him.

A strangled cry emerged from Corey's throat. It had all happened so quickly. She looked from Fraser to Mark to Boyd and back to Fraser. He was eyeing her with a cold glance of contempt, and for the first time Corey became aware of her dishevelled state: the open shirt with its exposure of bare bruised breast, the trousers parted at the zip. She was still on the ground where Boyd had thrown her. As she struggled to her feet, pulling her shirt together with shaking fingers, hot colour flooded her face and neck.

Fraser's attention returned to the two men. 'I'll have no fighting.' His voice was flat and harsh.

'You don't understand.' Some of the anger had left Mark's face. He looked shaken, and beneath his tan there was pallor.

'I understand.' Once more the glance went to Corey, and once more there was no attempt to disguise his contempt.

'I want to finish him off.' Boyd was sullen. 'He hit me first.'

'You know why.' Still the flatness. 'I don't want to hear reasons or excuses. We're a team; we have to live together. Fights are bad for the morale of the men as a whole.'

'Fraser's right.' Mark spoke into the tense stillness.

'Like hell he is!' Boyd was unrepentant.

'You'll shake hands and that will be the end of it.' Fraser released his grip on Boyd. His manner was that of a man who took it for granted that his orders would be obeyed.

Boyd shook his head, ignoring Mark's reluctant outstretched hand. 'Never!'

'Now.' There was steel in the vibrant voice. 'I insist.'

For the first time Boyd looked uncertain. His belligerence was still in evidence, but with it there was hesitation. It was obvious that the decisive firmness of the man who was his leader had made an impression on him. Confused and unhappy as she was, Corey realised that there would be few people, if any, who would have the courage or the desire to cross Fraser.

'Okay.' A hand went out to Mark's. 'But it's a mistake to bring a dame along on a trip like this.'

'I think we all realise that.' Fraser turned to Corey and gestured towards the camp. 'If you're quite ready....'

'I prefer to go back on my own.' The small oval face was mutinous. Now that the danger had passed Corey resented Fraser's manner.

'Your preferences are quite irrelevant.' A firm hand went to her arm. 'See you at lunch, Mark, Boyd.'

CHAPTER EIGHT

Now the scolding would come, Corey thought, as they walked out of earshot of the two men. It would spare her nothing in the way of disdain or contempt. Well, she was ready for it. Whatever Fraser might think, she had not invited Boyd to follow her. For once she would answer his insults.

He did not say a word. The hand that had held her arm had dropped back to his side. There was no proper path, just a gap between the grasses. It was too narrow to walk side by side, and Corey was content to let Fraser walk ahead. Not once did he turn his head, as if he was confident that she would not dream of defying him. Impishly Corey wondered what he would do if she turned and joined Mark. Not that she seriously considered it; there was something in Fraser's manner which demanded compliance. It was a quality Boyd had sensed when he had given in and taken Mark's hand. Corey sensed it now.

Not for the first time she realised that Fraser was different from anyone she had ever known. His authority and strength, his virility and sheer maleness, were such that she wondered if there existed the man who could match him. Unbidden came the wondering what it would be like to be his wife.

She tried to push the thought from her. She did *not want* to know the answer. It did not concern her, nor was she interested. Any woman who married Fraser Mallory would have a hard time; she would have a husband who was domineering and insufferable, who would expect her to follow his lead at all times.

The question was rhetorical anyway, for though women would be drawn to Fraser like moths to a flame, none would be brave enough to marry him. She tried to ignore the little voice that told her that a woman who was loved by Fraser, and who loved him in return, would know a happiness that would be rare indeed.

Finally, crossly, she decided that the matter was of no importance to her. Since she could never be that woman—Fraser's dislike of her had never been in question—she would do better to concentrate her energies on more positive things. It was almost time for lunch, and the men would be expecting a meal.

As they reached the camp Corey took a step towards the kitchen tent. She was caught off guard when Fraser turned. 'Where do you think you're going?'

'Why should you care?' Her tone was more defiant than necessary. Did Fraser have to make her feel at a disadvantage all the time, so that she could never answer him normally? 'I'm safe and sound now.' On a new thought she paused. 'I suppose I should thank you.'

'You could thank Mark,' he suggested easily. 'Come, Corey.'

He was watching her. She saw the devilment in his eyes, the amusement in the curve of the lips, and took a step backwards. 'Where to?'

'Our tent.'

There was a subtle inference in the word 'our'. Corey took a breath. She had been naïve to think Fraser would let her off. With sheer effort of will she controlled the quivering of her lips.

'I've nothing to do there,' she told him lightly. 'And I do have duties in the kitchen. See you later, Fraser.'

'No, my dear.' There was steel in the long line of the jaw, relentlessness in the chiselled mask of the well-cut face. 'You don't get out of it so easily. We have things to say, Corey, and we'll say them now.'

There was no escaping him. Corey understood how Boyd must have felt when he had found himself giving in. Fraser dictated, and Fraser was obeyed.

One last effort. 'I have nothing to say to you,' she managed breezily.

An eyebrow lifted sardonically. 'I have things to say to *you*.'

She did not fight him, not now, not in full view of several members of the team. There was no way she could win, so she might as well keep her dignity and save her strength for when she really needed it.

Something told her that she *would* need it.

Fraser closed the tent flap behind them. It was dim in the tent, and hot; there was no reason for Corey to shiver. She looked once, very briefly, at the tall figure towering above her, close to her, too close, and then looked away. She did not need to study the ruthless set of the jaw, the glint in the eyes, the power in the broad shoulders. Every detail of Fraser Mallory's appearance was etched all too clearly on her mind.

She tried to step back, and found the canvas wall in her way. Tension seemed to crackle and spark in the tiny space which separated her from Fraser—surely he must feel it and hear it as she did?—and it was becoming increasingly difficult to swallow.

'You said there was something you wanted to say.' There! she had managed to speak, and only a very acute ear would have detected her nervousness.

'I told you to be careful.' Flatness in his tone.

'I . . . I was.'

'. . . .not to cause any trouble.'

'I didn't.' Tears trembled behind her eyelids. She could not let him see them, could not let him know that she was frightened. No, not frightened, at least not in the usual way. She was experiencing fear all right, but in the sense of excitement and apprehension and anticipation all mixed together. She dropped her eyes quickly, letting long lashes fall on soft flushed cheeks.

When a hand touched her chin she trembled.

Lean fingers cupped it, lightly yet inexorably, so that she could not pull away. A thumb slid down the length of her throat as her chin was pushed upwards, forcing her to look at him.

'What did you think would happen when you walked away from the camp?' His voice was soft now, and with the softness came a heightened sense of danger.

'I didn't think ... I mean, how could I know that Boyd would follow me?'

'You knew it.' Still that softness.

It was becoming very hard to keep the tears back. 'No.' A choked whisper. 'You have to believe me.'

'Cut the innocence.' Now there was cruelty in his tone. 'You should know by now that it doesn't go over well with me. We both know what you are, Corey. Boyd knows it too. Only Mark doesn't see the hard-bitten playgirl behind the soft brave exterior of the young woman who's undertaken this arduous mission on behalf of her ailing father.'

She tried to twist away from him, but the gentle hold tightened. 'Leave me alone, Fraser!'

'When I've given you what you've been wanting.'

'I only want to get out of this tent.'

'What you went looking for on that lonely trail.' He jerked her towards him.

Corey threw back her head, violet eyes blazing. 'Don't taunt me, Fraser! You saw me fighting Boyd off.'

Her eyes had grown accustomed to the dimness in the tent. She could make out the expression in the lean stern face; it was unexpectedly bleak. The corners of mobile lips curved in a mirthless smile. 'You could have been playing hard to get.'

'Boyd revolts me,' she threw at him bitterly.

'But Mark doesn't. Was it Mark you were waiting for, or were you hoping one of the other men would follow you? There's more fun in numbers, isn't there?'

'Fraser. . . .' she began desperately.

Relentlessly he cut her off. 'Whoever you hoped for, your fun was cut short.' A pause. There was a new inflection in his tone when he continued. 'That's why I intend to give it to you now.'

She had fought him before, and she fought him now. But it was a losing fight, she knew that from the start, not only because he was stronger than she was, but because her body betrayed her with a desire that left her weak. As his lips closed on hers a shiver of excitement coursed through her. It was humanly impossible to stop herself from responding to his kiss, even though, when sanity returned, she would realise that it stemmed only from contempt and revenge. It was impossible to fight the melting feeling in her bones when hard hands slid beneath her shirt to move across her back and down to her hips. As he moulded her to him, the soft pliant feminine curves against the angular male lines, there was only a desire to get closer, still closer.

Later she might hate herself for the way she had let him have his way, but now there was only the wish that this physical contact would never end.

She could no more stop her body arching towards his than she could stop breathing. She heard the hiss of breath, and felt the tightening of his muscles. Fraser did what he did because he wanted to hurt her, but at the same time he wanted her as much as she wanted him, and a tiny corner of her mind rejoiced in the knowledge.

She did not resist him when he lifted her from the ground. His arms were tight bands of steel around her back, and she could feel every inch of her body against his. She did not resist him either when he put her down on her camp-bed and began to undress her. The last barriers of her resistance had crumbled. There was only sensation now, a wild pounding in her blood, and a desire such as she had never dreamed existed.

She lay quite still, vulnerable and suddenly very uncertain, and yet proud too that he should see her as she really was. His own shirt was off now, and she watched him unbuckle his belt. And then he looked down at her. For a moment that seemed to have no meaning in time grey eyes searched violet ones, and Corey saw an expression she had never seen in Fraser before, one she had never dreamed she would ever see. Her heart raced for a moment of incredible happiness, and then the expression vanished, and the hard tightness that replaced it was in such contrast that Corey felt cold despite the heat in the tent.

'Fraser....' An involuntary whisper.

'No.' He was buckling his belt. She saw him reach for his shirt.

She could feel the earlier tears at the back of her eyes once more. 'What's wrong?' she whispered. 'What have I done?'

'Played true to type, my dear.' His tone was a whiplash, hard and stinging. He went on, ignoring Corey's visible flinching. 'I knew your innocence was assumed. You led Boyd on, just as you led Mark on. You can't do it to me, Corey. I'm too old a hand at this game to fall for it.

'You started this,' she tossed at him furiously, her tears vanishing with her anger. 'I didn't ask you to make love to me.'

'Love!' A hoarse expletive. 'Don't confuse what just happened with love, Corey. It was just a game played between two adults who both knew the score.'

There was something here that she did not understand; even through her terrible hurt and anger Corey knew that. 'Then why draw back at this point?' she demanded recklessly, unconcerned for the moment that she was playing with a fire that she already knew she was unable to control.

'Because I choose to.'

He looked down at her. He was fully dressed now. His eyes raked her contemptuously, lingering insolently on the soft rounded body. Ashamed, all at once, she tried to cover herself with her hands.

'Don't bother. You're very beautiful, Corey Latimer, very tempting. But not to me—at least not at this moment.' The corners of his mouth lifted mockingly. 'There's a name for girls like you. Perhaps the gentle Mark doesn't know it, but I do, and I have no doubt Boyd does too. Get dressed, Corey. The men will be waiting for their lunch.'

He strode out of the tent without a backward glance. Corey lay very still. The heat had left her body and and she was cold again, but her limbs felt so weak, so drained, that she did not have the strength to crawl into her sleeping-bag.

What was this craziness which had taken hold of her? she asked herself despairingly. She did not love Fraser, she *could not* love him. He was the very antithesis of the kind of man she respected and wanted—a man like Mark. Yet Mark did not stir her, did not provoke the wildness that could raise her to ecstasy at one moment and plunge her to despair the next. She did not want such a man, she told herself. If he could make her feel feminine and vital and alive, he also made her vulnerable and uncertain and more unhappy than she had ever been.

She did not want him in her mind or in her emotions. If such a thing were possible, she wished there was a way she could never see him again. But it was not possible.

As she lay there, Corey realised that even if by some miracle the expedition were to end today she would still not be rid of him. The lean chiselled face would appear in her thoughts during the day, and in her dreams at night. There were ways in which no man would ever measure up to him; she would be unable to prevent herself making comparisons. Despairingly she wondered if she was fated to have Fraser haunt her for the rest of her life.

She did not prepare lunch that day. If the men wondered what had happened to her, they did not seek her out. She thought that Fraser might fetch her and insist that she come to the tent kitchen. When he did not she assumed that such was his contempt for her that he would not lower himself to a second encounter in one day.

Perhaps an hour had passed when a voice called from just beyond the tent flap. 'Corey?'

'Mark?'

'Are you all right?'

'Yes, thanks.'

'You didn't come for lunch.' She could just see the side of his head. He was bending towards the tent opening, but seemed hesitant to come inside.

She raised herself on one arm. She was dressed now; some time ago she had put on fresh slacks and a shirt. 'I had a headache. You can come in, Mark.'

'No....' He sounded troubled. 'You're sure there's nothing wrong, Corey? Boyd didn't hurt you?'

'You saw to it that he didn't.' She laughed shakily. 'I haven't even thanked you.'

'I'd have killed him if he'd hurt you.' A strangeness in his tone, as if something bothered him. 'And Fraser ... Fraser didn't....' He stopped, as if he could not bring himself to voice his thoughts.

'I'm fine, Mark, really.' She spoke with as much conviction as she was able.

Three days passed, days that were flat and uneventful, and yet, for Corey, filled with strain. Fraser ignored her. He did not speak to her, did not touch her. They shared a tent, they spent eight hours of every night stretched out in their sleeping-bags no more than a few feet from each other, and yet for all the notice he took of her she might not have existed.

Corey did everything she had to. She took photographs and prepared meals. She spent the evenings at the campfire, talking with the men. Mark was her constant companion, and more than ever she was grateful for his friendship. Now and then, when she happened to come face to face with Boyd, he glowered at her resentfully, and Corey guessed that Fraser had told him in no uncertain terms to keep away from her. Not for her own good, she told herself wryly, but for his.

She was growing used to Fraser's silence. Save for a numb pain somewhere in the region of her chest, she began to accept his blank-faced treatment. She learned to change her own behaviour in accordance with his. She spoke to him only when she had to, and then in monosyllables. At night, in the tent, she gave no indication that she was unhappy and unable to sleep.

When he said her name on the fourth day, she could only look at him in amazement.

'Well, Corey?'

He was looking down at her. At her unconcealed surprise he smiled, and she saw the warmth that lit the grey eyes, making him look not only very attractive but also very human. His teeth were white and strong against the deep tan of his face. The thrust of his throat was strong and straight above the collar of the safari jacket, and where the top buttons were left open she saw a narrow expanse of muscled chest.

She had tried so hard not to think of him. Yet now, when he stood so close to her, she was powerless to prevent herself remembering. As if he was touching her, she could feel again the hardness of his chest against her soft breasts, the tautness of the long thighs, the seductiveness of the mobile lips.

Over and over in the past three days she had told herself to put out of her mind. There could be no future with the man, and if she allowed herself to dwell on what had been there would be no future for her alone either. If there was a man who was Fraser Mallory's equal she had never met him. She doubted that she ever would. Yet if she was to find happiness one day with someone else she must learn not to make comparisons. Accepting the fact was one thing; putting it into practice another. Fraser Mallory could not be allowed to haunt her. If he did, she was lost.

All her rationalising did not help her at this moment. Exposed now to the full virile force of his personality, she found her senses surging in response. As she looked back at him, she did not know that her eyes were lit with a violet radiance.

'Hello, Fraser,' she said unsteadily.

'You've been working hard the last few days.'

'Hard enough,' she acknowledged carefully.

'And you haven't given a moment's trouble. Not one lonely walk.'

After the brief moment in which their gaze had met his she had looked down again. Now his words brought her head swiftly up. He was watching her, his eyes sparkling with laughter.

'No lonely walks,' she agreed warily, wondering what was coming.

'That adventurous spirit of yours must need a respite.' He was still laughing at her.

Forgetting the caution that was not a natural part of her nature, Corey slanted him a provocative look. 'What exactly do you have in mind?' she asked.

'A little trip.'

She wondered at the new note in his tone. 'We're breaking camp?' she asked.

'No, we haven't finished here.'

'Then.... I don't understand.... What sort of trip, Fraser?'

'Further into the desert. We'll be away for a night.'

Nothing in his words gave cause for the sudden racing of her heartbeats. 'You're making up a smaller party, then?'

'You could call it that.' His voice was very smooth. 'A party of two.'

'You mean . . .?' She looked at him incredulously. He was watching her still, his eyes narrowed now, and alert. 'Just you and me?'

'That's right.'

'No!' The protest burst from her lips like a pistol shot. And then, 'Why me?'

'I need a photographer.'

She shook her head, violently, as if to escape from a danger that threatened to engulf her. 'No!'

'Yes.' No softening.

Don't put me through this, she wanted to say, to scream. You don't know what you're doing to me. Or, yes, you *do* know, and you're enjoying it.

Aloud she said, 'Mark can go with us.'

'Just you and I, Corey.' She heard the sound of steel.

She could be stubborn too. 'I won't go.'

'No?' A lifting of one eyebrow. 'So, Corey Latimer, you're so frightened of me?'

Frightened? She was terrified. The mere thought of being alone with Fraser, quite alone with no other person within miles of them, threw her in turmoil.

Would Fraser try to make love to her, as he had done before? Perhaps. But that was something she could cope with. What terrified her more than anything else was herself. Just standing with him now, talking to him, was enough to kindle the desire to have him touch her. Alone with him in the desert, would she be able to summon the strength to resist him? She could not go, she would not.

'Don't flatter yourself,' she threw the words at him. 'I'm not frightened of you, Fraser. I simply don't care to be alone with you.'

The warmth vanished from his eyes, and his face became once more a chiselled mask of spare stern lines. She saw the momentary tightening in the long jaw. When Fraser spoke again his tone was smooth and dangerous. 'We leave tomorrow at sunrise.'

CHAPTER NINE

In the grey light of dawn the awakening camp had a look of sleep about it. Pete stood by the Land-Rover, confirming last-minute instructions with Fraser; he would be in charge of operations in Fraser's absence. Mark emerged from his tent and hovered near the Land-Rover, his forehead puckered in a frown, his expression unhappy. Corey had the feeling that he would have liked to stop her from going, but all he said was goodbye, and to take care of herself.

I'll be all right, she wanted to tell him. As far as physical safety is concerned nothing will happen to me. Already she had seen the precautions Fraser had taken. There was extra fuel and a spare tank of water; there was a rifle and a first-aid box; there was more than enough food. Fraser had anticipated all contingencies.

Only as far as her emotional well-being was concerned was she in any danger. A sleepless night had not succeeded in resolving her doubts on that score. But this was not something she could discuss with Mark.

The sky was translucent with the first light of the approaching day when the Land-Rover left the camp. It was cold still, and Corey huddled in the colourful Basuto blanket Fraser had given her. She sat quietly on the extreme side of the seat, and wondered what the next days would bring. Somehow she sensed that nothing would ever be quite the same again when they were over.

Fraser was silent too. The terrain they covered was rough and unknown, and needed all his concentration. Now and then, when it seemed safe to do so unobserved, Corey turned her head to look at him. Like the rest of him, his profile was arresting, the lines clear and well-defined. Over his safari suit he wore a thick suede bush-jacket, on his feet were boots which emphasised the length and strength of his legs. The Land-Rover pulled its way through rock and sand; it could be no easy matter to drive it, Corey surmised. But the hands that held the wheel were relaxed, and there was no sign of strain in the long lean body in the driver's seat.

Fraser was in control of the Land-Rover as he was in control of every other aspect of his life. Corey wondered again what marriage would be like with this man. He would be the dominant partner, perhaps, but she had the feeling that his wife, if she loved him, would be content to have him so. For with thc dominant side of his personality there would be security also, a feeling of safety, of knowing that whatever the problems that might arise they would be dealt with.

Would his wife accept the more difficult parts of his nature? It came to Corey that the answer could only be yes. Coupled with his superiority there would be compensations; love and happiness and excitement. There would be tenderness too. Corey had never glimpsed this tenderness, she doubted that she ever would, but some instinct told her it existed. She envied the girl who would experience it. In a man like Fraser love and tenderness would be two very wonderful qualities.

'Daydreaming?' His voice came to her through the stillness and she looked at him in surprise. She had been so sure that his concentration was fixed on the difficult road that he could have had no inkling that he was observed. Strange, she reflected wryly, that she never ceased to underestimate his perceptiveness.

'Just thinking,' she told him. 'This desert is so different from anything I ever expected.'

'That happens sometimes,' he said dryly. He turned his head a moment, and as their eyes met Corey had the distinct feeling that they were talking about something other than the desert.

Confused, all at once, she turned her eyes to the window. 'So much grassland. And the swamps.... All I expected was sand.'

As if he understood her need to stick to the subject, he returned his eyes to the road. 'There's sand too,' was his comment. 'As much sand as you'd want to see in a lifetime. But it's true that there's variety in the desert. That perhaps is what those who've never been here don't understand.'

Corey did not turn her head again. His voice reached her across the narrow expanse of seat, filling her mind and reaching to her heart. For days now she had tried to ignore certain realities; it was becoming more and more difficult to do so.

'Dad would love this,' she said once, as a herd of gemsbok lifted their heads and stared, then galloped across the dry grass plains in unison.

'He would,' agreed a quiet tone. Corey heard understanding as well as sympathy. She felt a sudden lump form at the back of her throat.

'You don't hate him, then?' she asked, still without turning.

'I never did. We had a difference of opinion, but I've never had anything but respect for your father.' A hand touched one of hers. 'Look, Corey—elephant, do you see them?'

It was hard to concentrate on anything while long lean fingers still lingered on hers. She swallowed. 'Those shapes beyond the bushes? Fraser, I thought they were rocks.'

'Elephants.'

'Dangerous?' She sat forward, taut with sudden excitement.

'Potentially always, but not if we behave with care.'

A double meaning again? Suddenly she did not care. She knew only that she was alone in the desert with a strange disturbing man who, one way or another, was beginning to mean more to her than she had dreamed possible. She also felt alive and exhilarated and more intensely vital than she could remember in years.

As if he read her thoughts, Fraser tightened his fingers around her hand. 'Enjoy these days, Corey.'

She turned then, meeting his gaze full-on. He was smiling, and for the first time she smiled back at him. 'I intend to.'

The atmosphere different after that. They still talked little, but when there was silence it was without strain. Fraser knew the desert well. He pointed out things which Corey, left to herself, would have missed.

Once he stopped the Land-Rover to gesture towards a little bird that flew in front of them flapping its wings. 'A honey-bird,' he told her. 'Follow it, and you'll find a store of honey.'

There were legends woven about the honey-bird, and Corey listened fascinated as he told her of the bird's revenge when men became greedy.

He stopped again to show Corey a bushman encampment. Not genuine bushmen these, he explained to her, as they left the vehicle and walked a little way through the bush. These people were descendants of the original bushmen, people who had intermarried with other tribes. But the bushman blood was evident in their appearance. They were little people, with yellow skin and broad shoulders and faces that were creased and wrinkled. Shyly they looked at Corey out of eyes that were alert and intelligent.

Corey thought of all she knew about the bushmen; that they managed to live for years on meagre supplies of water; that ostrich eggs filled with water lay hidden beneath the desert sands, emergency caches awaiting thirsty hunters. She knew of the poisoned arrows with which they speared the game. Her father had spoken to her of music that was unlike anything he had ever heard, and of the paintings through which a way of life had become immortalised. Wishing that there was a way in which she could exchange a few words with the bright-eyed people around their little fire, Corey was filled with admiration for the ingenuity with which they made their lives in the harshness of the desert.

Leaving the encampment, they drove further. The sun rose in the sky, burning down on bush and sand. Now and then Corey had glimpses of game—once some giraffe, more elephants, and more frequently than anything else the magnificent gemsbok with its powerful horns.

In the distance she saw a line of low hills, and, closer at hand, what looked like an immense pile of rock. Fraser seemed to be making straight for the rock.

'Camera ready?' he asked after a while.

He stopped the vehicle a little way from the rocks, where the sand was not so thick that he would not be able to get it started again. As they left the car and began to walk a hand slid beneath Corey's arm, cupping her elbow. She did not need his help. The sand was soft and dragged at the feet, but she could have managed. Yet she did not shrug him away. The gentle pressure beneath her elbow gave her a warm feeling of pleasure.

An unsuspecting stranger might never have discovered the paintings, but Fraser knew where to find them. As he led her to a sprawl of rock, Corey drew in her breath.

It was one thing to see her father's photographs, or to study pictures in books, quite another to see bushman paintings actually on rock. For a long time she stood before the first one, a scene depicting hunters and fleeing buffalo. It was not the first time Corey had seen bushman paintings, but these were a little different from the others she knew.

There were several paintings. The paint had dulled a little, but the scenes were vivid and graphic. Each told its own story. As she looked at them, Corey could only only marvel at the natural skill of the artists who had lived so many centuries ago.

It was a while before she remembered the camera which hung on her shoulder. It did not matter that many of these paintings were ones her father had already recorded. She wanted photographs of her own.

And then it was time to go on. Deeper into the desert they drove, and deeper. There were more rock piles, more paintings. Corey took photographs while Fraser busied himself with his own work.

The sun climbed higher and higher, it reached its zenith while the burning land below gasped for air. The day wore on, shadows began to form. It came to Corey, quite suddenly, that night was almost on them, and that they were many miles from camp. She had known when they started out that morning that they would spend the night alone together in the desert. For the first time that fact became reality.

Fraser stopped the Land-Rover near another pile of rock and turned off the ignition. 'Time to strike up camp,' he said.

'Yes.' She was suddenly breathless.

He glanced at her. 'You're as rigid as a tightly-coiled spring. Nervous, Corey?'

'Don't be ridiculous!' she managed.

'Is it ridiculous?' he asked softly. His hand went to her throat, one finger starting a slow stroking movement from her chin down to the little hollow where a pulse beat frenziedly. His gaze lingered on eyes that were very bright and, despite all Corey's efforts, a little scared; then it descended past the rapid pulse to breasts that rose and fell with Corey's breathing. 'Is it ridiculous?' he asked again, more softly.

'Yes. We've shared a tent before.' She tried to pull away, to break contact with fingers which were too seductive in their sensuousness. 'It gets dark so quickly. Hadn't we better make a start, Fraser?'

She heard the laughter that bubbled in his throat. He knows exactly how I feel, she thought wildly, and there's nothing I can do about it.

'An excellent idea,' Fraser agreed, and dropping his hand he turned to open the door.

The tent was pitched quickly. Corey watched as Fraser worked. His movements were streamlined and economical; he seemed to know at every moment just what he had to do. She watched him carry their bedding into the tent. Inside her every nerve was quivering. Very deliberately she turned away and went to the Land-Rover where the food supplies were boxed.

The fire was lit before the sun went down and the leaping flames gave Corey a feeling of reassurance. The tent looked so small, so isolated. The land was flat around them. A few stunted trees stood near the tent, but beyond that the sand stretched on and on, seemingly for ever.

However primitive the previous camps had been, from this distance they represented an oasis of civilisation. There had been more than one tent, more than one Land-Rover. There had been people, but now they were quite alone. Corey thought of the roars that sounded sometimes in the night, and shivered. The flames of the fire were high; she hoped Fraser would keep them so. The leap and hiss of the flames would keep any lions at bay.

Yet it was not the solitary lion which she feared most. Her thoughts were on the night ahead, on an intimacy which, all at once, seemed more seductive and basic than ever before. Fraser passed her on his way from the Land-Rover. In his arms was a box. It must have been heavy, for the calves of his legs were braced as he walked, and his head was thrust back. He grinned as he came alongside her, and at his devil-may-care expression Corey felt an odd twist of pain at the back of her throat.

Darkness was gathering as they ate their meal. Corey had imagined she was too strung up to swallow a morsel, but to her surprise she ate well. For once Fraser prepared the meal. Corey had not known that dehydrated rations and meat dried and salted by an expert could taste so good.

It was peaceful by the fire. The flames leaped and danced. Now and then Fraser threw on extra kindling, and there would be a sputtering hiss as the fire soared then settled.

She must remember this, Corey thought, as she watched the orange glow and the dark figure of the man silhouetted against it. She must remember this night. When the expedition ended her memories would be all that remained of a time when she had been crazily in love.

For she loved Fraser—she knew that now. She thought that she had known it for some time, and that in her stubbornness she had refused to acknowledge the fact. She had taken her feelings for infatuation, for emotions that were based purely on chemistry. She knew now that she had been mistaken. Fraser did have an appeal that played havoc with her senses, but she loved him for more than that. She loved his strength and his compassion—she had seen that compassion in his dealings with his men. She loved his mind and his integrity.

Once or twice in her life she had been stirred by a man, but never in this manner. Eric had disillusioned her, but her grief had been relatively fleeting. She did not think of him any more.

Fraser she would love always. She knew that now, and recognised that in that fact lay the seeds of unhappiness. For she meant nothing to him. He had kissed her and held her and she had felt the depth of his wanting, but Fraser was a normal man with normal desires. His wants were physical; they did not extend to his emotions.

She tried to push unhappiness from her mind. Soon there would be all the time in the world for unhappiness and regrets; the rest of her life, maybe. For tonight there must be only the joy of being with the man she loved.

They began to talk, and Corey realised how much they had in common. They both loved the life of the outdoors. They enjoyed the same music, even the same books. Fraser told her of his plans for his farm, the problems of merino sheep-farming, as well as the compensations. As he spoke of his dreams and ambitions Corey fell silent. There was such intense pleasure in hearing him talk that she wished the hours at the fire could go on for ever.

After a while he grew silent. 'What about you, Corey?' he asked, and she heard a new inflection in his voice. 'You must be longing to get back to the world of glitter and lights.'

'That's only how the public views modelling.' Her voice was deliberately light to hide the ache of the tears that had gathered in her throat.

'You *are* longing to get back?' he persisted.

No, she wanted to say, I don't want to go back, at least not to the kind of world I knew. I want to go with you to your farm and live with you always.

What would be his reaction? Contempt. Mockery. And then an icy withdrawal that would be worse than anything else. She could not bear the thought of withdrawal, not now while they were in such harmony. Aloud she said, 'It's my work, Fraser.'

He did not answer immediately. She saw him lift a piece of wood and throw it on to the flames. Perhaps it was only her heightened senses that endowed the movement with a violence that was unjustified. 'You have your work,' he said at length, and his tone was so controlled that she knew she had been mistaken after all. 'Just as I have mine.'

'Do you think we'll see each other again?' She did not know what made her ask the question.

'I don't frequent fashion shows.' He stood up, looking taller and more gaunt than usual in the darkness. 'It's getting late, Corey. Time for bed.'

She went into the tent before he did. That had become their custom. She would get undressed and crawl into her sleeping-bag. After a reasonable interval Fraser would come in and get undressed himself.

This time Corey procrastinated. She was not entirely conscious of what she did. Her movements were slow, deliberately so. She lingered over brushing her hair and her teeth and cleaning her face. She began to undress, but slowly. All her movements were infused with a languorous slowness which she seemed unable to do anything about. She took off her blouse and folded it, and then, as if she was dissatisfied with what she had done, she folded it again. She took off her slacks and took great pains to keep the creases quite straight. That too took time.

She was just putting her slacks down beside her shirt and shoes when there was a movement at the opening of the tent, and she turned. Her heart seemed to miss a beat as her gaze met Fraser's. He stood very still, his body almost rigid. In the light of the lantern she saw that a muscle tightened in his jaw and that his eyes became suddenly narrow. She thought she heard a hissing intake of breath.

His gaze held hers for a long moment, and then it descended to her body, moving over curves and outlines glowing softly in the swaying light. Corey's heart was beating so fast that she could feel it thudding against her rib-cage.

'Corey....' Her name was a husky exclamation in a tone she had never thought to hear from him.

Later she was never to remember who made the first move. Perhaps they met half-way. She knew only that he was holding her against him, his hands caressing her bare body. Through the fabric of his safari suit she could feel the demanding heat of his body and the tightness of his muscles. If she wanted him, he wanted her too. A heady feeling of love and happiness and warm desire swept through her. She put her arms around his back and pressed herself closer to him.

She heard him groan as his mouth came down and covered her lips. There was passion in the kiss, but tenderness too. And then his lips were descending to the sensitive column of her throat, stirring up fresh torrents of need. They lingered a moment at the little hollow where the pulse beat too quickly, and then went down to the hard swell of her breasts.

When he lifted her in his arms to put her down on the ground she could only cling to him. There were no thoughts in her mind now, no rationalising or remorse or reminders of what the consequences could be of their lovemaking. There was only the aching need of her body, and a love which was stronger than anything she had ever imagined possible.

Fraser lifted himself away from her very suddenly. She looked up uncomprehendingly. Even through the passion that blurred her eyes she could see the bleakness in his face.

'Fraser?' she whispered, not understanding what had happened. 'Fraser, what's wrong?'

'This can only end one way.' She saw the torment etched around his mouth.

'I know.' She was beyond shame, beyond embarrassment. She knew only that she loved this man and that she needed him more than she had needed anyone or anything in her life. If she had offended him in some way she did not know it. She leaned towards him, her arms reaching for him.

She had pressed herself against him again when he pushed her away, roughly this time. 'Do you know what you're doing? My God, Corey, I'm not a plaything, I'm a normal hot-blooded male!'

'I know. Fraser, don't you ... I thought we....' Her words trailed away in confusion.

'You thought I wanted to sleep with you.' There was no mistaking the mockery in his tone. It intended to hurt. She was unable to prevent herself flinching.

'Don't you?' The words were out before she could stop them.

'Damn right I do! What man wouldn't?' He was standing now, towering above her like some menacing Satanic figure. 'Boyd—Mark—they'd all be panting for the same thing.'

'You think ... you think all I was after was sex...?' The pain in her throat was so bad that she could hardly speak.

'Isn't it?' he taunted. 'It's what you've been after from the first.'

'You haven't been so reluctant yourself.' Slow anger was building inside her, driving her to say words she had no time to consider. 'There've been times when you forced yourself on to me.'

'Correct.' The chilling tone was a whiplash. 'But only when I wanted it. I told you once that I control the situation, Corey, and nothing has happened to change that.'

She stared at him, as if through a daze. No man had the right to speak to her like this, not even Fraser—least of all Fraser. 'Get out of here!' she snapped.

'You're a schemer, Corey.' There was a twist to

his lips. 'You schemed your way into the expedition. You schemed to cause a rift between two of my men. What scheme are you up to now?'

'Get out of here!' she shouted. And as he still stood there she seized a shoe and flung it at him, cursing when he side-stepped and the shoe bounced against the wall of the tent. 'Get out and stay out!'

'I will not stay out and you know it.' Still the same hateful tone. Hard eyes insolently raked the bare female figure. 'Get some clothes on, Corey, and be quick about it. It's been a long day and I want some sleep.' He strode out of the tent.

Her hands shook so much that she struggled to put on her pyjamas. Her whole body shook. Only minutes ago she had felt as if she was burning. Now she was shivering so that even her teeth chattered. Outside the chill of the night air was settling over the sands of the desert. Inside the tent it was cold too. But the iciness that gripped Corey stemmed from a rejection that was more hurtful than anything she had ever experienced.

She was in her sleeping-bag when Fraser came into the tent. Her eyes were closed, her body still. Only a superhuman effort kept her limbs from shivering.

Fraser could not have believed that she was asleep, but he did not speak to her. She heard him get ready for bed, the sound of his movements quick and angry. It was some time before even breathing filled the tent. It gave Corey some satisfaction to know that Fraser had difficulty sleeping too.

For once she woke before he did. She raised herself on one elbow and looked at him.

Dark hair fell untidily across a high forehead and long eyelashes cast shadows over the lean cheeks. One hand was flung loosely backwards, and his lips moved momentarily in a half-smile, as if he was dreaming. She had never seen him like this, so defenceless, so vulnerable, and a great wave of love and longing surged through her.

She grimaced wryly. What was wrong with her? This man made no secret of his contempt. He had hurt her more with his unjustified mockery than anyone, even Eric, had ever hurt her. Yet even now, knowing what he was, what he thought of her and what he was capable of, she still loved him. Love should be sane and reasoning, appropriate. Irrational longings should have no part in it. So she told herself—and knew that while her mind accepted the reasoning, her emotions did not.

She did not know when she became aware of the movement on her sleeping-bag. Hardly a movement, more a gentle gliding, a momentary thing that lasted no more than seconds. She looked down, but as the scream welled in her throat blind instinct stopped it.

A snake lay stretched across the bag. The long body was sleek and coiled: a cobra. Corey knew the distinctive markings, knew too that its bite could be fatal.

She must not move. One jerky movement and the reptile would strike. That it had not done so when she had raised herself just minutes ago was probably due to a sleep-induced relaxation. Now, however, she was anything but relaxed.

Should she wake Fraser? Dared she? What if he startled the cobra? Whatever she did, she had to be certain. There would be no second chance.

Another movement as the snake coiled a further section of its body. It was the same movement as the one which had claimed her attention initially. It was just above her stomach. An iciness gripped her. She wanted to hurl the snake from her, she wanted to scream. But through it all she knew the importance of control.

'Fraser.' Her tone was as quiet as she could make it.

He came awake instantly. He looked across at her, and for a moment the tautness that was with him at all times was absent. As his eyes met hers there was an expression, very briefly, which in other circumstances might have set her heart beating.

'Well, Corey?'

'Hush!' Her voice was just barely loud enough for him to hear. Her eyes dropped to her sleeping-bag. 'Cobra.'

She saw him mouth the words, 'My God!' He was wide awake now. The lassitude of sleep had left him. He was taut once more, yet quiet with it. There was no fear in his expression, only a rigid determination.

He was in control of the situation. Instinctively Corey understood that he knew what to do.

'Be very quiet.' Again the mouthing of words. 'Don't move.'

All his movements were smooth. If he felt any fear he did not show it. Only the whiteness around his nose and lips revealed his awareness of the urgency of the situation. One false movement, one premature startling of the reptile, and it would strike.

He used a stick. In two movements that were so fast as to be one, he pushed the cobra from the sleeping-bag and crushed its head on the ground.

Seeing the long body in the writhing which preceded death, Corey was unable to take in fully that she was safe. The whole incident, from the moment she had noticed the cobra till the moment when Fraser had hurled it from her, had lasted no more than minutes, but it seemed much more.

Through it all she had maintained an icy calm. Now, with safety, the calm was shattered. Fraser left the tent with the dead snake impaled at the end of the stick. When he came back in she was shaking.

'You're all right, Corey?' His eyes were warm with concern.

The concern was her undoing as much as the reaction to the calm she had managed to preserve through the minutes of terror. She looked at him. She opened her mouth to speak, but no words came. She fell back against the ground, crumpled and weeping.

'Corey....' Strong hands lifted her against him. There was gentleness in his hands, and tenderness too. He was stroking her hair, her back, softly, soothingly. She heard him say her name, over and over again, and through her tears she heard a broken quality in his tone. Once she thought she felt his lips in her hair.

The weeping stilled at last. As the shock of the cobra faded, new sensations came into play. An aura of maleness seemed to envelop her, the hardness of thighs and chest, a virile smell filling her nostrils. Fraser was in his pyjamas, and the jacket was open. The hairs that covered his chest were rough against her cheek. Last night's rejection should have been fresh still in her memory, but for some reason it wasn't. She turned her face so that her lips nuzzled against the rough hardness of his chest, and gradually her shivering quietened completely. Cradled against Fraser, there was only safety and security.

Imperceptibly there was a change in the hands that held her. She felt a tensing in the fingers, a tautening in the chest muscles and in the thighs, a stronger beat of the heart against her cheek. There was a change in the mood of his caresses. The tenderness was still there, but passion was beginning to take over, and she could feel her own passions responding to his.

'Corey,' she heard him say, 'look at me.' And

when she did not heed him a hand cupped her head and drew it from his chest.

'Fraser....' It was hard to meet the gaze that burned in the grey ones. There was no mockery this time, no dislike, only an expression which sent the blood surging like fire through her veins.

'Last night,' she whispered, as the hurtful memories flooded back. 'Last night you....'

'I was mad—angry.'

'Angry?' Violet eyes were confused. 'What did I do?'

'Nothing, my darling. You were just being yourself. Warm and feminine and unbearably desirable.'

'Then...?'

'I'll explain it all another time, if you'll let me. But now....' His lips came down, claiming hers with the thirst of a man who has been holding himself back for too long.

It came to Corey that Fraser had been hurt, badly hurt, by a woman. She would make him forget, she thought, with a forgiving surge of love and eagerness. She parted her lips beneath his and felt him shudder.

His kiss deepened. His lips tasted and explored the sweetness of her mouth, sending heat flaming through her nerve-stream. She was still lying across his thighs, in the position where he had cradled her for reassurance. As his lips and hands became infused with a life of their own, there was no more thought for reassurance in the man who held her.

Now there was only passion and need.

He pushed aside the top of her pyjamas, and then his mouth burnt a trail along throat and shoulders and breasts and down further to the flatness of her stomach. There was gentleness in the expert lips, and an expertise that was so tantalisingly seductive that it left her breathless.

His lips returned to hers as he lifted her and laid her flat on her sleeping-bag. No words were needed as he undressed first her and then himself. And then he was lowering himself on to her, moulding the shape of her body to his.

'No regrets?' he asked once, lifting his head to look down at her.

She shook her head mutely. There was no voice in her to say that she loved him, and that she wanted him to make love to her fully.

'Corey . . . darling. . . .' This time the break in his voice was not imagined. 'Last night I fought you, but now. . . . Don't ever be sorry.'

Later, when they had dressed, Fraser stoked the fire which had burned through the night, and they had breakfast. The sun was lifting above the horizon, and the desert was still gripped in its nocturnal chill. Corey and Fraser sat by the fire, close together. Now and then they exchanged a few words, but not many. Over steaming mugs of coffee their eyes met frequently, rendering verbal speech unnecessary.

Don't be sorry, Fraser had said in the moment

before he had taken full possession of her. She would never be sorry, Corey knew, even though what had happened had violated all the principles she had thus far held dear. She loved Fraser. What had happened between them had been beautiful, fitting too. Whatever happened she would never be sorry.

Only later, much later, would she remember that Fraser had not told her he loved her too.

CHAPTER TEN

TOWARDS mid-morning they approached a small clump of hardy desert trees. There was no road leading to it, and the Land-Rover had to plough its way through sand and over scrub. When Fraser stopped the vehicle Corey looked at him expectantly. The sun had been burning down mercilessly for many hours and she was hot and sticky and thirsty. She wondered if they had stopped for something cool to drink.

'The cups are behind the cardboard box,' she began. And then, seeing a tight expression on the tanned face, she said hesitantly, 'Fraser....'

'Stay here.' His words were clipped.

She watched him leave the Land-Rover and walk towards the trees. Involuntarily the muscles of her stomach tightened.

When he came back to the vehicle and opened her door she was not surprised. She looked up at him, wondering if he would speak, but when he did not she was content to take the hand he held out to her.

She followed him to the trees. It was so hot that the sand burned through the soles of her shoes. Beneath the leafless trees there was a sprinkling of shade, but there was no time to loiter, for Fraser was pulling her further.

She did not see the rocks till they were almost upon them. They were in a depression of ground and hidden by the trees.

Fraser turned, and gestured. He had not spoken yet, but there was an odd glimmer in his eyes, and a tautness about his mouth and jaw. The feeling that had been building up in Corey since he had stopped the car intensified.

She stopped in mid-step. There was a pounding in her temples, and she put a hand to her head. Instinctively she guessed what to expect. Now that the time had come she was oddly frightened, as if the reality might be anticlimactic after her expectations.

As if Fraser guessed her thoughts his expression changed. The light was still in his eyes, but there was a softening around the mouth. 'Come,' he said softly.

They walked through the narrow opening and Corey understood why this spot had remained secret for so long. It was not easily discernible. Even had she known the location she might have missed the cave itself.

A pile of rock hid the opening to the cave. Stones slithered beneath Corey's feet, but Fraser took her hand once more, and supported her when she might have slipped.

Then they were in the cave itself, and Corey clapped a hand to her mouth. The frieze was almost as her father had said it would be—a long expanse of rock depicting a hunting scene. Till now she had wondered what made the frieze so special that her father should have hankered after it for so many years, but with the evidence before her eyes she knew the answer.

It was like the other bushman paintings she had seen, and yet it was different. It was long, very long, stretching across more than one rock. The variety of animals was staggering, and Corey saw that each one had been depicted with great attention to detail. In all the other figures she had seen thus far, she had been struck by the angularity of the lines. That angularity existed here too, but with it there was a sense of movement, a fluid grace and vitality that suggested the brush of a master painter.

Wind and weather seemed hardly to have affected the painting, for the colours were still vivid. Corey thought of her father, firm in his adherence to an ancient dream, and she wished with all her heart that he was here.

She glanced at Fraser. He was watching her, a question in his eyes. She could not answer it, for the lump in her throat precluded all speech. His expression changed and he smiled, a smile that she had seen only rarely, and even then it had never been directed at her. It was a smile which changed the aspect of the lean stern face, giving it warmth and understanding. An arm went round her shoulders.

The lump in her throat deepened. Corey knew she had never been more moved. There was the painting in front of her, the vision of one man executed thousands of years earlier, and there was the arm that held her, and a warmth and human contact that were very much a part of the present. The two realities seemed somehow linked.

They went back to the Land-Rover for the camera. Corey shot the picture many times, from many angles. If there had been a way of communicating with her father she would have done so. She would have liked to tell him that now there was nothing more to hold up the completion of his life's work.

The warmth was with her still when they went back to the Land-Rover, also the excitement. She was silent as Fraser turned the vehicle and began to drive back along the way they had come. There was a question in her mind, and though she meant to ask it, she thought she already knew the answer.

'Did you know we'd find the frieze?' The clump

of trees was almost out of sight, and the spell which had seemed to be upon her was broken now, making it possible for her to speak again.

'I hoped so.'

'That's why we made this trip?'

He was silent, and Corey wondered if he meant to ignore the question. She turned in her seat to look at him. It was strange how the chiselled profile had taken on a different aspect in her mind. Once she had thought it strong and stern and arrogant. The strength was still there, and some of the sternness, but she was no longer bothered by the arrogance. Instead, in the features that she was growing to love more all the time, she saw the warmth and understanding of a man who was in every respect superior to all other men she had known.

Taking his eyes from the road, he smiled at her. 'Partly,' he agreed.

'Then you did believe the frieze existed?' Corey breathed.

The smile deepened. She saw the laughter lines around the lips and eyes, and felt an urge to reach out a finger to trace their contours.

'I reckoned if John Latimer had such strong feelings about a picture there must be something in it. Your father is a stubborn man, Corey—I've told you that before. But he's also wise and shrewd.'

'So all the time....' She could not go on.

A hand went to a soft flushed cheek, then upwards to ruffle through short dark hair that clung in wisps to a smooth forehead. 'Let's say I wanted to satisfy myself,' Fraser said.

She should have realised earlier why they had undertaken this trip. True, they had stopped here and there, and Corey had taken photographs which were important in the research project. But the main purpose of the trip had been to find the frieze that was her father's dream. The warmth that filled her now was only partly due to gratitude.

They were nearly back at camp, the animal frieze many hours behind them, when Fraser stopped the car once more. They were in a wooded area now, a tract of land that reminded Corey of the bushveld with its density of thorn trees and scrub.

She was not surprised when Fraser told her there was a spot he wanted to explore. His mind was never far from the work that was also his hobby; she knew already that many of the notes he had made on this trip could provide the basis for future expeditions. Pain tugged briefly at her chest when she remembered that these would be expeditions in which she would have no part.

There were still a few shots left on the spool she had begun for the frieze. Not knowing how many photographs Fraser would need, she tucked a new spool in the pocket of her slacks.

They came to a pile of rock that looked different from anything Corey had seen thus far. As Fraser showed her what he needed recorded, she saw the alertness in his eyes. This place was interesting.

While Corey photographed, Fraser measured and examined and made notes. There was no conversation between them. Later Corey would ask him the significance of these rocks, but for the moment they were both absorbed in their work.

Corey heard the sound quite suddenly, and her head jerked up at the same moment as she heard Fraser's urgent 'Don't panic!'

The elephant was ominously near. An old elephant, Corey saw that in a moment, an old bull, rejected perhaps by the herd. Ears flapped back, and long tusks lowered menacingly. It seemed to be looking straight at Corey, the tiny eyes, incongruous in such an enormous beast, mean and boding no good.

For a moment Corey was transfixed. Then, as the elephant lifted its great head and let out a thunderous roar, she jerked to her feet. Elephants could run quickly, she knew that. She had to run faster. She stepped blindly backwards, oblivious of Fraser and his urgent commands. She swivelled and ran. Once her foot hit a twisted root. She lurched against a tree, breaking her fall, but the camera was knocked from her hand.

Corey and Fraser beat the elephant in the race to the Land-Rover. Fraser spent no time in comfort. Every moment was important. It was only as the Land-Rover got under way and the angry trumpeting beast was left behind that he turned a grim face.

His expression made an impact and Corey

clapped a hand to her mouth. 'My camera!' she whispered.

'I know.'

'Fraser, I must have left it....'

'It broke against a rock.' His voice was flat, without inflection.

'The spool....'

'Exposed to the light.' A hand left the wheel, covering one of hers, and in the touch there was an attempt at comfort. 'I'm sorry, Corey.'

Sorry.... When her father's dream lay shattered on the thorny sunbaked ground. Numbly Corey stared at the hand that held hers a moment longer before returning to the wheel. If she had a spare camera with her she could ask Fraser to go back, but her cameras were at camp, and she knew already that the expedition was almost at an end. The weather was turning. There were parts of the desert where rain could be heavy. No more precious days could be wasted. Fraser wanted to be out of the desert before they were stranded.

They had been back in camp only a day and already Corey saw a change in Fraser's attitude. There was an aloofness that reminded her of his manner when he had first discovered she was a girl. There was a reserve, almost a withdrawal. While she was hurt by it, she was puzzled also. For her, the time spent alone with him had been a time of magic, of enchantment. The love which had nurtured slowly inside her had flowered. Fraser, that strange disturbing man, had seemed changed too; there had been a tenderness in his lovemaking, a different expression in his eyes and voice. There had been times when Corey had actually allowed herself to dream that her feelings could eventually be reciprocated.

Now, just one day after they had rejoined the others, it was as if the interlude of togetherness had never been. He devoted himself almost exclusively to the men. Corey could understand that he wanted to know what progress they had made in his absence. That was natural. His almost deliberate ignoring of herself was not.

Driven by her pain to retaliate, Corey did likewise. Mark was happy to see her back, and she spent more time than was necessary talking with him. She talked about the desert and the things she had seen. But there were two things she never mentioned; the animal frieze and the precious moments when she had become fully a woman. Inside her, constant and raw, was pain.

Fraser's attitude did not improve with the passing of the days, and Corey was glad that the expedition was ending soon. She could not stand much more. The days were bad enough. Whenever Fraser was nearby she could feel herself tauten; her voice would become too brittle, her manner too vivacious. When he was not near she wondered constantly what he was doing.

The nights were an ordeal. Perhaps if she had

never known the fullness of Fraser's lovemaking Corey would have adjusted, somehow, to the new sterility of their relationship. But she had known it. As if it had just happened, she could still feel the hardness of his arms and legs against her own soft ones, the strength of his chest against her breast, the taste of his lips. She could still remember the sweet wild rapture of the moment that had changed her life.

Through the long silent desert nights Corey lay rigid, her body aching with need, while from the camp-bed next to hers the steady sound of breathing filled the tent.

Fraser left the camp early one morning. Corey heard the men say he must have gone ahead to check on refuelling points; that was part of his duty as leader of the expedition. But Corey wished that he had thought of saying goodbye to her. When he came back it would be time to start packing up camp, and after that it would be no more than a matter of days till they emerged from the desert and the team dispersed. She had no illusions that they would see each other again.

To disperse the feelings of helplessness and despair Corey accepted Mark's invitation to go for a walk. With Mark she could relax; he was kind and gentle and there were no awkward silences when they were together. No man could take Fraser's place in her heart—unhappily Corey was forced to acknowledge the fact that perhaps no man ever would—but at least when she was with Mark her misery was lessened for a while.

They walked as far as the desert heat permitted. Mark asked her what she planned to do when she returned to Cape Town, and not altogether surprisingly Corey did not find the answer simple. Before embarking on the expedition she had decided to leave the modelling world and turn to photography. Now she was no longer sure what she wanted. She had a suspicion that it would be a long while before she could handle a camera without thinking of Fraser.

There were a few alternatives she was considering, she said, and she asked Mark what he would do next. It was more than a change of subject. She had a genuine affection for the gentle scientist, and was therefore interested in his plans.

'You'll be joining another expedition?' she wanted to know.

'Not for a long while.' Had she not been quite so absorbed in her own concerns she might have heard the change in his tone.

'Oh?' she said casually.

'I want to settle down. I'm hoping to get married, Corey.'

'Oh, Mark!' She turned to him in pleasure. 'That's good. You never mentioned it before.'

There was an odd little pause. 'The time wasn't right before now.' He stopped walking and took her hand. As she looked up at him she felt herself tensing. She sensed what was coming. She realised, when it was too late, that she could have done something to prevent it.

'Will you marry me, Corey?'

'Mark—dear Mark!' Her voice was as gentle as she could make it. 'I wish I could say yes, but I can't.'

The hand that held hers tightened. 'I'd make you happy.'

'I know that.'

If only she had never met Fraser, never fallen in love. Mark was nicer than any other man she had met. Without Fraser's spectre in the background she might have loved him. She might never have known the wild passion and throbbing excitement she had experienced with Fraser, but life could have been lived happily enough without those emotions. Mark was everything she had ever thought she wanted in a husband.

Yet she could not have him. It would not be fair to marry him while she yearned with all her heart and body for someone else. It would not be fair to marry any man. Fraser, she wept silently, if only you hadn't shown me a glimpse of heaven, so that all other men have been spoiled for me.

'Corey?' There was distress in his tone.

'Mark, I can't. I'm so sorry.'

'There's someone else?' And when she did not answer, he continued on a harder note. 'Fraser?'

Violet eyes were swimming with tears when she

looked up at him again. She heard the muttered oath, alien to Mark, and saw that the hardness had extended to his expression. 'He's not for you, Corey.'

'No....'

'He's not the marrying kind.'

'I know that.' The words came out on a sob.

'Then....' The harshness left Mark's tone as he drew her to him. 'You can't remain alone for ever. I love you, Corey.'

He gave her no time to answer. He was pulling her to him with a strength she had not suspected. She allowed him to kiss her. There was reassurance in his embrace, and a kind of hope too. Perhaps, by some miracle, she could love another man, could feel some stirring. His kiss grew harder, more passionate, and she felt the desire of a man who was aflame with need.

When he drew away from her she knew the worst. She had not felt repelled by the kiss. She could never be repelled by Mark. But she had not felt even a little of the abandoned excitement she had experienced with Fraser. She had not been stirred in the slightest. It was unlikely she would feel any different with another man.

'It's no good, is it?' She heard his sadness.

'No,' she whispered.

By tacit agreement they turned and began to make their way back to camp. They did not talk much now. Corey felt raw and drained, and she sensed that Mark felt much the same. Liking him as she did, she wished that she had not had to hurt him.

They were emerging from the trees at the edge of the camp when he stopped once more. 'Let's say goodbye now, Corey.' His voice was ragged. 'Chances are it'll be the last time we're alone together before the camp breaks up.'

She did not resist as he drew her to him again. This time his kiss was gentle. There was no passion; it was the kiss of two friends who were saying goodbye. Corey put her arms up around his neck, and in her lips was her own farewell.

Some instinct made her break from the kiss and swing round. Fraser was standing not more than three yards from them. She had not known he was back. For one time-stopping moment they stared at each other, and it was as if Mark did not exist. In Corey's eyes was a plea for understanding, naked and unashamed. In Fraser's eyes was only hardness. His lips were a narrow line and his jaw was rigid.

'Fraser....' The name was torn from her throat.

His lips curved in a mocking taunt. 'Having fun, Corey?'

'It's not what you think it is.' Mark spoke into the tension.

'No need to protect the lady.' The hardness deepened, and contempt was deliberate in the glance that raked the trembling body. 'Our Corey has never been one to miss out on any fun.'

'Damn you, Fraser!' Anger gave the edge to despair, as she stared at him furiously.

'And you, my dear.' He turned then, and strode away.

'I'm sorry, Corey.' Mark's tone was husky with distress.

But Corey hardly heard him. She was looking after a long lithe figure. Her chin was tilted defiantly, but inside she was weeping.

A thin line of mist hung over the top of Table Mountain. The sky was blue and almost cloudless. The sea, even from a distance, looked inviting. Driving up the mountain road, Corey saw the line of breakers edging the beaches. Near the horizon two ships were making their way towards the harbour.

She had always loved this stretch of road. There were great clumps of trees, mimosas and firs and the lovely silver trees which grew in such profusion. There were wild flowers, and here and there a protea bush, its waxy blooms spiky and perfect.

Through the open window of the car wafted the scents and smells of the mountain: the tangy aroma of a distant bush-fire, the mingled spiciness of the trees and undergrowth. It was one of those rare and perfect days when the people of Cape Town knew why they would trade their city for no other place on earth. It was contrary then that Corey should look down at all the beauty around her and wish that she was back in the desert.

She felt a little depressed as she negotiated the steep mountain bends. Would she never get Fraser out of her system? It was almost three weeks since she had returned from the desert, and the pain of parting from him had in no way faded. During the day she tried to push him from her mind. At night she was powerless to keep him from her dreams.

Her father's delight at her return had been some compensation. After he had got over his astonishment that she had not after all been on holiday on the Garden Route as she had told him, he listened avidly of her tales of the expedition. Her descriptions of the animal frieze had him riveted. In his joy at knowing that the painting he had dreamed of for so long did in fact exist, he was able to accept the fact that the camera had been broken and the spool destroyed. Over and over in the days that followed he asked Corey for more details about the frieze. Though the photographs would have added the final touch, at last he seemed able to complete his lifetime's work.

They spoke only once about Fraser. John Latimer had been interested in knowing about the man who had once been his friend, but Corey's replies had been guarded. She hoped her father did not hear the tiny break in her voice, or notice her heightened colour. Brown eyes had studied her perceptively, and Corey wondered if she saw a hint of compassion. It was after all her father who had first mentioned Fraser's fatal attraction for women.

After that first conversation Fraser was not discussed again.

Corey was tired as she drove the car up the drive that led to the house. She had still not decided what she wanted to do with her life. She had been offered two modelling assignments and was debating whether to accept them or whether to remain true to her original resolve of abandoning the modelling field. Some time soon she would have to make a final decision.

She frowned as she saw the car parked outside the house. It was long and low and silver-grey. She had never seen it before, and could only assume that her father had a visitor. She was not in the mood for conversation. She would make tea and then go to her room.

Voices came from the living-room. Corey walked to the door and then stood quite still, her body rigid. The room sparked with a tension which she had known only in a small tent on the edge of the Kalahari Desert. She could not see the face of her father's visitor, but her senses told her who he was.

Her first impulse was to run. Like a wounded animal she needed a place to hide. After a moment, when her limbs could move once more, she took a step away from the door.

'Corey!' It was her father's voice.

It was an effort to respond. 'Dad?'

'We have a visitor.'

Slowly, very slowly, she entered the living-room.

It was difficult to walk, each step was an effort. She felt the colour had drained from her face, and her legs were weak.

'Hello, Corey.' He turned and looked at her. His face was very tanned still, and in his eyes was the ghost of a smile.

'Hello, Fraser.' Was that really her voice, the sound so flat and controlled?

Why was he here? Never before had he thought of visiting her father. Why now? Had he come to torment her?

Something of her thoughts must have revealed themselves in her expression. She heard her father say, 'Fraser came to bring us a present.'

'A present?' she echoed hollowly.

'A very special present.'

Something in her father's tone penetrated the blur that filled her mind. She allowed herself to look from one man to the other. A very special present....

Her father gestured to the table where he and Fraser had been sitting, and reluctantly Corey dragged her eyes to the table. It was irrational, impossible, and yet some instinct told her what she would see there.

Photographs of the animal frieze lay scattered on the table. About a dozen in all, showing the painting from various different angles, highlighting the more spectacular details. Beautiful photographs, which would provide the pièce de résistance to her father's work.

Corey looked up. Both men were watching her. There was silence in the room, a hushed silence, expectant, waiting.

'The camera,' she said when she could speak, 'it wasn't broken, then ...?'

'It was.' There was a curious inflection in Fraser's tone.

'The spool.' She frowned, trying to think. 'You picked it up after all.'

It was the obvious explanation, the only one. And yet something was wrong. The spool had been exposed to the light, and these photographs were perfect.

'I don't think you understand. Fraser will explain.' It was her father who spoke. He was getting to his feet. 'I need some notes from my study. I'll go and look for them.'

A moment of panic as her father left the room. Corey took a deep breath. She looked at the broad-shouldered man whose presence seemed to fill the room. 'You took those photos?'

He inclined his head, the slightest hint of amusement curving his lips.

'But then.... You must have gone back.' And as understanding became complete, 'When you left camp ... I thought you'd gone to make arrangements for our return....' It was becoming difficult to speak once more. 'And then ... then when you came back . . . you saw Mark and me kissing.'

A gleam appeared in the grey eyes. 'I had to restrain myself from strangling you both.'

She looked at him, hope leaping inside her at what his words might imply. 'It meant nothing,' she said softly. 'Just a farewell between friends.'

'I know that now.'

'Fraser.' She swallowed. 'It was good of you to do this.'

'Good?' His tone mocked her.

'You knew what the frieze meant to Dad.' She stopped, groping for words. Then, because she had to know, she asked, 'You could have posted the photographs. Why did you come all this way just to bring them?'

The amusement deepened in the curves about the strong mouth, and the grey eyes were warm with laughter. 'Because, my darling, I wanted to see my future father-in-law's joy for myself.'

Her heart had leaped at the word darling. It did a double somersault at the rest of the statement.

'Fraser! You don't mean . . . you can't. . . .' She got no further, for the lump in her throat was so hard that she couldn't swallow.

'I do and I can.' She did not see him cross the room, she only knew that he was holding her, and that she had nuzzled her face against his chest, glorying in the familiar hardness, the clean male smell.

A hand went beneath her hair to draw her head

back. 'In my usual autocratic fashion I'm taking things for granted. Corey darling, you *will* marry me?'

'Oh, yes!' And then, when his lips left hers long enough for her to draw breath to speak again. 'Fraser, I thought in your life women were only good for one thing.'

'Till I met you they were.' He grimaced wryly. 'I didn't mean to fall in love with you, God knows, but you gave me no choice. Corey....' For the first time since she had known him he sounded uncertain. 'You haven't told me if you....'

'From the beginning,' she interrupted him, violet eyes shining up at him through happy tears. 'I loved you from the beginning, though I didn't want to believe it.'

She heard him groan, then he was kissing her with all the love and passion and tenderness she had yearned for.

At length he lifted his head. 'Let's go and tell your father our news, my darling. I think he's been tactful long enough.'

Mills & Boon
Classics

Doctor Nurse Romances

and August's
stories of romantic relationships behind the scenes
of modern medical life are:

PRIZE OF GOLD
by Hazel Fisher

It was the eminent surgeon, Sir Carlton Hunter, who told Sandie that love was the prize of gold – but she was determined to win the gold medal for the best student nurse, rather than lose her heart! Unfortunately, it was also Sir Carlton who was wrecking her chances of winning either prize . . . .

DOCTOR ON BOARD
(The Path of the Moonfish)
by Betty Beaty

To meet Paul Vansini at the very beginning of her first cruise as a hostess aboard the luxury liner *Pallas Athene*, should have made Cristie Cummings perfectly happy. And so it might have done, but for Doctor David Lindsay's cutting remarks!

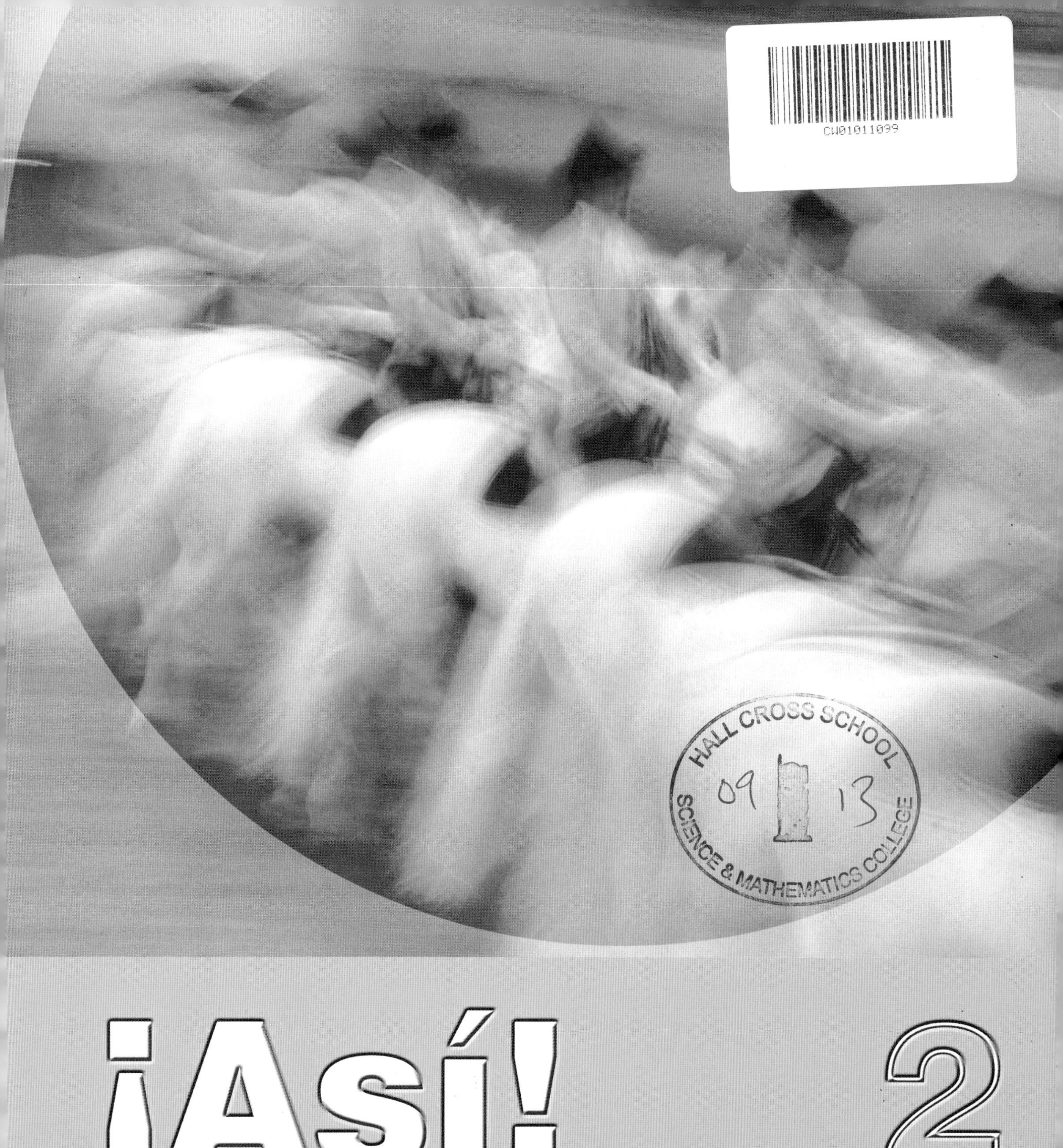

¡Así!

HELENA GONZÁLEZ-FLORIDO AND
JUAN PEDRO LÓPEZ-CASCANTE

Claro

Published in 2006 by:
Nelson Thornes Ltd
Delta Place
27 Bath Road
CHELTENHAM
GL53 7TH
United Kingdom

09 10 / 10 9 8 7 6 5 4 3

A catalogue record for this book is available from the British Library

ISBN 978 0 7487 9173 6

Illustrations by Mark Draisey, Mel Sharp, Yane Christensen, Richard Morris, Rupert Besley, Nigel Kitching, Mike Bastin, Theresa Tibbett, Gary Andrews, Jean de Lemos and Angela Lumley.

Page make-up by IFA Design Ltd., Plympton, Plymouth: www.ifadesign.co.uk

Printed in China by 1010 printing International Limited.

Welcome to ¡Así! 2 Claro

- **Most pages have the following features to help you:**

Gramática:
Examples of how you put Spanish words together to make sentences.

Pronunciación
Practice of Spanish sounds to improve your pronunciation and spelling.

A list of the key words and phrases you'll need to do the activities.

¡Así se hace!
Tips to help you learn better and remember more.

Activities in which you'll listen to Spanish.

Activities in which you'll practise speaking Spanish.

Activities in which you'll practise reading and writing in Spanish.

¡extra! **Activities that provide an extra challenge – have a go!**

Activities which give you the chance to recycle language from *¡Así! 1*.

- **The *Resumen* at the end of each unit lists the key words of the unit in Spanish and English. Use it to look up any words you don't know!**

Índice de materias *Contents*

1 De vacaciones

1A Tú, ¿qué haces?

- describe your holiday routine
- say what you like to do and where you like to go
- revise reflexive verbs in the present tense

1  **Mira y escucha. Une los diálogos y las fotos.**

Ejemplo: **1 B**

1
– ¡Hola, Carmen! ¿Qué haces de vacaciones?
– Hago esquí en las montañas.

2
– ¿Y tú, Raúl?
– En verano, yo juego al fútbol con mis amigos.

3
– Y tú, ¿qué haces, Marga?
– Siempre voy a la playa en agosto.

4
– Dime, Pablo, ¿qué haces de vacaciones?
– Hago windsurf en el mar.

5
– ¿Y tú, Conchi?
– Practico la equitación en el campo.

6
– ¿Qué haces tú, Luis?
– Normalmente hago excursiones con mi familia.

7
– ¿Y tú, Carolina?
– Juego al tenis en el parque.

8
– ¿Qué haces tú, Alfonso?
– Practico la natación en la piscina.

Gramática: verbs

- Find all the verbs in exercise 1. Complete the list below:
  jugar: *juego* ***ir:***
  hacer: ***practicar:***
- What does each verb mean?

2 ***Complete the sentences with the appropriate verb.***

1 ______ al volcibol.
2 ______ la equitación.
3 ______ excursiones.
4 ______ a la playa.
5 ______ al cine.
6 ______ esquí.

3 a **Practica el diálogo con tu pareja. Usa los dibujos.**

Ejemplo: **A** ¿Qué haces normalmente de vacaciones?
B Normalmente practico la natación en la playa.

3 b  ***Write 6 sentences saying what you do in the holidays.***

4 ¿Qué hora es?

Une las horas y el español.

1 Son las tres y veinte.
2 Es la una y diez.
3 Son las cinco y media.
4 Son las siete menos veinte.
5 Son las cuatro y cuarto.
6 Es la una menos cuarto.

5 a Lee la agenda de María cuando está en el instituto y en las vacaciones. Apunta las diferencias en inglés.

Ejemplo: **school day gets up at 7.15; holiday gets up at 11.30.**

lunes, 15 de enero
Me levanto a las siete y cuarto.
Voy al instituto a las ocho menos cuarto.
Hago mis deberes.
Ceno a las nueve y media.
Me acuesto a las once.

lunes, 16 de agosto
Me levanto a las once y media.
Juego al bádminton en la playa.
Como a las tres y media.
A las siete voy al cine.
Me acuesto a las dos.

5 b Escucha a María y apunta más información.

Gramática: reflexive verbs

Some of the verbs used to describe routine activities are reflexive and take *me* in front of them. The *me* here means 'myself'.

Example: ***Me** lavo* literally means '**I** wash **myself**', as opposed to washing somebody else – ***Le** lavo* = '**I** wash **him**'.

me levanto	I get up
me lavo	I wash myself
me ducho	I shower
me visto	I get dressed
me preparo	I get ready
me acuesto	I go to bed

- Make a list of verbs in each of María's descriptions which need *me* and those which do not.

6 a Une las preguntas y las respuestas.

Ejemplo: **1 d**

1 ¿A qué hora te levantas?
2 ¿A qué hora te acuestas?
3 ¿A qué hora te duchas?
4 ¿A qué hora te preparas para ir al colegio?
5 ¿A qué hora te lavas?
6 ¿A qué hora te vistes?

a Me ducho a las siete y media.
b Me visto a las ocho menos cuarto aproximadamente.
c Me acuesto normalmente a las diez.
d Me levanto a las siete y cuarto.
e Me lavo antes de acostarme – a las nueve y media.
f Me preparo para ir al colegio a las ocho y cuarto.

6 b Ahora practica las preguntas de 6a con tu pareja.

1B ¿Dónde vas a alojarte?

- talk about where to stay and give opinions
- learn the rules for stress and accentuation in Spanish

Si vas a América del Sur de vacaciones hay muchas posibilidades: hay hoteles, apartamentos, campings, cabañas y estancias.

A 

B 

C 

D 

E 

F 

1 a **Escucha (1–6). Empareja las personas con los dibujos.**

Ejemplo: **1 D, E**

1 b **Escucha otra vez. ¿Verdad (V) o mentira (M)?**

1. La persona 1 va a alojarse en un hotel o en un apartamento en la ciudad.
2. La persona 2 va a hacer camping.
3. La persona 3 va a alojarse en una tienda en un camping.
4. La persona 4 va a alojarse en una estancia.
5. La persona 5 va a alojarse en un hotel.
6. La persona 6 va a alojarse en las montañas.

Gramática: the immediate future

voy a ir	I am going to go
vas a ir	you (sing.) are going to go
va a ir	he/she/you (*usted*) is/are going to go

2 a **Lee los textos y rellena el cuadro.**

Nombre	Destino	Mes	Duración	Actividades
Miguel		julio		
Nuria			quince días	
Pepe				ir de compras

Miguel

Este año voy a hacer camping en julio. Voy a pasar tres semanas en el Camping Bellavista. Voy a ir a Santander en julio. Voy a hacer windsurf y excursiones. Tú, ¿adónde vas?

Nuria

Este año no voy a los Estados Unidos como normalmente. Voy a ir a Cuba. Voy a pasar quince días allí con mi familia en junio. Voy a hacer windsurf y practicar el esquí acuático.

Pepe

Voy a ir de vacaciones en mayo. Voy a ir a los Estados Unidos con el instituto. Voy a pasar una semana en Nueva York. Voy a ir de compras y voy a visitar los monumentos famosos. Tú, ¿qué vas a hacer?

2 b ¡extra! ***Interview your partner using the following:***

¿Adónde vas a ir de vacaciones este verano?

¿Cuándo vas a ir?

¿En qué mes vas a ir?

¿Qué vas a hacer?

¿Con quién vas a ir?

2 c ***Write down your partner's responses.***

Example:

If your partner says:

Voy a ir a la costa de Francia en verano.

Voy a ir en agosto.

Voy a ir a la playa y hacer windsurf.

Write:

Julie **va a** ir a la costa de Francia en verano.

Va a ir en agosto.

Va a ir a la playa y hacer windsurf.

2 d **Prepara una presentación de tus vacaciones (5–6 frases). Contesta a las preguntas de 2b.**

Ejemplo: **Este año voy a ir a Santiago de Chile.**

Stress and accentuation (1)

There are relatively simple rules about where the stress falls on a Spanish word. Remember this simple rhyme:

> **Vowel, *n* or *s* penultimate stress.**
> **All other words last vowel stress.**

hablo, hablas, hablan – stress on penultimate (next to last) syllable

Barcelona – ends in a vowel

hablar, hablad – stress on last syllable

Madrid – ends in a consonant (other than *n* or *s*)

Easy! But some words are stressed differently, such as *kilómetros, estación, televisión, teléfono, está* and *¡Así!*
The accents tell us where to put the stress.

¡Así se hace! Extended speaking and writing

Your aim is to say a few sentences about your holiday this year.

Step 1 Decide what you are going to say beforehand and include as much information as you possibly can.

For example, instead of saying *Voy a ir a muchos restaurantes*, say: *Voy a ir a muchos restaurantes y tomar platos típicos como paella o tortilla española.*

- Look at this person's holiday plans. How many questions have been answered?

  Where you are going? *Voy a…*

  When are you going? *Voy en…*

  How long are you going to stay? *Voy a pasar…*

  Who are you going with? *Voy a ir con…*

  What are you going to do? *Voy a… y…*

Voy a pasar tres semanas en Caracas en julio. Voy a ir con mis padres. Caracas es la capital de Venezuela. Está en la costa norte de América del Sur. Voy a visitar museos y el parque de atracciones. Tú, ¿qué vas a hacer?

Step 2 Write your sentences in full.

Step 3 Read your presentation aloud to your partner.

Step 4 Learn it by heart and practise saying it from memory.

3 a ***Write out the following words underlining where the stress goes and saying why.***

cabaña *semanas* *hacen* *deportes*
maravilloso *excursiones* *junio*

3 b ***Listen to your teacher pronouncing the following words. Put an accent on each one and practise pronouncing them correctly.***

asi	el autobus	el miercoles
el lapiz	Maria	el futbol
el dialogo	Mejico	tambien
la excursion	el interes	simpatico

1C ¿Adónde vas a ir y cuándo?

- find out about a holiday resort and suitable accommodation

1 **Lee las descripciones y apunta las diferencias entre España y Argentina en inglés.**

Ejemplo: **Spain – summer in June...,**
Argentina – summer in December.

2 a **Escucha los diálogos y rellena el cuadro.**

¿Adónde vas a ir?

¿En qué estación del año?

¿En qué mes?

Nombre	Lugar	Estación	Mes
Bea	Andorra	invierno	febrero
Antonio			
Elena			
Alberto			
Teo			

2 b **Habla con tu pareja. Usa las preguntas de 2a y los dibujos.**

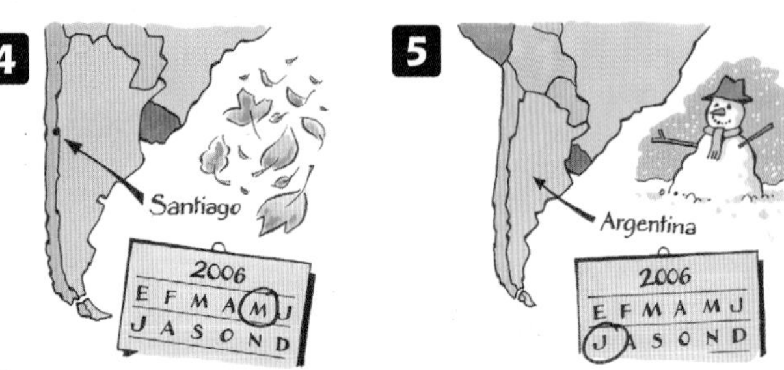

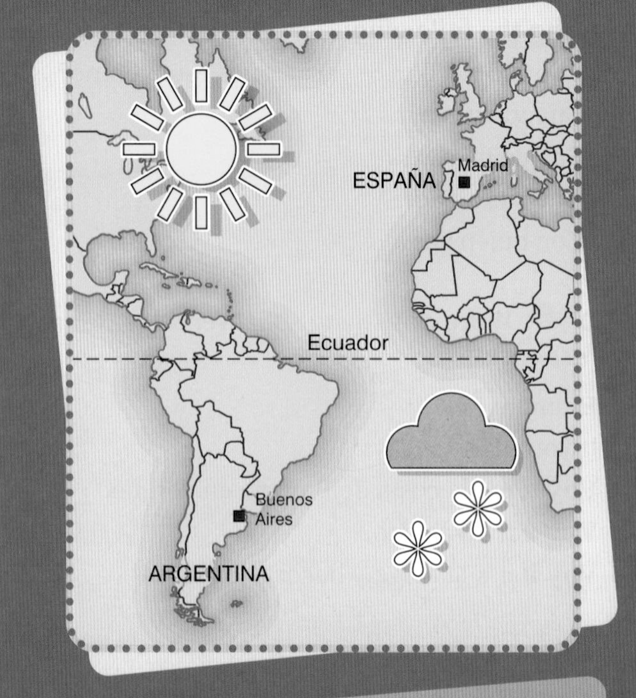

Si vas a **España** y buscas mucho sol, vas a ir en verano, en junio, julio y agosto. Muchos españoles van a la costa a pasar un mes. En España, el instituto empieza en septiembre. Los españoles hacen esquí en enero y febrero en las montañas.

Si vas a **Argentina**, su verano es en diciembre y enero. Muchos argentinos van a pasar un mes en la costa en enero. Es muy tradicional tener una casa en la costa. En Argentina, el instituto empieza en marzo. Los argentinos van a esquiar en invierno, en julio y agosto.

3 **Escribe unas frases sobre tus planes ideales.**

Ejemplo: **Voy a ir a los Estados Unidos. Voy a ir en agosto. Voy a ir a la playa. Voy a ir con mis amigos.**

¡Así se hace! *Creating longer sentences*

You can make your writing sound better by combining sentences together, therefore writing longer sentences.

Example: Voy a ir a los Estados Unidos en agosto con mis amigos. Voy a ir a la playa.

4 a ***Read this publicity about Argentina. Write 2 details for each site in English.***

Example: **1 Buenos Aires – 3 million inhabitants, ...**

1 Buenos Aires

Ven a visitar Buenos Aires. Ciudad de 3 millones de habitantes. Tiene música y arquitectura. Hay hoteles de todo tipo.

2 Los horneros

Situado en la costa, el camping 'Los horneros' ofrece camping y bungalows. Hay agua corriente, una barbacoa y sombra. En verano, hay muchos turistas.

3 Turismo rural

Si prefieres el turismo rural y la tranquilidad hay la pampa. Te puedes alojar en estancias. Hay sitio para grupos de 6 a 20 personas. Actividades: andar en bicicleta, montar a caballo y observar pájaros. En la capital, Santa Rosa, se puede practicar el golf, visitar museos, ir al casino y de compras.

4 Turismo aventuras

Safari fotográfico o trekking en el Parque Nacional. Hay posibilidades de navegar por el río, hacer piragüismo, dar paseos en la selva y hacer excursiones en 4x4.

5 Establecimiento La Alegría

En medio de la selva, todas las cabañas tienen tres dormitorios, comedor, salón, baño y cocina. Hay safari fotográfico, trekking, excursiones en bicicleta de montaña y aventuras en vehículos 4x4.

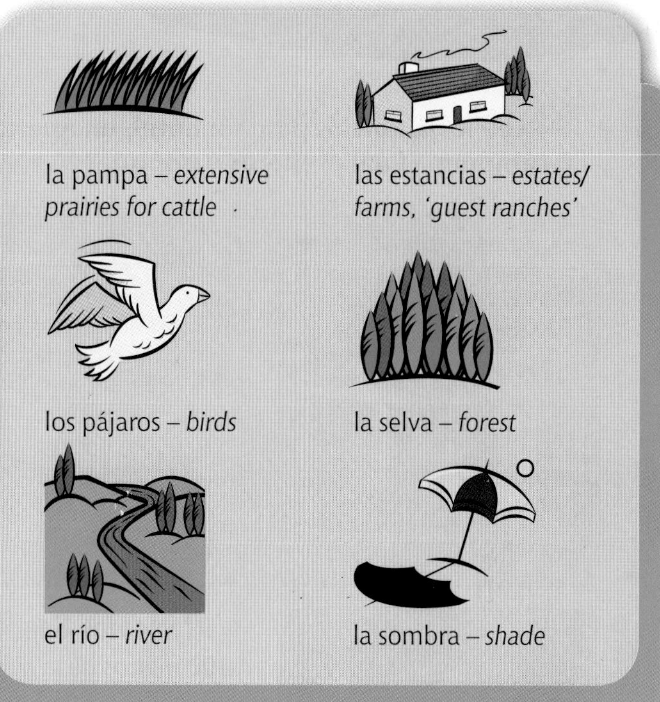

la pampa – *extensive prairies for cattle*
las estancias – *estates/ farms, 'guest ranches'*
los pájaros – *birds*
la selva – *forest*
el río – *river*
la sombra – *shade*

4 b **Prepara un póster publicitario para la oficina de turismo. Elige un sitio, por ejemplo Palma de Mallorca. Usa 4a como modelo.**

Ejemplo:

1 D ¿Qué alojamiento prefieres?

- express a preference in terms of accommodation
- learn ways of avoiding using the dictionary

1 a Lee los anuncios para un hotel, un apartamento y un camping. ¿Cuál prefieres y por qué?

Hotel Miramar ****

A un kilómetro de la playa y a dos kilómetros del centro. 250 habitaciones con baño completo. Hay TV con satélite, teléfono y terraza. Se puede practicar la natación en las dos piscinas. Hay bar y dos restaurantes. Hay gimnasio y sala de juegos.

Apartamentos San Roque

A 100 metros de la playa y a mil metros del centro. Cien habitaciones con vistas al mar y terraza. Hay baño completo, kitchenette, lavadora, frigo, teléfono y televisión. Se puede practicar la natación en la piscina. Hay discoteca.

Camping Sol

Situado al lado de la playa. Hay sitio para 180 personas. El camping tiene un supermercado, una lavandería, un restaurante-cafetería y hay parque infantil.

1 b ¿Verdad (V) o mentira (M)?

1 En el Camping Sol, hay actividades para niños.
2 El Hotel Miramar está situado a 100 metros de la playa.
3 Los Apartamentos San Roque no tienen vistas a la playa.
4 En el Camping Sol, hay sala de juegos.
5 En los Apartamentos San Roque, se puede preparar las comidas.

1 c ¡extra! Corrige las frases mentirosas.

¡Así se hace! *Avoiding the dictionary*

- Dictionaries are extremely useful but before you look up a word, ask yourself:
  1 How many words in a sentence do I need to know before I can work out what it means? For example, you do not need to understand all the words in this English sentence to be able to guess how it will end:

     I get up at around 9 o'clock. Then I have breakfast. Generally I eat *** or ***, but sometimes ***.

  2 Can I work out the meaning of the word from: **titles**, **headings**, **picture clues**, **spelling** similarities with English, **sound** patterns in Spanish (or other languages I know) etc.?
- Look at the adverts in exercise 1 and make a list of the words that you have not met but can work out the meaning of. For example, *centro* looks like 'centre'. It means the town centre. Words like these are called near cognates.
- Work out the meaning of the following: *piscina*, *sala de juegos*, *vistas al mar*, *lavadora*, *parque infantil*. (They have been underlined for you to find easily.) How did you work out the meaning?

2 Escucha (1–4) y rellena el cuadro. ¿Dónde van a alojarse?

	Hotel	Apartamento	Camping
1		✔	
2			

3 Mira la conversación y practícala con tu pareja. Cambia las palabras.

Ejemplo:

A ¿Cuál prefieres?
B Prefiero el hotel.
A ¿Por qué?
B Porque hay televisión con satélite. ¿Cuál prefieres tú?
A Prefiero los apartamentos.
B ¿Por qué?
A Hay piscina.

Las actividades	Activities
hacer trekking	*to go trekking*
hacer excursiones	*to go on trips*
hacer alpinismo	*to go climbing*
hacer esquí	*to go skiing*
hacer windsurf	*to go windsurfing*
practicar el esquí acuático	*to go water-skiing*
practicar la equitación	*to go horseriding*
practicar la natación	*to go swimming*
practicar el golf	*to play golf*

Un día típico	A typical day
Me levanto a...	*I get up at...*
Voy al instituto	*I go to school*
Ceno a...	*I have dinner at...*
Me acuesto a...	*I go to bed at...*

Ir de vacaciones	Going on holiday
¿Adónde vas a ir?	*Where are you going to go?*
Voy a ir a Mallorca	*I'm going to go to Majorca*
¿Cuándo vas a ir?	*When are you going to go?*
En agosto	*In August*
¿Qué vas a hacer?	*What are you going to do?*
Voy a ir a la playa	*I'm going to go to the beach*

Alojamiento	Accommodation
¿Dónde vas a alojarte?	*Where are you going to stay?*
un hotel	*hotel*
un apartamento	*apartment*
un camping	*campsite*
un bungalow	*bungalow*
una estancia	*estate*
una cabaña	*cabin*
una tienda	*tent*
una terraza	*terrace*
una sala de juegos	*games room*
una piscina	*swimming pool*
un parque infantil	*children's play area*
situado	*situated*

Gramática:
present tense
reflexive verbs
the immediate future

¡Así se hace!

- ★ Extended speaking and writing
- ★ Combining sentences
- ★ Avoiding the dictionary

Stress and accentuation

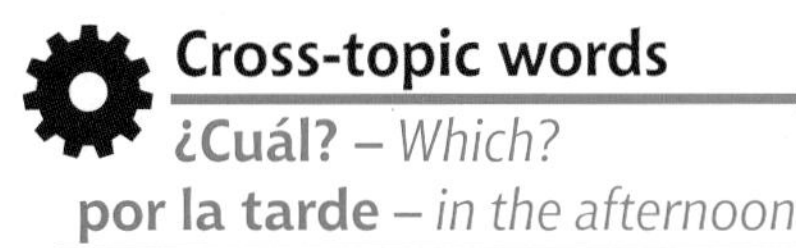

Cross-topic words
¿Cuál? – Which?
por la tarde – in the afternoon

2 ¡Me duele la cabeza!

2A El cuerpo

- learn the vocabulary of some parts of the body
- use *doler* to say that something hurts

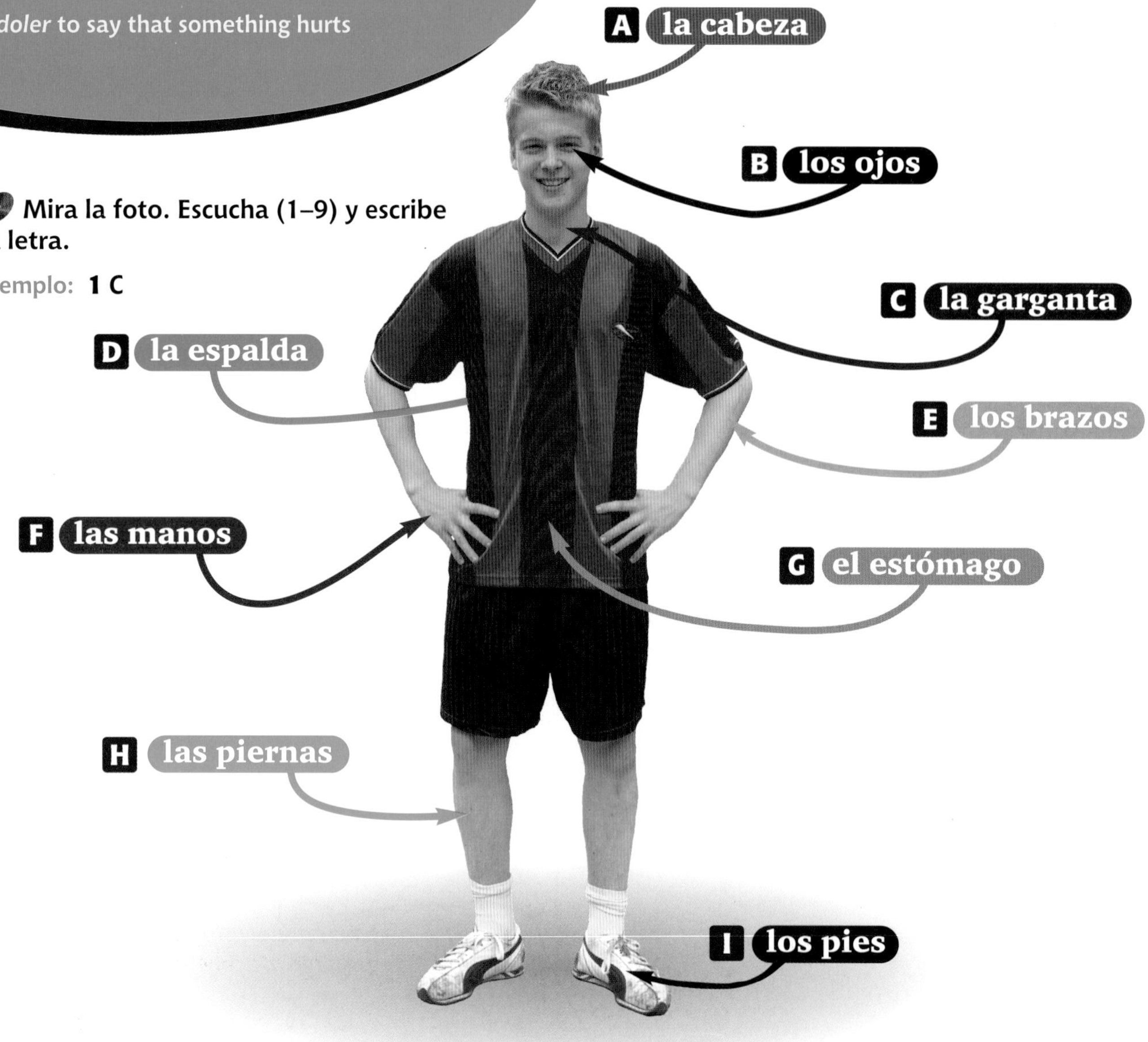

A la cabeza
B los ojos
C la garganta
D la espalda
E los brazos
F las manos
G el estómago
H las piernas
I los pies

1 **Mira la foto. Escucha (1–9) y escribe la letra.**

Ejemplo: **1 C**

2 **Trabaja con tu pareja. Toca una parte del cuerpo y tu pareja dice la palabra.**

Ejemplo:

3 **Juego de memoria. Juega con tu pareja.**

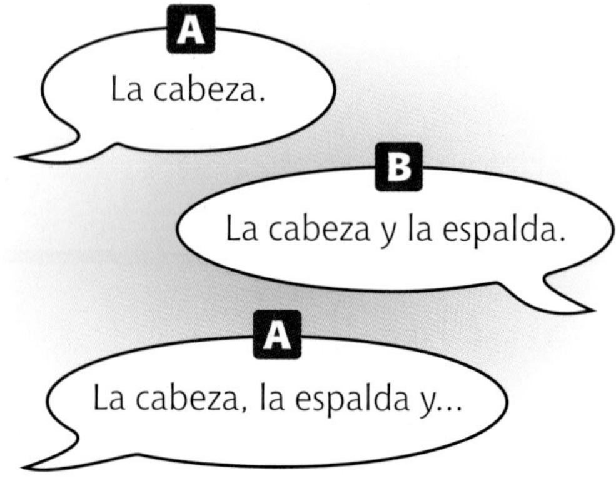

A
La cabeza.
B
La cabeza y la espalda.
A
La cabeza, la espalda y...

4 a Lee el artículo. ¿Verdad (V) o mentira (M)?

Ejemplo: **1 V**

¡Invasión de los Extraterrestres!

Noticias de última hora. Hay un extraterrestre en Madrid, en el centro de España. <u>El extraterrestre tiene</u> seis piernas largas y tres brazos muy cortos. <u>Tiene</u> cuatro ojos marrones <u>y</u> dos verdes, una cabeza grande con mucho pelo rojo. <u>También tiene</u> dos manos muy pequeñas en cada brazo. <u>En el centro de la cabeza tiene</u> una nariz enorme. La policía está en alerta. Si tiene alguna información, llame al 091.

1. El extraterrestre está en Madrid.
2. Madrid está en el sur de España.
3. El extraterrestre tiene cinco piernas largas.
4. El extraterrestre tiene tres brazos muy cortos.
5. El extraterrestre tiene cuatro ojos marrones y dos azules.
6. La cabeza es grande.
7. El extraterrestre tiene mucho pelo rubio.
8. El extraterrestre tiene seis manos.

4 b ¡extra! **Corrige las frases mentirosas.**

Ejemplo: **2 Madrid está en el centro de España.**

4 c **¡Diseña tu propio extraterrestre! Dibújalo y escribe una descripción. Usa las palabras <u>subrayadas</u> en 4a para ayudarte.**

5 **Escucha y pon en orden.**

a Me duele la garganta

b Me duele la pierna

c Me duele la espalda

d Me duele la cabeza

e Me duelen las manos

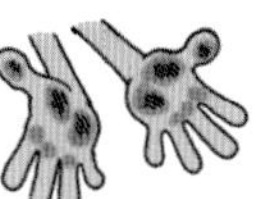

f Me duelen los pies

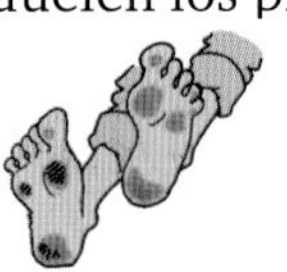

g Me duele el estómago

Gramática: ***me duele(n)* – my ... hurt(s)**

Me duele + singular noun (*el/la*)

Me duele el estómago.
Me duele la cabeza.

Me duelen + plural noun (*los/las*)

Me duelen los ojos.
Me duelen las piernas.

- ***Complete these sentences with duele or duelen.***

1. – ¿Te ______ la cabeza?
   – No, me ______ los ojos.
2. A mi madre siempre le ______ las manos.
3. Me ______ mucho la espalda.
4. – ¿Qué te pasa?
   – No sé, no estoy bien.
   Me ______ la garganta y la cabeza.

2B Tengo un resfriado

- learn the vocabulary related to illnesses
- listen for gist

A

B

1 a Une las frases y los dibujos.

1 Tengo mucho frío.

2 Tengo una insolación.

3 Tengo un resfriado.

4 Tengo tos.

5 Estoy mareado/a.

6 Tengo fiebre.

7 Tengo gripe.

8 Tengo dolor de estómago.

1 b Escucha (A–H).
¿Cuál es el problema? Escribe el número.

Ejemplo: **A 2**

1 c Escucha otra vez. ¿Qué dicen? Escribe en español.

Ejemplo: **A Tengo una insolación.**

2 Pon las letras en orden. ¿Qué problema es?

Ejemplo: **1 Estoy mareado**

1 ysEto omaeard
2 gTeon umoch rfoí
3 gTeon tso
4 gTeon nu driesfroa
5 gTeon nau sinnoalció
6 gTeon rldoo ed setmoagó
7 gTeon efireb
8 gTeon rgiep

3 a Lee el correo electrónico. Rellena los espacios.

Querida Carmen:

¿Qué tal el instituto? Yo no estoy bien. Me duelen [ ] y la [ ]. Tengo [ ] y [ ].

¡Hasta mañana!

Javier

3 b Escribe tu propio correo electrónico.

4 a Mira las soluciones para los problemas.

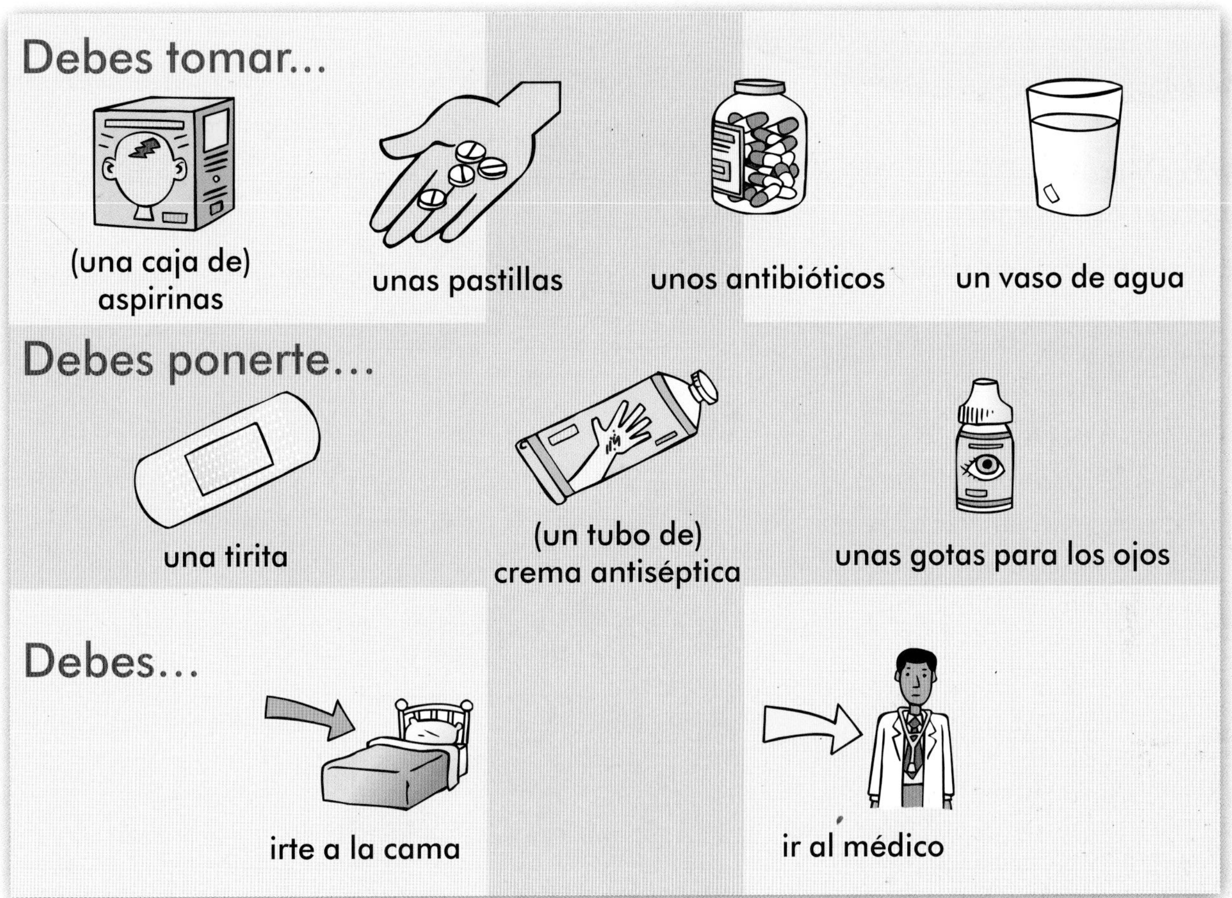

Gramática: ***debes* + infinitive**

debes + infinitive = you must (do)

4 b Escucha (1–4). Copia y rellena el cuadro.

	Problema	Solución
1	Me duele la cabeza	Aspirinas

4 c Escribe las soluciones más apropiadas a los problemas.

Ejemplo: **1 Debes tomar unas aspirinas.**

1 Me duele la cabeza.
2 Me duele la garganta.
3 Tengo gripe.
4 Tengo un resfriado.
5 Tengo los ojos rojos.
6 Me duele el estómago.

5 a Lee la conversación con tu pareja.

A
¡Hola! ¿Qué te pasa?
B
Me duele mucho la cabeza.
A
Debes tomar una aspirina.
B
Pero también me duele la garganta, y tengo fiebre.
A
¡Uf! Debes ir al médico.
B
¡Gracias!

5 b Escribe y practica otra conversación similar a 5a. Cambia las palabras.

2C No estoy bien, doctor

- learn the vocabulary needed at the chemist's/doctor's
- develop role-play skills
- cope with longer reading texts

1 Lee y escucha. Busca las expresiones.

Ejemplo: **Está muy inflamada.**

1. It is very inflamed
2. This cream
3. We have these tablets
4. You must take three a day
5. These tablets are very good
6. There are small or large tubes
7. I have some aspirin
8. A bottle of twenty

– ¡Hola! ¿En qué puedo ayudarle?
– Bueno, me duele esta mano. Está muy inflamada. ¿Qué me recomienda?
– Esta crema es muy buena.
– Estupendo, ¿cuánto cuesta?
– Son 6.

– Buenas tardes, ¿en qué puedo ayudarle?
– Me duele muchísimo el estómago. ¿Tiene algo?
– Sí, tenemos estas pastillas. Debe tomar tres al día.
– Muchas gracias.

– ¡Hola! ¿Tiene algo para la tos?
– Estas pastillas son muy buenas. Hay tubos pequeños y grandes.
– El grande, por favor.
– Aquí tiene. Son 8.

– ¡Buenos días! ¿Qué desea?
– Me duele muchísimo la cabeza.
– Tengo estas aspirinas. Tengo de 20 y 40 unidades.
– Un bote de 20, por favor.
– Aquí tienes. Son 2,80.

¡Así se hace! *Guessing vocabulary*

When reading, you can use your knowledge of the world to guess what different expressions might mean. For example, in **1** on this page, there are a lot of new words, but you should be able to apply your knowledge of going to the doctor's to guess the meaning of many of them.

2 Haz conversaciones con tu pareja. Usa el cuadro.

Farmacéutico	Cliente	Farmacéutico	Cliente
¿Puedo ayudarle? ¿Qué desea?	¿Tiene algo para el dolor de... ? cabeza/espalda/ojos ¿Tiene algo para... ? la gripe/la insolación/el resfriado	Debe... ponerse una venda ponerse una crema ir al médico Tengo... estas pastillas estas aspirinas	De acuerdo, gracias Muchas gracias, adiós Deme un bote/una venda/ la crema

3 Lee la conversación con el médico. Contesta a las preguntas en inglés.

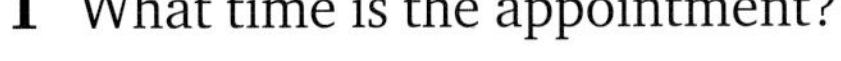

1 What time is the appointment?
2 What is wrong with Silvia?
3 How long has she been feeling ill?
4 Does she have a temperature?
5 What is the doctor's diagnosis?
6 What is the prescription?

1
¿Cómo se llama?
Me llamo Silvia González.
¿A qué hora es su cita?
A las cuatro.
Siéntese, por favor.
2
¿Qué le pasa?
Bueno, me duelen mucho la garganta y la cabeza, y tengo mucha tos.
¿Desde cuándo tiene tos?
Desde hace dos días.

3
¿Tengo fiebre?
Sí, tiene un poco de fiebre. Posiblemente es gripe.

Bien, aquí tiene una receta. Debe tomar antibióticos durante una semana.

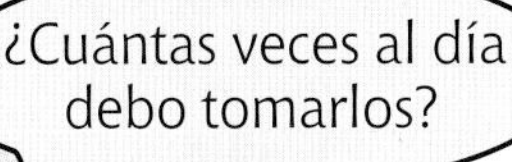

¿Cuántas veces al día debo tomarlos?

4

Tres veces al día, con las comidas.

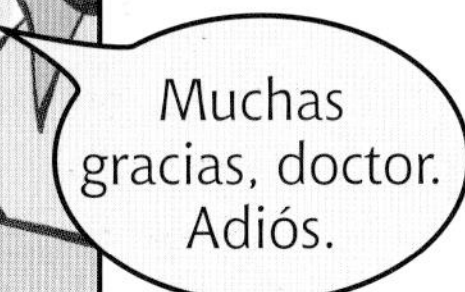

Gramática: how long

Look at the text in exercise **3** again.
How do you say 'How long...?'?
And 'for (x days)'?

desde cuándo, desde hace

4 Escucha (A–D). Elige el número correcto en el cuadro.

Ejemplo: **A** 1, 7...

2D La vida sana

- talk about healthy lifestyles
- use the command form of regular verbs

1 a **Mira el folleto sobre la vida sana.**

1 b **Escucha (1–4). ¿Llevan una vida sana (✔) o no (✘)?**

Ejemplo: **1 ✔**

¡extra! **¿Qué actividades mencionan de la lista de 1a?**

Gramática: the command form of regular verbs

The command form for *tú* is created as follows: *-ar* and *-er* regular verbs drop the final *-r* of the infinitive; *-ir* regular verbs drop the *-r* and change the *i* into an e:

pasar – pasa *beber – bebe* *vivir – vive*

For the negative command form, endings need to change:

-ar > -es *pasar > no pases*
-er > -as *beber > no bebas*
-ir > -as *vivir > no vivas*

- ***Put the verbs in brackets into the correct command form.***
  1. (Pasar) menos tiempo en casa.
  2. (Vivir) en el campo en vez de la ciudad.
  3. (Disfrutar) la compañía de tus amigos.
  4. (Beber) poco alcohol.
  5. (Practicar) algo de ejercicio todos los días.
  6. (Beber) mucha agua y (comer) mucha fruta y verdura.

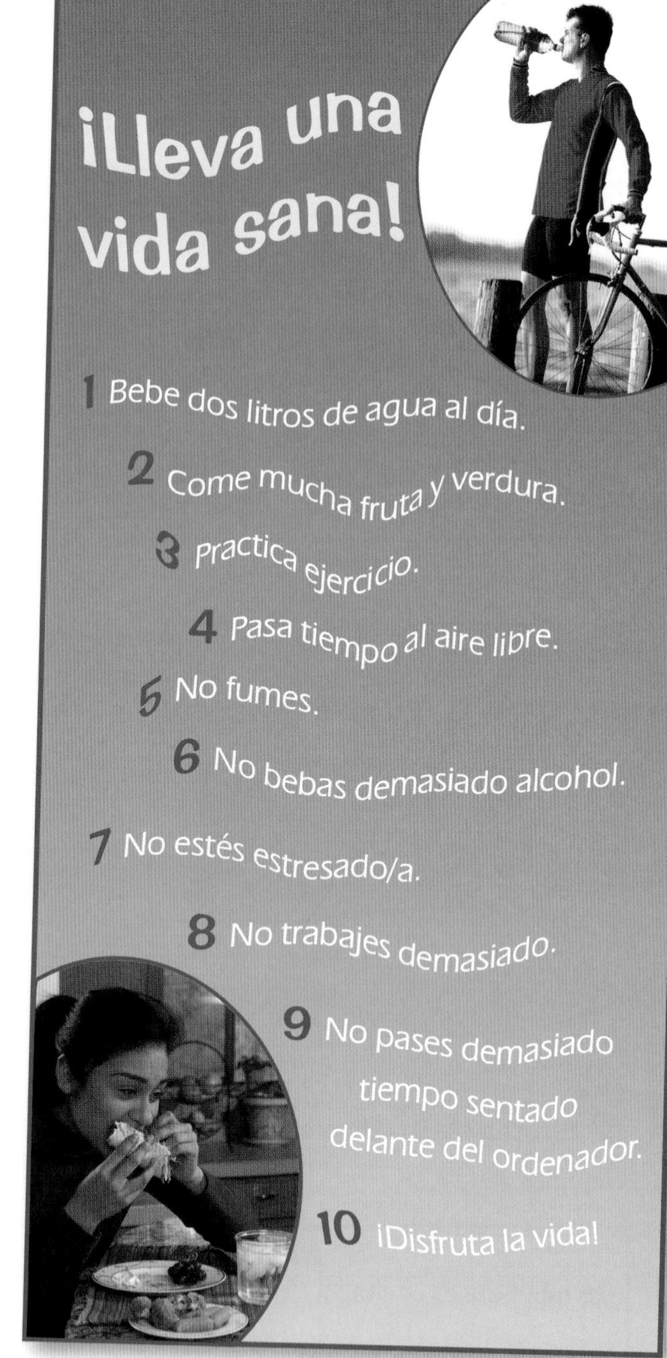

¡Lleva una vida sana!
1 Bebe dos litros de agua al día.
2 Come mucha fruta y verdura.
3 Practica ejercicio.
4 Pasa tiempo al aire libre.
5 No fumes.
6 No bebas demasiado alcohol.
7 No estés estresado/a.
8 No trabajes demasiado.
9 No pases demasiado tiempo sentado delante del ordenador.
10 ¡Disfruta la vida!

2 a **Trabaja con tu pareja.**

A	B
¿Bebes mucha agua?	Sí/No, (no) bebo...
¿Comes fruta y verdura?	Sí/No, (no) como...
¿Practicas ejercicio?	Sí/No, (no) practico...
¿Pasas tiempo al aire libre?	Sí/No, paso...
¿Fumas?	Sí/No, fumo...
¿Bebes?	Sí/No, bebo...
¿Estás estresado/a?	Sí/No, estoy...
¿Trabajas demasiado?	Sí/No, trabajo...
¿Pasas mucho tiempo sentado delante del ordenador?	Sí/No, paso...

2 b ¡extra! **Escribe un párrafo sobre ti.**

Como... Bebo... Practico... Fumo... Estoy... Trabajo... Paso...

3 ¡extra! **Diseña tu propio folleto sobre la vida sana.**

¿Pasas tiempo al aire libre?

Sí/No, paso...

Las partes del cuerpo	***Parts of the body***
la garganta	*throat*
los brazos	*arms*
la cabeza	*head*
el estómago	*stomach*
la espalda	*back*
las manos	*hands*
la nariz	*nose*
los ojos	*eyes*
las piernas	*legs*
los pies	*feet*

Enfermedades	***Illnesses***
Tengo un resfriado	*I have a cold*
Tengo tos	*I have a cough*
Tengo fiebre	*I have a temperature*
Tengo gripe	*I have flu*
Tengo dolor de estómago	*I have stomach ache*
Tengo una insolación	*I have sunstroke*
Estoy mareado/a	*I feel dizzy*

Remedios	***Remedies***
Debes tomar...	*You must take...*
(una caja de/unas) aspirinas	*(box of/some) aspirin*
unas pastillas	*tablets*
un vaso de agua	*a glass of water*
unos antibióticos	*antibiotics*
Debes ponerte...	*You must put on...*
una tirita	*a plaster*
(un tubo de) crema antiséptica	*(a tube of) antiseptic cream*
una gotas para los ojos	*some eyedrops*
Debes...	*You must...*
irte a la cama	*go to bed*
ir al médico	*go to the doctor's*

En la farmacia	***At the chemist's***
¿En qué puedo ayudarle?	*How can I help you?*
¿Tiene algo para el dolor de espalda?	*Have you got anything for backache?*
¿Cuánto cuesta?	*How much is it?*

En el médico	***At the doctor's***
¿A qué hora es su cita?	*What time is your appointment?*
¿Qué le pasa?	*What is wrong?*
¿Desde cuándo le duele?	*How long has it been hurting?*
desde hace dos días	*for two days*
Aquí tiene una receta de...	*Here you have a prescription for...*

La vida sana	***Healthy living***
Bebe al menos dos litros de agua al día	*Drink at least two litres of water a day*
Come mucha fruta y verdura	*Eat a lot of fruit and vegetables*
Practica ejercicio	*Do exercise*
Pasa tiempo al aire libre	*Spend time outdoors*

Gramática:

The verb *doler*

you must: *debes* + infinitive

How long: *desde hace*

The command form of regular verbs

¡Así se hace!

★ Using your knowledge of the world to aid in reading comprehension

Cross-topic words

debes – *you should*

me duele... – *my... hurts*

Unidad 1 (¿Problemas? Mira la página 13.)

1 **Escucha (1–4). ¿Adónde van a ir, cuándo y durante cuánto tiempo? Rellena el cuadro.**

	¿Adónde?	¿Cuándo?	¿Cuánto tiempo?
1		abril	
2			un mes
3	Méjico		
4			quince días

2 **Rellena los espacios con el verbo correcto.**

1 ____________ al fútbol.
2 ____________ windsurf en el mar.
3 ____________ a la discoteca.
4 ____________ la equitación en el campo.
5 ____________ la televisión.
6 ____________ música.

practico veo voy hago escucho juego

Unidad 2 (¿Problemas? Mira la página 21.)

3 **Une los dibujos y las frases.**

Ejemplo: **1 F**

1 Me duele el pie.
2 Me duele la garganta.
3 Me duele la cabeza.
4 Me duele la espalda.
5 Me duele la pierna.
6 Me duele el estómago.

4 a **En la farmacia. Escribe este diálogo en el orden correcto.**

¿Qué le pasa?
¿Desde cuándo le duele?
Buenos días.
Desde hace dos días.
Debe tomar unas pastillas.
Gracias, adiós.
Me duele la garganta.

4 b **Practica el diálogo de 4a con tu pareja.**

1 ***Read Cristina's letter then answer the questions in English.***

1 Where does Cristina live?
2 Where does she go on holiday?
3 When does she go on holiday?
4 Why?
5 Where does she normally stay?
6 What other sort of accommodation does she like?
7 What is special about Puerto Madryn?
8 What can you do there?
9 Name two sorts of wildlife you can find there.

¡Hola!

Vivo en Buenos Aires y normalmente voy de vacaciones a la Patagonia en el sur de Argentina. Voy a ir en enero porque no hay clases en enero y febrero. Normalmente nos alojamos en hoteles pero me gusta también hacer camping.

Voy a ir a Puerto Madryn. Hay una colonia de pingüinos allí. Me encantan los pingüinos. ¿Y tú? ¿Qué haces de vacaciones normalmente? Puerto Madryn es la capital subacuática de Argentina. Se puede practicar la pesca y la exploración para la fotografía submarina. De julio a diciembre hay ballenas en la bahía.

Mira unas fotos de mis vacaciones.

Un abrazo,

Cristina

la bahía – *bay*
las ballenas – *whales*
la pesca – *fishing*

2 **Une los meses y su descripción.**

3 **Escribe los meses en orden.**

Los nombres de los meses

Une los meses y su descripción.

abrilnoviembremayoseptiembreagostojuliomarzodiciembreenerojuniofebrerooctubre

Ejemplo: Es el primer mes del año = enero

Navidad cae en este mes.
Normalmente empieza el año escolar en este mes.
Es el mes que viene después de marzo.
Este mes cae antes de septiembre.
Es el tercer mes del año.
En Gran Bretaña celebramos con fuegos artificiales durante este mes.
Este mes está entre septiembre y noviembre.
Este es el sexto mes que viene justo antes de julio.
Es el mes más corto del año.
Este mes está dedicado al emperador Julio César.
Es el mes que menos letras tiene en español.

cae – *falls*
antes – *before*
después – *after*
Navidad – *Christmas*
fuegos artificiales – *fireworks*

3 ¿Qué hiciste en tus vacaciones?

3A ¿Adónde fuiste?

- talk about what you did on a past holiday
- revise the preterite tense of regular verbs and learn some highly common irregular preterites

1
Hola, Vanesa. ¿Qué tal tus vacaciones?
¡Fantásticas! Fui a París una semana. ¿Y tú? ¿Qué tal?
¡Horrible! Fui a un pueblo muy pequeño en las montañas. ¡Fue muy aburrido!
2
Y además me alojé en un camping. Fue un rollo.
Pues yo me alojé en un hotel de lujo, con una piscina y con gimnasio. Fue estupendo.
3
¿Y qué hiciste en París, Vanesa?
Jugué al tenis y tomé el sol en el hotel, y también compré ropa muy bonita. ¡Fue genial! ¿Y tú?
Bebí Coca-cola y di una vuelta por el pueblo. ¡Fue horrible!

1 a **Lee y escucha la conversación entre Fede y Vanesa. Hablan de sus vacaciones.**

di una vuelta – *I went for a walk*

1 b **Haz una lista de las expresiones de opinión de 1a. Di si son positivas o negativas.**

Ejemplo: **¡Fantásticas! = positiva**

1 c **Mira los dibujos. ¿Quién dice las frases? Escribe 'Vanesa' o 'Fede' y escribe la frase.**

Ejemplo: **1 Vanesa. Compré ropa.**

1
2
Coca
3
4
5
×7
6
7
HOTEL

Gramática: the preterite

The preterite is the tense used to express something that happened in the past.

The regular endings are:

-ar verbs	**-er/-ir verbs**
comprar	*beber*
compré	*bebí*
compraste	*bebiste*
compró	*bebió*

Ir (to go) is one of the most common irregular verbs and it shares its preterite form with the verb *ser*, ('to be'):

fui	I was/went
fuiste	you (sing.) were/went
fue	he/she/it was/went

Another very common irregular verb is *hacer* (to do):

hice	I did
hiciste	you (sing.) did
hizo	he/she/it did

2 ***Fill in the gaps with one of the verbs from the box.***

1 El año pasado ________ a España.
2 ________ paella todos los días.
3 ________ agua con gas.
4 ________ con mis hermanos y mis padres.
5 ________ muchas actividades.
6 ________ al fútbol.
7 ________ el sol.
8 ________ genial.

bebí comí fue fui fui jugué hice tomé

3 a **Mira el cuadro. Escucha (A–D) y escribe los números correctos.**

Ejemplo: **A** 3, 6...

¿Adónde fuiste?	**1** Fui a España.	**2** Fui a Perú.	**3** Fui a Bolivia.	**4** Fui a Cuba.
¿Dónde te alojaste?	**5** Me alojé en un hotel.	**6** Me alojé en un camping.	**7** Me alojé en una caravana.	**8** Me alojé en un apartamento.
¿Qué compraste?	**9** Compré una camiseta.	**10** Compré unos regalos.	**11** Compré una gorra.	**12** Compré una postal.
¿Qué comiste?	**13** Comí paella.	**14** Comí pescado.	**15** Comí fruta.	**16** Comí comida típica.
¿Qué hiciste?	**17** Jugué al tenis.	**18** Di una vuelta.	**19** Nadé en el mar.	**20** Tomé el sol.
¿Cómo lo pasaste?	**21** Lo pasé genial.	**22** Lo pasé bastante bien.	**23** Lo pasé mal.	**24** Lo pasé fatal.

3 b **Escribe sobre tus últimas vacaciones. Contesta a las preguntas. Usa el cuadro de 3a.**

1. ¿Adónde fuiste?
2. ¿Dónde te alojaste?
3. ¿Qué compraste?
4. ¿Qué comiste?
5. ¿Qué hiciste?
6. ¿Cómo lo pasaste?

4 **Lee la carta y contesta a las preguntas en inglés.**

1. Where did Marta go on holiday?
2. How long did she stay there?
3. What sport did she play?
4. What else did she do?
5. What two things did she buy?
6. Who did she visit?

¡Hola, Pilar!

¿Qué tal? Fui de vacaciones a la costa. Mis padres tienen un apartamento en la playa y pasé allí dos semanas.

Fui a la playa todos los días y tomé el sol. Nadé mucho en el mar. Mis hermanos y yo jugamos al voleiplaya también. ¡Es un buen ejercicio!.

Compré unas gafas de sol y camisetas de muchos colores diferentes. Visité a mis abuelos que viven cerca, y a mis amigas Ester y Alicia.

¿Y tú? ¿Qué hiciste en tus vacaciones?

Escríbeme pronto, un beso

Marta

3B ¿Con quién fuiste?

- give more details about your holiday
- practise using questions with prepositions
- practise the intonation of questions

1 a Lee y escucha el diario de vacaciones de John.

lunes	Llegué al Arroyo de la Miel con mis padres y mi hermana Karen. Es un pueblo muy bonito. Comí un helado en la playa.
martes	Fui a la playa con mi hermana para tomar el sol. La playa es muy tranquila y está bastante limpia. Fue divertido.
miércoles	Fui a Torremolinos en autobús para ir de compras. Compré unos CDs y una revista de música. Todo es más barato que en Inglaterra.
jueves	Fui al parque temático *Tívoli* con mis amigos. Conocí a una chica española que se llama Isabel. Tengo su número de teléfono.
viernes	Llamé a Isabel. Fui con ella a una cafetería y al cine. Fue fantástico.
sábado	Fui de excursión a Málaga con mi familia, para visitar la catedral y el castillo árabe. Málaga es muy bonita. Compré una pulsera para Isabel.
domingo	Fuimos al aeropuerto para volver a Inglaterra. Fui a la playa para decir adiós a Isabel. Tengo su dirección de correo electrónico.

un helado – *ice cream*
limpia – *clean*
más barato que – *cheaper than*
conocí – *I met*
una pulsera – *bracelet*
decir adiós – *to say goodbye*

1 b ¿Verdad (V) o mentira (M)?

1 John fue de vacaciones con su hermano.
2 El pueblo es muy bonito.
3 El martes fue a la playa para nadar en el mar.
4 Fue a Torremolinos para visitar el castillo.
5 Tívoli es un pueblo cerca de Torremolinos.
6 John fue con Isabel al cine y a una cafetería.
7 Fue a Málaga con su familia.
8 John volvió a casa en ferry.

1 c Corrige las frases mentirosas.

Ejemplo: **1 (M) John fue de vacaciones con su hermana y sus padres.**

2 Copia el cuadro. Escucha (1–4) y rellénalo.

	¿Adónde fue?	¿Con quién fue?	¿Para qué fue?
1	Ecuador		
2		con familia	
3			visitar padres y amigos

Gramática: questions with prepositions

In questions with prepositions, the preposition must appear before the question word in Spanish. In English, it usually appears at the end of the question.

- Compare the questions
  ¿***Con*** *quién fuiste?* Who did you go **with**?
  ¿***Para*** *qué fuiste?* What did you go **for**?
- Remember that when you ask 'where…to?' the preposition **a** is joined to the question word in Spanish:
  ¿***Adónde*** *fuiste?*

3 ***Insert the prepositions in brackets in the appropriate place in the questions.***

Example: **1 ¿Para qué fuiste a España?**

1 ¿Qué fuiste a España? (para)
2 ¿Quién jugaste al fútbol? (con)
3 ¿Dónde fuiste el verano pasado? (a)
4 ¿Quién fuiste a Francia? (con)
5 ¿Qué fuiste a Irlanda? (para)

4 a Trabaja con tu pareja. Haz preguntas y respuestas.

Ejemplo:

A ¿Adónde fuiste de vacaciones?

B Fui a España.

¿Adónde fuiste de vacaciones?	Fui a…	España Francia
¿Con quién fuiste?	Fui con…	mis padres mis amigos
¿Para qué fuiste?	Fui para…	tomar el sol visitar la familia relajarme
¿Qué hiciste?	Tomé el sol Salí con amigos Visité la catedral Jugué al tenis Comí en restaurantes Compré ropa	

4 b ¡extra! **Escribe sobre tus vacaciones y las vacaciones de tu pareja.**

Yo	Mi pareja
Fui a…	Fue a…
Fui con…	Fue con…
Fui para…	Fue para…
Tomé el sol	Tomó el sol
Nadé en el mar	Nadó en el mar
Jugué al tenis…	Jugó al tenis…

Pronunciación: questions

When you pronounce a question in Spanish, intonation is very important, since the order of words is often not different between a statement and a question.

- ***Practise the following pairs of sentences. Then listen and repeat, imitating the intonation.***
  1 A mi hermano le gusta ir a Francia.
  2 ¿A tu hermano le gusta ir a Francia?
  3 Tus padres fueron a Florida.
  4 ¿Tus padres fueron a Florida?
  5 Fui a Egipto.
  6 ¿Fuiste a Egipto?
  7 Jugué al tenis.
  8 ¿Jugaste al tenis?

3C ¿Qué tiempo hizo?

- describe the weather in the past
- practise common irregular preterites

B

1 Une las frases y los dibujos.

Ejemplo: **1 D**

1 hizo frío

2 hizo calor

3 hizo viento

4 hizo buen tiempo

5 hizo mal tiempo

6 hizo sol

7 llovió

8 nevó

9 heló

10 hubo tormenta

11 hubo niebla

2 a Une las dos mitades de las frases sobre las vacaciones de Arturo. Escucha y comprueba tus respuestas.

Ejemplo: **1 b**

1 El lunes hizo mucho frío
2 El martes nevó en las montañas
3 El miércoles hizo sol
4 El jueves llovió
5 El viernes hizo mucho viento
6 El sábado hubo una tormenta
7 El domingo heló

a así que fui a patinar sobre hielo cerca del hotel.
b así que jugué a las cartas en el hotel.
c así que fui a un restaurante y luego al cine.
d y como me encantan las tormentas, saqué muchas fotos en la ciudad.
e y fui a la costa para hacer windsurf.
f y fui a esquiar.
g así que fui a la playa a tomar el sol.

2 b ¡extra! Escucha otra vez y rellena el cuadro.

Día	Tiempo	Actividad y dónde
lunes (el primer día)	frío	jugar a las cartas, hotel

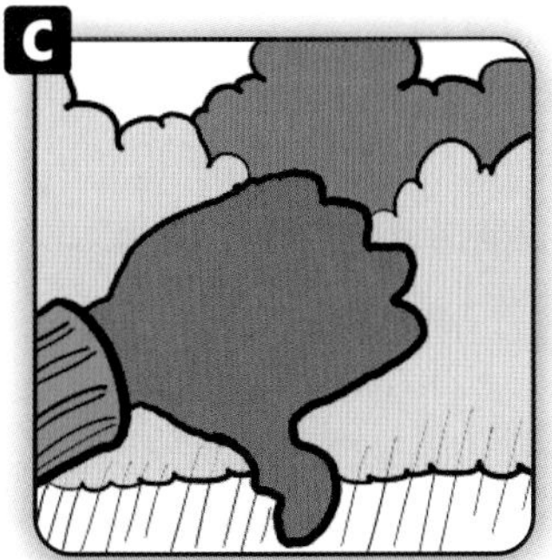

3 a Escucha el sondeo y rellena el cuadro.

hizo frío		llovió	
hizo calor	✔	nevó	
hizo viento		heló	
hizo buen tiempo		hubo tormenta	
hizo mal tiempo		hubo niebla	
hizo sol	✔		

3 b **Sondeo de clase. Pregunta qué tiempo hizo. Usa el cuadro de 3a.**

Ejemplo:

A ¿Qué tiempo hizo en tus vacaciones, Robert?

B Hizo frío y mucho viento.

4 a **Mira los dibujos de las vacaciones extraordinarias. ¿Qué tiempo hizo cada día y qué hiciste? Usa el cuadro.**

Ejemplo: **El lunes hizo frío. Me quedé en el hotel y jugué a las cartas.**

Fui a esquiar	Leí un libro
Fui a la playa	Saqué fotos
Fui al cine	Nadé en la piscina
Comí en un restaurante	Hice windsurf
Me quedé en el hotel	Fui de compras
Jugué a las cartas	Tomé el sol
Vi la tele	Visité el castillo

4 b **Describe unas vacaciones reales o imaginarias. ¿Qué tiempo hizo y qué hiciste?**

¡Así se hace! *Connectives*

When you are writing in Spanish, you can make your text more interesting by using connectives.

- What connectives can you think of that you could use in **4b**?
- Make a list of the following connectives in Spanish: after(wards), next, then, but, also, and, in the afternoon.

3D ¿Lo pasaste bien?

- express opinions about a past holiday
- discuss plans for your next holiday
- practise the intonation of exclamations

1 Lee las expresiones de opinión. Copia y rellena el cuadro.

a ¡Fue horrible!
b Lo pasé bien
c ¡Lo pasé fatal!
d ¡Lo pasé genial!
e ¡Lo pasé muy bien!
f Lo pasé bastante mal

Positivas	Negativas
Lo pasé bien	¡Fue horrible!

Pronunciación: exclamations

Exclamations, like questions, have the same word order as statements in Spanish. That is why your intonation has to show you are pronouncing an exclamation.

- *Listen to and repeat these exclamations.*

1 ¡Lo pasé genial!
2 ¡Fue horrible!
3 ¡Lo pasé bomba!
4 ¡Mis vacaciones fueron fantásticas!
5 ¡Lo pasé fatal!

2 Escucha (1–6). ¿Cómo pasaron sus vacaciones? Escribe la letra.

Ejemplo: **1** c

3 ¿Y tú? ¿Cómo lo pasaste en tus vacaciones? Pregunta a tus compañeros.

¿Qué tal tus vacaciones?

Lo pasé muy bien.

4 a Lee el correo electrónico y contesta a las preguntas en inglés.

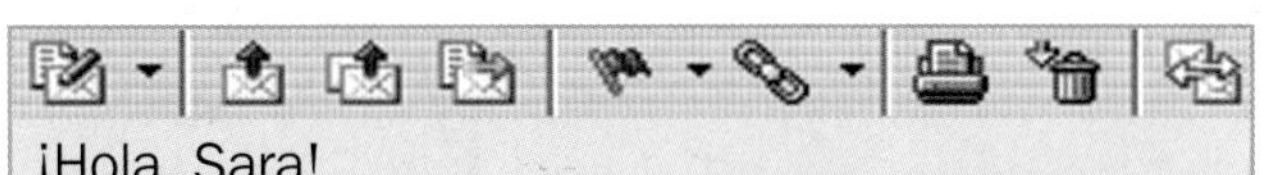

¡Hola, Sara!

¿Qué tal? Fui de vacaciones hace un mes y lo pasé fatal. Fui a Costa Rica para ir a la playa y tomar el sol, pero el tiempo fue horrible y la comida no me gustó nada.

El año próximo voy a ir a las Islas Canarias. Voy a ir a la playa y practicar el esquí acuático. Voy a alojarme en un apartamento en Lanzarote, una semana. Voy a comer mucho mojo picón, que es un plato típico. Voy a pasarlo muy bien.

¿Qué vas a hacer tú?

Escribe pronto.

Ana

mojo picón – *a spicy sauce from the Canary Islands*

1 What was Ana's holiday like?
2 Where did she go?
3 What did she not like about it?
4 Where is she going next year?
5 What is she going to do?
6 Where is she going to stay?
7 What is she going to eat?

4 b Contesta a la carta de Ana. Explica tus planes para tus próximas vacaciones.

El año pasado fui de vacaciones a…	España Londres		
Lo pasé…	muy bien fatal muy mal	porque…	hizo buen tiempo no me gustó la comida el hotel fue horrible
El año próximo voy a ir a…	Francia Irlanda		
Voy a alojarme en…	un hotel un apartamento un camping		
Voy a jugar…	al tenis al fútbol		
Voy a practicar…	la equitación la natación		
Voy a comer…	comida típica pescado mucha fruta fresca		
Voy a pasarlo…	muy bien mal		

¿Qué hiciste en tus vacaciones?	***What did you do on your holidays?***
¿Dónde te alojaste?	*Where did you stay?*
¿Qué compraste?	*What did you buy?*
¿Qué comiste?	*What did you eat?*
¿Qué hiciste?	*What did you do?*
¿Adónde fuiste?	*Where did you go?*
¿Con quién fuiste?	*Who did you go with?*
¿Para qué fuiste?	*What did you go for?*
Jugué al tenis	*I played tennis*
Tomé el sol	*I sunbathed*
Compré ropa	*I bought clothes*
Bebí Coca-cola	*I drank Coca-cola*
Di una vuelta por el pueblo	*I went for a walk around the village*
¡Fue muy aburrido!	*It was very boring!*
¡Fue un rollo!	*It was boring!*
Me alojé en un pueblo pequeño	*I stayed in a small village*
Fui a un pueblo	*I went to a town/village*

¿Qué tiempo hizo?	***What was the weather like?***
Hizo frío	*It was cold*
Hizo calor	*It was hot*
Hizo viento	*It was windy*
Hizo buen tiempo	*The weather was good*
Hizo mal tiempo	*The weather was bad*
Hizo sol	*It was sunny*
Llovió	*It rained*
Nevó	*It snowed*
Heló	*It was icy*
Hubo tormenta	*It was stormy*
Hubo niebla	*It was foggy*

¿Cómo lo pasaste?	***What kind of time did you have?***
¡Fue horrible!	*It was terrible!*
Lo pasé bien	*I had a good time*
¡Lo pasé fatal!	*I had an awful time!*
¡Lo pasé genial!	*I had a great time!*
¡Lo pasé muy bien!	*I had a very good time!*
Lo pasé bastante mal	*I didn't have a very good time*

¿Qué planes tienes?	***What plans do you have?***
Voy a ir a España	*I'm going to go to Spain*
Voy a alojarme en...	*I'm going to stay in...*
Voy a jugar...	*I'm going to play...*
Voy a practicar...	*I'm going to do...*
Voy a comer...	*I'm going to eat...*

Gramática:

The preterite of regular verbs

The preterite of some common irregular verbs (*ir*, *ser* and *hacer*)

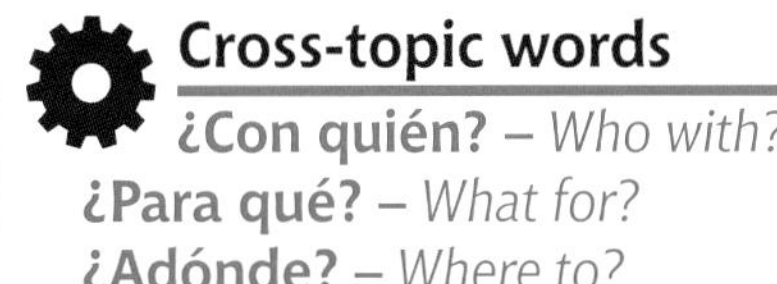

Cross-topic words

¿Con quién? – *Who with?*

¿Para qué? – *What for?*

¿Adónde? – *Where to?*

¡Así se hace!

- ★ Pronunciation: the intonation of questions and exclamations
- ★ Connectives

4 ¡Que aproveche!

4A ¿Qué te gusta comer?

- describe what you like eating and when you eat
- practise using negatives
- develop your listening and speaking skills

1 a Trabaja con tu pareja. Haz la encuesta de una revista española. Mira las respuestas.

1 b Mira y busca:

3 comidas
3 desayunos
3 bebidas
3 ejemplos de comida rápida

Eres lo que comes. ¿Eres sano?

Contesta a las preguntas.

1 ¿Comes

a mucha fruta y ensalada todos los días?
b un poco de fruta y ensalada?
c un poco de fruta?
d ni fruta ni ensalada?

2 ¿Comes carne

a todos los días y mucha?
b tres veces a la semana?
c solamente los domingos?
d nunca?

3 ¿Comes pescado

a todos los días?
b tres veces a la semana?
c una vez a la semana?
d nunca?

4 ¿Qué desayunas?

a Cereales, zumo de fruta y tostadas
b Tostadas y café
c Nada
d Bacón y huevos fritos con salchichas y tomates

5 ¿Cenas muy tarde?

a Todos los días.
b Muy frecuentemente.
c Si es un día especial.
d No, nunca.

6 Tienes hambre en la calle. ¿Comes

a una hamburguesa o un perrito caliente?
b un bocadillo de jamón y queso?
c un trozo de pizza?
d una pera o una manzana?

7 Tienes sed. ¿Bebes

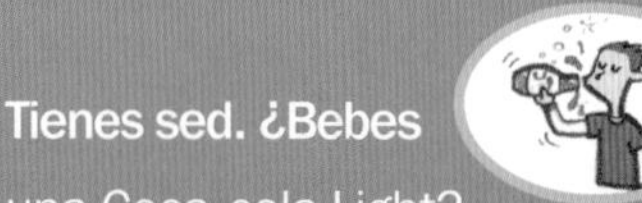

a una Coca-cola Light?
b una Coca-cola?
c un zumo de naranja?
d una botella de agua mineral?

	a	b	c	d
1	15	10	5	0
2	0	5	10	5
3	10	15	5	0
4	15	5	0	5
5	0	5	10	15
6	0	10	10	15
7	5	0	15	15

Más de 75

¡Comes muy bien! Pero ¡cuidado! Si haces mucho deporte, necesitas más calorías.

Más de 60

Comes bastante bien. Pero hay que beber mucha agua también.

Más de 40

No comes muy bien. Hay que cambiar tu dieta.

Menos de 40

Comes muy mal. También vas a tener problemas en el futuro si no haces más ejercicio.

Gramática: negatives

Simple negatives are formed by adding *no* in front of the verb: *como* > *no como*.

- There are three other negative words in the quiz. Can you find them? What do they mean?

  No como nunca pescado.

  No desayuno nada.

  No me gustan ni los perritos calientes ni los bocadillos.

Normally, *nada* (nothing), *nunca* (never) and *ni… ni* (neither… nor), follow the verb and the word *no* goes before.

- Note that when you are saying 'No, I don't...' you use *no* twice: *¿Te gusta la fruta? No, no me gusta.*

2 ***Choose* no, nunca, nada *or* ni... ni *to complete the sentences.***

1. ¿Comes el desayuno a las ocho?
   No, _____ como el desayuno a las ocho.
2. ¿Vas al parque los martes?
   No, _____ voy al parque los martes.
3. ¿Comes fruta o ensalada?
   No, no como _____ fruta _____ ensalada.
4. ¿Qué desayunas los domingos?
   No desayuno _____ los domingos.
5. ¿Comes carne los domingos?
   No, _____ como carne los domingos.
6. ¿Te gustan los cereales?
   No, no me gustan _____ los cereales _____ los productos de pan.

3 **Haz las preguntas a tu pareja. Mira los ejemplos.**

¿Qué comes en el desayuno?	Como tostadas en el desayuno.
¿Qué bebes?	Bebo té.
¿Qué comes en el instituto?	Como/No como...
¿Cenas tarde?	Ceno/No ceno...
¿Qué comes en la calle?	Como/No como...
¿Qué bebes normalmente?	Bebo/No bebo...
¿Comes carne o pescado?	Como/No como...

4 ¡extra! **Escribe una encuesta con 5 preguntas. Usa 1a como modelo.**

¡Así se hace! *Anticipating language*

It is so much easier to understand people speaking if we can anticipate what they are likely to say. Before you listen to the recording in **5**, write down as many words as you can for things you can eat and drink. Check your list with a partner.

5 **Escucha (1–8) y escribe la letra para cada uno.**

¡Así se hace! *Extended answers*

The questions in **3** have very short answers. Look at these expressions that you could use to make a more detailed answer.
A good way of starting is to say something like: *Depende…* (It depends). It also gives you 'thinking time'.

When

A las ocho	At 8 o'clock
Por la mañana	In the morning

Where

En casa	At home
En la cantina	In the canteen

How often

A veces	Sometimes
Normalmente	Usually

Who with

Con mis padres	With my parents
Con mis amigos	With my friends

Why

Porque me gusta(n)	Because I like it/them
Porque es sano	Because it's healthy

- Now give more detailed answers to the questions in **3**.

For example:
¿Qué comes en el instituto?
Depende. Normalmente no como nada pero a veces como pizza o un perrito caliente porque tengo hambre. Como con mis amigos en la cantina.

4B ¿Adónde vamos a comer?

- describe what type of food you like
- learn more about accents

1 a **Lee el artículo y busca las palabras españolas:**

1 there is/there are
2 and
3 a lot of
4 also
5 more than

Mucho de todo: la comida argentina

En Buenos Aires hay muchos restaurantes de todos tipos. Hay mucha variedad de cocina italiana, francesa, española, china, mejicana y argentina. A los argentinos les encanta la carne, el bife, sobre todo. ¡Es buenísimo!

Hay también mucha influencia italiana. Se come mucha comida italiana: lasaña, pizza y pasta en general. La pizza es el fastfood por excelencia con más de treinta variedades. ¡Y es riquísima!

Hay muchos restaurantes españoles. Se come mucho pescado y allí se come mucha paella, claro.

Gramática: *-ísimo*

-ísimo just means 'very, very…'.

bueno > *buenísimo*	good > very, very good
caro > *carísimo*	expensive > very, very expensive
lento > *lentísimo*	slow > very, very slow
N.B. *rico* > *riquísimo*	rich/tasty (of food) > very, very rich/tasty

1 b ***Translate these sentences.***

1 El caviar es carísimo.
2 La pizza es baratísima.
3 El tren es rapidísimo.
4 El español es facilísimo.
5 El alemán es dificilísimo.
6 La montaña es altísima.

1 c **Une las preguntas españolas con las inglesas.**

Ejemplo: 1 b

1 ¿Qué tipo de comida hay en los restaurantes argentinos?
2 ¿Qué comida les gusta muchísimo a los argentinos?
3 ¿Qué tipo de comida italiana se come?
4 ¿Por qué es popular la pizza?
5 ¿Qué plato español se come mucho?
6 ¿Cuál es riquísima: la comida española o la italiana?

a Why is pizza popular?
b What type of food is served in Argentinian restaurants?
c Which is very, very tasty: Spanish food or Italian food?
d What type of Italian food is eaten?
e Which food do Argentinian people like very much?
f Which Spanish dish is eaten a lot?

1 d **Contesta a las preguntas de 1c.**

Ejemplo: 1 En los restaurantes argentinos hay comida italiana, francesa, española, china, mejicana y argentina.

1 En los restaurantes argentinos…
2 A los argentinos les gusta…
3 Se come…
4 La pizza es popular porque…
5 Se come mucho…
6 La comida…es riquísima.

2 a Escucha (1–5). ¿Adónde van los clientes?

Ejemplo: **1 E**

Restaurantes de Buenos Aires

A

Cocina francesa

Chez Christophe

Lunes a domingo. Platos clásicos y comida riquísima.

B

Lunes a sábado. Típicas comidas rusas. Especialidades: el caviar y el salmón. $50 por persona.

C

Comida rápida

Angelín

Lunes a sábado. Sirven sandwiches, ensaladas, hamburguesas y pizzas. $5 a $10 por persona.

D

Comida italiana

Cara Napoli

Lunes a viernes. Lo mejor de Italia. Pizzas y pastas. $15 a $30 por persona.

E

¡Viva Méjico!

Lunes a domingo. Cocina tradicional mejicana. Tacos, tortillas y chile con carne.

Gramática: agreement of adjectives

Remember that adjectives agree with the noun they describe!

Examples: ***cocina mejicana*** **– because *cocina* is feminine**
judías verdes **– because *judías* is plural.**

- Write a list of the adjectives used in the adverts to describe food.

2 b *Can you put the following phrases into Spanish?*

Example: **1 hamburguesas caras**

1 expensive hamburgers
2 cheap dishes
3 long menus
4 tall drinks
5 lots of variety
6 lots of different dishes

2 c Lee los anuncios. ¿Adónde van a ir?

Ejemplo: **1 B**

1 Busco un restaurante para el martes. Me gusta mucho el pescado. ¿Adónde voy?
2 Sólo tengo una hora. Quiero algo rápido.
3 Busco un restaurante un poco clásico y de lujo.
4 Voy a comer comida latinoamericana.
5 Me encantan la lasaña y los espaguetis.

2 d Habla con tu pareja. Cambia las palabras.

Ejemplo:

A ¿Qué tipo de comida te gusta?
B Me gusta la comida española.
A ¿Qué platos te gustan?
B Me gustan la paella, la tortilla española y los calamares.
A ¿Qué plato te gusta más?
B Mi plato preferido es la paella.

argentina mejicana
italiana la pasta la pizza
los tacos las patatas fritas
la lasaña la hamburguesa
el perrito caliente
el pollo la carne

Bajo la lupa Accentuation (2)

We saw earlier (page 9) how there are rules as to where to put the stress on a word. We also saw that for words that are stressed differently, we had to put an accent. For example: *jamón, típico*. There is another reason why you might use a written accent.

- Look at the following examples:

*Para **mí**, el pollo.*
***Mi** pollo está bueno.*

*¿Quieres **té**?*
*¿**Te** gusta el chocolate?*

*Vamos a tomar **esta** mesa.*
*Prefiero **ésta**.*

In these cases, the accent does not change the stress. It is there to remove confusion between two words that are spelt the same. We write *para mí* but in *para ti*, the word *ti* does not need an accent because there is not another word that could be confused with it.

4C ¡Camarero!

- understand a menu and order food
- devise ways of learning new vocabulary
- learn how to use disjunctive pronouns

1 a **Mira el menú y apunta las palabras que no entiendes. Busca las palabras en el diccionario.**

Restaurante El Faro
Almuerzo de 12 a 15
Menú turístico 30
Primer plato
sopa de pescado
ensalada verde
ensalada mixta
cóctel de gambas
tortilla española
tortilla francesa
Segundo plato
Carnes y aves:
bistec pollo
Pescado:
merluza bacalao salmón paella
Postres
flan
arroz con leche
ensalada de fruta
helados
Pan, vino, agua incluidos.
El servicio no está incluido.

1 b **Escucha (1–5). ¿Qué piden?**

¡Así se hace! *Learning new vocabulary*

How can you remember new words?

- Make a list and cross off words once you are sure you can say, write, understand and use them correctly.
- Test yourself and others. If testing yourself, have the word in English on one side of a card and the Spanish on the other.
- Create a sentence to help you remember, e.g. **b**ig **e**lephants **c**an't **a**lways **u**se **s**mall **e**xits (because).
- Take five words and do the following: look, say, write, cover, check.
- Create a mind map of a menu and try to add as many dishes as you can. Then compare with your partner.

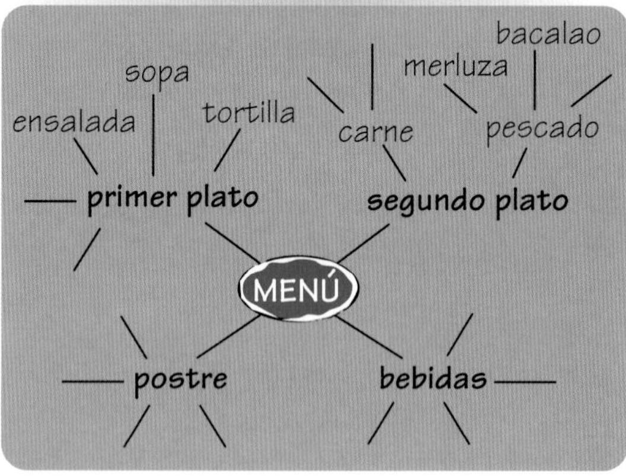

Pizzería
GIUSEPPE
¡Camarero! ¿Qué recomienda?
Recomiendo el restaurante italiano.

1 c Haz un test con tu pareja. Nombra un plato y tu pareja dice un ejemplo. Recibe un punto para cada respuesta correcta. No se puede repetir un plato. Mira el menú en la página 36 para ayudarte.

Ejemplo:

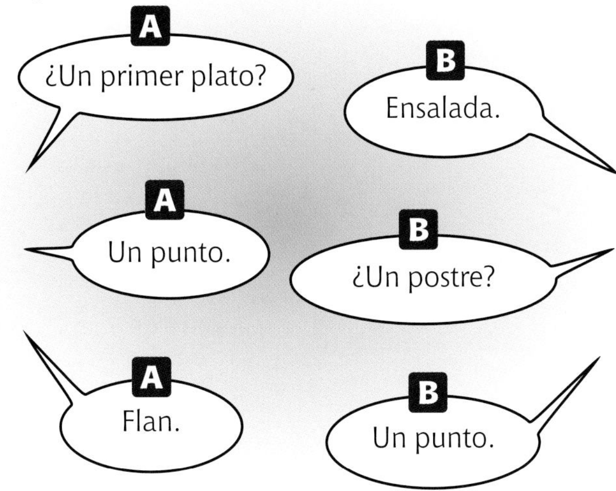

A ¿Un primer plato?
B Ensalada.
A Un punto.
B ¿Un postre?
A Flan.
B Un punto.

1 d ¡extra! Haz un test más complicado.

Ejemplo:

A ¿Dos segundos platos?
B Merluza y bacalao.
A Muy bien, un punto.
B ¿Dos primeros platos?
A Ensalada verde y… no sé.

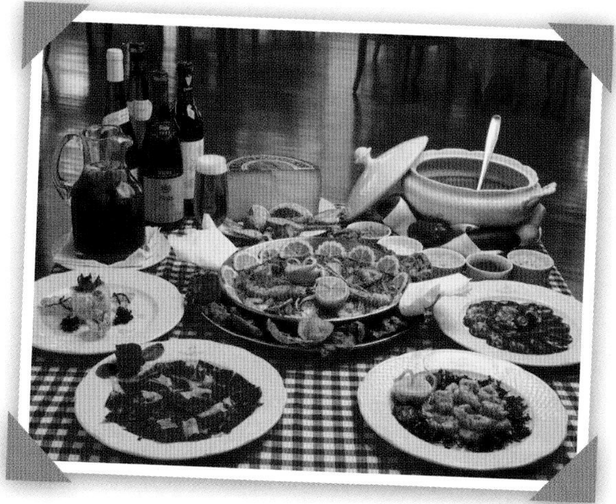

2 Mira los dibujos y escucha (1–6). Escribe la letra correcta.

Ejemplo: **1 C**

3 a Pon las frases en orden para hacer un diálogo.

Vino blanco.
¡Camarero!
Aquí tiene. ¿Qué desea?
¿Sí, señor?
El menú, por favor.
Para mí, la ensalada.
Muy bien. ¿Y para beber?
Nada más, gracias.
¿Algo más?

3 b Habla con tu pareja. Cambia las palabras.

Gramática: disjunctive pronouns

When you have a preposition (*para, delante de*), you need to use a special pronoun to say 'me', 'you', 'her' or 'him', etc. Look at the list below before attempting **4**.

mí	me
ti	you (fam)
él/ella	him/her

4 *Fill in the gaps with the correct pronoun.*

1 Para ________, la ensalada y el pollo. (*me*)
2 Papá, ¿para ________ el vino tinto o el vino blanco? (*you*)
3 Para ________ el pescado. (*Cristina*)
4 La sopa es para ________ . (*Raúl*)
5 La paella es para ________ . (*me*)
6 María, para ________ la sopa, ¿verdad? (*you*)

4D La gastronomía en España

- learn about Spanish food
- describe the contents of a dish

1 a 

Mira el mapa y contesta a las preguntas.

Ejemplo: **1 En la costa.**

1 ¿Dónde se come mucho pescado?
2 ¿Dónde se come mucho arroz?
3 ¿Cómo se llama el queso famoso?
4 ¿Dónde se sirve mucha carne?
5 ¿Cómo se llama la sopa famosa?

el marisco – *shellfish*

El centro es la zona de los asados: hay muchos platos de carne asada. El queso famoso de La Mancha se llama manchego.

El este es la zona del arroz: es la base de muchos platos.

En la costa hay mucho pescado y marisco muy famoso en España.

En Andalucía se toma el gazpacho que es una sopa fría.

1 b Escucha (1–5). Apunta los ingredientes.

Ejemplo: **1 tomate, pan**

patatas pan
ensalada tomate pescado
arroz carne

2 a ¿Con qué se hacen los platos?

Ejemplo: **1 El gazpacho se hace con tomates, aceite de oliva, cebolla, vinagre, pan y ajo.**

1 ¿Con qué se hace el gazpacho?

2 ¿Con qué se hace la paella?

3 ¿Con qué se hace la tortilla española?

4 ¿Con qué se hace el arroz con leche?

5 ¿Con qué se hace el flan?

6 ¿Con qué se hace la ensalada mixta?

2 b Juego. Trabaja con tu pareja. Di un ingrediente y tu pareja adivina el plato.

Ejemplo:

A Leche. **B** ¿Flan?
A No. **B** ¿Arroz con leche?
A Sí.

La comida	Food
la comida rápida	*fast food*
el plato	*dish/course*
el primer plato	*first course*
el segundo plato	*second/main course*
el postre	*dessert/sweet course*
la sopa de pescado	*fish soup*
la ensalada verde	*green salad*
la ensalada mixta	*mixed salad (with tuna and egg)*
el gazpacho	*cold tomato soup*
el bistec	*steak*
el pollo	*chicken*
la merluza	*hake*
el salmón	*salmon*
la paella	*paella*
la pizza/pasta	*pizza/pasta*
el flan	*egg custard*
el arroz	*rice*
la ensalada de fruta	*fruit salad*
los helados	*ice creams*

Ingredientes	Ingredients
¿Con qué se hace?	*What is it made with?*
Se hace con…	*It is made of…*
patatas	*potatoes*
cebolla	*onion*
tomate	*tomato*
marisco	*shellfish*
leche	*milk*
azúcar	*sugar*
aceite de oliva	*olive oil*
atún	*tuna*

Las bebidas	Drinks
el vino tinto	*red wine*
el vino blanco	*white wine*

¡Camarero!	Waiter!
El menú, por favor	*The menu, please*
Para mí…	*For me…*
¿Y para beber?	*And to drink?*
Mi plato preferido es…	*My favourite dish is…*

Opiniones	Opinions
Está bien	*It's fine*
¡Buenísimo!	*Really good!*
¡Muy rico!	*Very tasty!*
¡Riquísimo!	*Very, very tasty!*
¡Fue delicioso!	*It was delicious!*
¡Fabuloso!	*Great!*
lo mejor	*the best*

Gramática:
Negatives: *no, nada, nunca, ni… ni*
-ísimo
Disjunctive pronouns: *para mí, para ti, para él/ella.*

¡Así se hace!
- ★ Extending your answers
- ★ Anticipating language in listening texts
- ★ Ways of learning new vocabulary

- Use of accents to avoid ambiguity

Cross-topic words
sobre todo – *above all*
una vez – *once*
nunca – *never*
nada – *nothing*

Unidad 3 (¿Problemas? Mira la página 31.)

1 a Habla con tu pareja.

Ejemplo: **A** ¿Qué tiempo hizo ayer en Francia?
B Hizo calor.

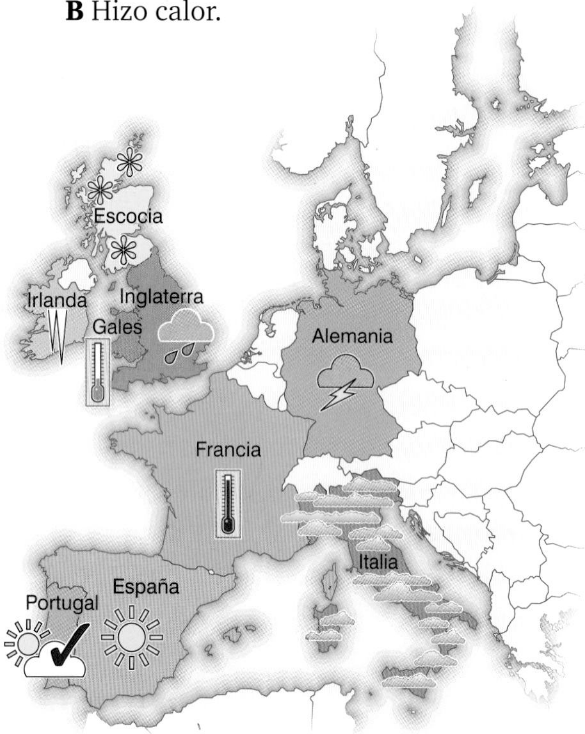

1 b Contrarreloj

Mira el mapa otra vez. En dos minutos escribe el país y el tiempo.

Ejemplo: **En Francia, hizo calor.**

2 Escucha (1–5) y rellena el cuadro.

	1	2	3
País	Estados Unidos		
Tiempo	buen tiempo		
Comida	hamburguesas		
Actividades	parque temático		
Opinión	¡genial!		

Unidad 4 (¿Problemas? Mira la página 39.)

3 Lee la carta y contesta a las preguntas en inglés.

1 When was Bea's birthday?
2 How did she celebrate the event?
3 Why was the visit a disaster?
4 What did she do yesterday?
5 What does Bea have to say about the Spanish restaurant?
6 What did she eat?
7 What two things is she going to do in the future?
8 Why?

¡Hola, amigo!
El sábado fue mi cumpleaños y como siempre fuimos a cenar en el restaurante italiano que está cerca. Fue un desastre. Lo pasé fatal porque no me gustó nada la comida. Ayer, fuimos al centro a un restaurante español. Los camareros son españoles y la cocina es muy típica. ¡Lo pasé genial! Comí gambas, una paella y de postre un helado de fresa. Fue buenísimo todo. Voy a volver al restaurante español con mis amigos. También voy a visitar España porque me gusta mucho la comida española.
¿Hay muchos restaurantes donde vives tú?
Bea

4 Escribe un párrafo en español sobre lo que te gusta comer y beber. Usa las frases y palabras de abajo para ayudarte.

Mi plato favorito es...
También me gusta comer... y me gusta beber...
No me gusta nada comer... y odio beber...
La semana pasada fui a un restaurante... con...
Comí... y bebí...
Me lo pasé...

Una receta fácil

En España la tortilla española es un plato muy popular. No se hace muy rápidamente, pero es delicioso, y un plato que a casi todos les gusta compartir.

Hacer una tortilla deliciosa es bastante fácil. Sólo hay que seguir las instrucciones:

Ingredientes

6 huevos

8 patatas medianas

Una cebolla

Medio litro de aceite de oliva

Sal

Instrucciones

1 Cortar las patatas y la cebolla en trozos pequeños.
2 Freír las patatas y la cebolla a fuego lento en el aceite de oliva.
3 Cuando estén blandas las patatas y la cebolla, retirarlas del fuego.
4 Batir los huevos.
5 Añadir un poco de sal a los huevos.
6 Mezclar los huevos con la mezcla de patatas y cebolla.
7 Freír la masa en una sartén. Dar vueltas a la tortilla de vez en cuando.
8 Servir en un plato y partir en trozos o lonchas.

1 ¿Verdad (V) o mentira (M)?

Ejemplo: **1 V**

1 Es un plato típico español.
2 Se tarda muy pocos minutos en prepararla.
3 Es un plato apropiado para vegetarianos.
4 Se necesita un par de huevos.
5 Se necesita más de una patata.
6 Hay que cocinar las patatas y la cebolla juntas.
7 Se cocinan los huevos separados.
8 Esta receta es para una persona sólo.

compartir – *share*
seguir – *follow*
trozos – *pieces*
a fuego lento – *on a low heat*
blandas – *soft*

2 *Now match up the Spanish phrases and the English ones.*

1 No se hace muy rápidamente
2 Hacer una tortilla es fácil
3 medio litro de aceite de oliva
4 cuando estén blandas
5 Batir los huevos
6 Freír la masa en una sartén

a half a litre of olive oil
b when they are soft
c It's not quick to make
d Making a tortilla is easy
e Fry the mixture in a frying pan
f Whisk the eggs

3 *Find out what the ingredients for the following dishes are and make a list in Spanish. Look up words you don't know in the dictionary.*

Example: **gazpacho – Los ingredientes son: tomates, cebollas...**

1 gazpacho **2** enchiladas **3** paella

5 Intercambio

5A Dime más sobre tu familia

- say more about yourself and your family
- give more detailed descriptions

1 a Mira el dibujo y escucha. Pon las letras en orden.

Ejemplo: **C, ...**

1 b ¡extra! Escucha y lee. ¿De quién habla la chica?

Ejemplo: **1 abuelos**

1 No trabajan. Están jubilados. Viven en casa con nosotros.
2 Está casado con dos hijos. No vive con nosotros.
3 Tiene cincuenta años.
4 No trabaja. Prefiere estar en casa.
5 Va al colegio conmigo.
6 Tiene cinco años. ¡Es un perro guardián!
7 Es viuda. Vive sola en un piso cerca. Su marido, mi abuelo, murió hace 15 años.

la viuda – *widow* jubilado – *retired*
morir (murió) – *to die (died)*

Gramática: the use of masculine for mixed genders
Notice that *abuelos* can mean 'grandfathers' but is used here to describe grandfather and grandmother. When there is more than one gender together, the **masculine** form is used.

2 a Escucha y lee las cartas. ¿Quiénes viven con ellos? Rellena el cuadro.

Nombre	Padre	Madre	Hermanos (¿cuántos?)	Hermanas (¿cuántas?)	Otros (¿quién?)
Andrés	✔	✔			
Carolina					
Nuria					

2 b ¿Qué significan las palabras *mujer*, *separado*, *novios*, *hija única*, *divorciados*, *casadas*?

2 c Lee las cartas otra vez. ¿Quién habla?

Ejemplo: **1 Carolina**

1 No tengo hermanos. Somos dos en casa.
2 Mis padres tienen cuatro hijos.
3 Mi madre tiene novio.
4 Soy tía.
5 Mis hermanas no están casadas.
6 Mi hermano se casó pero no vive con su mujer.
7 Mi padre no vive con nosotros.

¡Hola! Te voy a presentar a mi familia. Hay seis en mi familia: mis padres, mi hermano, mis dos hermanas y yo. Mi hermano Ignacio es ingeniero. Está separado de su mujer. Mis hermanas, Paula y Conchita, tienen novios pero no están casadas. Mándame una foto de tu familia.
Un abrazo de tu buen amigo,
Andrés

¡Hola! Me llamo Nuria. Mi familia es muy grande. Vivo con mi padre, mi madrastra y mi hermana en una casa pequeña en Barcelona. Tengo dos hermanas y un hermanastro. Mi hermana mayor, Sonia, tiene un bebé. Mi hermana menor, Amelia, vive con nosotros.
Besos y abrazos,
Nuria

Me presento. Yo soy Carolina y tengo 16 años. Soy hija única. Vivo con mi madre. Mis padres están divorciados. Mi padre vive en Honduras. Mi madre tiene novio pero es un secreto.
Besitos,
Carolina

3 a Contesta a las preguntas sobre tu familia.

¿Cuántas personas hay en tu casa? — En mi casa hay cinco personas.
¿Tienes hermanos? — Tengo dos hermanas.
¿Cómo se llaman? — Se llaman Rosa y Carla.
¿Cuántos años tienen? — Rosa tiene 15 años. Carla tiene 17 años.
¿Están casados/as? — No están casadas.
¿Tienen hijos? — No tienen hijos.
¿Tienes abuelos? — Tengo un abuelo y dos abuelas.
¿Dónde viven? — Viven en Valencia.

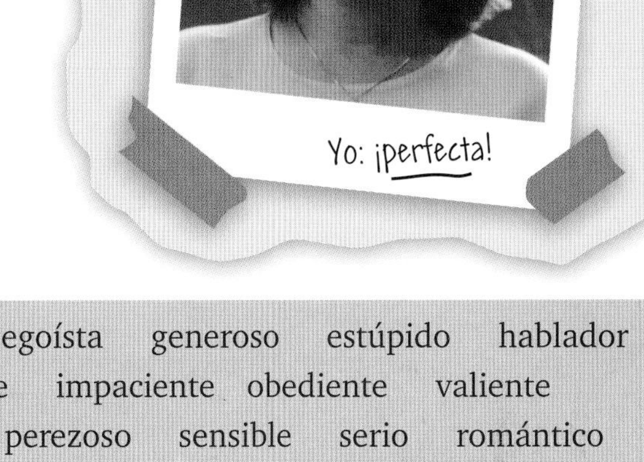

3 b Contrarreloj

Prepara 5 frases sobre tu familia.

4 *Look at the adjectives in the box. Work with a partner. What do they mean? What strategies will you use to find out? Examples: sounds/looks like an English word, look it up in a dictionary.*

antipático egoísta generoso estúpido hablador
paciente impaciente obediente valiente
nervioso perezoso sensible serio romántico
simpático cruel desobediente extrovertido
tímido trabajador honesto súper guapo

Bajo la lupa **Word patterns**

- You will notice some patterns in the adjectives. These patterns can help you to understand words you do not know.

5 a Habla con tu pareja. Apunta los detalles.

Ejemplo:
¿Cómo te llamas?
Me llamo Fernando.
¿Cuántos años tienes?
Tengo catorce años.
¿Dónde vives?
Vivo en Madrid.
¿Cuántas personas hay en tu familia?
Hay cuatro personas en mi familia: mi padre, mi madre, mi hermana y yo.
¿Cómo se llama tu hermana?
Mi hermana se llama Ana.
¿Cuántos años tiene?
Tiene doce años.
¿Cómo es tu hermana?
Es simpática y generosa.

Gramática: verbs

Notice the changing patterns in verbs. Some of these have been highlighted in **5a**.

5 b *Complete the table with the missing parts of each verb.*

	yo	tú	él / ella	ellos / ellas
llamarse	me llamo			
tener		tienes		
vivir	vivo		vive	
ser	soy	eres		son

5 c *Insert the correct form of each verb in the following sentences.*

Example: 1 ¿Dónde vives?

1. ¿Dónde ________? (vivir)
2. Mi padre ________ en Málaga. (vivir)
3. Mi abuela ________ generosa. (ser)
4. Yo ________ un amigo muy simpático. (tener)
5. Mis hermanos ________ Paula y Tito. (llamarse)
6. ¿________ hermanos? (tener)
7. Mis padres ________ simpáticos. (ser)

5B Estás en tu casa

- introduce people and welcome a visitor
- say what you need

1 a Lee y escucha.

1 b Mira los dibujos y haz el diálogo con tu pareja.

Ejemplo: **¡Hola! ¿Qué tal?**
¡Estupendo!

2 Mira la foto y haz un diálogo con tu pareja.

3 a Escucha y lee.

1
Aquí está tu dormitorio. Si te hace falta algo...

2
... hay otra almohada o más sábanas si tienes frío. Las toallas están en la cama.

3
Y aquí el cuarto de baño. Hay champú, jabón, pasta de dientes.

4
Me hace falta un secador de pelo.
No hay problema.

5
Muchas gracias.

6
¿A qué hora te levantas por la mañana?

7
A las siete. Y si te hace falta un despertador, hay uno en la mesita de noche.

Gramática: ***me hace falta***

Hacer falta is a way of saying 'to need'. Literally it means 'it is lacking to me'.

Me hace falta una toalla. I need a towel.

If what you need is plural, add an 'n' to the verb:

Me hacen falta dos toallas. I need two towels.

3 b Escucha (1–7) ¿Qué te hace falta?

Ejemplo: **1 D**

3 c Juego de memoria. Cierra el libro y haz frases con tu pareja.

Ejemplo:

A Me hace falta una toalla.

B Me hacen falta una toalla y una sábana.

A Me hacen falta una toalla, una sábana y...

5C ¿Qué hace tu madre?

- describe what jobs people do
- prepare for questions

1 a Contrarreloj

Une los trabajos y las descripciones.

1 Sirve a los clientes en el bar.

2 Arregla coches.

3 Escribe a máquina y habla mucho por teléfono.

4 Asiste a clase.

5 Trabaja con jóvenes.

6 Trabaja en una tienda.

7 Es el jefe/la jefa.

8 Trabaja en un hospital.

9 Tiene pacientes.

10 Hace un trabajo práctico.

11 Tiene mucho dinero pero no es rico.

¡nuevo!

A profesor(a)
B médico
C secretario/a
D empleado/a de banco
E director(a)
F ingeniero/a
G camarero/a
H dependiente/a
I enfermero/a
J mecánico
K estudiante

1 b Escucha (1–11). ¿Tus respuestas son correctas?

2 a Juego. Adivina dónde trabaja tu pareja y qué hace.

Remember: verb endings change according to who speaks.

A ¿Trabajas en un hospital?
B No, no trabajo en un hospital.
A ¿Sirves a clientes?
B Sí, sirvo a clientes.
A ¿Trabajas en una tienda?
B No.
A ¿Trabajas en un bar?
B Sí.
A Eres camarero/a.

2 b Adapta el diálogo. ¿Qué hace tu familia? Trabaja con tu pareja.

A ¿Qué hace tu madre?
B Mi madre es médico.
A ¿Dónde trabaja?
B Trabaja en un hospital en Cambridge.

Gramática: dropping *un/una* with jobs

In Spanish you do not use *un* or *una* when describing what people do.

Mi madre es médico. My mother is **a** doctor.

3 **Escucha (1–5) y apunta sus detalles personales.**

	Family member A	Family member B
1		Father – engineer
2		

Gramática: question words

In Spanish all the question words have accents on the stressed syllable: *¿Dónde? ¿Qué?* And, don't forget, all questions need two question marks: *¿?*

4 ***Add accents and correct punctuation to the following questions.***

1 Donde viven sus abuelos
2 Cuando juegas al fútbol
3 Que hace tu madre
4 Como se llama su madrastra
5 Cual es más importante
6 Cuando vas a Madrid

¡Así se hace! ***Preparing for questions***

If you go to visit or stay with a family in Spain or a Latin American country, they are bound to ask you about obvious things like your family and what the journey was like. Always have your answers ready in Spanish. It will make conversation easier and calm your (and their) nerves! Have some photos of family and pets to show them too.

5 a ***Match up the questions and answers.***

1 ¿De dónde eres?
2 ¿Dónde está exactamente?
3 ¿Cuánto tiempo vas a estar aquí?
4 ¿Desde cuándo estudias español?
5 ¿Qué tal?
6 ¿Qué tal el viaje?
7 ¿Tienes hermanos?
8 ¿Cuántos años tiene(n)?
9 ¿Qué hacen tus padres/hermanos?
10 ¿Dónde trabaja(n)?

a Fue muy largo.
b Voy a estar dos semanas.
c Soy de York.
d Mi hermano tiene 18 años.
e Trabaja en Leeds.
f Muy bien, gracias.
g Está en el norte de Inglaterra.
h Tengo un hermano y no tengo hermanas.
i Mi padre es ingeniero.
j Desde hace dos años.

5 b ***Answer the questions for yourself.***

5 c ***Now practise with a partner. Imagine you are speaking to a Spanish-speaking family on your arrival at their house.***

5D La amistad

- talk and write about friendship

1 Mira los anuncios en una revista. Apunta los adjetivos.

1 Chica guapa de 15 años busca a un chico simpático, divertido y sincero. Soy sensible y honesta.

Barcelona. Buzón 189934 SMS.

2 Chica de 17 años busca amigo tranquilo.

Toledo. Buzón 198755 SMS.

3 Chica deportista y activa de 16 años busca chico divertido e inteligente.

Teruel. Buzón 198756 SMS.

4 Chica de 14 años busca a un chico atractivo y divertido. Me gustan los conciertos, ir al cine y jugar al tenis.

Ávila. Buzón 198757 SMS.

5 Chico de 18 años busca chica sincera y guapa. Soy tímido pero no soy aburrido. Escríbeme.

Madrid. Buzón 198758 SMS.

6 Chico atlético busca chica entre 15 y 20 años para amiga. Yo soy alto, 1,90, y delgado. No fumadora, por favor.

Salamanca. Buzón 198759 SMS.

7 Chico muy romántico. Tengo buen sentido de humor. Mándame un mensaje.

Ciudad Real. Buzón 198757 SMS.

2 Haz una lista de las características de un buen amigo/una buena amiga. Ponlas en orden. Compara tu lista con la de tu pareja.

3 Escribe un anuncio. Usa los anuncios en **1** como modelo.

Chico/a de...

busca un(a) chico/a...

Soy...

Me gusta(n)...

Resumen

La familia	***The family***
el padrastro	*stepfather*
la madrastra	*stepmother*
la mujer	*wife, woman*
el bebé	*baby*
los tíos	*uncle and aunt*
el/la novio/a	*boy/girlfriend*
divorciado	*divorced*
separado	*separated*
casado	*married*
jubilado	*retired*
el/la viudo/a	*widower/widow*
muerto	*dead*

Presentar a alguien	***Introducing someone***
el intercambio	*exchange*
presentar	*to introduce*
mucho gusto	*pleased to meet you*
encantado/a	*pleased to meet you*

Estás en tu casa	***Make yourself at home***
¿Te hace falta algo?	*Do you need anything?*
Me hace falta una toalla	*I need a towel*
la sábana	*sheet*
el champú	*shampoo*
la pasta de dientes	*toothpaste*
el secador de pelo	*hairdryer*
la toalla	*towel*

El trabajo	***Work***
el/la profesor(a)	*teacher*
el/la médico	*doctor*
el/la secretario/a	*secretary*
el/la empleado/a de banco/oficina	*bank/office worker*
el/la director(a)	*manager*
el/la ingeniero/a	*engineer*
el/la camarero/a	*waiter/waitress*
el/la dependiente/a	*shop assistant*
el/la enfermero/a	*nurse*
el/la mecánico	*mechanic*
el/la estudiante	*student*

Gramática:
Using the masculine for mixed genders
Verb patterns
Hacer falta (to need, to be necessary)
Dropping *un/una* with jobs: *Soy profesor*
Question words: accents and punctuation

Cross-topic words
desde hace – *for (with expressions of time)*
hace falta – *is necessary*

Patterns of words as an aid to understanding

¡Así se hace!
★ Anticipating and preparing for questions

6 El instituto

6A ¿Se puede comer chicle?

- talk about rules in a school
- express what you can, cannot, have to or don't have to do

1 Mira la lista de reglas del instituto.

Instituto San José

1. Hay que llevar uniforme.
2. No se puede comer chicle.
3. En el recreo no se puede salir del colegio.
4. Hay que llegar a clase a tiempo.
5. No se puede entrar en el polideportivo sin zapatillas de deporte.
6. No se puede tirar basura.

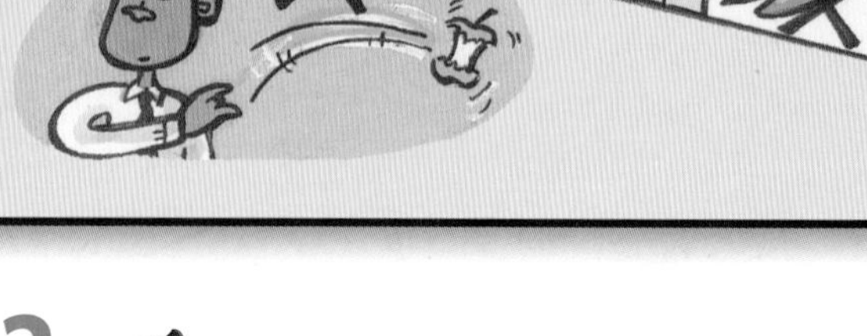

2 a ***Listen*** **(A–F)** ***and give the expression used to say something is allowed or not.***

Example: **A hay que**

2 b ¡extra! **Escucha otra vez. ¿Qué reglas mencionan?**

Ejemplo: **A 4**

Gramática: saying what you can and cannot do

- Look at the text in **1**. How many ways of saying what is and is not allowed can you list?

  A very common way of expressing what is allowed is *se puede/no se puede*. Another one is *hay que* which means 'you have to' and *no hay que*, 'you don't have to'. Both must be followed by a verb in the infinitive.

2 c **Escribe tu lista de reglas ideal.**

Se puede...
- comer chicle en las clases
- hablar en las clases
- comer dulces y beber Coca-cola en las clases
- salir del colegio en el recreo

No hay que...
- llevar uniforme
- hacer los deberes
- ir a todas las clases
- llegar a clase a tiempo

3 a Escucha y lee.

1

¡Hola!
Soy Claudio, de Chile. En los institutos de Chile, hay que llevar uniforme. Normalmente no es muy estricto, pero hay que llevar colores específicos.
En los recreos se puede ir al patio o a la biblioteca, pero no se puede estar dentro de las clases.
Llegar tarde a clase es una falta leve. Una pelea es una falta grave, y hay que ir al apoderado, que a veces expulsa a los alumnos.
En Chile el colegio es obligatorio hasta los dieciséis años.

2

¿Qué tal?
Soy Pilar y soy española.
En los colegios en España, no hay que llevar uniforme; sólo hay uniforme en los colegios privados.
No se puede llegar tarde a clase.
El trato con los profesores es muy informal. No se puede comer chicle. Si tu comportamiento no es bueno, el colegio llama por teléfono a tus padres, o el director te regaña: depende del colegio.
El colegio en España es obligatorio hasta los dieciséis años.

3 b Busca las palabras en español.

1 Arriving late to a lesson is a less important offence.
2 Fighting is a serious offence.
3 He sometimes expels pupils.
4 In schools in Chile you have to wear a uniform.
5 The relationship with the teachers is very informal.
6 The head teacher tells you off.
7 The school telephones your parents.
8 You have to wear specific colours.
9 You mustn't arrive late to lessons.
10 You mustn't be inside the classrooms.
11 You can't chew gum.

el patio – *playground*
una pelea – *fight*
el apoderado – *teacher in charge of discipline in Chilean schools*
el trato – *relationship*
el comportamiento – *behaviour*
el director – *head teacher*
te regaña – *tells you off*
expulsa – *expels*
una falta leve – *less important offence*
una falta grave – *serious offence*

3 c ¿Es Claudio, Pilar o los dos?

1 No hay uniforme.
2 No se puede estar dentro de las clases en el recreo.
3 El colegio es obligatorio hasta los 16 años.
4 El trato con los profesores es muy informal.
5 En el recreo se puede ir al patio o a la biblioteca.
6 No se puede comer chicle.
7 El director te regaña.

3 d ¡extra! Escribe una carta parecida sobre las reglas de tu colegio. Usa las cartas en 3a para ayudarte.

6B ¿Cómo es tu uniforme?

- describe your uniform and give your opinion
- revise adjectival agreement

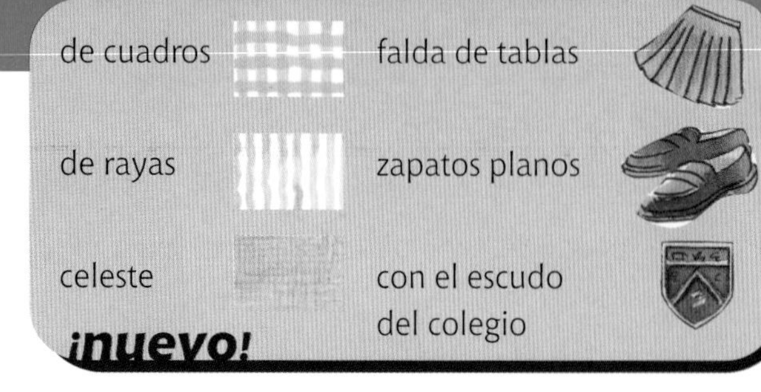

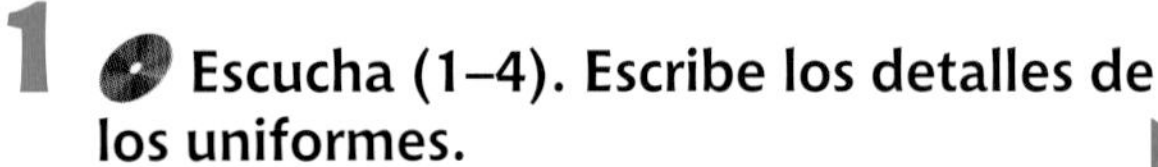

1 **Escucha (1–4). Escribe los detalles de los uniformes.**

Ejemplo: **1 falda azul…**

calcetines	pantalón	azul	negro
camisa	polo	blanco	rojo
chaqueta	top	gris	verde
falda	zapatos		
jersey	medias		

2 **Une las descripciones y los dibujos.**

A

B

1 ¡Hola! Me llamo Pablo y soy uruguayo.
En Uruguay hay que llevar un uniforme muy extraño: una gran túnica blanca con una moña grande y azul. Es horrible, pero es obligatorio.

C

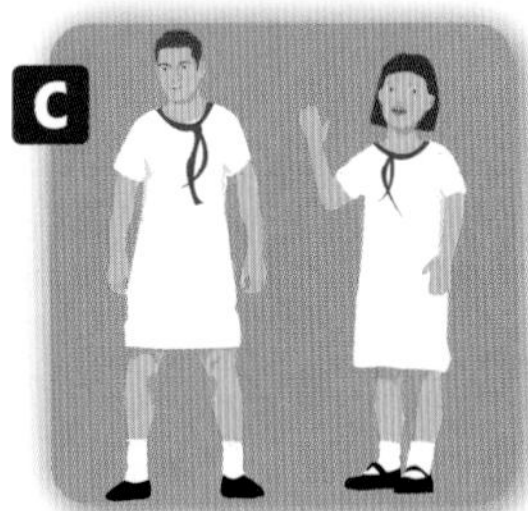

2 ¿Qué tal? Soy Paula, de Chile. En Chile hay que llevar uniforme. Normalmente es una chaqueta gris o azul, una camisa blanca, una corbata azul, y unos pantalones grises o una falda gris. Es un poco aburrido, pero bastante elegante.

3 ¡Hola! Soy Nuria, de España. En España no hay que llevar uniforme: sólo en los colegios privados. Normalmente llevo vaqueros y una camiseta, porque es más cómodo.

Gramática: agreement of colour adjectives

Type 1 (most adjectives)

They change their endings to match the noun in **gender and number**:

m sing	f sing	m pl	f pl
blanco	*blanca*	*blancos*	*blancas*

Type 2

They change their endings to match the noun in **number** but not gender:

m/f sing	m/f pl
azul	*azules*

Type 3

They **do not change** their endings to match the noun in gender or number:

naranja *lila* *rosa*

3 ***Choose the right form for each colour.***

1. Mi uniforme consiste en una camisa (blanco/blanca) y unos pantalones (gris/grises).
2. – ¿Te gusta tu uniforme?
   – No, hay que llevar un jersey (amarillo/amarilla) y odio ese color.
3. No hay uniforme en mi colegio: llevo unos vaqueros (azul/azules) y una camiseta (blanca/blanco) o (rojo/roja).
4. Me gusta mucho mi uniforme: consiste en una chaqueta (azul/azules), una corbata (azul/azules) y (celeste/celestes) y unos pantalones (azul/azules). Es muy elegante.

4 **¿Y tú? ¿Llevas uniforme? Escribe una descripción. Usa el cuadro de 1 para ayudarte.**

Ejemplo: **Mi uniforme es un/una…**

5 a **Escucha (1–5). ¿Tienen una opinión positiva (P) o negativa (N) de su uniforme?**

Ejemplo: **1 P**

5 b ¡extra! ***Listen again. Which opinion from the grid do they use?***

Example: **1 Me gusta mucho.**

Positiva	Negativa
Me gusta	No me gusta
Me gusta mucho	No me gusta nada
Me gusta bastante	Lo odio
Me encanta	

5 c **Haz un sondeo. ¿Qué piensan del uniforme?**

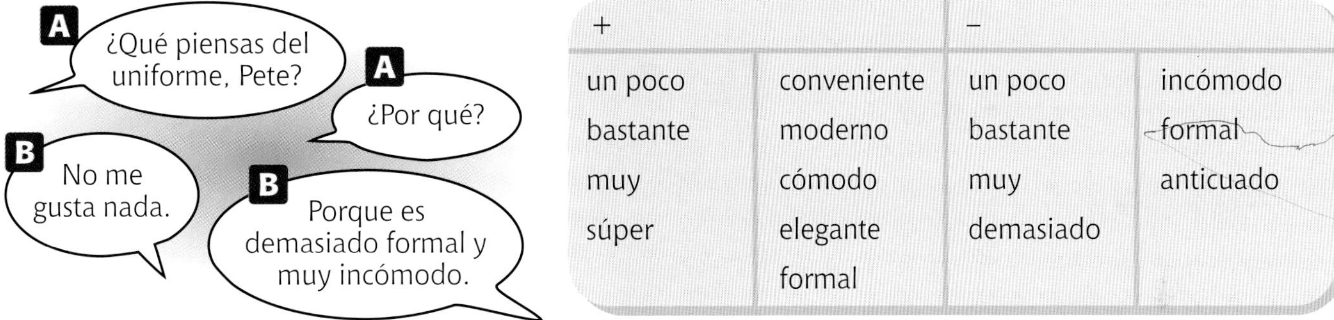
A ¿Qué piensas del uniforme, Pete?
B No me gusta nada.
A ¿Por qué?
B Porque es demasiado formal y muy incómodo.

+		–	
un poco	conveniente	un poco	incómodo
bastante	moderno	bastante	formal
muy	cómodo	muy	anticuado
súper	elegante	demasiado	
	formal		

5 d **Escribe tu opinión sobre tu uniforme. Usa el cuadro de 5c.**

Ejemplo:

Me gusta mucho mi uniforme porque es muy cómodo y elegante.

Odio mi uniforme porque es demasiado formal y un poco anticuado.

6 a **Lee el texto. Rellena los espacios con las palabras del cuadro.**

No me gusta el uniforme de mi (1) colegio porque es muy (2) _________. Mi uniforme ideal es (3) _________ y conveniente. Tiene unos (4) _________ azules y una (5) _________ de muchos colores. Cuando hace frío tiene una chaqueta de (6) _________ blancas y (7) _________. En verano las chicas llevan una falda (8) _________. Los chicos llevan unos calcetines (9) _________ y zapatillas de (10) _________.

aburrido camiseta colegio
cómodo deporte negras negros
rayas rosa vaqueros

6 b **¿Cómo es tu uniforme ideal? Escribe una descripción y haz un dibujo. Usa el cuadro.**

Mi uniforme ideal es	elegante informal cómodo
Tiene	una falda azul una camisa de rayas unos pantalones deportivos
Los chicos llevan	unos pantalones cortos unas zapatillas de deporte
Las chicas llevan	una falda de rayas rosa unas medias negras

6C ¿Qué harás en tus exámenes?

- say what options you will take and why
- discuss future plans and careers
- use the future tense

A
¡Hola, Jack! ¿Qué haces?
¿Qué tal, Miguel? Pues mira, escribo mis opciones para mis exámenes.
2
¿Qué estudiarás?
Bueno, estudiaré español, porque es muy útil. ¡Siempre vamos de vacaciones a España!
3
¿Y qué más?
Pues estudiaré historia, ciencias, matemáticas, física, inglés y diseño. ¿Y tú?
También estudiaré español, porque me encanta. Y estudiaré inglés, matemáticas y geografía.
4
¿Estudiarás algo más?
Sí, también estudiaré historia y alemán.
¡Muy bien!

1 a **Lee y escucha la conversación entre Miguel y su amigo inglés, Jack.**

1 b **Qué asignaturas estudiarán Jack y Miguel?**

Jack	Miguel
español	español

1 c **¿Y tú? ¿Qué estudiarás el año próximo? Escribe una lista.**

Ejemplo: **El año próximo estudiaré...**

Gramática: the future tense

To form the future tense, you need to add the ending -é to the infinitive.

estudiar (to study) – *estudiaré* (I will study)
ser (to be) – *seré* (I will be)
ir (to go) – *iré* (I will go)

There are a few, very common irregular verbs:

salir – *saldré* (I will go out)
hacer – *haré* (I will do)
poder – *podré* (I will be able)
venir – *vendré* (I will come)

2 ***Read the sentences and write down the verbs which are in the future tense. Match up each sentence with its English translation.***

1. El año que viene iré a la universidad de Madrid.
2. Mañana desayunaré un té.
3. Esta noche saldré con mis amigas Irene y Pilar.
4. Estudiaré esta noche para el examen de mañana.
5. Me encantan las ciencias. Seré médico en el futuro.
6. Ahora no hago ciclismo, pero el año próximo sí lo haré.
7. Vendré a España de vacaciones este verano.
8. Viviré en Valencia dentro de tres meses.

a I don't cycle now, but next year I will do.
b I love science. I will be a doctor in the future.
c I will come to Spain on holiday this summer.
d I will live in Valencia in three months' time.
e I will study tonight for tomorrow's exam.
f Next year I will go to Madrid University.
g Tomorrow I will have tea for breakfast.
h Tonight I will go out with my friends Irene and Pilar.

3 ¿Quién habla?

Who...

1 wants to be a psychologist in the future?
2 likes active subjects?
3 wants to be an engineer?
4 thinks that languages are useful?
5 wants to be an artist?
6 will study biology?

El año próximo estudiaré idiomas porque son muy útiles. Quiero ser traductor.

Nicolás

Inés

En el futuro seré artista. Estudiaré arte y diseño para mis exámenes.

¿En el futuro? Seré psicóloga, así que necesitaré estudiar biología y matemáticas.

Voy a estudiar física e informática. Son muy interesantes y seré ingeniero en el futuro.

Paco

¿Qué estudiaré el año próximo? Estudiaré educación física. Me encantan las asignaturas activas y seré profesor en el futuro.

¡nuevo!

Las profesiones	
abogado/a	escritor(a)
arquitecto/a	psicólogo/a
artista	soldado
científico/a	traductor(a)

4 Escucha. Copia y completa el cuadro.

	¿Asignaturas?	¿Por qué?	¿En el futuro?
José			
Anabel			
Blanca			
Sergio			

5 a Habla con tu pareja.

A ¿Qué estudiarás el año próximo?
B Estudiaré (francés, diseño y español).
A ¿Por qué?
B Porque (me gustan los idiomas) y (creo que el español será muy útil).
A ¿Qué quieres ser en el futuro?
B Me gustaría ser (profesora).

5 b Escribe un párrafo con tus respuestas.

Ejemplo: **Yo estudiaré... porque... Me gustaría ser...**

6D Un buen profesor debe ser...

- give your opinion on subjects and teachers
- learn dictionary skills: finding the stem of a word

A estricto

B relajado

C organizado

1 **Mira las cualidades. Escribe una lista con las cualidades que un profesor debe o no debe tener, en tu opinión.**

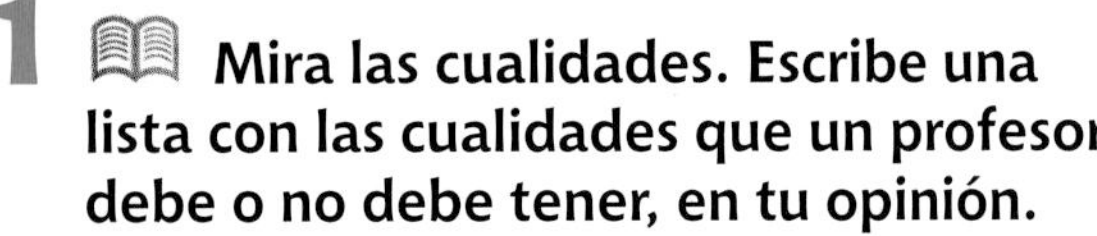

Ejemplo:
En mi opinión, un buen profesor debe ser...
En mi opinión, un buen profesor no debe ser...

D desorganizado

E hablador

F tímido

G inteligente

H atractivo

i simpático

j antipático

k justo

2 **Escucha (1–4). ¿Cómo es un profesor perfecto? Copia y rellena el cuadro.**

	Debe ser	No debe ser
1	justo, hablador	desorganizado, antipático
2		
3		

3 **Haz un sondeo. ¿Cuáles son las cualidades más importantes de un profesor?**

Tom, ¿cuáles son las cualidades más importantes de un profesor?

En mi opinión, debe ser paciente y relajado.

Hannah, ¿cuáles...?

¡Así se hace! *Dictionary skills: looking for the stem*

Words in the dictionary appear in the simplest form: in the masculine form, nouns in the singular and verbs in the infinitive.

When you want to find a new word, you need to change it into these forms, otherwise you will not always be able to find it.

For example, if you wanted to know the meaning of the word *antipáticas*, you would need to change it first into *antipático*.

This is particularly difficult with verbs: for example, to find *fui* you would need to look for *ser* or *ir*.

- ***Look at the following list of words. Put them in the form you will find in the dictionary and then look up their meaning.***

Word	Form in dictionary	Meaning
asignaturas	*asignatura*	subjects
canté	*cantar*	I sang
velas		
piñas		
comeré		
lagartos		
sombrillas		
viajaré		
tenedores		

Las reglas	Rules
Hay que llevar uniforme	You have to wear a uniform
No se puede comer chicle	You can't chew chewing gum
En el recreo no se puede salir del colegio	You can't go out of school at break times
Hay que llegar a clase a tiempo	You have to arrive in class on time

El uniforme	Uniform
consiste en...	consists of...
de cuadros/de rayas	checked/striped
una falda de tablas	pleated skirt
zapatos planos	flat shoes
con el escudo del colegio	with the school's badge
celeste	light blue

Opiniones sobre el uniforme	Opinions on uniform
Me gusta/No me gusta mi uniforme porque es...	I like/don't like my uniform because it is...
cómodo/incómodo	comfortable/ uncomfortable
elegante/formal	elegant/formal
conveniente/moderno	convenient/modern
anticuado	old-fashioned

Las profesiones	Professions
Me gustaría ser/seré...	I would like to be/I will be...
traductor(a)	a translator
ingeniero/a	an engineer
artista	an artist
psicólogo/a	a psychologist
soldado	a soldier
científico/a	a scientist
escritor(a)	a writer
arquitecto/a	an architect
profesor(a)	a teacher
médico	a doctor
abogado/a	a lawyer

Opiniones sobre las asignaturas	Opinions on subjects
Me gustan las matemáticas porque...	I like maths because...
son muy útiles	it's very useful
son muy interesantes	it's very interesting
Me encantan las asignaturas activas	I love active subjects
Me gustan los idiomas	I like languages
Me encanta leer	I love reading

Las cualidades de los profesores	Qualities of teachers
estricto/relajado	strict/relaxed
organizado/desorganizado	organised/disorganised
hablador/tímido	talkative/shy
inteligente	intelligent
atractivo	attractive
simpático/antipático	nice/unpleasant
justo	fair

Gramática:

Saying what you can and cannot do: *se puede/no se puede*

Saying what you have to and don't have to do: *(no) hay que*

Saying what qualities someone ought to have: *deber ser.../no debe ser...*

Agreement of colour adjectives

The future tense

Cross-topic words

(no) hay que – *you (don't) have to*
normalmente – *normally*
¿por qué? – *why?*
un poco – *a little*
bastante – *quite*
muy – *very*
demasiado – *too*

¡Así se hace!

★ Dictionary skills: looking for the stem

Repaso

Unidad 5 (¿Problemas? Mira la página 49.)

1 **Mira la lista de adjetivos en el cuadro. Escucha y escribe cómo son los miembros de la familia.**

Ejemplo: **Madre:** muy extrovertida, …

antipático	generoso	paciente	super guapo
cruel	hablador	perezoso	tímido
desobediente	honesto	romántico	trabajador
egoísta	impaciente	sensible	valiente
estúpido	nervioso	serio	
extrovertido	obediente	simpático	

Unidad 6 (¿Problemas? Mira la página 57.)

2 **Une el inglés y el español. Después une las preguntas y las respuestas.**

1 ¿Qué asignaturas vas a estudiar el año próximo?
2 ¿Llevas uniforme?
3 ¿Cómo es tu uniforme?
4 ¿Cómo debe ser un profesor?
5 ¿Qué hace tu padre?
6 ¿Cómo es tu hermano?

a Do you wear a uniform?
b What does your father do?
c What is your uniform like?
d What is your brother like?
e What should a teacher be like?
f What subjects are you going to study next year?

i Mi hermano es desobediente y antipático.
ii Mi padre es abogado.
iii Mi uniforme es un vestido blanco y azul, unos calcetines blancos y zapatos negros.
iv Sí, llevo un uniforme horrible.
v Un profesor debe ser estricto pero justo.
vi Voy a estudiar matemáticas, español y física.

3 a **Entrevista a tu pareja. Mira los ejemplos.**

A ¿Qué asignaturas vas a estudiar el año próximo?
B Voy a estudiar español y matemáticas.
A ¿Cómo es tu uniforme?
B Mi uniforme es horrible pero elegante.
A ¿Cómo debe ser un profesor?
B Un profesor debe ser simpático y divertido.
A ¿Qué hace tu padre/madre/hermano?
B Mi [padre]es camarero.
A ¿Cómo es tu padre/madre/hermano?
B Mi [padre] es hablador y trabajador.

Max es muy deportista

3 b **Escribe tus respuestas a las preguntas de 3a.**

Colegio Sierra Blanca

El colegio Sierra Blanca, en el sur de España, ofrece una gran variedad de actividades para sus alumnos. Es un colegio mixto con ochocientos alumnos. Los grupos son pequeños, con un máximo de quince alumnos por clase. Las notas son las mejores de la región.

Reglas

El colegio Sierra Blanca tiene las siguientes reglas:

- Hay que llegar a clase a tiempo.
- No se puede comer chicle.
- No se puede tirar basura.
- En el recreo no se puede salir del colegio.
- Hay que llevar el uniforme correcto.
- No se puede entrar en el polideportivo sin zapatillas de deporte.

El uniforme

El uniforme en Sierra Blanca consiste en una chaqueta azul con el escudo del colegio, una camisa blanca, una corbata de rayas, unos calcetines azules y zapatos negros planos, una falda de cuadros para las chicas y unos pantalones grises para los chicos.

Instalaciones

El colegio Sierra Blanca tiene instalaciones fantásticas. El colegio tiene dos gimnasios, pistas de tenis, bádminton y squash, piscina climatizada y pistas atléticas. También hay muchos ordenadores. Todas las aulas tienen vídeos y DVDs.

Contactos

La dirección del colegio es:

Colegio Sierra Blanca
Camino de los Tilos 26
29312 Mijas
Málaga
España
contactos@colegiosierrablanca.es

Lee el texto y contesta a las preguntas en inglés.

1. Where is the school?
2. How many pupils are there?
3. How many pupils are there per class?
4. What are the results like?
5. What is the uniform like?
6. What facilities does the school have?
7. What two things do all the classrooms have?
8. What rules must all the pupils follow?

7 De compras

7A Las tiendas

- talk about what you can buy in what shops
- say where things are

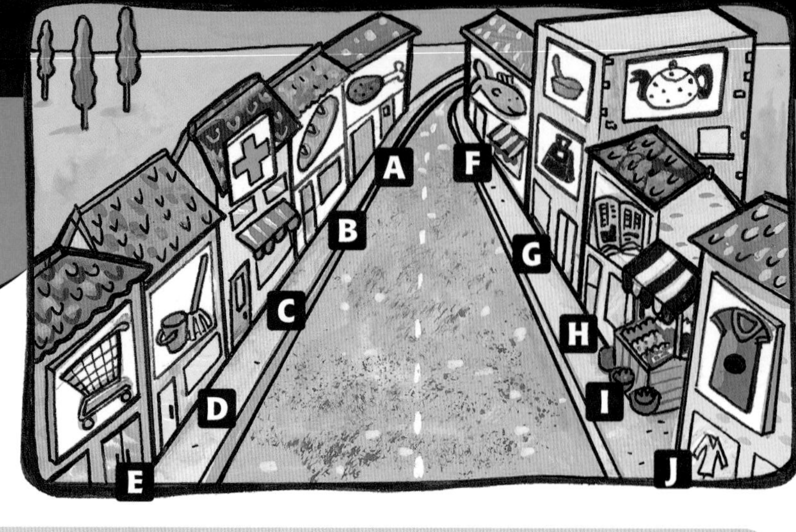

1 a **Escucha (1–7). Escribe las letras de las tiendas mencionadas.**

la carnicería	el quiosco	los grandes almacenes	la droguería	el mercado
el supermercado	la tienda de ropa	la pescadería	la farmacia	la panadería

1 b **Mira los dibujos y completa las tiendas.**

1 c **Habla con tu pareja. Menciona un producto y tu pareja adivina la tienda.**

Ejemplo:

A Pescado.
B Supermercado.
A ¡No!
B Pescadería.
A ¡Sí!

2 a **Mira los productos. ¿En qué tiendas los puedes comprar? Escribe la lista.**

Ejemplo: **En (<u>una</u> carnicería) se puede comprar: (carne, salchichas...)**

aspirinas	filetes	pasta de dientes	salchichas
café	fruta	pescado	salmón
camisas	jabón	periódicos	té
carne	pan	pollo	tiritas
calamares			

2 b ¡extra! **Añade más productos que se pueden comprar en cada tienda.**

3 **Escucha (1–5). ¿Qué van a comprar y dónde? Copia y rellena el cuadro.**

	¿Productos?	¿Dónde?
1	pasta de dientes, jabón	droguería
2		

Gramática: *se puede* – you can

To say that 'they' or 'you' can do something, in Spanish you normally use *se puede*.

Se puede comprar jabón en el mercado.
You can buy soap at the market.

4 a Read the text about shops in Spain. How many examples of *se puede* can you find?

4 b Lee el texto otra vez. ¿Qué tiendas y qué productos se mencionan? Haz una lista.

Ejemplo: **tiendas** | **productos**
supermercado | fruta
…

4 c ¿Qué se puede encontrar en las tiendas en Gran Bretaña? Escribe un texto.

¿Dónde se puede comprar pasta de dientes?

En los barrios en España hay muchas tiendas pequeñas. En un supermercado se puede comprar fruta, verdura, detergente, carne y pescado…

Normalmente en España hay supermercados pequeños en los barrios, pero los grandes hipermercados están en las afueras de la ciudad.

Los españoles compran los productos frescos, como la carne, el pescado y la fruta, en un mercado.

En los barrios hay droguerías. Aquí se puede comprar detergente, jabón, pasta de dientes… En las panaderías se puede comprar pan, pasteles y tartas.

barrios – *neighbourhoods* frescos – *fresh*
en las afueras – *in the outskirts*

¡Así se hace! *Adapting phrases from a text*

You can adapt sentences from the article in **4a** to write your own text about shops in Great Britain.

En Gran Bretaña	en los barrios hay…	supermercados	
	en las ciudades hay…	tiendas pequeñas panaderías	
	se puede comprar…	pan ropa carne y pescado productos frescos	en los supermercados en los mercados en los grandes almacenes en la farmacia

5 a Mira la calle principal. Adivina las tiendas. Usa las pistas.

La droguería está a la derecha de la carnicería.
El mercado está entre el quiosco y la tienda de ropa.
La farmacia está enfrente del supermercado.
La pescadería está a la izquierda de la carnicería.
La tienda de ropa está al final de la calle, enfrente de la panadería.
Los grandes almacenes están entre la farmacia y el quiosco.
La panadería está al final de la calle a la izquierda, enfrente de la tienda de ropa.

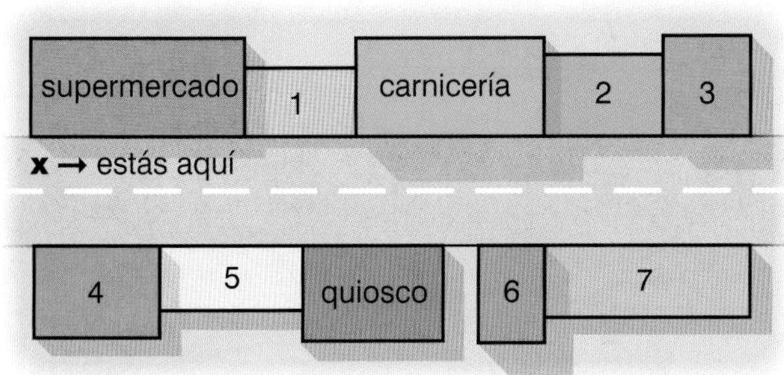

5 b Habla con tu pareja.

Ejemplo:

A
¿Dónde está el quiosco?
B
Está entre los grandes almacenes y el mercado.

Gramática: prepositions to express where places are

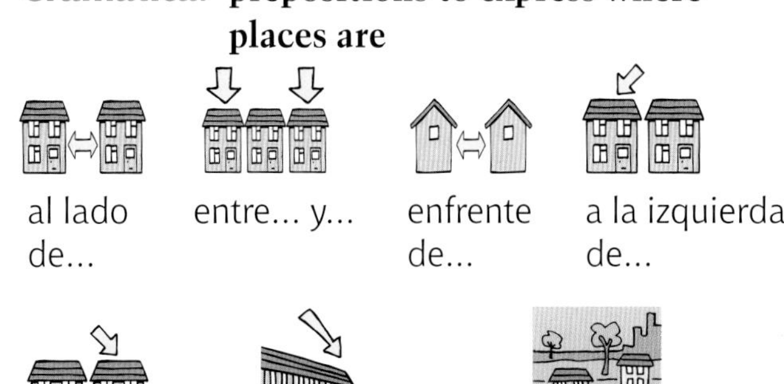

al lado de… | entre… y… | enfrente de… | a la izquierda de…

a la derecha de…

al final de la calle

en las afueras del pueblo/de la ciudad

7B La lista de la compra

- say quantities and prices of food
- buy fruit and vegetables

Gramática: expressions of quantity

In Spanish, expressions of quantity are followed by de.

un kilo de…	one kilo of…
un paquete de…	a packet of…
100 gramos de…	*100 grams of…*

1 a Mira los dibujos. Escucha (1–9) y escribe la letra.

Ejemplo: **1 I**

A

un tubo de pasta de dientes

B

una caja de té

C

una docena de huevos

D

una barra de pan

E

un kilo de pollo

F

medio kilo de salchichas

G

100 gr de jamón

H

un paquete de café

I

una lata de Coca-cola

1 b Escucha otra vez. Apunta el producto y el precio (1–9).

Ejemplo: **1 Coca-cola 9**

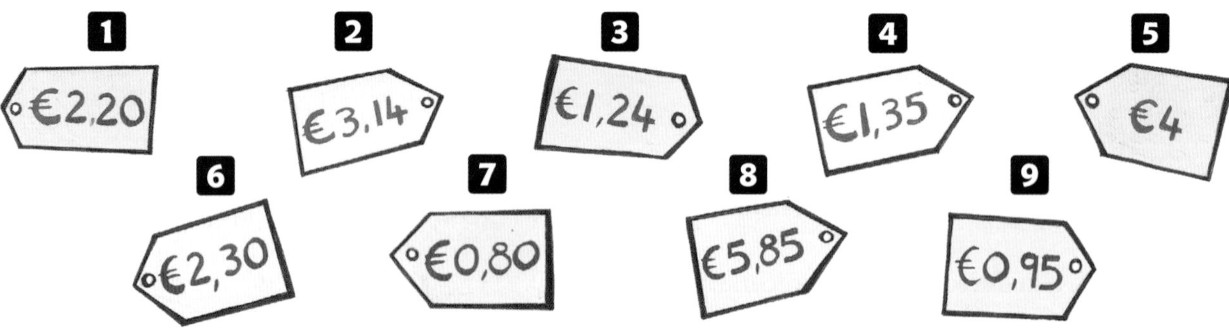

1 c Habla con tu pareja.

Ejemplo: **A** Número cinco.
B Cuatro euros.

2 a Escucha y lee.

– Buenos días, ¿qué desea?
– Quisiera un kilo de salchichas, por favor.
– ¿Algo más?
– Sí, medio kilo de pollo.
– ¿Es todo?
– Sí, es todo. ¿Cuánto es?
– Son 15,50.
– Aquí tiene. Gracias.
– Adiós.

2 b Practica la conversación de 2a con tu pareja.

2 c Escribe las otras 3 conversaciones. Cambia la palabras.

1

2

3

4

3 a Escucha (1–10). ¿Qué productos se mencionan?

Ejemplo: **1 I**

3 b ¡extra! Escucha otra vez. ¿Qué cantidades quieren?

Ejemplo: **1 cuatro limones**

4 a Une las conversaciones y los recibos.

A

– ¿Qué desea?
– Quisiera un kilo de limones.
– ¿Algo más?
– Sí, dos kilos de naranjas y una lechuga.
– ¿Es todo?
– Sí, ¿Cuánto es?
– Son tres con veinte euros.
– Aquí tiene, gracias.

B

– Buenos días, ¿qué desea?
– Quisiera una lechuga, por favor.
– ¿Algo más?
– Sí, dos kilos de peras y un kilo de cebollas.
– ¿Es todo?
– Sí, es todo. ¿Cuánto es?
– Son tres con cuarenta euros.
– Aquí tiene, adiós.

C

– Hola, ¿qué desea?
– Quisiera un kilo de limones, por favor.
– ¿Algo más?
– Sí, dos kilos de patatas y medio kilo de tomates.
– Aquí tiene, ¿algo más?
– No, eso es todo. ¿Cuánto es?
– Son cuatro con sesenta euros.
– Aquí tiene, adiós.

A
2 kg peras
1 lechuga
1 kg cebollas
total 3,40
B
1 kg patatas
2 kg limones
1/2 kg manzanas
total 4,70
C
2 kg naranjas
1 kg limones
1 lechuga
total 3,20
D
1/2 kg tomates
1 kg limones
2 kg patatas
total 4,60

4 b Escribe el diálogo para el recibo que falta. Practica con tu pareja.

7C ¿Qué comes?

- say how often you eat different things
- say what you should eat in order to have a healthy diet

1 a Escucha y lee.

¿Con qué frecuencia comes dulces?

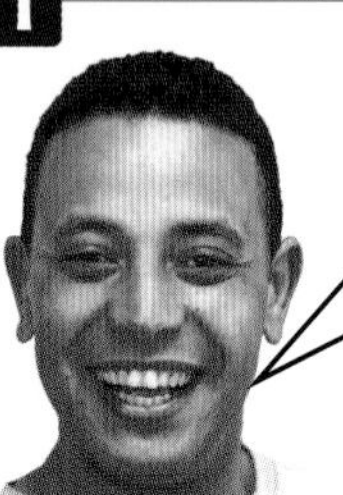

1 Como dulces todos los días. También me gusta la fruta. Siempre como fruta.

¿Y tú? ¿Con qué frecuencia comes pescado y carne?

2 Bueno, nunca como carne pero me gusta mucho el pescado, lo como tres o cuatro veces a la semana.

Y tú, ¿con qué frecuencia bebes té o café?

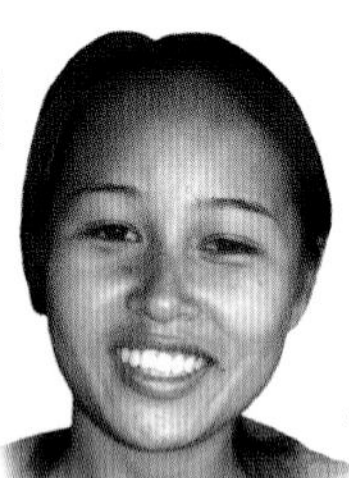

3 Nunca bebo té o café, no me gustan nada. Bebo Coca-cola dos veces a la semana. Me gusta mucho.

A ver, otro joven. ¿Con qué frecuencia comes verduras?

4 ¡Uf! Nunca como verduras.

Gramática: saying how often you do something

siempre		always	
a veces		sometimes	
nunca		never	
una vez	*a la semana*	once	a week
dos veces	*al día*	twice	a day

A veces como verduras.	I eat vegetables sometimes.
Nunca bebo Coca-cola.	I never drink Coke.
Como pescado tres veces a la semana. (◄◄ p.33)	I eat fish three times a week.

1 b Busca las expresiones.

1 I eat sweets every day
2 I always eat fruit
3 I like fish a lot
4 I eat it three or four times a week
5 How often do you eat vegetables?
6 I never eat vegetables

1 c ¿Con qué frecuencia comen los jóvenes? Usa los textos de 1a.

Ejemplo: **dulces – todos los días**
fruta – siempre

2 a  Habla con tu pareja y escribe las respuestas.

A	B
¿Con qué frecuencia comes verduras? / carne? / dulces?	Siempre como/bebo...
¿Con qué frecuencia bebes té y café?	Como/Bebo...
	una vez/dos veces... a la semana/al día/todos los días
	Nunca como/bebo...

2 b Escribe tus propias respuestas.

Ejemplo: **Siempre como verduras. Como carne todos los días y pescado una vez a la semana. Nunca bebo café.**

¡Así se hace! Recycling words

Where possible, try to use words you have already learnt (e.g. una hamburguesa).

3 a ¿Verdad (V) o mentira (M)?

1 Para estar sano debes comer una pieza de fruta o verdura.
2 Debes picar entre comidas.
3 No debes comer muchos dulces.
4 No debes hacer ejercicio.
5 No debes comer mucha grasa.
6 Debes beber dos litros de agua al día.

picar entre comidas – *to snack between meals*

Gramática: what you should or shouldn't do

Debes…/No debes…	+ infinitive
Debes comer verduras.	You should eat vegetables.
Debes comer fruta.	You should eat fruit.

¡La vida sana!
Para mantenerte sano

Debes…
comer cinco piezas de fruta o verdura
hacer ejercicio
beber dos litros de agua al día
dormir ocho horas por la noche

No debes…
comer mucha grasa
picar entre comidas
comer muchos dulces

3 b Diseña un póster para la vida sana.

Nunca Siempre	Debes	comer verduras comer fruta comer carne comer pescado hacer ejercicio dormir ocho horas beber dos litros de agua	todos los días una vez a la semana dos veces al mes tres veces al año con frecuencia
	No debes	beber té beber café beber Coca-cola picar entre comidas comer mucha grasa	

7D ¿Qué compraste?

- describe a shopping trip in the past
- revise the preterite tense

1 Ayer fui de compras.

2 Fui a la zapatería y compré unos zapatos marrones muy bonitos.

3 Después, fui a los grandes almacenes y compré una botella de perfume. Costó 20.

1 a Lee y escucha.

4 La botella de perfume se rompió.

5 Más tarde fui a la frutería y compré mucha fruta.

6 Comí toda la fruta y me dolió el estómago.

7 Por último fui al quiosco y compré mi revista favorita, que se llama *Superpop*.

8 Volví a casa y tomé una aspirina.

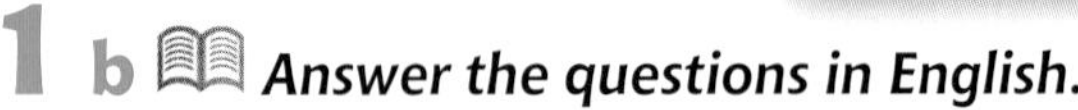

1 b *Answer the questions in English.*

1 When did Maria go shopping?
2 What shop did Maria visit first?
3 What did she buy first?
4 How much did she pay for the perfume?
5 What problem did she have with the perfume?
6 Where did she go next?
7 What happened?
8 What was the effect?
9 What did she buy in the newsagent's?
10 What did she have to do in the end to recover from the shopping trip?

1 c *Find the following in the text:*

- 8 preterite tenses
- 4 shops
- 4 products

2 a Escribe sobre un día de compras real o imaginario.

Ejemplo: **Ayer fui a la zapatería. Compré...**

¿Cuándo fuiste?	¿Adónde fuiste?	¿Qué compraste?	¿Cuánto costó?	¿Qué problemas hubo?
Esta mañana	Fui...	Compré...	Costó...	Fue muy caro/a
El sábado	a la zapatería	unos zapatos	30	pequeño/a
La semana pasada	a los grandes almacenes	una chaqueta	2,50	Se rompió
Ayer	al supermercado	fruta		Me dolió el estómago
	a la tienda de ropa	perfume		Me dolió la cabeza

2 b Habla con tu pareja sobre tu día de compras. Cambia las palabras.

Ejemplo:

A ¿Adónde fuiste? **B** Fui al supermercado.
A ¿Cuándo fuiste? **B** Ayer.
A ¿Qué compraste? **B** Compré fruta.
A ¿Cuánto costó? **B** Costó 7.
A ¿Qué problemas hubo? **B** Me dolió el estómago.

Gramática: the preterite

(◄◄ p.24)

hay problemas	there are problems
hubo problemas	there were problems

Las tiendas	Shops
el supermercado	*supermarket*
la droguería	*hardware shop*
la farmacia	*chemist's*
la panadería	*bakery*
la carnicería	*butcher's*
la pescadería	*fishmonger's*
el quiosco	*newsagent's*
el mercado	*market*
la tienda de ropa	*clothes shop*
los grandes almacenes	*department store*

Los productos	Products
las aspirinas	*aspirin*
el café	*coffee*
los calamares	*squid*
la camisa	*shirt*
la carne	*meat*
el cómic	*comic*
los filetes	*fillets*
la fruta	*fruit*
el jabón	*soap*
el pan	*bread*
la pasta de dientes	*toothpaste*
el periódico	*newspaper*
el pescado	*fish*
el pollo	*chicken*
la revista	*magazine*
las salchichas	*sausages*
el salmón	*salmon*
el té	*tea*
las tiritas	*plasters*

Los contenedores	Containers
un tubo de pasta de dientes	*tube of toothpaste*
una caja de té	*box of tea*
una docena de huevos	*dozen eggs*
una barra de pan	*loaf of bread*
un kilo de pollo	*1 kg chicken*
medio kilo de salchichas	$^{1}/_{2}$ *kg sausages*
100 gr de jamón	*100 g ham*
un paquete de café	*packet of coffee*
una lata de Coca-cola	*can of Coke*

La fruta y la verdura	Fruit and vegetables
las naranjas	*oranges*
las manzanas	*apples*
las peras	*pears*
las uvas	*grapes*
las patatas	*potatoes*
los tomates	*tomatoes*
los limones	*lemons*
las cebollas	*onions*
los pimientos	*peppers*
la lechuga	*lettuce*

Un día de compras	A shopping day
ayer	*yesterday*
el sábado pasado	*last Saturday*
la semana pasada	*last week*
Fui a la zapatería	*I went to the shoe shop*
Compré	*I bought*
Fue	*He/She/It was*
Hubo un problema	*There was a problem*
Fue muy caro	*It was very expensive*
Se rompió	*It broke*

Gramática:
The impersonal *se puede*
Prepositions of place
Expressions of quantity
Expressions of frequency
deber

¡Así se hace!

★ Recycling words

Cross-topic words
debes – *you should*

8 En tren, autobús y metro

8A El transporte público

- talk about means of transport
- learn how to say *I usually*

1 **Pilla al intruso. Hay varias posibilidades.**

1 metro tren tranvía autobús
2 taxi autocar coche autobús
3 tren autocar barco bicicleta
4 tranvía tren taxi autobús
5 avión taxi autocar autobús
6 tren avión autocar taxi

2 a **Mira el plano. Escucha y une los diálogos (1–6) y las fotos.**

Ejemplo: **1** B, …

2 b ¡extra! ***Listen again. How many ways are there to ask for directions?***

Example: **¿Para ir al…?**

A el autobús

B el taxi

C el metro

D el avión

E la bicicleta

F el autocar

G el tranvía

H el coche

I el tren

3 a Lee las descripciones. ¿Quién habla?

Ejemplo: **Si voy a otra ciudad no voy en tren.**
= Cristina

En Buenos Aires hay autobuses y hay el metro. Hay muchos problemas porque hay mucho tráfico y muchos accidentes. El metro es bueno pero no suelo coger el autobús. Los trenes son muy malos. Si voy de una ciudad a otra, voy en autocar. Es muy bueno, no me gusta ir en tren.

Cristina

1 No suelo ir en autobús.
2 Los autocares son buenos.
3 El metro es muy práctico para mí.
4 Es mejor no ir en tren.
5 Si voy a Barcelona, por ejemplo, suelo coger el autocar.

En Madrid hay el metro, autobuses y muchos trenes. Yo prefiero el metro porque hay una estación de metro muy cerca de mi casa. Si vas a otra ciudad hay autocares. Son muy cómodos. Tienen vídeo y se sirven bebidas y comidas. Cuando voy a Sevilla por ejemplo, suelo coger el AVE. Es un tren rápido. Si estoy con mis padres voy en coche.

Carlos

3b Une las frases en español en 3a y las frases en inglés.

Ejemplo: **1 No suelo ir en autobús. = B**

A The coaches are good.
B I don't usually go by bus.
C It's better not to go by train.
D If I go to Barcelona, for example, I usually go by coach.
E The underground is very practical for me.

Gramática: *suelo…* – I usually…

Soler + infinitive is used to describe what you usually do:

Suelo coger el autobús.		I usually catch the bus.
suelo	+ infinitive	I usually
sueles		you usually
¿sueles…?		Do you usually…?

4 a Habla con tu pareja. Cambia las frases.

A ¿Cómo sueles ir al colegio?
B Suelo ir al colegio en coche.
A ¿Y sueles ir a casa de tus amigos en coche?
B No, suelo ir a casa de mis amigos en bici.
A ¿Cómo sueles ir al polideportivo?
B Suelo ir al polideportivo en autobús.

4 b Une el español y el inglés.

1 porque	**a** it's too expensive
2 es muy práctico	**b** it's very slow
3 es muy rápido	**c** it's very (un)comfortable
4 es muy barato	**d** it's very practical
5 es muy lento	**e** it's very fast
6 es muy (in)cómodo	**f** it's very cheap
7 es demasiado caro	**g** because

4 c Ahora repite 4a y di por qué.

Ejemplo:

A ¿Cómo sueles ir al colegio?
B Suelo ir al colegio en coche porque es muy práctico.

5 Escribe 5 o 6 frases sobre los transportes que usas.

Ejemplo: **Suelo ir al colegio en autobús con mis amigos porque...**

8B ¿A qué hora sale...?

- understand bus and train timetables
- understand announcements
- form adverbs with *-mente*

Gramática: saying the time

A la una.	At one o'clock.
A las tres y diez.	At ten past three.
A las seis y media.	At six thirty.
A la una y cuarto.	At quarter past one.
A las ocho menos cuarto.	At quarter to eight.

1 a Une las frases y los dibujos.

1 a las 10.20
2 un billete sencillo
3 el tren llega
4 el tren sale
5 ¿Cuánto cuesta?
6 a las 10.40
7 el viaje dura veinte minutos
8 un billete de ida y vuelta

A 
B 
C 
D 
E 
F
G 
H 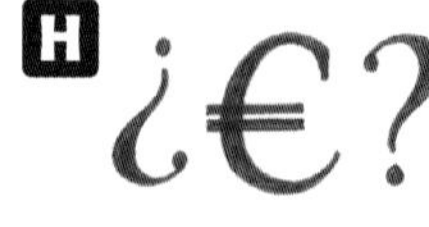

1 b Mira el horario y contesta a las preguntas.

Ejemplo: **1 El primer tren sale a las ocho y veinte.**

1 ¿A qué hora sale el primer tren de Girona?
2 ¿A qué hora llega a Barcelona? Llega a Barcelona...
3 ¿A qué hora llega a Barcelona el tren de las nueve? Llega a Barcelona...
4 ¿Cuánto tiempo dura el viaje del tren que sale a las 10.40? El viaje dura...
5 ¿Cuánto cuesta un billete sencillo en el Delta? Un billete sencillo cuesta...
6 ¿Cuánto cuesta un billete sencillo en el Catalunya Expres? Cuesta...

Tren	Girona	Barcelona	Precios (billete sencillo)
Delta	8.20	10.00	5,60
Arco	8.30	9.40	15,00/9,00 niño
Catalunya Expres	9.00	10.15	5,85
Mare Nostrum	10.40	11.40	15,50/9,30 niño
Delta	11.25	12.55	5,60

¡nuevo!

primer(o) – *first* último – *last* próximo – *next*

2 Escucha (1–4). Une las preguntas y las respuestas.

Ejemplo: **1 B, D**

A sale a las 8.30 **B** sale a las 8.20 **C** 5 con 85 euros **D** a las diez
E a las 11.25 **F** a las 12.55 **G** una hora y diez minutos

Gramática: adverbs with *-mente*

- Look at the following table:

aproximado	aproximadamente	approximately
exacto	exactamente	exactly
normal	normalmente	normally
difícil	difícilmente	with difficulty

1 What is the equivalent of *–mente* in English?
2 How do you form Spanish adverbs when the adjective ends in o?
3 How do you form Spanish adverbs when the adjective ends in a letter other than o?

3 a Escucha y lee.

A Buenos días. Quiero ir a Madrid.
B ¿Cuándo quiere viajar?
A El martes, 22.
B ¿A qué hora quiere viajar?
A A las nueve aproximadamente.
B Hay un tren a las nueve diez.
A Muy bien. ¿Cuánto tiempo dura el viaje?
B Tres horas. ¿Quiere un billete sencillo o un billete de ida y vuelta?

3 b Escribe el diálogo que sigue 3a en el orden correcto.

– Vale, gracias.
– Adiós.
– Un billete sencillo.
– ¿Fumador o no fumador?
– No fumador. ¿Cuánto cuesta?
– Aquí tiene. Gracias.
– 50.

3 c Practica los diálogos con tu pareja. Cambia las palabras de 3a y 3b.

1 Quiero viajar el lunes 28 por la tarde. Quiero salir a las tres de la tarde aproximadamente y llegar a las ocho. Quiero un billete de ida y vuelta en un compartimento no fumador.

2 Quiero viajar el domingo 27 por la mañana. Voy a coger el tren a las doce y llegar a la una aproximadamente. Quiero comprar un billete sencillo en un compartimento fumador.

3 d ¡extra! Escribe otro diálogo como el modelo.

¡Así se hace! *Understanding announcements*

Announcements are always extremely difficult to understand (even in your own language). The sound quality is often poor and the announcements are so unpredictable. It helps if you can anticipate the sort of language you are going to hear and then listen out for key words such as:

próximo (next) *vía* (the platform the train is arriving at)
procedente de (from) *retraso* (delay) *con destino* (to)

4 a *Read the announcements (1–3) and write down in English what they are about.*

1 El tren procedente de Sevilla con destino Valencia va a entrar por vía 3.

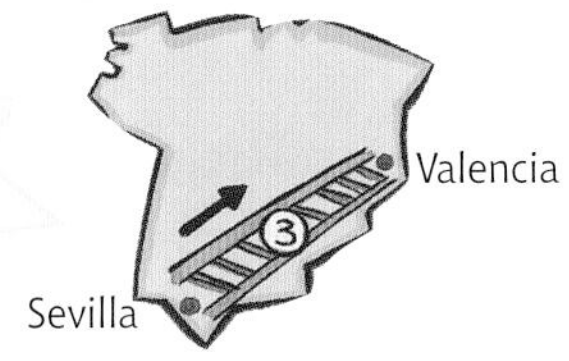

2 El tren de las diez con destino Madrid está a punto de salir de la vía 6.

3 El tren de las 8.50 procedente de Valladolid lleva un retraso de cincuenta minutos. Disculpe las molestias.

4 b Escucha (1–5) y apunta la información.

	Procedente de	Con destino	Hora	Vía	Observaciones
1	—	Tortosa	17.50	6	Sale dentro de 4 minutos
2	Valencia		18.05		—
3		—	—	—	15 minutos de retraso
4	Madrid	—	—		va a llegar dentro de unos minutos
5	—	Málaga			—

8C ¡Qué viaje!

- describe a journey in the past
- recognise the imperfect tense

1 a Lee la carta y rellena el cuadro.

Past (preterite)	English	Present	English	Past (imperfect)	English
fui	I went	voy	I go		
salí	I left		I leave		
	I had breakfast	desayuno	I have breakfast		
llegué		llego	I arrive		
vi	I saw	veo			
me levanté	I got up	me levanto	I get up		
		son las nueve	it is 9 o'clock	eran las nueve	it was 9 o'clock
		tengo hambre	I'm hungry		I was hungry
		hace mucho calor	it is very hot	hacía mucho calor	it was very hot
		hay	there is/are	había	

Gramática: the imperfect tense

The imperfect tense describes what something or somebody was like in the past, e.g. what the weather was like or what time it was.

For now, you just have to **recognise** this past tense.

infinitive	*ser*	*tener*	*hacer*	*estar*
I	*era*	*tenía*	*hacía*	*estaba*
you	*eras*	*tenías*	*hacías*	*estabas*
he/she/it/you	*era*	*tenía*	*hacía*	*estaba*

Note:

a) *era* becomes *eran* for all times other than ones related to one o'clock: *eran las dos*.

b) *había* (there was) is the imperfect tense of *hay* (there is).

Madrid, 2 de mayo

¡Hola!

Gracias por tu carta sobre tu viaje a Roma.

A Hace dos años fui a Sevilla en autocar. ¡Mi primera visita y fui solo! Eran las nueve de la noche. Salí de la Estación del Sur de Madrid y llegué a las cuatro de la mañana.

B Hacía mucho calor pero había aire acondicionado en el autocar. Los autocares son muy buenos, muy cómodos y más baratos que los trenes. Había vídeo, bebidas, comidas y aseo en el autocar. No había paradas – el autocar era directo. Comí bocadillos y dormí un poco. Cuando llegué a Sevilla hacía frío y tenía hambre.

C La semana pasada fui a Sevilla en tren con mis padres. Me levanté temprano y cogí el AVE de Madrid a las siete de la mañana. Llegué dos horas y media más tarde. No había muchos viajeros en el tren. Desayuné en el coche restaurante, vi una película y escuché música.

D Hacía mucho sol en Sevilla. El tren es más caro que el autocar, pero es rápido y me gustó mucho. Hay un restaurante. Yo prefiero el tren porque es rápido y cómodo.

Un abrazo,

Juan

1 b *Match each title with the correct paragraph(s) in the letter.*

1 Juan's trip with his parents
2 Juan's journey to Seville
3 What Juan thinks about trains and coaches
4 Why Juan prefers trains

2 a Escucha (1–4). Une los diálogos y los dibujos. Sobran dos dibujos.

Estaba en la estación sola.

Hubo un retraso al aeropuerto porque nevó.

No habiá aire acondicionado en el autocar.

La cafetería estaba cerrada.

¡El viaje fue horrible! Hubo una tormenta.

El autobús no llegó. Hacía mucho viento.

2 b Practica los diálogos. Inventa diálogos para los dibujos que sobran. Usa las frases en rojo como modelo.

Ejemplo:

¿Qué tal el viaje?
A
Mal.
B
¿Por qué?
A
Porque el autobús no llegó. Hacía mucho frío.
B

2 c Escribe 5 frases sobre un viaje real o inventado.

Ejemplo: **La semana pasada fui a Sevilla en autocar con mis amigos. Cogí el AVE de Madrid a las cinco de la mañana. Llegué a las siete. Había muchos viajeros en el tren. Desayuné en el restaurante, vi una película y escuché música.**

8D Un poco de historia

- learn about the history of Spain

1 La historia de España es una historia de conquista. En 206 antes de Cristo, llegan los Romanos y se quedan hasta el siglo quinto (V). Construyen acueductos, carreteras, anfiteatros y monumentos impresionantes.

A

B

1 a Escucha y lee. Une los textos y los dibujos.

2 En 408 comienzan las invasiones germánicas. En 711 los árabes llegan de África y se quedan 700 años. Controlan casi toda España pero en Asturias empieza la reconquista. Hay muchas batallas. En 1492 los árabes son vencidos por fin y son expulsados de España.

3 Los árabes también han contribuido muchísimo a la arquitectura y cultura de España, lo que es evidente hoy día.

C

4 En 1492 Cristóbal Colón descubre América y la conquista de las Américas empieza. Colón vuelve a España con mucha riqueza como oro. España es un país muy rico e importante.

D

5 España tiene una flota muy grande y hay muchas guerras contra Francia y contra Inglaterra.

E

F

6 Entre 1936 y 1939 hay una guerra civil y gana Franco. El dictador reina hasta su muerte en 1975. El Rey Juan Carlos sube al trono.

se quedan – *they stay*	batallas – *battles*	flota – *fleet*
siglo – *century*	vencidos – *beaten*	guerras – *wars*

1 b Lee y contesta a las preguntas en inglés.

1. For approximately how long did the Romans occupy Spain?
2. What did they leave behind in the way of architecture?
3. How long were the North Africans in Spain?
4. When were they defeated and expelled?
5. What other famous historical event happened in the same year?
6. Who won the Spanish civil war and carried on ruling the country for almost forty years?

1 c ¡extra! *Write down 5 examples of plural verb forms in Spanish and English.*

Example: *Los Romanos llegan*. The Romans arrive.

2 *Draw a time line to show important landmarks in Spain's history.*

- *206BC The Romans arrive.*
- *408*
- *711*

El transporte público	***Public transport***
el autobús	*bus*
el taxi	*taxi*
el metro	*underground*
el tren	*train*
el tranvía	*tram*
el autocar	*coach*
el avión	*plane*
el barco	*boat*
la bicicleta	*bike*

Opiniones	***Opinions***
Cojo normalmente el tren porque es más rápido	*I normally take the train because it is faster*
Suelo ir en tranvía	*I usually go by tram*
Prefiero el metro porque es más cómodo	*I prefer the underground because it is more comfortable*
No me gustan los autobuses porque son muy lentos	*I don't like buses because they are very slow*

En la taquilla	***At the ticket office***
¿A qué hora sale el tren para Salou?	*What time does the Salou train leave?*
¿A qué hora llega?	*What time does it arrive?*
¿Cuánto cuesta un billete sencillo?	*How much is a single ticket?*
¿De qué andén sale?	*What platform does it leave from?*
la vía	*track (on which train is coming in)*

Anuncios	***Announcements***
El tren procedente de…	*The train coming from…*
… con destino…	*… going to…*
sale del andén 2 dentro de 2 minutos	*… is leaving from platform 2 in 2 minutes*
… lleva una hora de retraso	*… is running an hour late*

Gramática:
Soler
Adverbs with *-mente*
Recognising the imperfect tense

Cross-topic words
era – *was*
había – *there was*
hacía – *was doing/what the weather was like*

¡Así se hace!
★ Understanding announcements

Unidad 7 (¿Problemas? Mira la página 67.)

1 **Escucha el diálogo y completa la lista de compras.**

Mercado:
1 de tomates
2 un kilo de
3 naranjas
Supermercado:
4 una lata de
5 de agua mineral
6 huevos

2 **Habla con tu pareja. Cambia las frases.**

Ejemplo:

A ¿Adónde fuiste de vacaciones?
B Fui a Francia.
A ¿Qué hiciste?
B Leí un libro y escuché música.
A ¿Qué tiempo hacía?
B Hacía mucho calor.
A ¿Qué había en Francia?
B Había monumentos, playas y discotecas.

Unidad 8 (¿Problemas? Mira la página 75.)

3 a **Lee la carta de Laura.**

Montevideo, 14 de marzo

¡Hola! Me preguntas sobre el transporte público en Uruguay. En Uruguay, hay una compañía de omnibuses. Todos van al centro de Montevideo, la capital. Es difícil ir de una zona a otra. El omnibús es caro para los pobres. No hay trenes. No hay vuelos directos entre Europa y Uruguay. No hay demanda y la seguridad no es suficiente. Argentina está al lado. Debes volar a Buenos Aires que está a 20 minutos.

¿Cómo es el transporte público en tu pueblo? ¿Es caro o barato? ¿Hay muchos trenes y autobuses? ¿Hay un metro o tranvía? ¿Hay un aeropuerto cerca de tu casa? ¿Adónde van los aviones?

Un abrazo,

Laura

3 b **Contesta a la carta de Laura como el modelo. Cambia las palabras.**

Querida Laura,

Donde vivo hay autobuses, trenes y autocares. También hay taxis.

En mi pueblo cojo un tren para ir a otras ciudades bastante lejos como Londres. Se puede ir en autocar también.

Para ir a sitios cerca o dentro del pueblo hay autobuses. El problema es que son caros y pocos. Salen cada hora.

Tenemos aeropuerto, pero no hay vuelos para el público.

Yo prefiero ir a todos los sitios en bici. Es muy barato y rápido.

Muchos besos,

Jacoba

Lee el texto y contesta a las preguntas.

Los tranvías

Hace muchos años había muchos tranvías. Hay un tranvía antiguo en Barcelona que se llama *Tranvía Blau* (tranvía azul) que va a Tibidabo. Como este tranvía, los antiguos son normalmente para los turistas.

Hay unos problemas con los tranvías. Hoy, la gente prefiere ir en coche o en autobús. Pero en Barcelona, por ejemplo, el tranvía es totalmente nuevo. Hay sitio para 218 personas y tiene una velocidad máxima de 70 kilómetros por hora. Son buenos para el medio ambiente: no son ruidosos; no usan gasolina y llevan muchos viajeros.

hace muchos años – *a long time ago*
los antiguos – *the old ones (trams)*
nuevo – *new*
velocidad – *speed*
el medio ambiente – *the environment*
llevan – *they carry*

¿Verdad (V) o mentira (M)?

1 There used to be many trams a long time ago.
2 The old trams are popular with tourists.
3 The old trams reach a maximum speed of 70 km per hour.
4 Modern trams are noisy.
5 Modern trams don't use petrol.
6 Modern trams are kind to the environment.

9 Los medios de comunicación

9A ¿Qué medio de comunicación prefieres?

- say what media you like and why
- learn how to say *more/less than, the most/least*

1 a Escucha y lee.

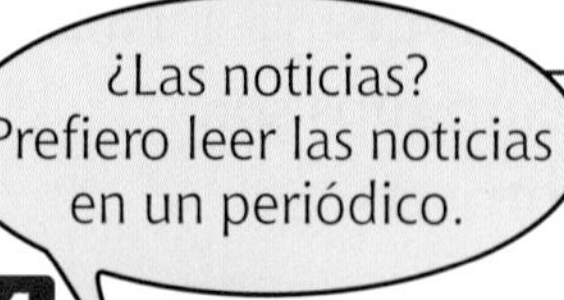

1
Hola, Pilar. ¿Qué tal?
Muy bien, Marina. Me gustaría ir al cine esta tarde. ¿Te gusta el cine?
2
¿El cine? Uf, no me gusta nada. Es aburridísimo. Yo prefiero la televisión. Es genial.
¿Ves mucho la tele?
Sí, dos o tres horas al día. ¿Y tú?
3
No, no me gusta la tele, los programas son muy malos. Yo prefiero escuchar la radio. Me gustan mucho los programas de música, y también los debates. Es lo más interesante.
¿Los debates? ¡Qué rollo! Prefiero Internet. Me gusta chatear con mis amigos por messenger, o leer las noticias por Internet.
4
¿Las noticias? Prefiero leer las noticias en un periódico.
¡Uy, no! Los periódicos son aburridos. Prefiero las revistas.
5
¡A mí también me gustan las revistas!
¡Bien! ¡Por fin estamos de acuerdo!

1 b Mira los dibujos. ¿En qué orden se mencionan?

A 
B 
C 
D 
E 
F 

1 c Copia y rellena el cuadro.

Medio de comunicación	Opinión de Pilar	Opinión de Marina
cine	+	–

2 Habla con tu pareja. ¿Qué le parecen los medios de comunicación? ¿Por qué?

Ejemplo: **A** ¿Qué te parecen las revistas?
B Me gustan mucho. Son geniales

	+	–
¿Qué te parece... ? el cine la televisión la radio Internet	Me encanta Es genial Me gusta mucho Creo que es interesante educativo/a divertido/a/ emocionante	No me gusta nada Lo/La odio Es muy aburrido/a Los programas son muy malos Creo que es un rollo un desastre demasiado caro/a
¿Qué te parecen...? los periódicos las revistas	Me encantan Son geniales Me gustan mucho Creo que son interesantes educativos/as divertidos/as baratos/as	No me gustan nada Los/Las odio Son muy aburridos/as Creo que son un rollo un desastre demasiado caros/as

Gramática: more/less than, the most/least

... *es más* (adjective) *que...*	... is more... than...	*La televisión es* ***más divertida que*** *la radio.*
... *es menos* (adjective) *que...*	... is less... than...	*Internet es* ***menos educativo que*** *los periódicos.*
... *es el más* (adjective) *(de...)*	... is the most... (in...)	*El cine es* ***el medio de comunicación más emocionante****.*
... *es el menos* (adjective) *(de...)*	... is the least... (in...)	*Las revistas son* ***el medio de comunicación menos interesante****.*

3 ***Match up the sentences. Then decide which ones are true for you and change the ones which are not.***

A Cinema is more exciting than TV.
B I like radio less than TV.
C The Internet is the cheapest media.
D Magazines are more expensive than the cinema.
E Radio is the most boring media.
F The media which is the most fun is magazines.

1 El medio de comunicación más divertido son las revistas.
2 La radio me gusta menos que la televisión.
3 Las revistas son más caras que el cine.
4 El cine es más emocionante que la televisión.
5 La radio es el medio de comunicación más aburrido.
6 Internet es el medio de comunicación más barato.

4 a **Une los títulos 1–5 y los párrafos A–E.**

1 Introducción
2 Las noticias
3 Opinión de la radio
4 Opinión de la televisión
5 Opinión del cine

4 b **Contesta a las preguntas en inglés.**

1 How old is Almudena?
2 What director and film does she mention?
3 Why does she not like Spanish TV?
4 How does she keep up with the news?

A Almudena Ibáñez es la nueva revelación del cine español. Tiene diecinueve años.

B Almudena. ¿Qué haces en tu tiempo libre? ¿Te gusta el cine?

Sí, me encanta. Creo que el cine es más divertido que la televisión. ¡Pero no me gusta ver mis películas! Me encanta el cine español, por ejemplo los directores como Amenábar. Su película *Los otros* es fantástica, en mi opinión. Los directores españoles son más creativos que los ingleses.

C ¿Y te gusta la televisión?

No, no me gusta mucho la televisión española, porque los programas no son buenos. Prefiero ver la tele en Inglaterra. Creo que hay más variedad en la televisión inglesa.

D ¿Escuchas la radio?

Sí, mucho. En mi coche escucho música y en casa escucho los debates. Son muy interesantes, pero la música es más entretenida.

E ¿Dónde lees las noticias? ¿Lees periódicos?

No, porque no tengo tiempo. Normalmente leo las noticias en Internet, y chateo con mis amigos. Internet es más divertido que los periódicos. Pero leo revistas, en el avión.

9B La televisión

- talk about TV programmes
- give reasons for liking a programme
- reach an agreement on what to watch

1 a Mira la programación de la televisión. Busca las palabras.

1 debate
2 documentary
3 film
4 news programme
5 quiz show
6 series
7 soap opera
8 weather forecast

TVE1	TVE2	Antena3	Canal+	Tele5
18:00 Noticias	**17:30** Concurso: El precio justo	**18:00** Noticias	**18:00** Serie: Friends	**18:00** Salsa rosa
18:30 Los Simpson	**19:00** Documental: El África Occidental	**18:30** Telenovela: Paso Adelante	**19:00** La cartelera	**19:00** Telenovela: Machos
19:00 Concurso: Gran Hermano	**21:00** Noticias	**20:30** La cocina de Arguiñano	**20:00** Noticias	**20:00** Las noticias de la 5
21:00 Película: La Roca	**22:00** Debate: La clonación	**21:30** Película: Piratas del Caribe	**20:30** Serie: Los mejores años de nuestra vida	**20:50** El tiempo
24:00 Serie: Expediente X		**24:00** Serie: CSI	**21:00** Estreno: El retorno del Rey	**21:00** Documental: Historia de España
				22:30 Cine Español: La Regenta

1 b Lee la programación otra vez. Contesta a las preguntas en inglés.

1 Which channels are showing a series at 12 o'clock?
2 What time is the film *The Rock* on?
3 What is the name of the documentary on TVE2?
4 What new film is being shown on Canal+?
5 What time is the soap opera on Tele5?
6 On which channel is a documentary on the history of Spain being shown?
7 At what time is there a cookery programme on Antena3?

2 Escucha (1–5). Copia y rellena el cuadro.

	Programa	Canal	Hora
1			

documental	noticias	película	serie	telenovela
TVE1	TVE2	Antena3	Canal+	Tele5
7.30	8.15	8.30	10.00	11.30

¡Así se hace! *Discussing and agreeing*

One very important skill is discussing your opinions and finally being able to reach an agreement after listening to somebody else's arguments. Here are some useful phrases:

Giving your opinion	Asking somebody else's opinion	Expressing a different point of view	Reaching an agreement	Agreeing
En mi opinión...	¿Qué crees?	No estoy de acuerdo	Entonces vamos a...	Vale
Creo que...	¿Qué piensas?	Creo que es mejor...	Podemos...	Muy bien
Me gustaría...	¿Prefieres... o...?	Prefiero...		
Pienso que...	¿Qué te gustaría?			

3 a **Mira los dibujos. Escribe las conversaciones.**

Ejemplo:

A Me gustaría ver la tele. ¿Qué crees?
B No estoy de acuerdo. Es mejor ir al cine. ¿Qué piensas?
A Vale.

escuchar la radio	jugar al fútbol
ir a un restaurante	leer una revista
ir al cine	ver un concurso
ir de compras	ver un documental
ver la tele	

1

2

3

4

5

3 b **Habla con tu pareja. Practica las conversaciones.**

3 c **Escribe tu propia conversación.**

9C ¿Quieres ir al cine?

- talk about films and your opinions on them
- arrange to meet to go to the cinema

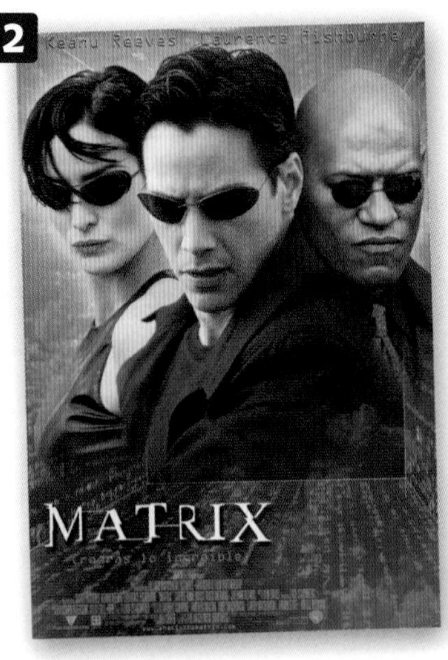

1 a Une las frases y los dibujos.

A una comedia
B una película de acción
C una película de aventuras
D una película de ciencia ficción
E una película de dibujos animados
F una película de suspense
G una película de terror
H una película romántica

1 b Escucha (1–8). Escribe la letra.

Ejemplo: **1 C**

2 a Escribe tus opiniones sobre los diferentes tipos de películas.

Ejemplo:

Me encantan las películas de acción porque son entretenidas y rápidas.

No me gustan las películas de dibujos animados porque son infantiles y tontas.

2 b Habla con tus parejas. ¿Qué tipo de película prefieren?

Ejemplo:

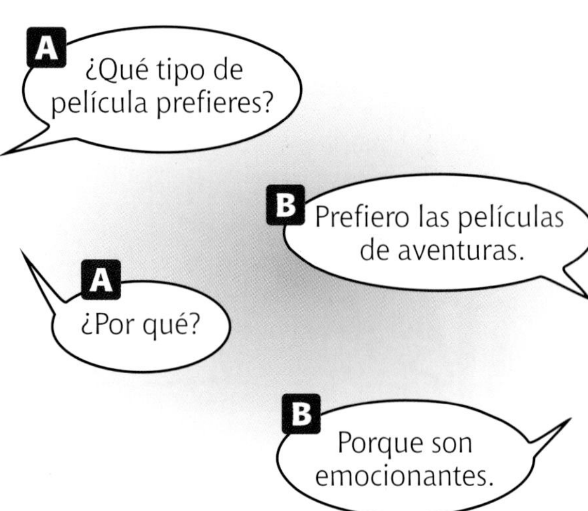

+	–
Me gustan (mucho) Me encantan Me apasionan Adoro	No me gustan (nada) No soporto Odio No aguanto Detesto
las películas de aventuras	las películas de terror
porque son... divertidas emocionantes fantásticas entretenidas rápidas inteligentes	porque son... aburridas lentas infantiles insoportables tontas

4

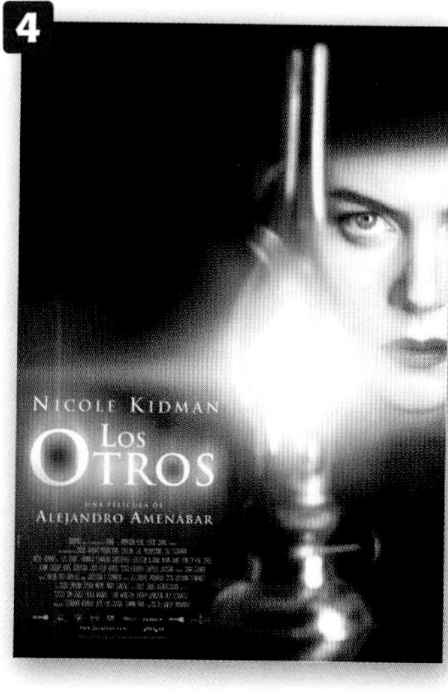

8

LA GUERRA DE LAS GALAXIAS

STAR WARS

3 a Lee la conversación. Busca las expresiones entre las expresiones subrayadas.

1. at the door of the cinema
2. Do you fancy coming to the cinema this evening?
3. At 8.30
4. Where shall we meet?
5. They're showing a very good romantic film.
6. we can see
7. What time?

Hola, Pablo.

Hola, María. ¿Qué tal?

Muy bien. ¿Quieres venir al cine esta tarde?

Bueno, ¿qué ponen?

Ponen una película romántica muy buena.

Oh, no, no me gustan nada las películas románticas. Podemos ver una película de aventuras.

Vale, ¿a qué hora?

A las ocho y media.

¿Dónde nos encontramos?

En la puerta del cine.

¡Fantástico! Hasta luego entonces.

Adiós.

3 b Escribe otra conversación como en 3a. Practícala con tu pareja. Usa el cuadro.

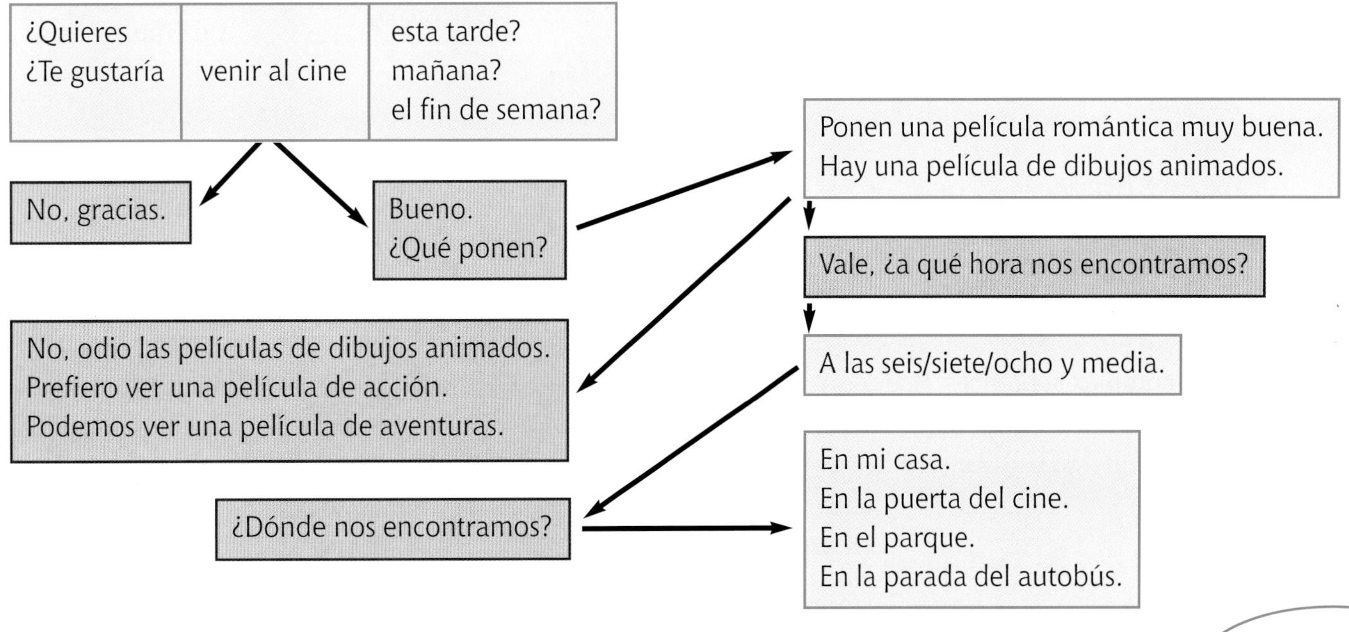

¿Quieres
¿Te gustaría
venir al cine
esta tarde?
mañana?
el fin de semana?
No, gracias.
Bueno.
¿Qué ponen?
Ponen una película romántica muy buena.
Hay una película de dibujos animados.
Vale, ¿a qué hora nos encontramos?
A las seis/siete/ocho y media.
No, odio las películas de dibujos animados.
Prefiero ver una película de acción.
Podemos ver una película de aventuras.
¿Dónde nos encontramos?
En mi casa.
En la puerta del cine.
En el parque.
En la parada del autobús.

9D Mis novelas favoritas

- practise extended reading
- practise imaginative writing

B

C D

las reseñas – *reviews*

1 Une las reseñas y las novelas. Usa un diccionario si es necesario.

A

el brujo – *wizard*	el personaje – *character*	el anillo – *ring*
brujería – *wizardry*	los amantes – *lovers*	llevar – *to take*
el argumento – *plot*	triste – *sad*	el Monte del Destino – *Mount Doom*

1 La historia del brujo Harry Potter que va a la escuela de brujería para perfeccionar sus habilidades y tiene muchas aventuras. El argumento es emocionante y los personajes son fascinantes.

2 Esta es una obra de teatro clásico. Los dos amantes más famosos de la historia sufren un destino trágico. Una obra perfecta aunque triste.

3 Esta fantástica novela es la historia del Anillo de Poder. Frodo debe llevar el anillo al Monte del Destino con Sam, mientras Gandalf participa con los elfos por la victoria.

4 La historia de Bridget, una mujer de treinta y dos años. Busca al hombre perfecto. Esta novela es en forma de diario y tiene muchos momentos cómicos. Ahora una película famosa.

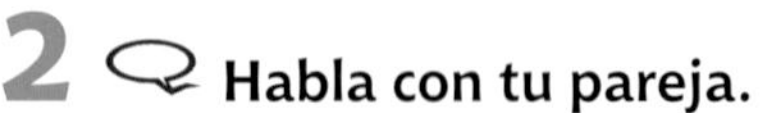

2 Habla con tu pareja.

A	B
¿Cuál es tu novela/película favorita?	Mi novela/película favorita es…
¿Quién es el autor/director?	El autor/director es…
¿Dónde tiene lugar?	Tiene lugar en…
¿Quiénes son los personajes?	Los personajes son…
¿Por qué es tu novela/película favorita?	Es mi novela/película favorita porque es emocionante romántica interesante entretenida

¡Así se hace! *Writing longer sentences*

When writing or talking about a book or film you like, think about the following basic questions:

What? Where? Who? Why?

- For example, if you are writing about the film *Spider-Man*, you could write something like:
  (what) *Spider-Man es una película de acción.*
  (where) *Tiene lugar en América.*
  (who) *El protagonista es un chico que tiene poderes especiales.*
  (why) *Me gusta porque es muy interesante y divertida, y tiene escenas de acción muy emocionantes.*
- This will be the basis of your review. Then make up longer, more complex sentences. Use connectors such as:

Lo mejor/peor es que…	The best/worst thing is that…
Prefiero… porque… y también	I prefer... because... and also...
pero	but
que	who/that e.g. *un chico que busca a alguien* a boy who is looking for somebody

3 Escribe una reseña sobre tu novela o película favorita.

La novela... del autor/de la autora... La película... del director/de la directora... es la historia de...	un chico y su familia una mujer de 30 años un hombre que vive en América.
El argumento es...	emocionante entretenido lento/rápido
El final es...	espectacular sorprendente fantástico
Lo mejor es...	el argumento los personajes las descripciones
Es una novela... Es una película...	fantástica genial divertida

Resumen

Los medios de comunicación	***The media***
el cine	*cinema*
la televisión	*TV*
la radio	*radio*
(el) Internet	*internet*
los periódicos	*newspapers*
las revistas	*magazines*

Los programas	***Programmes***
el debate	*debate*
el documental	*documentary*
la película	*film*
las noticias	*news programme*
el concurso	*quiz show*
la serie	*series*
la telenovela	*soap opera*
el tiempo	*weather forecast*
¿En qué canal ponen la serie?	*On which channel do they show the series?*
¿A qué hora pone Antena3 el programa de cocina?	*What time does Antena 3 show the cookery programme?*

Las películas	***Films***
una comedia	*comedy*
una película de acción	*action film*
una película de aventuras	*adventure film*
una película de ciencia ficción	*sci fi film*
una película de dibujos animados	*animated film*
una película de suspense	*thriller*
una película de terror	*horror film*
una película romántica	*romantic film*

Una invitación al cine	***An invitation to the cinema***
¿Quieres... ?	*Do you want... ?*
¿Te apetece... ?	*Do you fancy... ?*
¿Te gustaría... ?	*Would you like... ?*
venir al cine	*to come to the cinema*
esta tarde	*this evening*
mañana	*tomorrow*
el fin de semana	*at the weekend*
¿Qué ponen?	*What are they showing?*
¿A qué hora nos encontramos?	*What time shall we meet?*
A las seis	*At 6 o'clock*
¿Dónde nos encontramos?	*Where shall we meet?*
En mi casa	*At my house*
En la puerta del cine	*At the door of the cinema*

Una reseña	***A review***
la novela	*novel*
el autor/la autora	*author*
Es la historia de...	*It's the story of...*
Los personajes son...	*The characters are...*
El argumento es...	*The plot is...*
El final es...	*The ending is...*
Lo mejor es...	*The best thing is...*
Es una novela...	*It is a... novel*

Gramática:
more/less than, the most/least

Cross-topic words

me apasiona – *I love*
detesto – *I detest*
no aguanto/soporto – *I can't stand*

¡Así se hace!

- ★ Discussing and agreeing
- ★ Writing longer sentences

10 ¡De fiesta!

10A Calendario de fiestas

- learn about different festivals in the Spanish calendar
- use *se* to say what people do

Fiestas de España

enero	febrero	marzo
1 Año Nuevo 6 Los Reyes	28 día de Andalucía	19 día del Padre Carnaval
abril	**mayo**	**junio**
Semana Santa, Feria de Sevilla	1 día de la Madre	24 día de San Juan
julio	**agosto**	**septiembre**
7 San Fermín	15 Feria de Málaga	
octubre	**noviembre**	**diciembre**
12 día de la Hispanidad	1 día de Todos los Santos 2 día de Todos los Difuntos	8 día de la Inmaculada 24 Nochebuena 25 Navidad 31 Nochevieja

1 a Lee el calendario de fiestas importantes de España. ¿Verdad (V) o mentira (M)?

1 Hay tres fiestas en diciembre.
2 No hay fiestas en julio.
3 El día de Andalucía se celebra el 28 de marzo.
4 La Semana Santa es normalmente en abril.
5 El día de la Madre y del Padre son diferentes que en Gran Bretaña.
6 El día de la Hispanidad se celebra en noviembre.
7 Hay tres fiestas en enero.
8 *Christmas* se dice Navidad en español.

fiesta – *festival*
se celebra – *it is celebrated*
la Semana Santa – *Holy Week*
día de la Madre – *Mother's Day*
día del Padre – *Father's Day*

1 b ¿Qué se hace en las fiestas? Une el español y el inglés.

1 A big dinner is eaten with all the family.
2 An effigy of Judas is burnt.
3 Dead relatives are remembered.
4 Flamenco dresses are worn.
5 Presents are given to fathers.
6 Presents are given to mothers.
7 The grapes of luck are eaten.
8 There are bull runs in the streets.
9 There are processions.

A

Se quema una imagen de Judas.

B

Se dan regalos a los padres.

C

Hay carreras de toros por las calles.

D

Se toma una gran cena con toda la familia.

E

Hay procesiones.

F

Se dan regalos a las madres.

G

Se toman las uvas de la suerte.

H

Se recuerda a los familiares que se han muerto.

I

Se llevan trajes de flamenco.

2 **Lee y escribe una descripción de las fiestas. ¿Qué se hace?**

Ejemplo: **En San Fermín se come y se bebe mucho y hay carreras de toros por las calles.**

carreras de toros – *bull running*
trajes de flamenco – *flamenco dresses*
se baila – *people dance*
se ven procesiones – *people watch processions*
fiestas – *parties*

Gramática: using *se* to say what people do

- Look at the captions in **1b** again. What is the first word in most of the sentences?

To say that people do something, you use:

se + third person singular of the present + singular noun
se + third person plural of the present + plural noun

Examples:

A big meal is eaten. (People eat a big meal.)	*Se come una gran comida.*
Presents are given. (People give presents.)	*Se dan regalos.*

Entrevista con Eduardo Mendiola, experto en fiestas y festivales en España.

Eduardo, ¿cuál es tu fiesta preferida en España?

Bueno, a mí me encanta San Fermín.

¿Y qué se hace en San Fermín?

Pues, se come y se bebe mucho y hay carreras de toros por las calles.

¿Y la Feria de Sevilla? ¿Qué se hace?

Se llevan trajes de flamenco y se baila flamenco. ¡Es fantástico!

¿Y qué pasa en Semana Santa?

Pues, se ven procesiones por las calles.

¿Y qué pasa la noche de San Juan?

Se celebran fiestas y se come y se bebe. También se quema una imagen de Judas.

Similar a nuestra 'Bonfire Night' entonces. Muchas gracias, Eduardo.

3 a **¿Qué se hace en las fiestas en Gran Bretaña? Habla con tu pareja.**

A ¿Qué se hace en el día de la Madre?
B Se dan regalos a las madres.

El día de la Madre	Se comen 'pancakes'.
El día del Padre	Se dan regalos a las madres.
Navidad	Se dan regalos a los padres.
Nochevieja	Se quema una imagen de Guy Fawkes.
Bonfire Night	Se toma una comida especial.
Pancake Day	Se va a fiestas.

3 b **Escribe 5 frases sobre una fiesta en Gran Bretaña o en otro país. ¿Qué se hace?**

Ejemplo: **En Irlanda en el día de St Patrick se bebe Guinness.**

En Gran Bretaña en *Pancake Day* se comen 'pancakes'.

10B ¡Feliz Navidad!

- learn about Christmas and New Year traditions in Spain
- revise the preterite of regular verbs

algunas familias – *some families*
postre – *dessert*
almendra – *almond*
un belén – *a crib*
las doce uvas – *the twelve grapes*
las doce campanadas del reloj – *the twelve chimes of the clock*

1 a Lee y escucha. Busca las palabras en azul.

1 Christmas **2** Christmas Eve **3** church **4** turkey **5** dinner **6** Christmas tree **7** parties **8** presents **9** New Year's Eve

1

Paul
Enrique
¡Hola, Enrique!
Hola, Paul. ¿Qué tal?

P: Fantástico. Dime, ¿qué se hace en Navidad en España?
E: La cena con la familia es el 24 de diciembre, el día de Nochebuena. Toda la familia come y después algunas familias van a la iglesia a las doce de la noche.

2

P: ¿Y qué se come en la cena?
E: Es muy tradicional el pavo y los postres tradicionales de almendra.
P: ¿Qué ornamentos se ponen en la casa?
E: Normalmente hay un belén, y también un árbol de Navidad.

3

P: ¿Y el día de Navidad? ¿Se dan los regalos?
E: No, el día de Navidad, el 25 de diciembre, es un día bastante tranquilo.
P: ¿Y cómo se celebra la Nochevieja?
E: El día 31 de diciembre se cena con la familia y a las doce se toman las doce uvas con las doce campanadas del reloj.

4

P: ¿Y después?
E: Se va a las fiestas.
P: ¿Y cuándo se dan los regalos?
E: El día 6 de enero.

1 b ***Find the underlined nouns in the text and put them in the right categories.***

Masculino singular (el/un)	Masculino plural (los/unos)	Femenino singular (la/una)	Femenino plural (las/unas)
día	postres	Navidad	campanadas

1 c Lee y escucha otra vez. Contesta a las preguntas en inglés.

1. When is the main family meal in Spain?
2. What is eaten traditionally?
3. What are the two most common decorations in the house?
4. What happens on New Year's Eve?
5. When are presents exchanged?

2 a Find the 13 preterite tenses in the letter.

Ejemplo: **cené, comí...**

15 de enero

¡Hola, Alison!

¿Qué tal? El día 24 de diciembre, Nochebuena, cené en casa con mi familia. Comí pollo con verduras y patatas. ¡Qué rico!

El día de Navidad vi la tele y por la tarde salí con mis amigos al centro.

El día de Nochevieja, el 31 de diciembre, fue muy divertido. Por la noche cenamos a las diez. A las doce, tomamos las doce uvas con las campanadas y después bebimos champán.

El día 5 de enero fui a la procesión de los Reyes Magos.

El día 6 de enero abrí mis regalos en casa. Recibí varios CDs y un i-Pod, una camiseta y una falda muy bonitas, unos libros y dinero. La falda me gustó mucho.

¿Y tú? ¿Qué hiciste en las Navidades? Escríbeme pronto.

Un abrazo,

Paula

los Reyes Magos – *the Three Wise Men*
abrí los regalos – *I opened the presents*

2 b Copia y rellena el cuadro.

¿Qué día?	¿Con quién?	¿Dónde?	¿Información extra?
24 de diciembre	Familia	En casa	Comí pollo con verduras y patatas.
	Amigos		
31 de diciembre			
	–	–	
	En casa		

2 c Escribe una carta a Paula. ¿Qué hiciste en las últimas vacaciones de Navidad?

El día 25 de diciembre...	Comí...	Fue fantástico
El día 31 de diciembre...	Bebí...	Fue sensacional
El día 1 de enero...	Salí...	Me gustó mucho
	Fui a...	Fue un desastre
	Recibí...	No me gustó nada
	Compré...	
	Vi...	
	Escuché...	

Gramática: the preterite

-ar verbs	-er/-ir verbs
comprar (to buy)	*beber* (to drink)
*compr**é***	*beb**í***
*compr**aste***	*beb**iste***
*compr**amos***	*beb**imos***

3 Entrevista a tu pareja.

1 ¿Dónde comiste la cena de Navidad el año pasado?	Comí la cena de Navidad en mi casa en la casa de mis tíos en un restaurante
¿Con quién?	Con mi familia mis padres mis amigos
2 ¿Qué comiste?	Comí pescado con verduras uvas y ensalada
3 ¿Qué regalos recibiste?	Recibí unos CDs ropa dinero
4 ¿Qué regalaste?	Regalé un perfume a mi madre una cámara a mi padre una camiseta a mi hermano
5 ¿Adónde fuiste el 31 de diciembre?	Me quedé en casa Fui a una fiesta con mis amigos al centro de la ciudad con mis hermanos a casa de mis primos

10C El verano pasado

- talk about what you did during the summer holidays
- use the preterite of regular verbs and some common irregular verbs

1 a Escucha y lee.

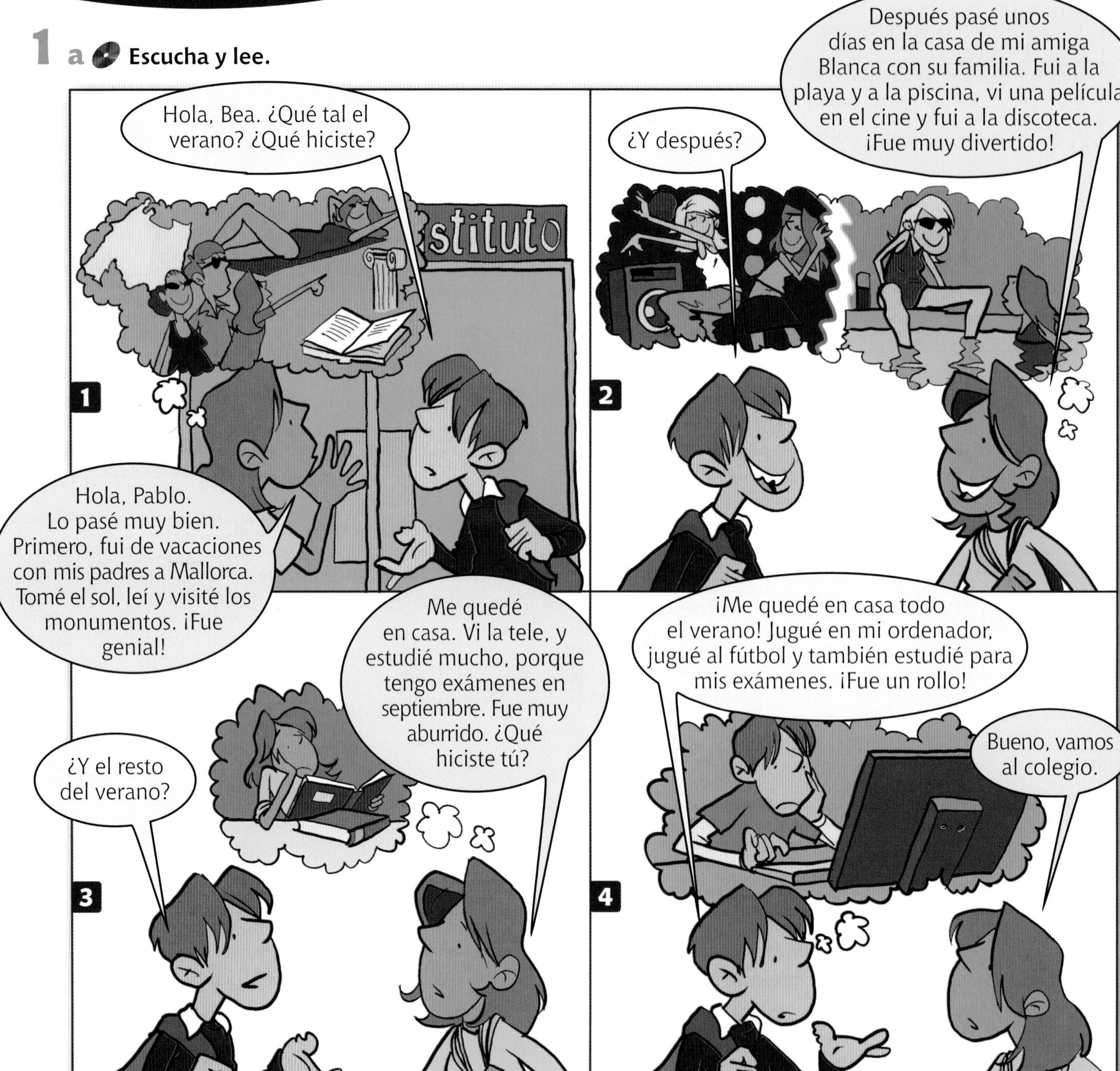

1
Hola, Bea. ¿Qué tal el verano? ¿Qué hiciste?
stituto
Hola, Pablo. Lo pasé muy bien. Primero, fui de vacaciones con mis padres a Mallorca. Tomé el sol, leí y visité los monumentos. ¡Fue genial!
2
¿Y después?
Después pasé unos días en la casa de mi amiga Blanca con su familia. Fui a la playa y a la piscina, vi una película en el cine y fui a la discoteca. ¡Fue muy divertido!
3
¿Y el resto del verano?
Me quedé en casa. Vi la tele, y estudié mucho, porque tengo exámenes en septiembre. Fue muy aburrido. ¿Qué hiciste tú?
4
¡Me quedé en casa todo el verano! Jugué en mi ordenador, jugué al fútbol y también estudié para mis exámenes. ¡Fue un rollo!
Bueno, vamos al colegio.

1 b ¿Es Bea, Pablo o los dos?

1 Me quedé en casa.
2 Fui de vacaciones a Mallorca.
3 Jugué en mi ordenador.
4 Fui a la piscina.
5 Vi la televisión.
6 Vi una película en el cine.
7 Visité monumentos.
8 Estudié mucho.

1 c Busca 5 expresiones de opinión.

1 d ¡extra! ***Can you remember any other ways to express your opinion about something that happened in the past?***

1 e ¡extra! ***How many verbs in the past tense can you find in the text on page 90?***

2 Describe las actividades y las opiniones según los dibujos.

1

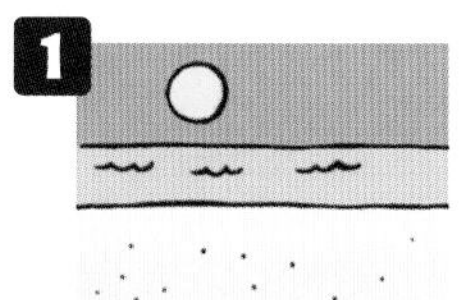
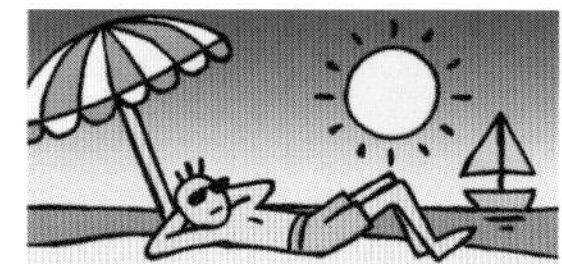

2

3

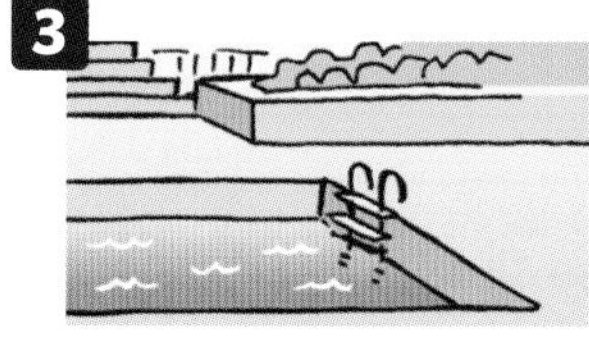

4

3 ¿Y tú? ¿Qué hiciste el verano pasado? Escribe un párrafo.

Primero Después Luego	fui a... me quedé vi una película/la tele jugué...
Fue .../Lo pasé...	

4 Entrevista a tu pareja.

1 ¿Qué hiciste el verano pasado? Fui a...
2 ¿Qué hiciste después? Visité...
3 ¿Cómo lo pasaste? Lo pasé...

10D Un día de desastre

- describe a disastrous day in the past
- recognise the imperfect tense
- read and write longer texts

1 Lee y busca las frases.

1 I decided to go to the café
2 I lost my money
3 I went to bed
4 I went to buy some shoes
5 I went to catch the bus
6 In the afternoon
7 It started to rain
8 It was too big
9 Last Saturday
10 The film was very boring
11 The shop was closed

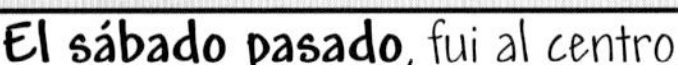

El sábado pasado, fui al centro.

Primero **fui a comprar unos zapatos**, pero eran demasiado caros.

Después fui a comprar un juego de ordenador, pero **la tienda estaba cerrada.**

Luego fui al parque a comer un bocadillo, pero **empezó a llover**.

Decidí ir a la cafetería a comer una pizza, pero fue horrible.

Por la tarde fui al centro comercial a comprar una camiseta, pero **era demasiado grande**.

Fui a coger el autobús, pero **perdí mi dinero**, así que fui a casa a pie.

En mi casa, vi la tele, pero **la película fue muy aburrida**, así que... **¡me fui a la cama!**

2 Escucha (1–6) y escribe las actividades y los problemas.

Ejemplo: **1 Fui a comprar unos pantalones. Eran demasiado grandes.**

comí en un restaurante
comí un bocadillo en el parque
Fui a comprar unos pantalones
fui al campo a pie
fui a la cafetería
fui a comprar un libro
eran demasiado grandes
empezó a llover
la tienda estaba cerrada
hizo mucho frío
la comida era horrible
perdí mi dinero

3 Escribe sobre un día de desastre real o imaginario. Usa **1** y **2**.

El sábado/lunes pasado/La semana pasada...
Primero... pero.... Después... pero... Luego... pero...
Por la tarde... pero... Al final... pero...

Las fiestas	***Festivals***
El Año Nuevo	*New Year*
La Nochebuena	*Christmas Eve*
La Navidad	*Christmas*
La Nochevieja	*New Year's Eve*
El día del Padre/de la Madre	*Father's/Mother's Day*
la feria	*fair*
Se celebra	*It's celebrated*
Se come	*It's eaten*
Se llevan trajes de flamenco	*Flamenco dresses are worn*
Hay procesiones	*There are processions*

¡Feliz Navidad!	***Happy Christmas!***
la cena de Nochebuena	*Christmas Eve dinner*
el belén	*nativity scene/crib*
Los Reyes	*the Three Wise Men*
el árbol de Navidad	*Christmas tree*
el pavo	*turkey*
las doce campanadas	*the twelve chimes of the clock (at midnight)*
Recibí...	*I received...*
Regalé...	*I gave...*
Compré...	*I bought...*

El verano pasado	***Last summer***
estudié mucho	*I studied loads*
fui a la piscina	*I went to the swimming pool*
fui a la playa	*I went to the beach*
me quedé en casa	*I stayed at home*
tomé el sol	*I sunbathed*
vi una película	*I watched a film*
visité monumentos	*I visited monuments*
fue aburrido	*it was boring*
fue divertido	*it was fun*
fue un rollo	*it was a pain*
lo pasé bomba	*I had a great time*

Gramática:

Using *se* to express what people do

Revision of the preterite tense

Understanding the imperfect tense

Cross-topic words

se come – *people eat*

se bebe – *people drink*

¿Qué se hace? – *What do people do?*

¡Así se hace!

- ★ Reading longer texts
- ★ Writing longer texts

Unidad 9 (¿Problemas? Mira la página 85.)

1 Mira la conversación y escribe otra conversación. Cambia las palabras. Practícala con tu pareja.

A ¿Quieres ir al cine esta tarde?
B Sí, ¿qué ponen?
A Ponen una película de dibujos animados muy buena.
B Odio las películas de dibujos animados porque son infantiles. Prefiero las películas de acción.
A Vale. ¿A qué hora nos encontramos?
B A las siete y media.
A ¿Dónde nos encontramos?
B En mi casa.
A Muy bien. Hasta luego.

a las nueve y media
aburridas
en el cine
esta noche
las películas románticas
una película de ciencia ficción

2 Lee la crítica de la película. Busca las palabras.

1 adventures
2 film
3 on at the cinema
4 prisoner
5 wizard
6 you have to go

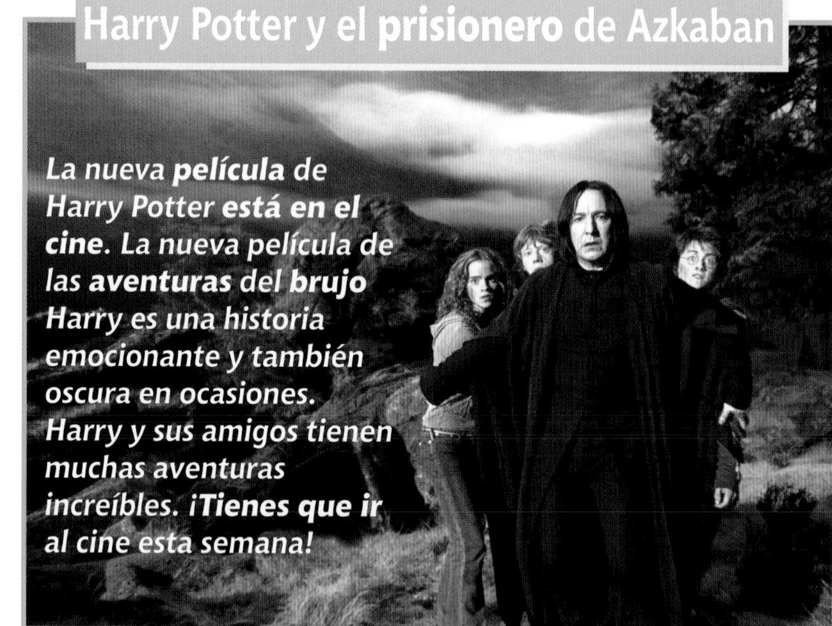

Harry Potter y el prisionero de Azkaban
La nueva película de Harry Potter está en el cine. La nueva película de las aventuras del brujo Harry es una historia emocionante y también oscura en ocasiones. Harry y sus amigos tienen muchas aventuras increíbles. ¡Tienes que ir al cine esta semana!

3 Contesta a las preguntas.

¿Te gusta el cine? ¿Ves mucho la tele?
¿Escuchas la radio? ¿Cómo lees las noticias?
(No) Me gusta... Prefiero...

Unidad 10 (¿Problemas? Mira la página 93.)

4 Escucha y busca la respuesta correcta.

1 El pueblo de Buñol está en Madrid/en Valencia.
2 La fiesta empieza a las once/doce de la mañana.
3 Se llevan pantalones cortos/largos.
4 Se tiran miles de/cientos de kilos de tomates.
5 Al final las calles se limpian con limonada/con agua.
6 La gente lo pasa genial/muy bien.

La Semana Santa de Málaga

La Semana Santa empezó en Málaga el doce de abril. Hay procesiones desde el domingo hasta el viernes.

El Domingo de Ramos, hay seis procesiones. Cada trono lo llevan doscientos cincuenta hombres. También hay nazarenos, y detrás de la procesión va la banda de música.

El lunes veremos la procesión con la imagen de la Virgen de la Trinidad, con su manto morado, y las miles de flores blancas en su trono.

La gente en las calles come las típicas *torrijas*, un dulce con pan y miel, normalmente con un café con leche. Los niños comerán algodón dulce y palomitas.

nazarenos – *penitents*
Domingo de Ramos – *Palm Sunday*
detrás de – *behind*
dulce – *sweet, pudding*
miel – *honey*
manto – *cape, coat*

Lee el reportaje. ¿Verdad (V) o mentira (M)?

1 La Semana Santa empezó el doce de marzo.
2 Las procesiones son desde el sábado hasta el viernes.
3 El domingo hay seis procesiones.
4 Cada trono lleva 260 hombres.
5 La banda de música va delante del trono.
6 El lunes hay la procesión de la Virgen de la Trinidad.
7 El manto de la Virgen es rojo.
8 El trono lleva muchas flores blancas.
9 La gente come la típica paella.
10 Los niños comen algodón dulce y palomitas.

Corrige las frases mentirosas.

11 En casa

11A Mi dormitorio

- describe your room
- make comparisons using *tan… como*
- say what are the best and worst things

1 a Busca las cosas en los dibujos. Juega con tu pareja.

la cama　el ordenador
la lámpara　el vídeo
el póster　el despertador
el equipo de música　la televisión
la revista　la silla

1 b Escucha y mira los dibujos. ¿Es el dormitorio de Pablo o de Antonio?

1 c Escucha otra vez y escribe dos listas.

Pablo	Antonio
una cama	una cama, …

1 d Mira los dibujos. Escribe una lista de 5–10 diferencias.

Ejemplo:
En el dormitorio de Antonio hay pósters en las paredes.
En el dormitorio de Pablo no hay pósters.

1 e ¡extra! Mira los dibujos. ¿Quién habla, Antonio o Pablo?

Ejemplo: **1 Antonio y Pablo**

1. Tengo una mesa en mi dormitorio.
2. Escucho música en mi dormitorio.
3. Me gustaría viajar en el futuro.
4. Prefiero un dormitorio práctico.
5. Me gusta la lectura.
6. Soy deportista.
7. Estudio mucho.

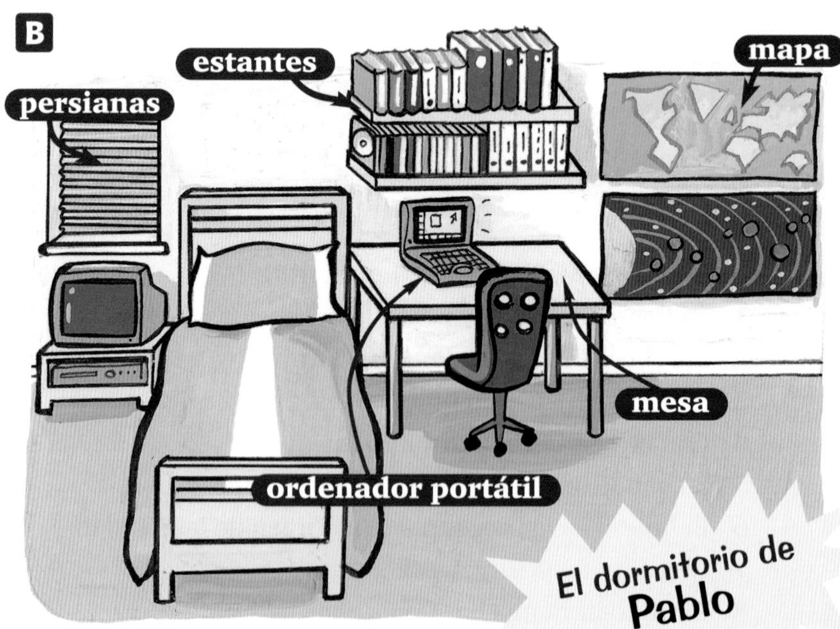

1 f Une el español y el inglés.

Ejemplo: **1 c**

1. El dormitorio de Antonio es más grande que el de Pablo.
2. El dormitorio de Pablo es tan cómodo como el de Antonio.
3. Las paredes del dormitorio de Pablo son menos atractivas que las de Antonio.
4. Pablo es tan deportista como Antonio.
5. El dormitorio de Antonio es más práctico que el de Pablo.
6. Antonio es tan trabajador en el colegio como Pablo.

a The walls in Pablo's bedroom are less attractive than Antonio's.
b Antonio's bedroom is more practical than Pablo's.
c Antonio's bedroom is bigger than Pablo's.
d Pablo's bedroom is as comfortable as Antonio's.
e Antonio is as hard-working in school as Pablo.
f Pablo is as sporty as Antonio.

Gramática: *tan… como – as… as*

Mi dormitorio es tan cómodo como el de mi hermana.*
My bedroom is as comfortable as my sister's.

*Notice how the word *dormitorio* isn't repeated. If the sentence were translated word for word it would be 'My bedroom is as comfortable as the (one/bedroom) of my sister.'

 *más… que* = more… than
menos…que = less… than

Gramática: *lo* + adjective

Lo + adjective *es que…*
= the… thing is that…

Lo mejor – the best thing
Lo peor – the worst thing
Lo aburrido – the boring thing

2 Habla con tu pareja. Cambia las palabras.

A ¿Compartes tu dormitorio o tienes tu propio dormitorio?
B Comparto mi dormitorio con mi hermana.
A ¿Cómo es tu dormitorio?
B Mi dormitorio es grande. Las paredes son azules. Hay muchos pósters.
A ¿Qué muebles hay en tu dormitorio?
B En mi dormitorio hay una cama, un armario, una silla, una mesa y un ordenador.
A ¿Qué hay en las paredes?
B En las paredes tengo pósters de Tom Cruise.

3 Lee y mira los dibujos. ¿A quién pertenece el dormitorio?

Bueno, mi dormitorio está muy ordenado y está limpio. Hay una cama, un armario y una mesa con una silla. Es suficiente. Lo mejor es que puedo hacer ejercicio. Hay mucho espacio. Tu dormitorio, Laura, es artístico, bien decorado y me gusta. Lo importante es que es cómodo. El dormitorio de Joaquín es una catástrofe. ¡Es un desastre! Lo peor es que no lo arregla nunca. ¡Es una pocilga!
Jaime
Laura
Joaquín

4 Escribe 5 frases para describir tu dormitorio.

Ejemplo: **Mi dormitorio es (grande). Tiene… También hay… No tiene… En mi opinión es…**

compartir – *to share*
ordenado – *tidy*
arreglar – *to tidy*
la pocilga – *pigsty*

11B Tareas en casa

- say what you have to do at home

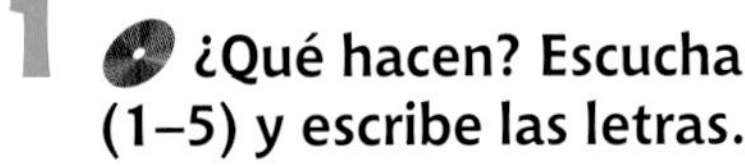

1 **¿Qué hacen? Escucha (1–5) y escribe las letras.**

Ejemplo: **1 E, …**

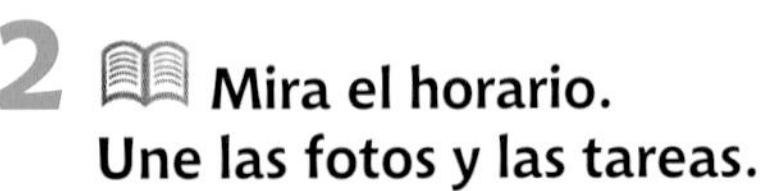

2 **Mira el horario. Une las fotos y las tareas.**

Ejemplo: **A quito el polvo**

	Yolanda	Juanjo	Mariluz
lunes	friego los platos	pongo/quito la mesa	quito el polvo
martes	pongo/quito la mesa	preparo la cena	limpio el salón
miércoles	preparo la cena	paso la aspiradora	friego los platos
jueves	plancho la ropa	quito el polvo	voy de compras
viernes	paso la aspiradora	preparo la cena	pongo/quito la mesa
sábado	voy de compras	lavo el coche	preparo el desayuno
domingo	hago las camas	arreglo mi dormitorio	preparo la comida

3 **Habla con tu pareja.**

A ¿Qué tareas haces el lunes?
B Arreglo mi dormitorio.
A ¿Qué tareas haces el martes?
B Hago la cama y friego los platos.

4 **Une las frases y las fotos de 1.**

Ejemplo: **1 B**

1 Lava el coche.
2 Quita el polvo.
3 Quita/Pone la mesa.
4 Prepara la cena.
5 Friega los platos.
6 Pasa la aspiradora.
7 Hace las camas.
8 Va de compras.

C

5 Mira el cuadro y rellena los espacios.

yo (I)	tú (you)	él/ella (he/she)
lavo	lavas	lava
friego	friegas	friega
pongo la mesa	pones la mesa	pone la mesa
…	quitas la mesa	… la mesa
preparo la comida	preparas la comida	… la comida
plancho	…	…
…	…	pasa la aspiradora
quito el polvo	…	…
…	lavas el coche	…
arreglo mi dormitorio	…	…
limpio	…	…
hago las camas	haces las camas	hace las camas
voy de compras	vas de compras	va de compras

6 Haz un horario de tareas para tu familia o tus hermanos (lunes a domingo). Escribe frases.

	lunes
Mi hermano	lava los platos
Mi hermanastra	prepara el desayuno
Yo	pongo la mesa

Ejemplo: **El lunes mi hermano lava los platos y mi hermanastra…**

7 a Lee al texto. ¿Verdad (V) o mentira (M)?

Se buscan chicos y chicas au pair.
¿Qué es un au pair?

Un au pair es un chico o una chica de 17 a 27 años que vive con una familia y cuida a los niños. No es un empleado doméstico. No recibe mucho dinero. Plancha, lava platos y cuida a los niños cinco horas al día. Tiene dos días de tiempo libre. También tiene tiempo libre para estudiar.

1. Un au pair es masculino o femenino.
2. Au pairs son jóvenes.
3. Les pagan bien.
4. Ayudan en casa y con los niños.
5. Estudian también.
6. Nunca tienen tiempo libre.

7 b *Read the e-mail and write a list of the things Maite does as au pair.*

Example: **Maite looks after the children…**

Querida amiga:

Yo trabajo como au pair y estoy muy triste. Trabajo con una familia. El padre es director de una compañía y viaja mucho. La madre trabaja en el hospital. Trabaja muchas horas.

Hay dos niños: de cinco y tres años. Me levanto a las seis para preparar su desayuno. Les lavo, les visto a los niños y les acompaño a la escuela.

Vuelvo a casa y quito el polvo, paso la aspiradora, lavo la ropa y hago las camas. A las tres y media voy a buscar a los niños y les cuido hasta las ocho.

Ceno con los niños normalmente. No tengo tiempo para estudiar inglés. Estoy libre el domingo pero el sábado estoy con los niños otra vez. Su madre trabaja y el padre juega al golf.

Estoy muy cansada. ¡Los padres son simpáticos pero trabajo demasiado!

Un abrazo,

Maite

11C Actividades

- how to say what you are doing
- revise how to structure a letter

1 a Lee y escucha. ¿Qué hacen?

Ejemplo: **Miguel is doing his homework.**

1 b Juego de memoria. Mira el dibujo durante 30 segundos y cierra tu libro. ¿Qué están haciendo?

Ejemplo: **Miguel está haciendo los deberes.**

2 Escucha. Apunta *a*, *b* o *c*.

1 a Alonso está preparando la comida porque no quiere ir al parque.
b Alonso está preparando la comida porque sus padres no están en casa.
c Alonso está preparando la comida porque sus padres están en el parque.

2 a Bea no quiere ir al polideportivo.
b Bea quiere ir pero está limpiando el cuarto de baño.
c Bea no quiere limpiar el cuarto de baño.

3 a Toda la familia está comiendo.
b José María no quiere ir a la casa de su amigo.
c José María está celebrando en la casa de su amigo.

4 a Isabel está viendo una película muy buena.
b Isabel no quiere ir al cine.
c Isabel quiere ver la película.

5 a Paco tiene un montón de deberes que hacer.
b Paco prefiere ir a la cafetería.
c Paco está haciendo los deberes en la cafetería.

Gramática: the present continuous

The present continuous is used to describe what is happening at the present time.

-*ar* verbs – e.g. *jugar*: **yo:** *Estoy jugando con mis amigos.* I am playing with my friends.

-*er* verbs – e.g. *beber*: **yo:** *Estoy bebiendo Coca-cola.* I am drinking Coke.

-ir verbs – e.g. *salir*: **yo:** *Estoy saliendo con Juan.* I am going out with Juan.

The present continuous is formed in two parts.

a The first part is the present tense of the verb *estar*:
(yo) estoy *(tú) estás* *(él/ella) está*

b The second part is the English '-ing' form in Spanish.
-ar *-ando* *limpiando*
-er/-ir *-iendo* *haciendo/saliendo*

Verbs ending in	present of estar	Remove	Add
-ar	estoy	-ar	-ando preparando
-er	estás	-er	-iendo comiendo
-ir	está	-ir	-iendo escribiendo

3 Escribe frases.
¿Qué están haciendo?

Ejemplo: **A Está escuchando música.**

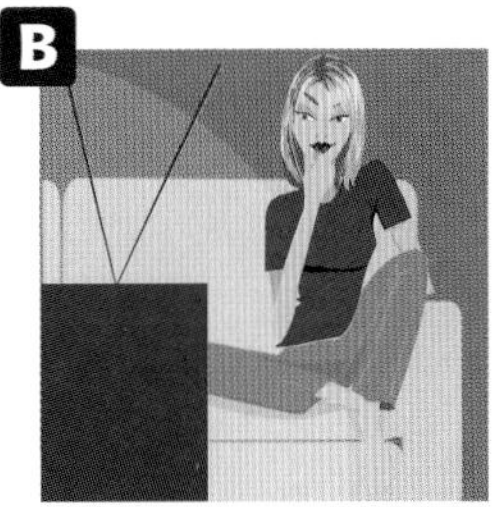

4 ¡extra! **Escucha (1–4).**
Escribe las excusas.
¿Son buenas [✔] o no [✘]?

Ejemplo: **1 Está hablando con Paco. [✘]**

5 **Habla con tu pareja.**

Ejemplo:

A ¿Qué estás haciendo?
B Estoy jugando al tenis. ¿Y tú?
A Estoy…

6 **Lee la carta y adáptala para describir un fin de semana típico.** Cambia **las frases.**

Salamanca, 2 de octubre

Querido Jorge,

¿Qué tal?

Yo estoy muy bien. Te voy a describir un fin de semana típico.

Los sábados me levanto a las nueve y paso mucho tiempo viendo la televisión y escuchando música.

Por la tarde voy al centro con mis amigos, comprando cosas, charlando en la cafetería y tomando tapas.

El domingo ayudo a mis padres: lavando el coche, arreglando mi dormitorio. Y paso la tarde haciendo los deberes, muchos deberes, y escuchando música. Tengo seis horas de deberes más o menos el fin de semana. ¿Tienes muchos deberes?

¿Qué haces tú en tu tiempo libre?

¿Ayudas en casa?

Escríbeme pronto.

Besos,

Sofía

¡Así se hace! *Answering a letter*

Before you answer a letter you must make sure that:

- you understand what it says
- you know what you have to respond to
- you identify what you can reuse from the text
- you know what you can say (and are sure is correct!) and in what order.
- Read through the text once to get the sense of it, and the second time note the things that you have to comment on/answer.
- Next, highlight words, expressions and structures that you can use in your reply. Finally, plan your letter on paper with separate paragraphs, for example, 1 introduction, 2 on Saturday, 3 on Sunday, 4 close.

11D ¿Cómo te entiendes con...?

- talk about relationships at home
- say what you can or can't do

A

puedo salir con mis amigos

B

puedo navegar por Internet

C

puedo ver la televisión en mi dormitorio

D

no puedo escuchar música

E

no puedo fumar

F

puedo invitar a mis amigos a casa

G

no puedo hacer nada

H

nos peleamos mucho

1 Lee y escucha (1–8). Pon los dibujos en orden.

Gramática: *poder* – to be able to

puedo – I can	*¿puedo?* – can I?
puedes – you can	*¿puedes?* – can you?
puede – he/she can	*¿puede?* – can he/she?

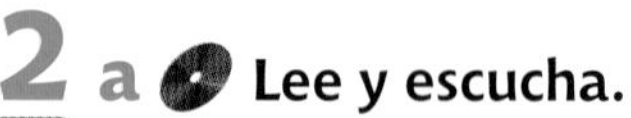

2 a Lee y escucha.

1
A ¿Te entiendes bien con tus padres?
B Sí, me entiendo bien. Son simpáticos y puedo hacer muchas cosas.
A ¿Por ejemplo?
B Puedo salir con mis amigos.
A ¿Algo más?
B Puedo invitar a mis amigos a casa.

2
A ¿Te entiendes bien con tus padres?
B No, no me entiendo con mis padres. Nos peleamos mucho. No son simpáticos. No puedo hacer nada.
A ¿Por ejemplo?
B No puedo navegar por Internet.
A ¿Algo más?
B Sí, no puedo salir con mis amigos.

2 b ¡extra! Habla con tu pareja. Cambia las palabras.

Ejemplo:
A ¿Te entiendes con tus padres?
B Sí, me entiendo bien. Son generosos.
A ¿Por ejemplo?
B Puedo ver la televisión en mi dormitorio.
A ¿Algo más?
B Sí, puedo navegar por Internet.

3 Con tu pareja contesta a las preguntas.

1. ¿Puedes salir con tus amigos? Sí, puedo/No, no puedo…
2. ¿Puedes fumar? Sí, puedo/No, no puedo…
3. ¿Puedes ver la televisión en tu dormitorio? Sí, puedo/No, no puedo…
4. ¿Puedes navegar por Internet? Sí, puedo/No, no puedo…
5. ¿Puedes escuchar música? Sí, puedo/No, no puedo…

amables · las tareas de casa · quince · una visita · jugar · ayudar en casa

4 a Lee la carta y contesta a las preguntas en inglés.

Santiago, 29 de octubre

¡Hola! No estoy muy contenta hoy porque no puedo salir. Normalmente mis padres son muy simpáticos y puedo salir pero hoy tengo que hacer los deberes para un examen mañana. Me entiendo bien con mis padres pero tengo catorce años y creo que puedo decidir si quiero estudiar o no. Y tú, ¿te entiendes bien con ellos? ¿Cómo son?

Un saludo,

Carmen

tengo que hacer los deberes – *I must do homework*

1. How is Carmen feeling today?
2. Why?
3. What does she have to do today?
4. Why?
5. Does she get on well with her parents?
6. What does she say about being 14?

4 b Escribe tu propia carta. Cambia las palabras.

Mi dormitorio	***My bedroom***
compartir	*to share*
mi propio dormitorio	*my own room*
la cortina	*curtain*
el despertador	*alarm clock*
las persianas	*blinds*
el espejo	*mirror*
el estante	*shelf*
la librería	*bookcase*
la mesa	*table*
la mesita de noche	*bedside table*
la pared	*wall*
el póster	*poster*
el ordenador portátil	*laptop*

Tareas	***Chores***
pasar la aspiradora	*to hoover, vacuum*
hacer las camas	*to make the beds*
ir de compras	*to go shopping*
quitar el polvo	*to dust*
lavar el coche	*to wash the car*
arreglar el dormitorio	*to tidy the bedroom*
preparar las comidas	*to prepare the meals*
poner la mesa	*to set the table*
quitar la mesa	*to clear the table*
fregar los platos	*to wash up*
limpiar	*to clean*
planchar	*to iron*

Entenderse en casa	***To get on at home***
entenderse	*to get on*
pelearse	*to fight*
Puedo salir	*I can go out*
¿Puedes escuchar música	*Can you listen to music?*
No puedo invitar a mis amigos	*I can't invite my friends*

Gramática:
Comparisons with *tan… como, más… que, menos… que*
Lo + adjective
The present continuous: *Estoy quitando el polvo*
Poder present tense

Cross-topic words

tan… como – *as… as*
más… que – *more… than*
menos… que – *less… than*

¡Así se hace!

★ Planning a response to a letter

12 El medio ambiente

12A Problemas globales

- understand key environmental issues
- understand and give opinions
- learn how to deal with unknown language

1 a **Lee y escucha. Une las fotos y las descripciones.**

1 El mundo en peligro

El aire, la tierra, el agua y las criaturas y plantas están en una situación cada día más difícil.

2 La contaminación atmosférica

Los gases de los vehículos y el humo de las fábricas contaminan el aire.

3 Los residuos químicos e industriales

Hay muchos residuos en el agua a causa de la industria y la agricultura.

4 La energía nuclear

Las centrales nucleares representan un riesgo. En cada momento hay la posibilidad de un desastre.

5 Las mareas negras

En la costa, accidentes con barcos llenos de petróleo producen mareas negras y una crisis ecológica y económica. El impacto es tremendo.

6 Desechos domésticos

Hay toneladas diarias de desechos domésticos: plásticos, metales, cartón, etcétera.

D

¡Así se hace! *Understanding unknown language*

- List the words on this page that you have never met before. Use the strategies below and then list the words that you still cannot understand. You may not even need the help of the vocabulary list to work out most of the meanings.

  Here is a list of the most common strategies that you can use:

  1. Use the context to work out meanings (topic and pictures help you).
  2. Work out meanings of words similar in Spanish and English (*producen* = produce).
  3. Use patterns within the language (*-dad* in Spanish = -ity in English).
- Check words you think you have worked out the meaning of in the dictionary and look up any you still don't understand. Work with a partner and see if you work out the same meanings. Make a vocabulary list of words you have discovered so far for this topic. Test each other to see if you have already learnt their meanings!

el peligro – *danger*   el humo – *smoke*
las fábricas – *factories*

1 b **Lee los textos otra vez. Pon los peligros en orden de importancia en tu opinión (1 = más importante).**

2 **Escucha y rellena los espacios.**

En mi opinión, el medio ambiente es muy importante.

Hay problemas muy graves.

Primero, la contaminación (1) __________.
El humo de los (2) __________ no es bueno para la salud.

Segundo, la polución del agua también me preocupa.

En la costa hay (3) __________ negras y muchos ríos están (4) __________ por los desechos industriales.

Finalmente, los desechos domésticos son también un (5) __________ muy grave. No se hace lo suficiente para salvar el (6) __________.

problema	planeta	atmosférica
mareas	coches	contaminados

3 a **Lee y escribe las frases en el orden correcto.**

Ejemplo: **1 No me gusta nada la polución porque afecta a la salud.**

1. nada polución no me salud a la afecta porque gusta la.
2. ríos contaminación porque preocupa me la de los el daña mundo.
3. gustan me animales los molestan porque no químicos los desechos.
4. afecta porque polución me la atmosférica miedo tengo.
5. negras animales preocupan me mareas gustan las los me porque.

3 b ¡extra! **Habla con tu pareja. Haz un sondeo.**

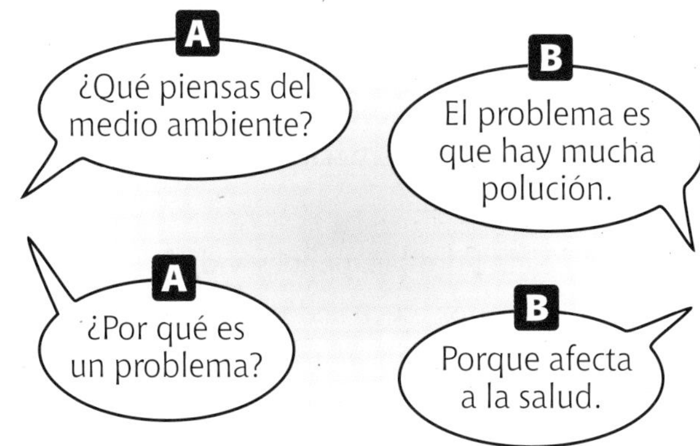
A
¿Qué piensas del medio ambiente?
B
El problema es que hay mucha polución.
A
¿Por qué es un problema?
B
Porque afecta a la salud.

No me gusta(n) nada	la polución atmosférica	porque	afecta(n) a la salud
Me preocupa(n)	la contaminación de los ríos		tengo miedo
Me molesta(n)	los desechos químicos		me gustan los animales, etcétera
Me afecta(n)	las mareas negras		daña(n) el mundo
	los desechos domésticos		no es bueno para la salud
	la energía nuclear		hay la posibilidad de un desastre

12B ¿Qué haces por el medio ambiente?

- understand what others do for the environment
- describe what you do for the environment

1 a Escucha (1–6) y une las instrucciones y los dibujos.

Ejemplo: **1 C**

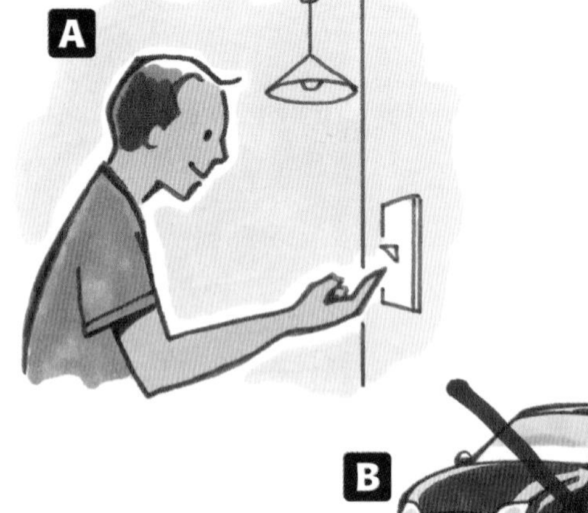
A

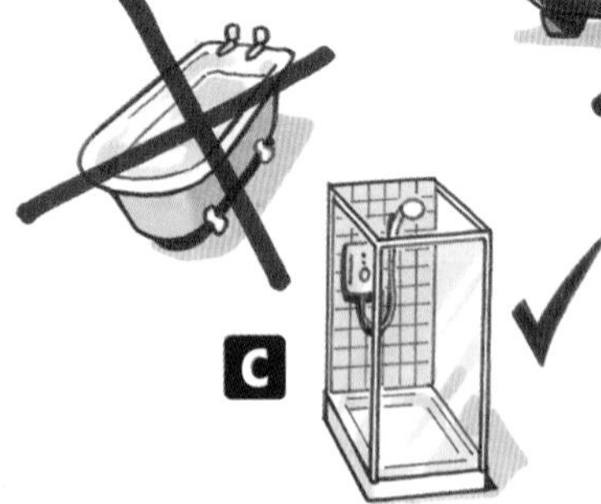
B

C D

E

F

1 b Lee las instrucciones. Une el español y el inglés.

Ejemplo: **1 d**

1 Recicla botellas, papel y vidrio.
2 Usa menos electricidad. Apaga las luces.
3 Dúchate en vez de tomar un baño.
4 No uses menos electricidad: ¡usa más!
5 Usa transporte público y ve andando o en bicicleta.
6 No recicles la basura.
7 No vayas en bicicleta. Ve en coche.
8 Cierra las puertas y ventanas cuando hace frío.
9 No cierres las ventanas y puertas.
10 Toma un baño dos veces al día. No te duches.

a Shower instead of having a bath.
b Have a bath twice a day. Don't shower.
c Use less electricity. Turn off the lights.
d Recycle bottles, paper and glass.
e Don't use less electricity. Use more!
f Don't go by bike. Go by car.
g Don't close windows and doors.
h Don't recycle rubbish.
i Use public transport and walk or go by bike.
j Close doors and windows when it's cold.

recicla – *recycle*
apagar – *to switch off, to put out*
el vidrio – *glass*
la basura – *rubbish*

1 c ¿Ayudan el medio ambiente o no?

Ejemplo: **1 Sí**

2 Escucha (1–6). ¿Qué hacen? Rellena el cuadro.

	¿Ayuda el medio ambiente?					
1	✔	✔				

3 a Lee. ¿Son ecológicos (✔) o no (✘)?

Ejemplo: **Felipe** ✔

A Soy bastante ecológico. Uso menos electricidad. Cuando salgo de una habitación, apago las luces.

B Soy ecologista. Es muy importante. Primero, no voy en coche si es posible. Cojo el autobús o voy andando.

C Francamente no soy ecologista. Me gusta ir en coche y no me gusta ir en bicicleta.

D Soy bastante ecológica porque reciclo el papel y el vidrio.

E ¿Yo, ecológico? No mucho. Mi madre dice que no cierro las ventanas ni las puertas.

F Creo que soy ecologista. Normalmente apago las luces... cierro las ventanas... reciclo la basura...

3 b Habla con tu pareja.

A ¿Eres muy ecológico/a?
B (Sí, bastante.)
A ¿Qué haces en casa?
B (Me ducho. No me baño.) ¿Y tú?
A (Francamente, no.)
B ¿Qué haces?
A (Me baño y no reciclo.)

12C El mundo del futuro

- recognise the future tense

	Español	Inglés
A	Descubriremos cómo eliminar la polución.	We will discover how to get rid of pollution.
B	No habrá suficiente comida.	There won't be enough food.
C	Todo estará bien.	Everything will be fine.
D	Produciremos suficiente comida.	We will produce enough food.
E	La gente no podrá respirar.	People won't be able to breathe.
F	Los ríos estarán contaminados.	The rivers will be contaminated.
G	Habrá animales en los zoos.	There will be animals in zoos.
H	No tendremos la selva.	We won't have any forests.
I	Tendremos tecnología.	We will have the technology.
J	Los animales y plantas desaparecerán.	Animals and plants will disappear.

1 a Lee y escucha (1–10). Pon las frases en orden.

Ejemplo: **1 C**

1 b *Which statements are positive (✔) and which are negative (✘)? Make two lists.*

Example:

Positiva	Negativa
Descubriremos cómo eliminar la polución.	No habrá suficiente comida.

Gramática: the future tense

estar	*comer*	*vivir*
estaré	comeré	viviré
estarás	comerás	vivirás
estará	comerá	vivirá
estaremos	comeremos	viviremos
estaréis	comeréis	viviréis
estarán	comerán	vivirán

Common irregulars:

haber ➡ *habrá*	there will be
hacer ➡ *haré*	I will do/make
poder ➡ *podré*	I will be able
tener ➡ *tendré*	I will have

2 Une el español y el inglés.

Ejemplo: **1 d**

1 En el mar habrá más mareas negras.
2 Yo viviré en la luna.
3 Iré al colegio en un coche eléctrico.
4 Los ríos estarán más limpios.
5 Tú no tendrás coche porque la gasolina será demasiado cara.
6 Podré ir a la playa todo el tiempo.

a I will live on the moon.
b I will be able to go to the beach all the time.
c You won't have a car because petrol will be too expensive.
d There will be more oil slicks in the sea.
e The rivers will be cleaner.
f I will go to school in an electric car.

3 ¡extra! Con tu pareja di unas frases sobre el futuro.

Ejemplo:

A No habrá gasolina.
B Las temperaturas serán más altas.
A …

4 ¡extra! Escribe unas frases sobre el futuro.

Ejemplo: **En el futuro no habrá polución porque los coches serán eléctricos.**

El medio ambiente	***The environment***
la contaminación atmosférica	*air pollution*
la polución	*pollution*
los residuos químicos	*chemical waste*
los desechos domésticos	*domestic waste*
el vidrio	*glass*
el riesgo	*risk*
el peligro	*danger*
grave	*serious*
ecológico	*ecological*
las centrales nucleares	*nuclear power stations*
la basura	*rubbish*
el desastre	*disaster*
la marea negra	*oil slick*
la selva	*forest*
los gases	*gases*
el humo	*smoke*
salvar	*to save*
reciclar	*to recycle*
usar	*to use*
producir	*to produce*
contaminar	*to contaminate*
afectar	*to affect*

Opiniones	***Opinions***
El mundo está en peligro	*The world is in danger*
Hay el riesgo de un desastre nuclear	*There is the risk of a nuclear disaster*
Es un problema muy grave	*It is a very serious problem*

Gramática:
The future tense

¡Así se hace!

★ Understanding unknown language

Cross-topic words

en mi opinión – *in my opinion*
primero – *firstly*
segundo – *secondly*
finalmente – *finally*
habrá – *there will be*

Unidad 12 (¿Problemas? Mira la página 109.)

1 a Escucha (1–5). ¿Qué les afecta? Contesta en inglés.

Ejemplo: **1 A – air pollution**

A air pollution
B danger of a nuclear disaster
C river pollution
D oil slicks
E rubbish in the street

1 b ¡extra! **Escucha otra vez y apunta en inglés por qué piensan así.**

Ejemplo: **1 suffers from asthma**

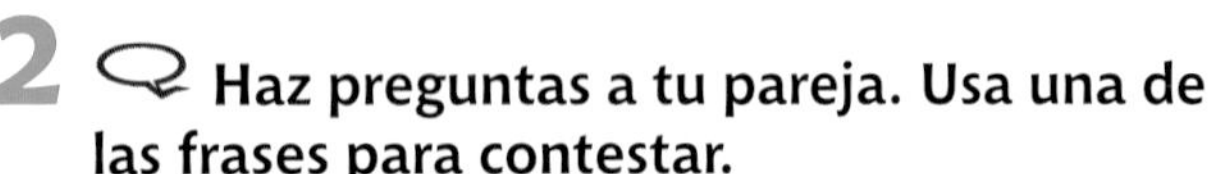

2 Haz preguntas a tu pareja. Usa una de las frases para contestar.

Para usar menos electricidad.
Para no usar mucha calefacción.
Porque voy a reciclarlas.
Porque es más ecológico.

1

A ¿Qué estás haciendo?
B Estoy cerrando las ventanas.
A ¿Por qué?
B …

2

A ¿Qué estás haciendo?
B Estoy buscando mi bicicleta en el garaje.
A ¿Por qué?
B …

3

A ¿Qué estás haciendo?
B Estoy poniendo las botellas en la bolsa.
A ¿Por qué?
B …

4

A ¿Qué estás haciendo?
B Estoy apagando las luces.
A ¿Por qué?
B …

3 Lee el artículo y contesta a las preguntas en inglés.

1 What is the weather like in Athens in the summer?
2 How does it affect people? (Name two ways.)
3 In which part of the city is the Acropolis?
4 What is affected in the Acropolis? How?
5 What does the last sentence say about how serious the problem is?

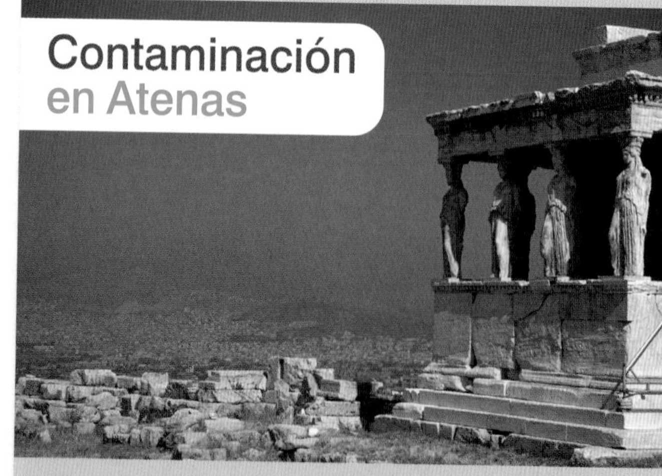

Contaminación en Atenas

En Atenas, en verano hace mucho calor y afecta a millones de personas. Muchas personas mueren durante el verano a causa del calor y la contaminación de los coches. La ciudad antigua sufre niebla y contaminación. En la Acrópolis los gases de los coches afectan mucho a las estatuas. Los problemas han aumentado durante los últimos veinte años.

mueren – *die*
niebla – *fog*
han aumentado – *have increased*

4 Escribe una lista de 6–8 cosas que tú haces en casa para ayudar el medio ambiente.

Ejemplo: **Reciclo latas y papel. Cierro las puertas.**

Juego: Salva el planeta

Juega por turnos. Tira el dado y avanza (>>) y retrocede (<<) según las instrucciones.

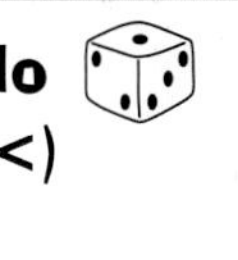

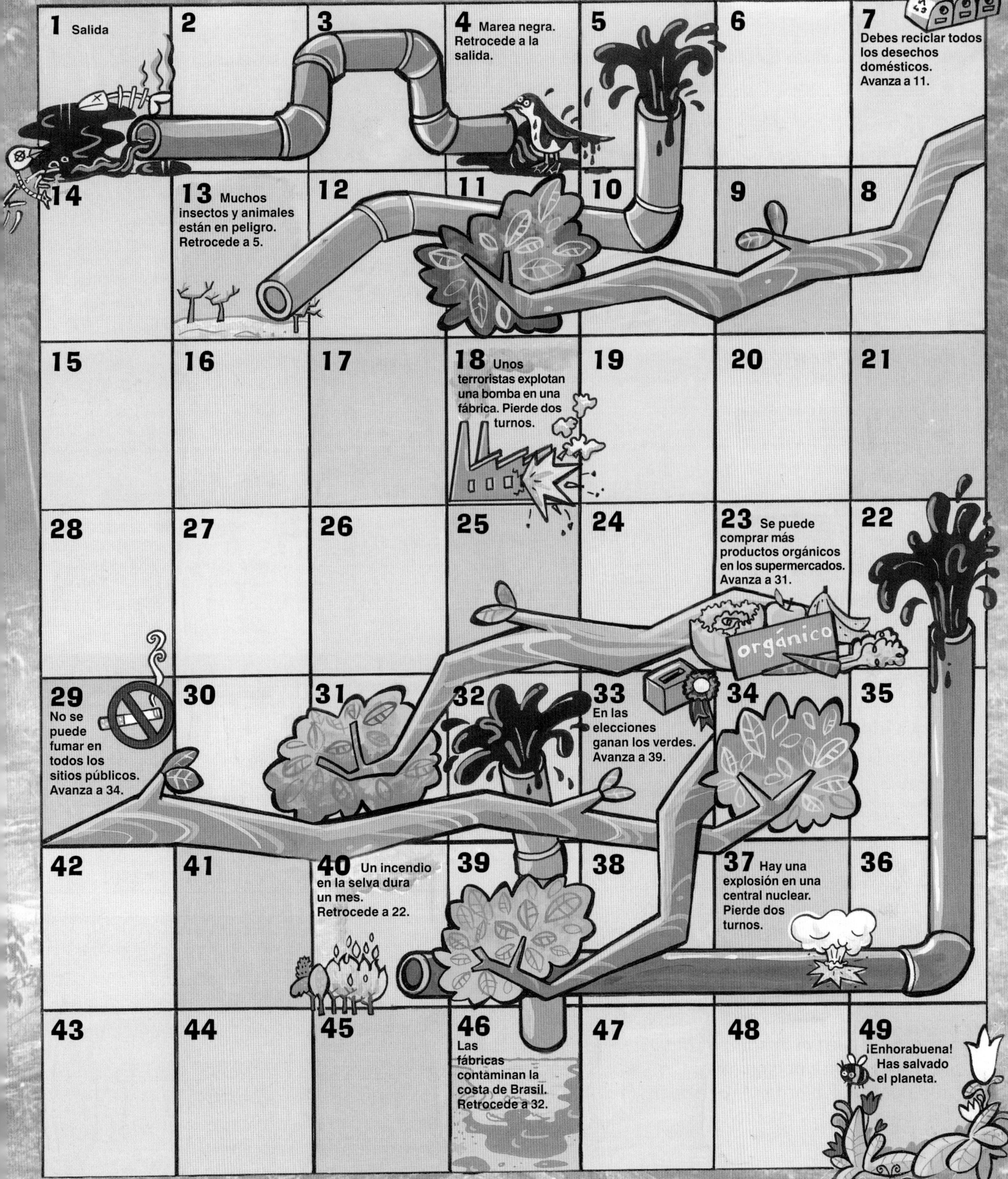

1 Salida	**2**	**3**	**4** Marea negra. Retrocede a la salida.	**5**	**6**	**7** Debes reciclar todos los desechos domésticos. Avanza a 11.
14	**13** Muchos insectos y animales están en peligro. Retrocede a 5.	**12**	**11**	**10**	**9**	**8**
15	**16**	**17**	**18** Unos terroristas explotan una bomba en una fábrica. Pierde dos turnos.	**19**	**20**	**21**
28	**27**	**26**	**25**	**24**	**23** Se puede comprar más productos orgánicos en los supermercados. Avanza a 31.	**22**
29 No se puede fumar en todos los sitios públicos. Avanza a 34.	**30**	**31**	**32**	**33** En las elecciones ganan los verdes. Avanza a 39.	**34**	**35**
42	**41**	**40** Un incendio en la selva dura un mes. Retrocede a 22.	**39**	**38**	**37** Hay una explosión en una central nuclear. Pierde dos turnos.	**36**
43	**44**	**45**	**46** Las fábricas contaminan la costa de Brasil. Retrocede a 32.	**47**	**48**	**49** ¡Enhorabuena! Has salvado el planeta.

¡Así se hace!

- The activities on these pages give you more practice in what you've learnt in each unit.
- Remember, you can look at the vocabulary list at the end of each unit for help if you need it.

1 ***Read what these young people say about what they do whilst on holiday. Match up the pictures and the activities mentioned.*** **(◄◄ p.6)**

ENTREVISTA VACACIONES

¿Qué haces cuando estás de vacaciones?

"Me encanta ir a esquiar en los Pirineos."
1 Maricarmen

"Siempre voy a la playa."
2 Ana

"Me encanta nadar."
Eduardo 3

"Hago windsurf. Es mi pasatiempo favorito."
Juan 4

"Voy de excursión en autocar con mis padres. Es muy aburrido."
Alonso 5

A 

B 

C 

D 

E 

2 ***Look at the picture diary below. Answer these questions.*** **(◄◄ p.7)**

1. ¿A qué hora te levantas?
2. ¿A qué hora te duchas?
3. ¿A qué hora te vistes?
4. ¿A qué hora desayunas?
5. ¿A qué hora te acuestas?

¡extra! ***Can you add some more questions and answers of your own?***

Hora	7:00	7:15	7:30	8:00	12:00
Actividad					

3 ***You find this advertisement for a hotel in Spain on the internet. Make a list in English of 10 things you find out.*** **(◄◄ p.12)**

Example: **It's called Hotel Dalmatos.**

Hotel Dalmatos

http://www.dalmatoshotel.com

Hotel Dalmatos

Abierto de abril a diciembre.
Cerca de la playa.
Todas las habitaciones con ducha, televisión y balcón.
Vistas al mar.
Piscina, restaurante, discoteca, tiendas, sala de juegos, piragüismo, windsurf, equitación y golf.
Excursiones en autocar disponibles cada día.
Ideal para familias.

4 ***Make a list in Spanish of the activities mentioned on this page and put them in order of personal preference (1 = first choice).*** **(◄◄ p.6)**

Example: **1 = el windsurf, 2 =**

1 ***Read the information about the activities. You have 100 euros. What are you going to do? Write a list.*** (◄◄ p.6)

Example: **photo safari 30 euros, water sports 30 euros...**

Camping Sueños
LUNES
Excursión a la montaña. Transporte en 4x4. Se puede observar los animales y los pájaros. Comida incluida. Salida: 6.00 de la mañana. 60.
MARTES
Equitación en la playa. Visita la costa y el campo. Cuatro horas a caballo. Salida: 10.00. 40.
MIÉRCOLES
¿Te gustan los deportes acuáticos? Hay excursiones para pescar, hacer windsurf e ir en barco. Comida (barbacoa) en la playa. Salida: 14.00. 30.
JUEVES
Safari fotográfico en el Parque Leones. Más de 300 animales salvajes. Excursión en autocar. Comida incluida. 30.
VIERNES
¡A bailar toda la noche! Discoteca desde las doce de la noche en la sala de juegos. 20.

2 ***Read this e-mail from Pablo. What plans does he have for this weekend and why?*** (◄◄ p.10)

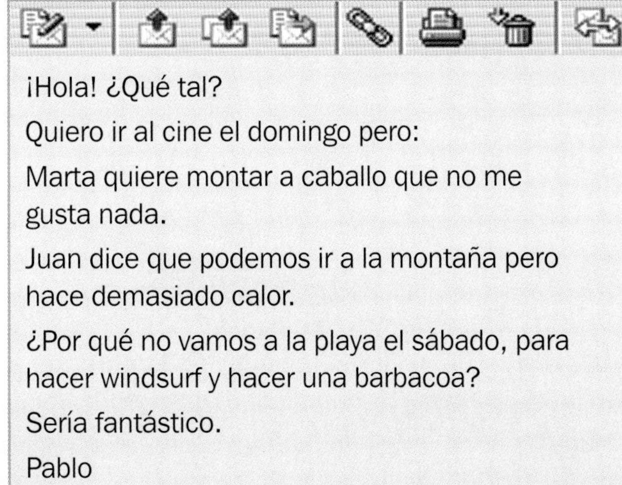
¡Hola! ¿Qué tal?

Quiero ir al cine el domingo pero:

Marta quiere montar a caballo que no me gusta nada.

Juan dice que podemos ir a la montaña pero hace demasiado calor.

¿Por qué no vamos a la playa el sábado, para hacer windsurf y hacer una barbacoa?

Sería fantástico.

Pablo

3 ***Look at the Camping Sueños leaflet again. Write some sentences about what you are going to do every day.*** (◄◄ p.10)

Example: **El lunes voy a ir a la montaña con mi hermano.**

4 ***Complete the postcard, using the leaflet above to help you.***

Martes, 13 de agosto

El lunes fui de ________ a la montaña. Viajé en ________. Saqué muchas fotos de los ________.

El ________ voy a ir a la ________. Voy a hacer todo tipo de deportes ________.

El jueves voy a ver muchos ________ en el Parque Leones.

Voy a ir en ________.

Hasta pronto,

Miguel

1 *Put the parts of the body in the appropriate column, depending on whether they are on the head, between the head and the waist, or between the waist and the feet.* (◄◄ p.15)

el estómago · la nariz · las piernas · los brazos · la garganta · la espalda · las manos · los ojos · los pies

Cabeza	Parte superior del cuerpo	Parte inferior del cuerpo

2 a *Copy the letter and replace the pictures with the appropriate words.* (◄◄ p.17)

¡Hola, Enrique!

¿Qué tal? Yo estoy fatal.

Estoy muy enfermo. [ ] y me duele [ ]. También tengo [ ] y me duele mucho [ ].

El médico dice que debo [ ] y también debo [ ].

¡Qué desastre de fin de semana!

Hasta pronto,

Miguel

2 b *Imagine you are feeling ill too. Answer the letter and explain to your friend what is wrong with you and what the doctor advised. Use the structure below.* (◄◄ p.17)

¡Hola, ____________!

¿Qué tal? Yo estoy fatal.

Me duele ____________ y también me duele ____________.

También tengo ____________.
El médico dice que debo ____________ y ____________.

Hasta pronto.

____

3 *Match up the questions and answers.* (◄◄ p.17)

1 ¿Qué te pasa?
2 ¿Qué te duele?
3 ¿Qué dice el médico?
4 ¿Cuánto es un paquete de aspirinas?
5 ¿Llevas una vida sana?

a El médico dice que debo irme a la cama.
b Me duele mucho la garganta.
c Sí, como muchas verduras y hago ejercicio.
d Son 3.
e Tengo una insolación.

1 ***Match up the problems with the most appropriate piece of advice. There might be more than one possibility.*** (◄◄ p.18)

1 Me duelen la cabeza y la garganta.

2 Tengo una insolación y tengo fiebre.

3 Me duele mucho la espalda.

4 Tengo mucha tos y me duele la garganta.

5 Me duelen mucho los ojos – están muy rojos.

A Debes ponerte una crema para el dolor de músculos.

B Debes tomar una aspirina y debes irte a la cama.

C Si tienes fiebre, creo que debes ir al médico.

D Debes ponerte unas gotas para los ojos.

E Debes tomar un vaso de agua o tomar una pastillas para la tos.

2 a ***Read the brochure on healthy living. Answer the questions in English.*** (◄◄ p.20)

1 What should your diet be like?
2 What should you eat and drink a lot of?
3 What should you not eat and drink a lot of?
4 How much exercise should you do?
5 How long should you sleep for?
6 What else should you not do?

2 b ***Design your own brochure to advertise healthy living.*** (◄◄ p.20)

equilibrada – *balanced*
suficiente – *enough*
grasa – *fat*
sal – *salt*
demasiada – *too much*
menos de – *less than*

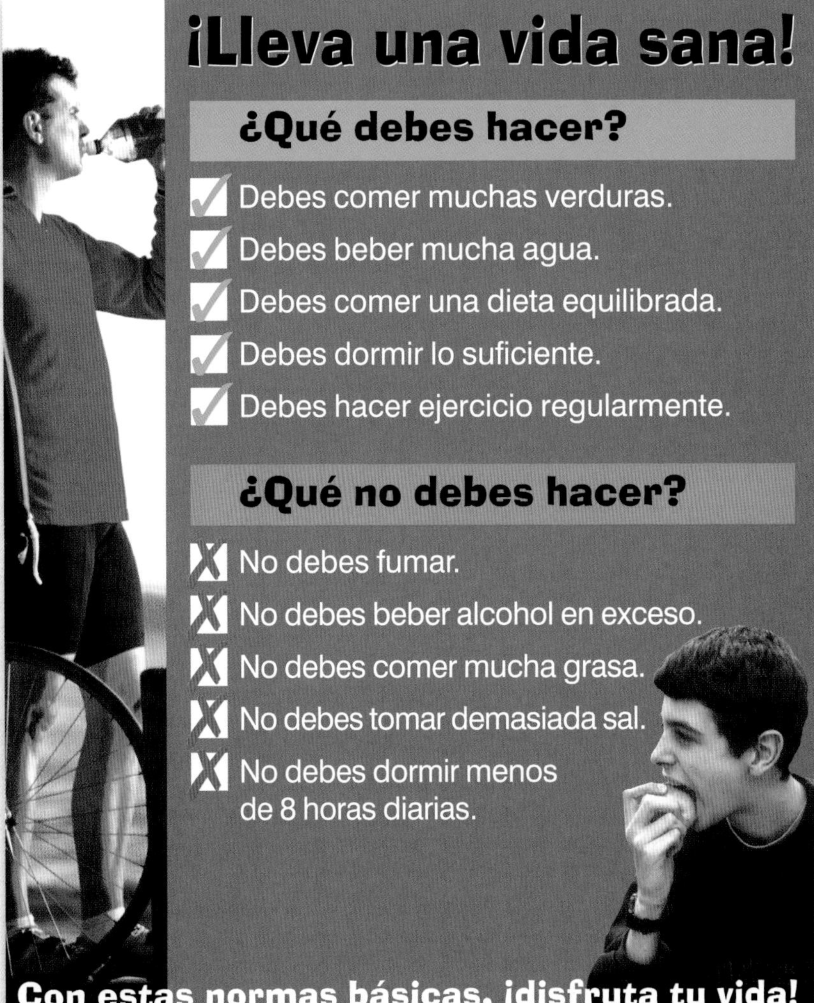

¡Lleva una vida sana!
¿Qué debes hacer?
Debes comer muchas verduras.
Debes beber mucha agua.
Debes comer una dieta equilibrada.
Debes dormir lo suficiente.
Debes hacer ejercicio regularmente.
¿Qué no debes hacer?
No debes fumar.
No debes beber alcohol en exceso.
No debes comer mucha grasa.
No debes tomar demasiada sal.
No debes dormir menos de 8 horas diarias.
Con estas normas básicas, ¡disfruta tu vida!

1 a ***Match up the questions and answers.*** (<< p.25)

1 ¿Adónde fuiste de vacaciones?
2 ¿Qué visitaste?
3 ¿Con quién fuiste?
4 ¿Qué comiste?
5 ¿Qué bebiste?
6 ¿Cómo lo pasaste?

a Bebí limonada.
b Comí pollo con patatas fritas.
c Fui a Portugal.
d Fui con mi familia y mi amiga Elena.
e Lo pasé muy bien.
f Visité monumentos y museos.

1 b ***Answer the questions for yourself talking about your own holidays. Change these words.*** (<< p.25)

2 ***Read the e-mail and say whether the statements are true (T) or false (F).*** (<< p.25)

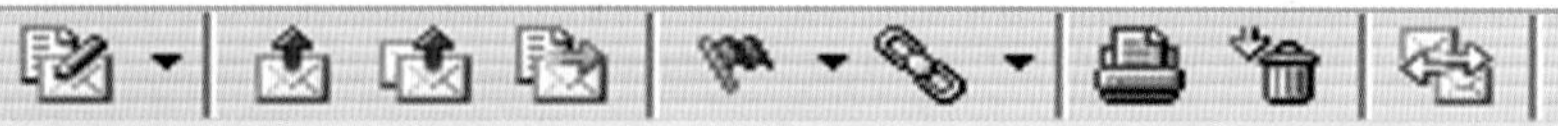

¡Hola, Ignacio!

¿Cómo estás?

Fui de vacaciones en julio. Fui con mis amigos Tom y Matt. Fuimos a España, porque me gustan mucho el sol y el windsurf.

Fui a un camping muy grande que se llama Las Palmeras. Visité los pueblos en la montaña y bebí sangría. Por la noche fui a las discotecas en la costa. Lo pasé fantástico.

¿Y tú? ¿Qué tal tus vacaciones?

Michael

1 Michael fue de vacaciones con su familia.
2 A Michael no le gusta el sol.
3 Fue a un hotel.
4 Visitó monumentos y museos.
5 Bebió mucha Coca-cola.
6 Por la noche fue a las discotecas.
7 Michael lo pasó fatal.

1 Match up the pictures and write the sentences. Use the box. Look at the example. (◄◄ p.28)

Example: **Nevó, así que fui a esquiar.**

2 Match up the pictures and sentences. (◄◄ p.30)

1. Bebí agua con gas.
2. Comí en un restaurante.
3. Fui a Francia.
4. Compré una camiseta.
5. Fui con mis amigos.
6. Hizo frío.
7. Lo pasé muy bien.
8. Me alojé en un hotel.
9. Visité París.

3 Answer the questions to describe your last holiday. (◄◄ p.30)

1. ¿Adónde fuiste? Fui a…
2. ¿Dónde te alojaste? Me alojé en…
3. ¿Con quién fuiste? Fui con…
4. ¿Qué compraste? Compré…
5. ¿Qué comiste? Comí…
6. ¿Qué hiciste? Jugué…/Escuché…/Tomé el sol…
7. ¿Cómo lo pasaste? Lo pasé…

1 a *Which word is the odd one out in each group? Can you give a reason?* (◄◄ p.36)

1 manzana pera huevo naranja
2 pollo pescado jamón bistec
3 desayuno comida cena plato
4 zumo bebida agua leche
5 cafetería supermercado restaurante pizzería

1 b *Check the meanings of these words. Put them into groups.* (◄◄ p.36)

Example: **manzana, pera, naranja = fruta**

atún bacalao sorbete flan *manzana* tomates pollo helado *pera* bistec jamón patatas *naranja* ensalada hamburguesa cebolla salmón gambas chocolate

2 a *Write your answers to these questions about food and drink.* (◄◄ p.35)

1. ¿Qué comes en el desayuno?
2. ¿Qué bebes?
3. ¿Cuál es tu plato favorito?
4. ¿Prefieres carne o pescado?
5. ¿Comes en el instituto todos los días?
6. ¿A qué hora cenas?
7. ¿Qué comes en la calle?

2 b *What can you remember? Write a list of four words to go under each of these headings.* (◄◄ p.35)

1 desayuno **2** comida rápida **3** bebidas **4** fruta **5** verduras

3 *Write menus for two of the following.* (◄◄ p.36)

a a fast food restaurant in Spain serving soft drinks
b a typical Spanish restaurant
c a restaurant in Spain serving Mexican or Italian dishes.

Use the following as examples.

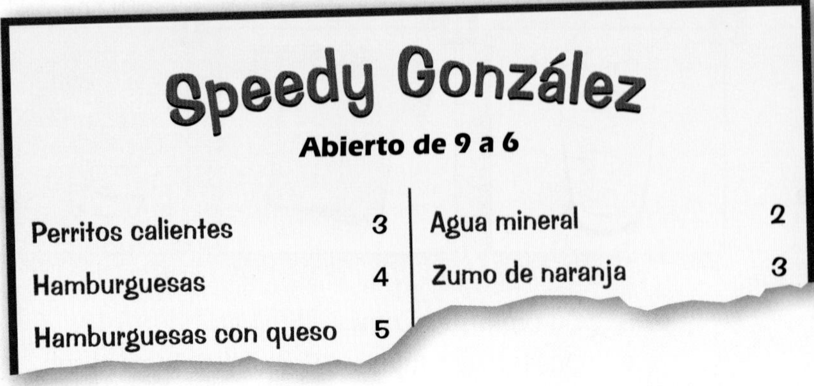

Speedy González
Abierto de 9 a 6
Perritos calientes 3
Hamburguesas 4
Hamburguesas con queso 5
Agua mineral 2
Zumo de naranja 3

Casa Miguel
Almuerzo 1–4
Menú turístico 35
Primer plato
Sopa de pescado
Tortilla española

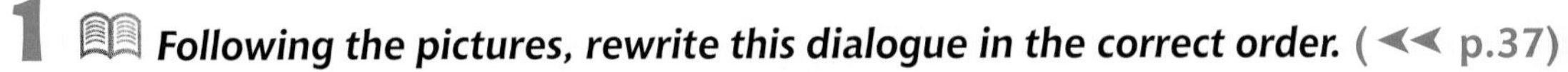

1 ***Following the pictures, rewrite this dialogue in the correct order.*** (◄◄ p.37)

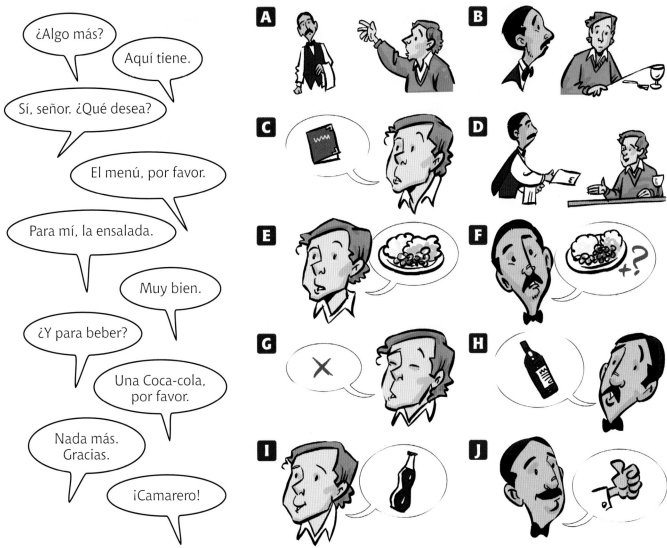

¿Algo más?

Aquí tiene.

Sí, señor. ¿Qué desea?

El menú, por favor.

Para mí, la ensalada.

Muy bien.

¿Y para beber?

Una Coca-cola, por favor.

Nada más. Gracias.

¡Camarero!

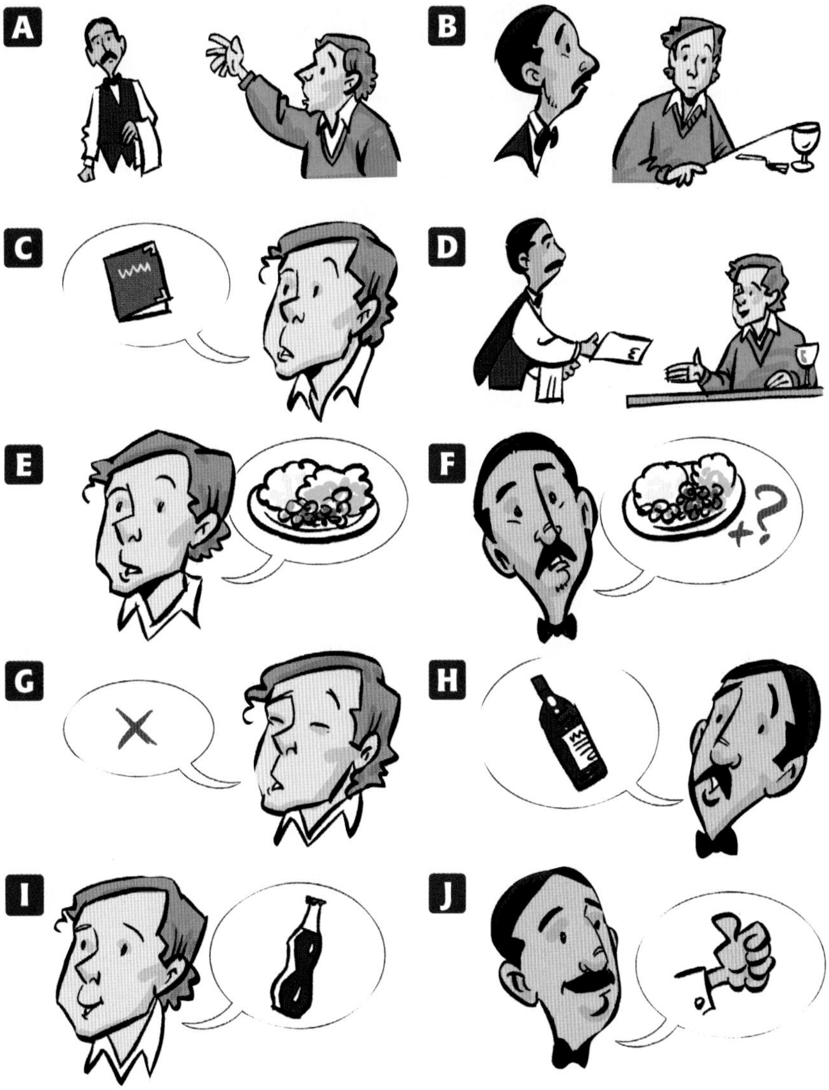

A B C D E F G H I J

2 ***Read the e-mail and complete it with the words provided.*** (◄◄ p.33)

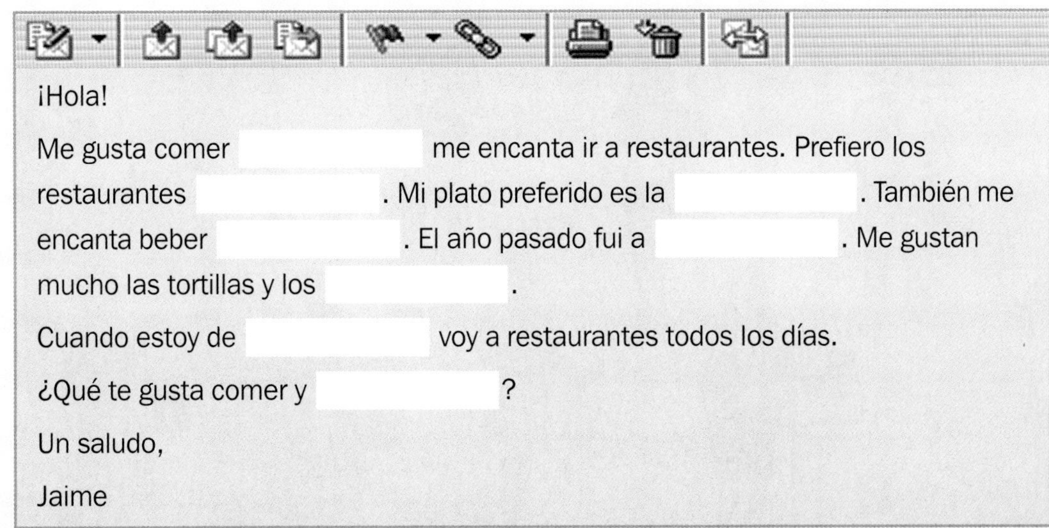

¡Hola!

Me gusta comer ______ me encanta ir a restaurantes. Prefiero los restaurantes ______. Mi plato preferido es la ______. También me encanta beber ______. El año pasado fui a ______. Me gustan mucho las tortillas y los ______.

Cuando estoy de ______ voy a restaurantes todos los días.

¿Qué te gusta comer y ______?

Un saludo,

Jaime

1 ***Look at this family tree. Complete the statements below by adding the correct name of each person described.*** (◄◄ p.42)

1 Mi abuelo se llama ________________.
2 Mi madre se llama ________________.
3 Mi hermano menor se llama ________________.
4 Te presento a mi abuela, ________________.
5 Mi padre, ________________, es muy alto.
6 Yo me llamo ________________.

2 a ***Find the meanings of these adjectives.*** (◄◄ p.43)

2 b ¡extra! ***Write a job advertisement for a ski instructor, a secretary and a babysitter.*** (◄◄ p.43)

Example:

Se busca instructor de esquí. Se busca persona trabajadora, atleta, simpática y positiva.

3 ***Match up the pictures and the jobs.*** (◄◄ p.46)

secretaria
mecánico
empleado de banco
enfermera
camarera
médico
dependienta
ingeniero
estudiante
director

1 Do this quiz. Answer the questions and look at the results. (<< p.43)

¿Qué tipo de persona eres?

1 ¿Qué color prefieres?
a Rojo
b Azul
c Negro

2 ¿Cuándo es tu cumpleaños?
a En verano
b En invierno
c En primavera

3 ¿Qué actividad prefieres?
a El fútbol
b La lectura
c Ver la televisión

4 ¿Prefieres salir...?
a Solo
b Con amigos
c Con tu familia

5 ¿Dónde prefieres trabajar?
a En una oficina
b En un instituto
c Al aire libre

6 ¿Cuál es tu número favorito?
a Uno
b Cinco
c Siete

7 ¿Ayudas en casa?
a No, nunca
b Sí, mucho
c Hago mi cama y nada más

8 ¿Qué tipo de música prefieres?
a La música pop
b La música romántica
c La música clásica

Resultados

	a	b	c
1	10	5	0
2	0	5	10
3	0	10	5
4	0	5	10
5	10	5	0
6	5	10	0
7	0	10	5
8	0	5	10

60–80 Eres sensible, honesto, paciente y serio.
30–55 Eres trabajador, práctico y simpático.
0–25 Eres egoísta y un poco antipático.

1 a *Match up the descriptions and the pictures.* (◄◄ p.52)

1 Mi uniforme consiste en una camisa blanca, un jersey rojo, una falda de cuadros, unos calcetines rojos y zapatos planos.

2 Mi uniforme es bastante elegante. Consiste en un jersey celeste, un polo blanco, una falda de cuadros, medias y zapatos de tacón negros.

3 Mi uniforme consiste en un polo blanco, unos pantalones grises, un jersey rojo y zapatos negros.

A

B

C

D

1 b *Write the missing description.* (◄◄ p.52)

Mi uniforme consiste en...

2 *Copy the letter and complete it with the appropriate words. Use the words in the box below.* (◄◄ p.54)

preocupada – *worried*
tengo que – *I have to*
elegir – *choose*
asignaturas – *subjects*

¡Hola, Eva!

¿Qué tal te va? Yo estoy un poco preocupada. Tengo que elegir mis asignaturas para el año próximo y es difícil.

Me gustaría estudiar un idioma. Me gusta el 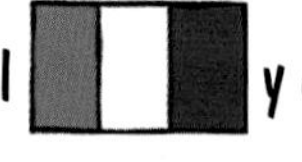 y el pero tengo que elegir. Es obligatorio estudiar 2+2=4 pero para mí son muy . Mi asignatura favorita es la  pero el profesor es muy . También tengo que elegir historia o . Creo que estudiaré tecnología, porque el profesor es muy .

¿Y tú? ¿Qué vas a estudiar el año próximo?

Escribe pronto.

Un beso,

María Luisa

difíciles
matemáticas
francés
desorganizado
geografía
música
divertido
inglés

1 *Put the words in the sentences into the correct order.* (◄◄ p.56)

1 asignatura el es es español favorita la Mi porque profesora simpática.
2 elegante. encanta es Me mi muy porque uniforme
3 de desorganizado. es estricto Mi muy muy pero profesor religión también
4 clases. colegio comer chicle En en las mi no puede se
5 a año El estudiar inglés matemáticas. próximo voy y
6 es gustaría ingeniero interesante. Me muy porque ser trabajo un

2 *Read the list of rules and match them up with the pictures.* (◄◄ p.50)

1 Hay que llevar uniforme.
2 No se puede comer chicle.
3 En el recreo no se puede salir del colegio.
4 Hay que llegar a clase a tiempo.
5 No se puede entrar en el polideportivo sin zapatillas de deporte.
6 No se puede tirar basura.
7 No se puede estar dentro de las clases en el recreo.
8 En el recreo se puede ir al patio o a la biblioteca.

A

B

C
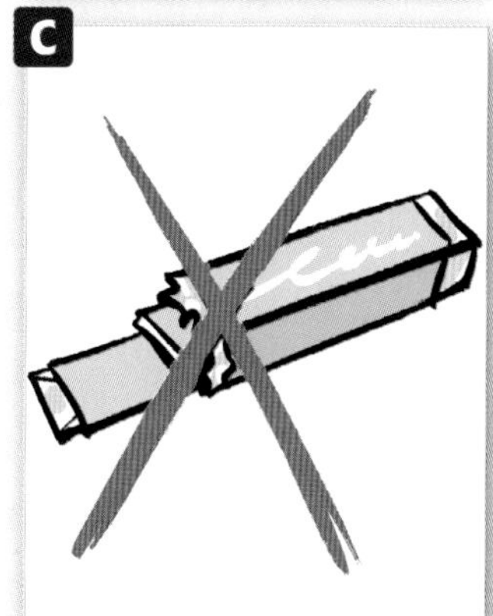

D

E

F

G
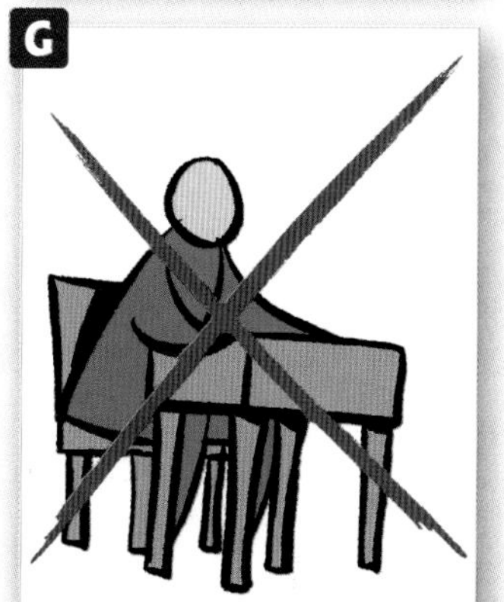

H

3 *Write a similar list of rules for your own school.* (◄◄ p.50)

1 ***Unscramble the names of the shops and match them up with the pictures.*** (◄◄ p.60)

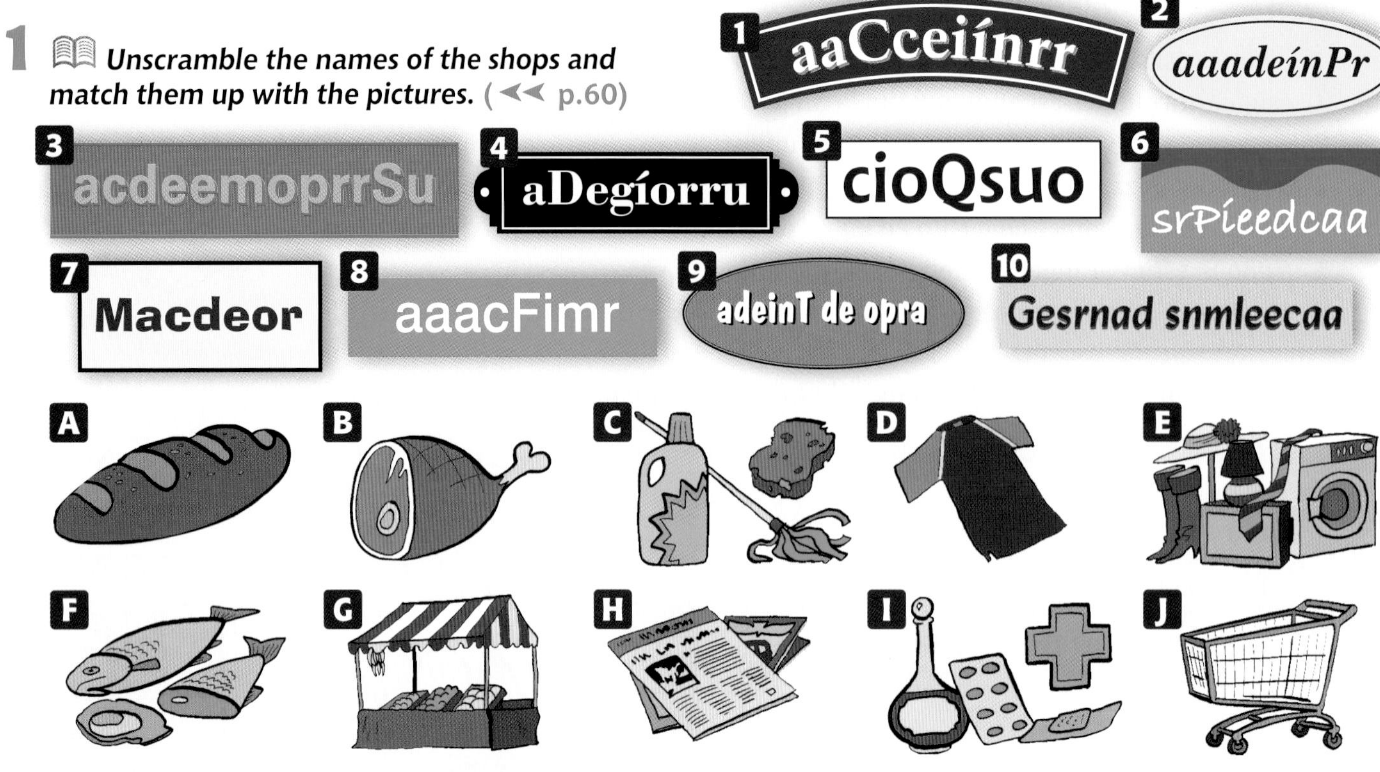

2 ***Match up the labels with the prices.*** (◄◄ p.62)

1 uno con treinta y seis euros
2 doce con veinticuatro euros
3 quince con cuarenta euros
4 dieciséis con doce euros
5 tres con sesenta y cinco euros
6 trece con setenta y cinco euros

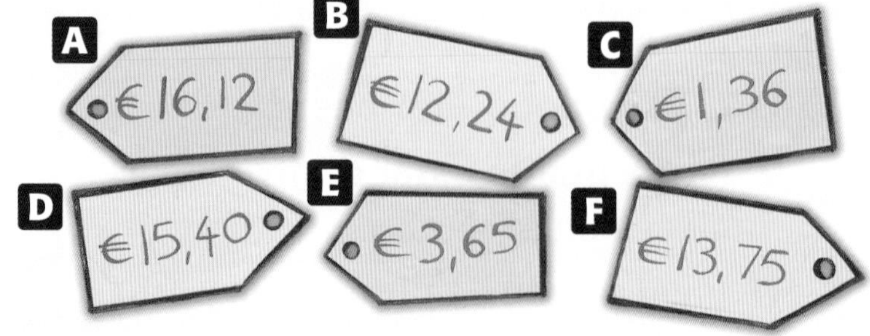

3 ***Write eight sentences to describe where the objects are.*** (◄◄ p.61)

Example: **Las naranjas están a la derecha de las manzanas.**

1 Match up the containers or amounts with the pictures. Then choose one of them for each product in the list. (◄◄ p.62)

1 una caja
2 una lata
3 200 gr
4 un kilo
5 una docena
6 un paquete
7 una barra
8 medio kilo
9 un tubo
10 3 kilos

pasta de dientes	tomates
Coca-cola	té
naranjas	huevos
limones	salchichas
café	pan
pollo	pescado
patatas	jamón

2 a Read about Marta's shopping trip and put the pictures into the correct order. (◄◄ p.66)

El sábado pasado fui al centro de la ciudad. Primero fui a una zapatería y compré unos zapatos negros muy bonitos. Después fui a los grandes almacenes y compré un perfume para el cumpleaños de mi madre. Salí del centro comercial y fui a una cafetería para beber un café. Finalmente, fui al supermercado. Compré unas salchichas y fruta, y también limonada. Fui a casa en autobús.

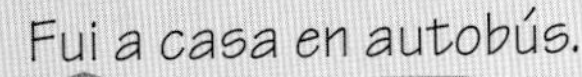

2 b Copy and fill in the grid. (◄◄ p.66)

Sitio	¿Para qué?
zapatería	Compré zapatos negros

1 *Unscramble the names of the 9 means of transport.* (◀◀ p.68)

2 *At the railway station. Write out the dialogue in the correct order.* (◀◀ p.71)

– Dos horas.
– ¿Quiere un billete sencillo o un billete de ida y vuelta?
– El jueves, 15.
– Hay un tren a las once y media.
– Vale, gracias.
– Muy bien. ¿Cuánto tiempo dura el viaje?
– Un billete de ida y vuelta.
– ¡Hola! Quiero ir a Sevilla.
– ¿Cuándo quiere viajar?

3 *Look at the timetable and answer the questions.* (◀◀ p.70)

Example: **1 El tren para Madrid sale a las ocho.**

1 ¿A qué hora sale el tren para Madrid?
2 ¿A qué hora llega el tren a Barcelona?
3 ¿Cuánto tiempo dura el viaje del tren para Málaga?
4 ¿Cuánto cuesta un billete sencillo para Gijón?
5 ¿Cuánto cuesta un billete para niño en el tren para Barcelona?

Horario de Trenes

http://www.horariodetrenes.com

Horario de Trenes

Destino	Salida	Llegada	Precios (billete sencillo)
Madrid	8.00	11.00	8,50
Barcelona	8.45	10.40	10,00/7,00 niño
Bilbao	9.07	12.15	6,20
Málaga	10.45	13.40	18,00/9,00 niño
Gijón	11.50	14.35	7,50

4 *How do you travel to school? Write a few sentences.* (◀◀ p.70)

Example: **Voy al... en... Es (cómodo). No voy en... porque es (lento).**

1 Match up sentences 1–6 with the most appropriate means of transport (a–f). (◀◀ p.71)

1 Quiero visitar a mi padre en Inglaterra.
2 Tengo prisa y quiero irme a casa.
3 Me encanta navegar por el mar.
4 Voy desde Madrid a Barcelona.
5 Quiero ir de excursión a las montañas.
6 Voy al colegio.

a Hay un tren directo.
b Coge un avión.
c Vete en barco.
d La parada de autobuses está a la derecha.
e Un taxi es lo mejor.
f Hay una excursión en autocar el sábado.

2 At the railway station. Complete the dialogue using the clues. (◀◀ p.71)

A Buenos días. Quiero ir a _______ por favor.
B ¿Cuándo quiere viajar?
A ______________________.
B ¿A qué hora quiere viajar?
A A _____________ por favor.
B ¿Un billete sencillo o de ida y vuelta?
A _____________ ¿Cuánto cuesta?
B 50.

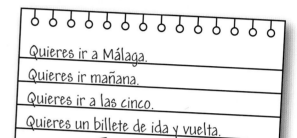

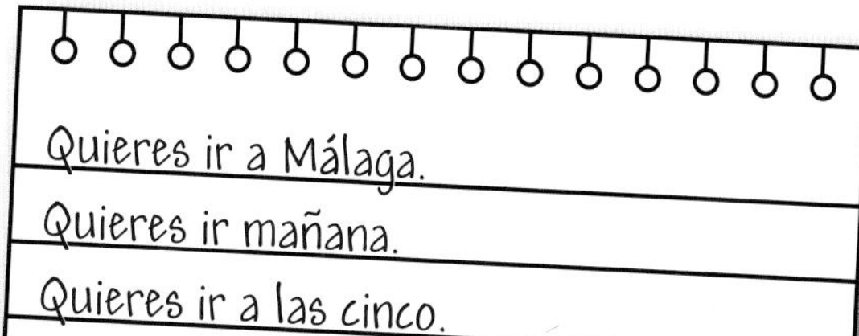

Quieres ir a Málaga.
Quieres ir mañana.
Quieres ir a las cinco.
Quieres un billete de ida y vuelta.

3 Complete the table with the advantages and disadvantages mentioned for each means of transport. (◀◀ p.69)

Transporte	Ventajas	Desventajas
autobús	barato, cómodo	
metro		ruidoso
coche		
taxi	–	
bicicleta		–

A En mi opinión el autobús es barato y bastante cómodo. Bien, no me gusta ir en metro. Es ruidoso y la gente me molesta.

B Suelo ir en coche porque es práctico y rápido. Pero es caro también. Y no me gusta ir en autobús, hay demasiada gente y es lento.

C Para mí lo mejor es el metro. Es más rápido que el autobús y es limpio y barato. Los taxis son muy caros y detesto los autobuses.

D Siempre voy en bicicleta. Es práctico y barato. También es buen ejercicio. Es muy sano.

4 Write 5 sentences about public transport using the words below. (◀◀ p.69)

Example: Me gusta ir en autobús porque es barato.

porque · prefiero · demasiado · no me gusta · me gusta · ruidoso · barato · cómodo · lento · muy

1 Write a sentence to express your opinion about the types of films below. Use the box to help you. (◄◄ p.82)

Example: **Odio las películas románticas porque son aburridas.**

Me encantan	las películas	porque son	entretenidas
Me gustan (mucho)	de dibujos animados		divertidas
No me gustan (nada)	de acción		aburridas
Odio	románticas		interesantes
	de horror		emocionantes
	de ciencia ficción		un rollo

2 Match up the questions and answers. (◄◄ p.81)

1 ¿Qué tipo de película prefieres?
2 ¿Prefieres la radio o la televisión?
3 ¿Te gustan las revistas?
4 ¿Qué te parecen los documentales?
5 ¿Qué programas ves los sábados por la tarde?

a No me gustan nada las revistas.
b Me encantan las comedias porque son muy divertidas.
c Normalmente veo la serie 'Embrujadas', que me gusta mucho.
d Prefiero la televisión porque es más entretenida.
e Me gustan los documentales porque son interesantes.

3 Match up the Spanish and the English sentences. Are they true for you? Change the ones which are not true for you. (◄◄ p.82)

1 Veo la televisión dos horas cada semana.
2 Mi autor favorito es Stephen King porque sus libros son increíbles.
3 Me gustan las series porque son muy divertidas.
4 Esta tarde voy a ver una película en el canal 2.
5 Odio las películas de acción porque son demasiado violentas.

a I hate action films because they are too violent.
b I like series because they are fun.
c I watch two hours of TV a week.
d My favourite author is Stephen King because his books are amazing.
e This afternoon I am going to watch a film on Channel 2.

1 *Read the interview with the author Blanca Pardo. Answer the questions in English.* (◄◄ p.84)

Hola, Blanca. ¿Qué tal?

Muy bien.

Tu última novela se llama *Sueños de Cristal*. ¿Qué tipo de novela es?

Bueno, tiene diferentes elementos. Hay mucha acción, también hay una parte romántica, y hay elementos de ciencia ficción.

¿Para qué público es?

Es una novela para gente bastante joven, entre quince y veinte años.

Y, ¿cómo es el protagonista, Miguel Bernal?

Es un chico de dieciséis años, que no es muy popular. Pero de repente entra en una historia de suspense y ciencia ficción, que se complica muchísimo.

¡Qué interesante! Muchas gracias, Blanca.

De nada. Hasta pronto.

Blanca

1 What is the novel's title?
2 What three different elements can be found in the novel?
3 Who is the novel aimed at?
4 What is the protagonist like?
5 What sort of story does the protagonist get mixed up in?

2 *Match up the texts with the different media.* (◄◄ p.78)

1 Son muy emocionantes y los actores son muy buenos. ¡Y muy guapos!

2 Es un libro que es difícil dejar de leer.

3 Hay muchos tipos de artículos: de moda, de belleza, de salud...

4 Hay diferentes programas a diferentes horas. Hay programas de música, debates y noticias.

5 Hay páginas con mucha información: sobre las noticias, el tiempo, literatura, programas de ordenador...

6 Hay programas de todo tipo: documentales, películas, series. Hay una gran variedad.

cine radio novelas revistas televisión Internet

3 *Match up the Spanish and the English sentences. Are they true for you?* (◄◄ p.78)

1 Me gusta la televisión porque es entretenida.
2 Odio la radio porque es muy monótona.
3 Me encantan las revistas pero son un poco caras.
4 No me gusta Internet, creo que es demasiado aburrido.
5 Me encantan los periódicos, son muy interesantes.
6 Mi medio de comunicación favorito es el cine, porque es muy emocionante.

a I don't like the Internet, I think it is too boring.
b My favourite media is the cinema because it is very exciting.
c I love newspapers, they are very interesting.
d I like TV because it is entertaining.
e I love magazines but they are a bit expensive.
f I hate the radio because it is monotonous.

4 *Write 5 sentences giving your opinions on the different media.* (◄◄ p.78)

Example: **Me encantan los periódicos. Son muy interesantes. Odio la radio porque es muy aburrida.**

1 a ***Match up the questions and the answers about last Christmas.*** (◀◀ p.89)

1 ¿Dónde comiste la cena de Navidad?
2 ¿Con quién comiste?
3 ¿Qué comiste?
4 ¿Qué bebiste?
5 ¿Qué regalos recibiste?
6 ¿Qué hiciste el 31 de diciembre?
7 ¿Cómo lo pasaste?

a Bebí limonada, y un poco de vino tinto.
b Comí pavo y patatas.
c Comí con mi familia: mis padres, mi hermana, mis tíos y mis primos.
d Fui a una fiesta con mis amigos.
e Lo pasé genial.
f Recibí dinero y un ordenador nuevo.
g Comí la cena de Navidad en la casa de mis tíos.

1 b ***Write a short description of what you did last Christmas. Use the answers in 1a to help you.*** (◀◀ p.89)

2 a ***Match up the Spanish festivals and the photos.*** (◀◀ p.86)

1 El día de la Madre
2 La Feria de Sevilla
3 El día del Padre
4 La Navidad
5 La Semana Santa
6 San Fermín

2 b ***Write sentences about what happens in the festivals in 2a. Use the box to help you. There are many different possibilities.*** (◀◀ p.86)

Se baila	a la iglesia	a las madres
Se bebe	carreras de toros	a los padres
Se come	procesiones	con la familia
Se dan	flamenco	con los amigos
Se va	pavo	por las calles
Se ven	vino dulce	
	regalos	

1 *Put the words in the sentences into the correct order.* (◄◄ p91)

1 con El España fui a mis padres. pasado verano
2 el en la playa. sol Tomé
3 a días. Fui la los piscina todos
4 a amigos. con discoteca fui la mis noche Una
5 al en fútbol Jugué la playa.
6 apartamento. en Me quedé un
7 genial. Lo pasé

2 a *A disastrous day. Fill in the gaps with the words provided.*
Watch out: You won't need all the words. (◄◄ p.92)

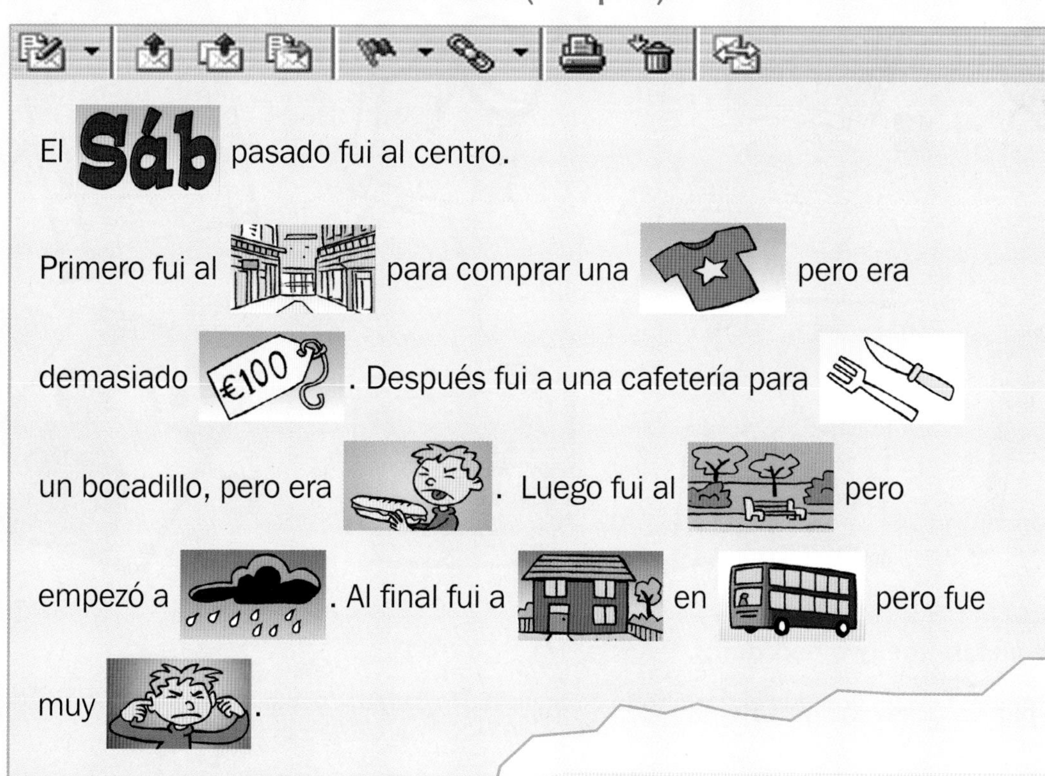
El Sáb pasado fui al centro.

Primero fui al para comprar una pero era demasiado €100. Después fui a una cafetería para un bocadillo, pero era . Luego fui al pero empezó a . Al final fui a en pero fue muy .

¿Y tú? ¿Qué hiciste el sábado?

autobús
camiseta
centro comercial
sol
horrible
cara
casa
coche
comer
ruidoso
llover
parque
sábado
tranquilo

El sábado pasado fui a...		
Primero...	fui...	al centro
Después...	compré...	con mis amigos
Luego...	comí...	un bocadillo
Al final...	bebí...	un café
	vi....	una película
Lo pasé	genial/muy bien/muy mal/fantástico/fatal	

2 b *Write an e-mail describing what you did last Saturday.* (◄◄ p.92)

1 *Match up the words and the pictures.* (≪ p.96)

1 la cama	**4** el vídeo	**7** el equipo de música	**10** la silla
2 el ordenador	**5** el póster	**8** la televisión	**11** la mesa
3 la lámpara	**6** el despertador	**9** la revista	**12** el espejo

A
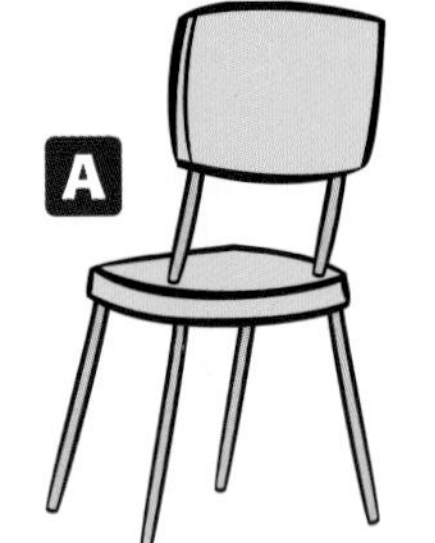
B

C

D
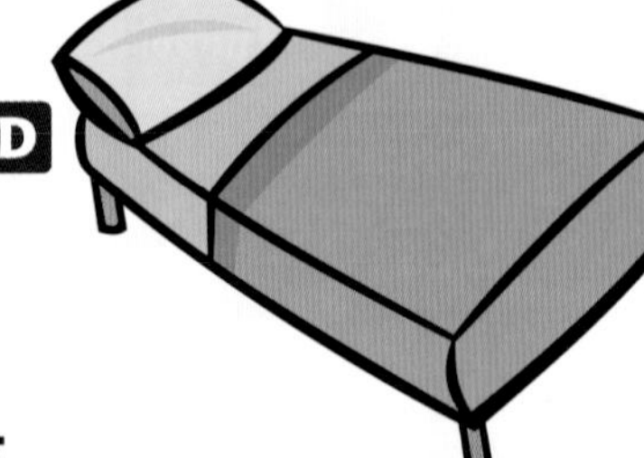
E
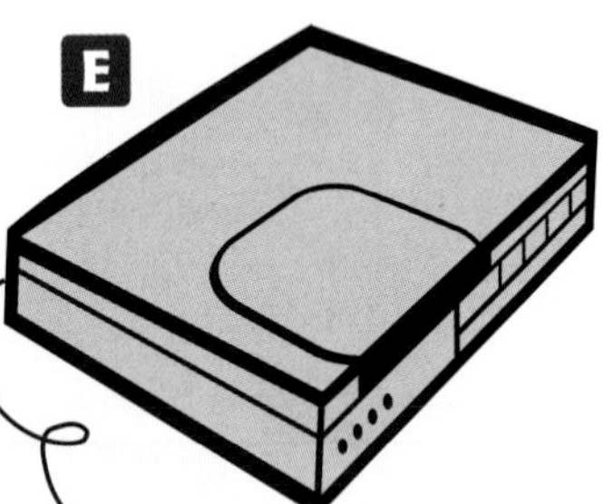
F

G

H

I

J

K

L

2 *Describe and compare the two bedrooms.* (≪ p.97)

Example: Mi dormitorio es más grande que el dormitorio de Ignacio. No es tan... como...

Mi dormitorio

El dormitorio de Ignacio

1 Look at the pictures. True or false? (◄◄ p.97)

1 **Mi hermano es tan alto como yo.**

2 **Ana es mayor que Marta.**

3 **Las ciencias son más interesantes que las matemáticas.**

4 **La casa roja es menos grande que la azul.**

5 **La lectura es peor que el fútbol.**

2 a Read the letter. Who does what to help at home? List the name of the person and the activities in English. (◄◄ p.98)

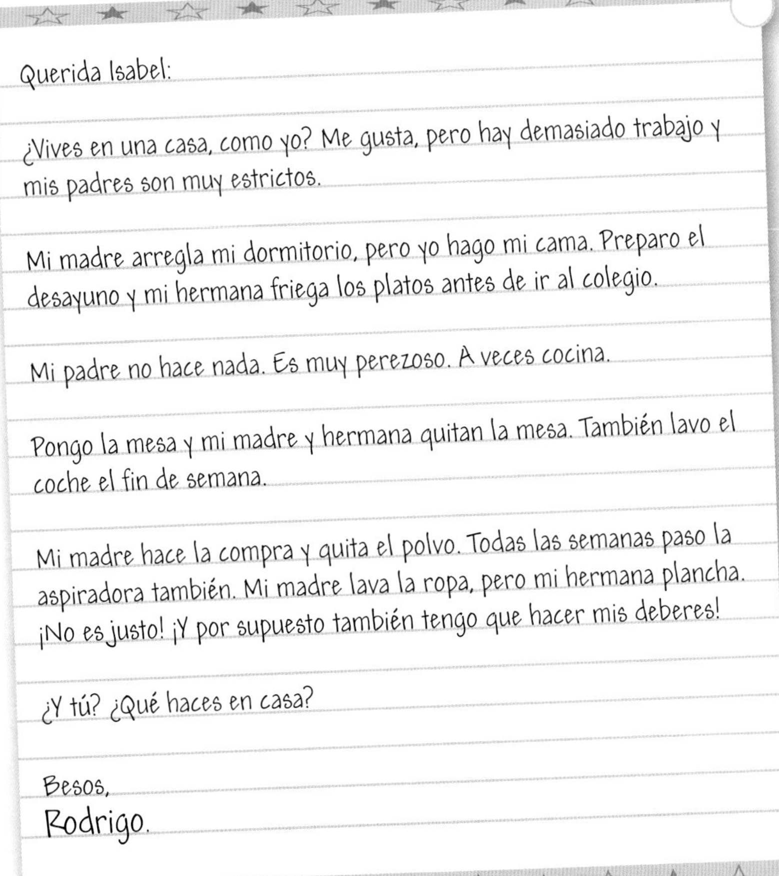

Querida Isabel:

¿Vives en una casa, como yo? Me gusta, pero hay demasiado trabajo y mis padres son muy estrictos.

Mi madre arregla mi dormitorio, pero yo hago mi cama. Preparo el desayuno y mi hermana friega los platos antes de ir al colegio.

Mi padre no hace nada. Es muy perezoso. A veces cocina.

Pongo la mesa y mi madre y hermana quitan la mesa. También lavo el coche el fin de semana.

Mi madre hace la compra y quita el polvo. Todas las semanas paso la aspiradora también. Mi madre lava la ropa, pero mi hermana plancha. ¡No es justo! ¡Y por supuesto también tengo que hacer mis deberes!

¿Y tú? ¿Qué haces en casa?

Besos,
Rodrigo.

2 b Write your reply, using the connectives below to help you. (◄◄ p.98)

todos los días
también
el lunes/martes... y
siempre
por la mañana/tarde

1 ***Look at the survey results and for each picture write the correct percentage.*** (<< p.106)

Example: **A** 50%

RESULTADOS DE ENCUESTA. VUESTRAS OPINIONES SON IMPORTANTES	
Usa menos electricidad	70%
Recicla botellas	60%
Usa transporte público	50%
Dúchate en vez de tomar un baño	40%
Ve en bicicleta	30%
Cierra las ventanas cuando hace frío	20%

2 ***Match what each person says with the correct heading.*** (<< p.104)

Paco: Me preocupa el agua sucia.

María: Me preocupan por los tigres y los osos.

Daniel: No uso un coche, sólo el autobús.

Claudia: Reciclo todas mis botellas y el papel.

- El mundo en peligro **A**
- La contaminación atmosférica **B**
- Los residuos químicos e industriales **C**
- Desechos domésticos **D**

3 ***What should we do to save the environment? Design a poster.*** (<< p.107)

1 ***Read this article about the environment. Answer the questions in English.*** (◄◄ p.104)

¿Dónde hay selvas tropicales?

Hay selvas en África, Asia y América.

¿Dónde exactamente están situadas?

En muchos países. Por ejemplo, las hay en América Central, América del Sur, Brasil, Colombia, Ecuador.

¿Cuáles son los productos típicos de las selvas?

Café, té, cacao, piñas, plátanos, pimientos y mangos.

¿Por qué son importantes las selvas?

Porque allí viven muchos animales, árboles y plantas muy raros e interesantes.

¿Es todo?

No, muchas drogas y medicamentos vienen de las selvas. También las selvas afectan al clima del planeta.

¿Qué pasa con las selvas?

Debido a los descuidos del hombre moderno, desaparecen.

¿Por qué?

Porque cortamos muchísimos árboles.

¿Por qué?

Para construir casas, etc.

1 Where can you find tropical rainforests?
2 What products grow there?
3 List at least 3 reasons why these forests are so important.
4 Why are they disappearing so fast?

2 ***Copy the sentences and choose the most appropriate word from each pair of alternatives so that each of the sentences reflects your own opinion about the future.*** (◄◄ p.108)

1 En el futuro habrá más/menos polución.
2 Los coches usarán gasolina/electricidad.
3 Habrá más/menos gente.
4 Habrá/No habrá hambre en el mundo.
5 Habrá/No habrá centrales nucleares.
6 Visitar la luna será/no será fácil.
7 La gente usará/no usará cosas recicladas.
8 Habrá/No habrá educación para todos.

Now put them in what you consider to be the order of importance, starting with the most important. Justify your choices.

Gramática

- Use these pages to check any grammar point you're not sure of.
- If you're still not sure, ask your teacher.

Glossary of terms

- ***Adjectives*** **los adjetivos**
  … are words that describe somebody or something:
  pequeño *small*
  verde *green*
- ***Determiners***
  … come before nouns and limit them:
  los *the*
  un *a*
  mi *my*
- ***The infinitive*** **el infinitivo**
  … is the name of the verb, as listed in a dictionary:
  jugar *to play*
  ir *to go*
- ***Nouns*** **los sustantivos**
  … are words for somebody or something:
  hermano *brother*
  música *music*
- ***Prepositions*** **las preposiciones**
  … are words or phrases used with nouns to give information about when, how, where, etc:
  a *to*
  con *with*
  en *in*
  encima de *on top of*
- ***Pronouns*** **los pronombres**
  … are short words used instead of a noun or name:
  yo *I*
  tú *you*
  él *he*
  ella *she*
- ***Singular and plural*** **singular y plural**
  – *singular* refers to just one thing or person:
    goma *rubber*
    hermano *brother*
  – *plural* refers to more than one thing or person:
    gomas *rubbers*
    hermanos *brothers*
- ***Tenses*** **los tiempos**
  … express an action or state in a particular time frame:
  como *I eat* (present)
  comí *I ate* (past)
  voy a comer *I am going to eat* (future)
- ***Verbs*** **los verbos**
  … express an action or a state:
  vivo *I live*
  tengo *I have*
  juega *she plays*

Gramática

The following abbreviations are used: *m.* = masculine, *f.* = feminine, *sing.* = singular, *pl.* = plural

A Masculine/feminine, singular/plural

A1 Nouns

A1.1 Singular and plural nouns

- As in English, Spanish nouns can be singular or plural.
  Nouns ending in a vowel (a, e, i, o, u) add *–s*:
  1 hermano, **2 hermanos** *1 brother, 2 brothers*
- Nouns ending in a consonant add *–es* in the plural.
  1 animal, **2 animales** *1 pet, 2 pets*
- There are some exceptions for words ending with a consonant:
  1 ratón, **2 ratones**
  1 mouse, 2 mice (the accent disappears)
  1 lápiz, **2 lápices**
  1 pencil, 2 pencils (the z becomes a c)
  1 hámster, **2 hámsters**
  1 hamster, 2 hamsters (words borrowed from English usually end with *–s*)

A1.2 Masculine and feminine nouns

- One key difference between English and Spanish grammar is that all Spanish nouns fall into one of two categories. We call these categories masculine and feminine. Most masculine nouns end in –o and most feminine nouns end in –a.
  For example: – **centro**, **supermercado**, **parque**, **fútbol**, **piano** are all masculine nouns.
  – **familia**, **música**, **geografía**, **televisión** are all feminine nouns.
- Some nouns have a masculine and a feminine form:
  el profesor *the male teacher*
  la profesora *the female teacher*

A2 Determiners

A2.1 ***el, la, los, las*** **the**

- The word for 'the' depends on whether the noun is masculine or feminine, singular or plural.

masculine singular	feminine singular	masculine plural	feminine plural
el	**la**	**los**	**las**
el gato *the cat*	la mesa *the table*	los pisos *the flats*	las tías *the aunts*

- **el**, **la**, **los** and **las** are sometimes used when we don't say 'the' in English.
  El español es importante. *Spanish is important.*
  Me gusta **la** historia. *I like history.*
- **el/los** are also used with expressions of time:
  el lunes *on Monday* **los** martes *on Tuesdays*

A2.2 un/una, unos/unas **a/an, some**

- Like the words for 'the', the words for 'a/an' and 'some' depend on whether the noun is masculine or feminine, singular or plural.

masculine singular	feminine singular	masculine plural	feminine plural
un	**una**	**unos**	**unas**
un libro *a book*	**una** casa *a house*	**unos** amigos *some friends*	**unas** reglas *some rulers*

After ***tener*** and ***hay*** in the negative, ***un/una*** is dropped:
¿Tienes una goma? *Have you got a rubber?*
No, no tengo goma. *No I haven't got a rubber.*
¿Hay un supermercado aquí?
Is there a supermarket here?
No, no hay supermercado en la aldea.
No, there isn't a supermarket in the village.

- Directly before feminine nouns beginning with *a–* or *ha–*, where the stress is on the first syllable, ***el*** and ***un*** are used instead of ***la*** and ***una***. This is just to make it easier to say:
  el agua mineral (f) *the mineral water*
- You don't use ***un*** or ***una*** when describing what people do.
  Mi madre es médico. *My mother is* ***a*** *doctor.*

A2.3 mi, tu, su, etc. **my, your, his/her**

- The word for 'my', 'your', etc. depends on whether its noun is masculine or feminine, singular or plural:
  mi hermano *my brother* **mi** hermana *my sister*
  mis tíos *my uncles* **mis** tías *my aunts*
  su cuaderno *his/her exercise book*
  sus libros *his/her books*

	masculine singular	feminine singular	masculine plural	feminine plural
my	**mi**	**mi**	**mis**	**mis**
your	**tu**	**tu**	**tus**	**tus**
his/her/ your (formal)	**su**	**su**	**sus**	**sus**
our	**nuestro**	**nuestra**	**nuestros**	**nuestras**
your	**vuestro**	**vuestra**	**vuestros**	**vuestras**
their/your (formal)	**su**	**su**	**sus**	**sus**

A3 Adjectives

A3.1 Masculine/feminine, singular/plural adjectives

- Adjectives are words that describe nouns. They agree in gender and number with the nouns they describe.
- In the dictionary, adjectives are usually listed in their masculine singular (*ms*) form: **small** *adj*. ***pequeño***
- Adjectives form their endings in several different ways.

Type 1 (the most usual)

Their endings show agreement in **gender** and **number**.

masculine singular	feminine singular	masculine plural	feminine plural
blanc**o** mejican**o**	blanc**a** mejican**a**	blanc**os** mejican**os**	blanc**as** mejican**as**

Type 2

The agreement shows in **number** but not in gender.

masculine and feminine singular	masculine and feminine plural
azul importante joven gris	azul**es** importante**s** jóven**es** gris**es**

Type 3

Adjectives of colour ending in *–a* **do not change** their endings to match the noun in gender or number.

masculine and feminine, singular and plural
naranja lila rosa

If a colour is followed by *claro*, *oscuro* or *marino* it does not change its ending.

- To say 'a lot of', use the adjective ***mucho/mucha/ muchos/ muchas***
- Where an adjective describes a group including both masculine and feminine people or things, use the masculine form.

  Los alumnos son ruidos**os**.
  The pupils (boys <u>and</u> girls) are noisy.

- Use ***lo*** before an adjective to mean 'the (...) thing...'

  Lo interesante es que... *The interesting thing is that...*
  Eso es **lo** difícil. *That's the difficult thing.*

A3.2 The position of adjectives

- The position of adjectives is different from in English. In Spanish, adjectives generally follow a noun:

  un vestido **rojo** *a red dress*
  una casa **adosada** *a semi-detached house*

A3.3 No capitals for adjectives of nationality

- Adjectives of nationality begin with lower-case letters:

  John es **inglés**. *John is English.*
  María es **italiana**. *María is Italian.*

A3.4 Comparative adjectives

- To make comparisons, use *más... que, menos... que*:

  Un vestido es **más** elegante **que** unos vaqueros.
  A dress is more elegant than jeans.

  Los zapatos son **menos** cómodos **que** las zapatillas de deporte.
  Shoes are less comfortable than trainers.

A3.5 Superlatives

- For superlatives – things that are 'the most' or 'the least' – use:

  ... el/la más (adjective) *(de...)* ... the most... (in...)
  ... el/la menos (adjective) *(de...)* ... the least... (in...)

  El cine es **el** medio de comunicación **más** emocionante.

  Las revistas son **el** medio de comunicación **menos** interesante.

  La radio es **el** medio de comunicación **más** aburrido.

  Internet es **el** medio de comunicación **menos** barato.

A3.6 tan... como

- *tan... como* means 'as... as':

  El dormitorio de Antonio no es **tan** grande **como** el de Pablo.
  Antonio's bedroom is not as big as Pablo's.

  Antonio es **tan** trabajador en el colegio **como** Pablo.
  Antonio is as hard-working at school as Pablo.

  Mi dormitorio es **tan** cómodo **como** el de mi hermana.
  My bedroom is as comfortable as my sister's.

A3.7 –ísimo

- *–ísimo* means 'very, very...'.

  bueno > buen**ísimo** good > very, very good
  caro > car**ísimo** expensive > very, very expensive
  lento > lent**ísimo** slow > very, very slow
  rico > riqu**ísimo** rich/tasty > very, very rich/tasty (of food)

B Verbs

B1 The present tense of regular verbs

- Spanish verbs have different endings according to who is doing the action.

  Examples of the present tense in English are: *I speak, I am speaking; we go, we are going.*

  The regular pattern is:

	–ar	–er	–ir
	habl**ar** (*to speak*)	com**er** (*to eat*)	viv**ir** (*to live*)
yo	habl**o**	com**o**	viv**o**
tú	habl**as**	com**es**	viv**es**
él, ella, usted	habl**a**	com**e**	viv**e**
nosotros/as	habl**amos**	com**emos**	viv**imos**
vosotros/as	habl**áis**	com**éis**	viv**ís**
ellos, ellas, ustedes	habl**an**	com**en**	viv**en**

- The present tense expresses what is happening and what usually happens:

  Hablo inglés y español. *I speak English and Spanish.*

  Eduardo siempre **come** mucho.
  Eduardo always eats a lot.

  Normalmente, **vivimos** en Madrid.
  Normally, we live in Madrid.

- It can also express what is happening at the moment:

  ¡**Hablas** muy rápido! *You are talking very fast!*

  Ella **come** demasiado chocolate.
  She's eating too much chocolate.

  Vivimos con mis abuelos ahora.
  We are living with my grandparents now.

- In questions and with negatives, English often uses *do*.

  This is not translated into Spanish:

  No **hablo** muy bien. *I do not/don't speak very well.*

  ¿**Comes** pescado? *Do you eat fish?*

  No **vivimos** cerca del centro.
  We do not/don't live near the centre.

B2 The present tense of irregular verbs

B2.1 Verbs which are irregular in the yo form only

- Some common verbs are irregular in the *yo* form, but regular in all other parts:

dar	*to give*	(yo) **doy**	*I give*
hacer	*to do, make*	(yo) **hago**	*I do, I make*
poner	*to put (on)*	(yo) **pongo**	*I put (on)*
salir	*to go out*	(yo) **salgo**	*I go out*
ver	*to see, watch*	(yo) **veo**	*I see*

Salgo los fines de semana. *I go out at weekends.*

No **veo** mucho la tele. *I don't watch much TV.*

B2.2 The present tense of tener and venir

	tener (*to have*)	**venir** (*to come*)
yo	**tengo**	**vengo**
tú	**tienes**	**vienes**
él, ella, usted	**tiene**	**viene**
nosotros/as	**tenemos**	**venimos**
vosotros/as	**tenéis**	**venís**
ellos, ellas, ustedes	**tienen**	**vienen**

Tengo dos hermanos. *I've got two brothers.*

Tienen un gato. *They have a cat.*

¿**Vienes** a la fiesta? *Are you coming to the party?*

Mis amigos **vienen** más tarde. *My friends are coming later.*

- *Tener* (to have) is used in the following phrases where English uses the verb *to be*:

  tener ... años — *to be ... years old*
  tener hambre — *to be hungry*
  tener calor — *to be hot*
  tener sed — *to be thirsty*
  tener frío — *to be cold*
  tener sueño — *to be sleepy*

  Tengo doce años. *I'm twelve years old.*

  ¿**Tenéis** frío, Carlos y Juan? *Are you cold, Carlos and Juan?*

B2.3 The present tense of estar and ser (to be)

- There are two verbs meaning 'to be' in Spanish: *estar* and *ser*.

	estar	**ser**
yo	**estoy**	**soy**
tú	**estás**	**eres**
él, ella, usted	**está**	**es**
nosotros/as	**estamos**	**somos**
vosotros/as	**estáis**	**sois**
ellos, ellas, ustedes	**están**	**son**

- Use ***estar*** to say where things are and to indicate temporary conditions:

  ¿Dónde **estás**, Ana? Estoy en el jardín.
  Where are you, Ana? I'm in the garden.

  El centro **está** muy ruidoso hoy.
  The centre is very noisy today.

- Use ***ser*** for describing people or things, and indicating more permanent conditions:

  Soy alto, pero mi hermano es bajo.
  I'm tall, but my brother is short.

  Los pueblos **son** blancos y muy bonitos.
  The villages are white and very pretty.

B2.4 The present tense of ir (to go)

- The verb *ir* is often followed by **a** (to).

	ir *(to go)*
yo	**voy**
tú	**vas**
él, ella, usted	**va**
nosotros/as	**vamos**
vosotros/as	**vais**
ellos, ellas, ustedes	**van**

¿**Vas** a la ciudad, Irene? *Are you going to town, Irene?*

Voy a la piscina todos los días.
I go to the swimming pool every day.

B2.5 Stem-changing verbs

- The stem of a verb is what is left when you take off the ending. This group of verbs have changes to some parts of their stem.
- The letter ***u*** or **o** in the stem changes to ***ue***:

	j**u**gar *(to play)*	p**o**der *(to be able to)*
yo	j**ue**go	p**ue**do
tú	j**ue**gas	p**ue**des
él, ella, usted	j**ue**ga	p**ue**de
nosotros/as	jugamos	podemos
vosotros/as	jugáis	podéis
ellos, ellas, ustedes	j**ue**gan	p**ue**den

Juego al fútbol. *I play football.*

Mi amigo **puede** jugar también.
My friend can play as well.

Other common verbs like *poder* where the *o* in the stem changes to *ue* are:

almorzar *to have lunch* encontrar *to find*
costar *to cost* llover *to rain*
dormir *to sleep* volver *to return*

- Here are two verbs where **e** in the stem changes to **ie**:

	qu**e**rer *(to want, like)*	pref**e**rir *(to prefer)*
yo	qu**ie**ro	pref**ie**ro
tú	qu**ie**res	pref**ie**res
él, ella, usted	qu**ie**re	pref**ie**re
nosotros/as	queremos	preferimos
vosotros/as	queréis	preferís
ellos, ellas, ustedes	qu**ie**ren	pref**ie**ren

¿**Quieres** beber algo? *Do you want anything to drink?*

Paca **prefiere** café. *Paca prefers coffee.*

Other common verbs like this are:

cerrar *to close* merendar *to have a snack*
empezar/comenzar *to begin* perder *to lose*

- In some verbs, the letter *e* in the stem changes to *i*. (This only happens in *–ir* verbs):

	p**e**dir *(to ask for)*
yo	p**i**do
tú	p**i**des
él, ella, usted	p**i**de
nosotros/as	pedimos
vosotros/as	pedís
ellos, ellas, ustedes	p**i**den

¿Qué **pide** tu hermana? *What is your sister ordering?*

Pedimos chocolate caliente.
We are asking for hot chocolate.

Other common verbs like this are:

repetir *to repeat* servir *to serve*

B3 Gerunds

- The gerund is the part of the verb ending in '–ing' in English: watching, dancing. It is formed in Spanish like this:

	Infinitive	Remove	Add	Gerund	English
–ar	ayudar	–ar	–ando	**ayudando**	*helping*
–er	vender	–er	–iendo	**vendiendo**	*selling*
–ir	escribir	–ir	–iendo	**escribiendo**	*eating*

Gano dinero **vendiendo** periódicos.
I earn money selling newspapers.

Paso mucho tiempo **escribiendo** cartas.
I spend a lot of time writing letters.

- The gerund of *servir* (to serve) is irregular: *sirviendo* (serving).

Trabajo en el bar **sirviendo** a los clientes.
I work in the bar serving customers.

- Although English often uses the gerund with verbs of liking/disliking, in Spanish you must use the infinitive form of the verb after *gustar*:

Me gusta **visitar** pueblos bonitos.
I like visiting/to visit pretty towns.

Me encanta **ir** a la costa. *I love going/to go to the coast.*

B4 The present continuous

- The present continuous is used to talk about an action that you **are doing** right now, an action which is ongoing: 'I am writing,' You are listening.'

Estoy haciendo los deberes.
I am doing my homework.

Estamos arreglando el dormitorio.
We are tidying the bedroom.

Están preparando la comida.
They are preparing food.

Estoy limpiando el cuarto de baño.
I am cleaning the bathroom.

¿**Estás leyendo** el periódico?
Are you reading the newspaper?

It is formed by using the present tense of *estar* plus the gerund.

yo	**estoy escribiendo**
tú	**estás escribiendo**
él, ella, usted	**está escribiendo**
nosotros/as	**estamos escribiendo**
vosotros/as	**estáis escribiendo**
ellos, ellas, ustedes	**están escribiendo**

B5 *Hay* – there is, there are

Hay un banco enfrente. *There is a bank opposite.*

Hay diez chicos en mi clase. *There are ten boys in my class.*

- After ***no hay***, you drop the indefinite article, ***un(a)***:

  Hay una piscina, pero no hay polideportivo.
  There is a swimming pool, but there isn't a sports centre.

  ¿Hay una bolera? No, no hay bolera en mi pueblo.
  Is there a bowling alley? No, there isn't a bowling alley in my town.

B6 *Gustar, encantar, doler*

- ***Gustar*** is the verb used when expressing 'to like'. Its exact meaning is 'to be pleasing to'. Look at the examples below.

Me *To me*	gusta *is pleasing*	el té *(the) tea*	=	*I like tea.*
Me *To me*	gusta *is pleasing*	leer *to read*	=	*I like to read.*

- When talking about one thing *(el ... la ...)* use **me gusta**. When talking about more than one thing *(los ... las ...)* use ***me gustan***:

  Me gusta el zumo de fruta.
  I like fruit juice. (To me is pleasing the fruit juice.)

  Me gusta la naranjada.
  I like fizzy orange. (To me is pleasing the fizzy orange.)

  Me gustan los churros.
  I like doughnuts. (To me are pleasing the doughnuts.)

  Me gustan las peras.
  I like pears. (To me are pleasing the pears.)

- If you are talking about an activity, use ***me gusta*** and the infinitive form of the verb:

  Me gusta salir al cine.
  I like to go out/going out to the cinema.

  Me gusta mucho **nadar**.
  I like to swim/swimming very much.

- Use ***encantar*** *(to love)* in a similar way:

one thing	*more than one thing*
me encanta (el ... la ...)	me encantan (los ... las ...)

Me encanta ir a la playa. *I love to go/going to the beach.*

Me encantan las uvas. *I love grapes.*

- You can express degrees of liking by using *mucho, bastante, un poco* and *no, no... nada*.

  Me gusta mucho el francés. *I like French a lot.*

  Me gustan bastante las ciencias. *I quite like science.*

  ¿La historia? **Me gusta un poco.** *History? I like it a bit.*

  No me gusta la geografía. *I don't like geography.*

  No me gustan nada los deberes.
  I don't like homework at all.

- To express someone else's likes and dislikes, use the following table to help:

me	*me*
te	*you (informal, sing.)*
le	*him, her, you (formal, sing.)*
nos	*us*
os	*you (informal, pl.)*
les	*them, you (formal, pl.)*

¿**Te** gusta el pan?
Do you like the bread? (Is the bread pleasing to you?)

¿Juan? Sí, **le** gusta el regalo.
Juan? Yes, he likes the present. (The present is pleasing to him.)

No **nos** gustan las gambas.
We don't like prawns. (The prawns are not pleasing to us.)

- The verb ***doler*** (to hurt) works in a similar way as the verbs *gustar* and *encantar*:

one thing	*more than one thing*
me duele (el ... la ...)	me duelen (los ... las ...)

Me duele la cabeza.
I have a headache./My head hurts.

Me duelen los pies.
My feet hurt.

If the person appears in the sentence, the preposition a is needed.

A Paula **le duelen** las piernas.
Paula's legs hurt.

A mis hermanos **les duele** el estómago.
My brothers have a bad stomach.

B7 *Soler* + infinitive

- ***Soler*** + infinitive is used to describe what you usually do.

  Suelo coger el autobús.
  I usually catch the bus.

  ¿Cómo **sueles** volver a casa si es tarde?
  How do you usually get home if it is late?

	soler *(to usually do something)*
yo	suelo
tú	sueles
él, ella, usted	suele
nosotros/as	solemos
vosotros/as	soléis
ellos, ellas, ustedes	suelen

B8 *Hay que…, Deber* + infinitive

- There are several ways of saying what you 'have to do' or 'must do' in Spanish.

  i You can use ***deber*** + infinitive:

	deber *(to have to)*
yo	debo
tú	debes
él, ella, usted	debe
nosotros/as	debemos
vosotros/as	debéis
ellos, ellas, ustedes	deben

Debe llevar una falda. *She has to wear a skirt.*

Debo estudiar. *I have to study.*

ii You can use ***hay que***… + infinitive:

Hay que comer mucha fruta.
You have to eat a lot of fruit.

Hay que ser cortés con los profesores.
You have to be polite to the teachers.

B9 The impersonal *se*

- To say that 'they' or 'you' do something, use **se** and the appropriate verb in the third person singular or plural.

Se puede comprar jabón en el mercado.
You can buy soap at the market.

El pan **se vende** en la panadería.
They sell bread at the baker's./Bread is sold at the baker's.

Las revistas **se compran** en el quiosco.
They sell magazines at the newsagent's.

B10 Reflexive verbs

- Reflexive verbs have an extra part at the beginning of the verb, called the reflexive pronoun.

	llamarse *(to be called)*
yo	**me** llamo
tú	**te** llamas
él, ella, usted	**se** llama
nosotros/as	**nos** llamamos
vosotros/as	**os** llamáis
ellos, ellas, ustedes	**se** llaman

Me llamo Ricardo. *I'm called Ricardo.*

¿Cómo **se llama** tu hermano? *What's your brother called?*

Mis padres **se llaman** Belén y Paco.
My parents are called Belén and Paco.

- Reflexive verbs often indicate an action done to oneself, e.g. to get (oneself) up, to wash (oneself). Other common reflexive verbs are:

bañarse *to have a bath, to bathe*
ducharse *to have a shower*
lavarse *to get washed*
lavarse los dientes *to clean one's teeth*
levantarse *to get up*
peinarse *to brush one's hair*
relajarse *to relax*

Me ducho rápidamente. *I have a shower quickly.*

¿Cómo **te relajas**? *How do you relax?*

- Some reflexive verbs are also stem-changing (see B2.5 on page 141).

acostarse (ue) *to go to bed*
despertarse (ie) *to wake up*
vestirse (i) *to get dressed*

Me acuesto a las once. *I go to bed at eleven.*

No me despierto temprano. *I don't wake up early.*

Me visto en seguida. *I get dressed straightaway.*

B11 The immediate future

The immediate future expresses what you are going to do soon or shortly.

- Use *ir a* (to go to) followed by an infinitive:

Voy a jugar al tenis. *I am going to play tennis.*

¿**Vas a salir** con Marisa?
Are you going to go out with Marisa?

Van a hacer los deberes.
They are going to do their homework.

- As in English, you can use part of *ir* followed by the infinitive *ir* to mean 'going to go':

Voy a ir al polideportivo.
I am going to go to the sports centre.

Vamos a ir a la cafetería.
We are going to go to the café.

B12 The future tense of regular verbs

- The future tense is used to express what **will** happen in the future. To form the future tense, add the following endings to the infinitive:

	–ar	**–er**	**–ir**
	estudiar *(to study)*	ser *(to be)*	ir *(to go)*
yo	estudiar**é**	ser**é**	ir**é**
tú	estudiar**ás**	ser**ás**	ir**á**
él, ella, usted	estudiar**á**	ser**á**	ir**emos**
nosotros/as	estudiar**emos**	ser**emos**	ir**éis**
vosotros/as	estudiar**éis**	ser**éis**	ir**án**
ellos, ellas, ustedes	estudiar**án**	ser**án**	

El año próximo **estudiaré** historia.
Next year I will study history.

Seré ingeniero en el futuro.
I will be an engineer in the future.

B12.1 The future tense of irregular verbs

- There are a few very common irregular verbs:

salir – saldré	poner – pondré	venir – vendré
hacer – haré	poder – podré	

B13 The preterite tense of regular verbs

- The preterite tense expresses what happened in the past:

  I went to a party last night. I met my friends and danced to the music.

  This is the pattern for regular verbs:

	–ar	–er	–ir
	habl**ar** (to speak)	com**er** (to eat)	viv**ir** (to live)
yo	habl**é**	com**í**	escrib**í**
tú	habl**aste**	com**iste**	escrib**iste**
él, ella, usted	habl**ó**	com**ió**	escrib**ió**
nosotros/as	habl**amos**	com**imos**	escrib**imos**
vosotros/as	habl**asteis**	com**isteis**	escrib**isteis**
ellos, ellas, ustedes	habl**aron**	com**ieron**	escrib**ieron**

Hablé con Juana por teléfono.
I spoke to Juana on the phone.

Comí con mis amigos en una pizzería.
I ate with my friends in a pizzería.

Escribí un mensaje de texto.
I wrote a text message.

- The spelling of the *yo* form of the verbs *jugar* (to play) and *navegar* (to surf) is slightly different. After the letter *g*, add *u* to keep the same hard (*'guh'*) sound:

  Yo **jugué** bien pero Martín jugó mal.
  I played well, but Martín played badly.

  Navegué por Internet toda la noche.
  I surfed the net all night.

B13.1 The preterite tense of irregular verbs

- The verb *ir* (to go)/*ser* (to be) is irregular in the preterite tense:

	ir *(to go)*/**ser** *(to be)*
yo	**fui**
tú	**fuiste**
él, ella, usted	**fue**
nosotros/as	**fuimos**
vosotros/as	**fuisteis**
ellos, ellas, ustedes	**fueron**

¿Adónde **fuiste** anoche? *Where did you go last night?*
Fui a casa temprano. *I went home early.*

- *Ir* shares its preterite form with the verb *ser*, to be.

  El año pasado **fue** a España.
  Last year she went to Spain.

  Fue estupendo.
  It was great.

- The verb *hacer* (to do) is also irregular in the preterite tense:

	hacer *(to do)*
yo	**hice**
tú	**hiciste**
él, ella, usted	**hizo**
nosotros/as	**hicimos**
vosotros/as	**hicisteis**
ellos, ellas, ustedes	**hicieron**

- The preterite form of *hay…*, there is/there are is *hubo…*, there was/there were.
- The preterite form of the verb *estar* is useful to talk about where people or places were situated when an action was finished.

	estar *(to be)*
yo	**estuve**
tú	**estuviste**
él, ella, usted	**estuvo**
nosotros/as	**estuvimos**
vosotros/as	**estuvisteis**
ellos, ellas, ustedes	**estuvieron**

Estuve en mi casa. *I was in my house.*
Estuvimos en el centro. *We were in the town centre.*
Estuvo en un restaurante. *He was in a restaurant.*

B14 The imperfect tense of regular verbs

- The imperfect tense **describes** what something or somebody was like in the past, e.g. what the weather was like. It is also used for actions that are repeated in the past and for actions that set the stage for another action.

  Hacía sol. *It was sunny.*
  Tenía hambre y mucha sed. *I was hungry and very thirsty.*
  Estaba sola. *I was alone.*

- To form the imperfect tense of *–ar* verbs, drop the *–ar* and add:

	estar *(to be)*
yo	est**aba**
tú	est**abas**
él, ella, usted	est**aba**
nosotros/as	est**ábamos**
vosotros/as	est**abais**
ellos, ellas, ustedes	est**aban**

- To form the imperfect tense of *–er* and *–ir* verbs, drop the *–er* or *–ir* and add:

	hacer *(to do)*	**vivir** *(to live)*
yo	hac**ía**	viv**ía**
tú	hac**ías**	viv**ías**
él, ella, usted	hac**ía**	viv**ía**
nosotros/as	hac**íamos**	viv**íamos**
vosotros/as	hac**íais**	viv**íais**
ellos, ellas, ustedes	hac**ían**	viv**ían**

B14.1 The imperfect tense of irregular verbs

- There are only three verbs that are irregular in the imperfect tense.

	ser *(to be)*	**ir** *(to go)*	**ver** *(to see)*
yo	**era**	**iba**	**veía**
tú	**eras**	**ibas**	**veías**
él, ella, usted	**era**	**iba**	**veía**
nosotros/as	**éramos**	**íbamos**	**veíamos**
vosotros/as	**erais**	**ibais**	**veíais**
ellos, ellas, ustedes	**eran**	**iban**	**veían**

Eran las tres de la tarde.
It was three o'clock in the afternoon.

- The imperfect tense of *hay* (there is/there are) is *había* (there was/there were).

No **había** muchos viajeros en el tren.
There weren't many people travelling on the train.

B15 Commands

- These are instructions to do something. The command form for *tú* is created as follows: *–ar* and *–er* regular verbs drop the final *–r* of the infinitive; *–ir* regular verbs drop the *–r* and change the *i* into an *e*:

pasar – **pasa** *(come in!)*
beber – **bebe** *(drink!)*
vivir – **vive** *(live!)*

B15.1 Negative commands

- For the negative command form, endings need to change:

–ar > –es	pasar > **no pases** *(don't come in!)*
–er > –as	beber > **no bebas** *(don't drink!)*
–ir > –as	vivir > **no vivas** *(don't live!)*

B15.2 Polite singular commands

- Polite or formal commands are made to someone to whom you would use *usted* – an adult you don't know, or someone in a position of authority.

Infinitive		Change last letter of the *usted* form		Singular command	English
–ar	hablar	habla	➞	habl**e**	*speak!*
–er	comer	come	➞	com**a**	*eat!*
–ir	escribir	escribe	➞	escrib**a**	*write!*

¡**Hable** más despacio, por favor! *Speak more slowly, please!*

Coma la paella, señor – es muy buena.
Eat the paella, sir – it's very good.

Escriba su apellido, por favor.
Write down your surname, please.

- Some commands have irregular forms:

Infinitive	Singular command	English
seguir *to follow, carry on*	**siga**	*carry on ...!*
torcer *to turn*	**tuerza**	*turn ...!*
cruzar *to cross*	**cruce**	*cross ...!*

Siga todo recto. *Carry straight on.*

Tuerza a la derecha. *Turn right.*

Cruce la calle. *Cross the street.*

B16 Infinitives

- In English, the infinitive of a verb begins with *to*: *to go, to have, to study* are all infinitive forms. In Spanish, the infinitive ends in one of three ways:

–ar e.g. hablar *(to speak)*

–er e.g. comer *(to eat)*

–ir e.g. vivir *(to live)*

This is the part of the verb you will find in the dictionary.

B17 In order to...

- To express 'in order to' in Spanish, use *para* and the infinitive form of the verb:

Ahorro dinero **para** viajar al extranjero.
I'm saving money in order to travel abroad.

Voy al centro **para** comprar ropa.
I'm going to the centre in order to buy clothes.

Hago deporte **para** estar en forma.
I do sport in order to keep fit.

C Other parts of a Spanish sentence

C1 Pronouns

C1.1 Subject pronouns

- Subject pronouns (I, you, he, she, etc) explain **who** is doing something. In Spanish, these are:

I	**yo**
you (informal, sing.)	**tú**
he	**él**
she	**ella**
you (formal, sing.)	**usted**
we	**nosotros/as**
you (informal, pl.)	**vosotros/as**
they (masc.)	**ellos**
they (fem.)	**ellas**
you (formal, pl.)	**ustedes**

- Spanish uses different words for 'you' depending on whether the relationship is informal or formal.

  Informal

  When talking to a young person or child, or an adult you know well, use

  tú when talking to one person

  vosotros when talking to more than one person

  If the people you're talking to are female, use **vosotras**.

  Estoy bien, gracias, Juana. ¿Y tú?
  I'm fine, thanks, Juana. And you?

  ¿Qué tal vosotros, Paco y Felipe?
  How are you, Paco and Felipe?

  ¿Y vosotras, Ana y María? *And you, Ana and María?*

  Formal

  When talking to an adult you do not know or who is in authority, use

  usted when talking to one person

  ustedes when talking to more than one person

  Estoy muy bien. ¿Y usted, Sr. Muñoz?
  I'm very well. And you, Mr. Muñoz?

  ¿Y ustedes, Sr. y Sra. Galván?
  And you, Mr. and Mrs. Galván?

- You don't normally need to use the subject pronouns, as the ending of the verb tells you who is speaking. Use them for emphasis or to make things clear.

  Él va al instituto, pero yo no voy.
  He is going to school, but I'm not going.

C1.2 Direct object pronouns

- Pronouns replace a noun. They are often used in order to avoid repetition:

  The jumper is very pretty – I'll take it (the jumper).

  I like the shoes – I'll take them (the shoes).

- Object pronouns *(it, them)* in Spanish match the number and gender of the noun they are replacing.

it	*(m. sing.)*	**lo**	¿El jersey? Me **lo** llevo. *The jumper? I'll take it.*
	(f. sing.)	**la**	¿La camisa? **La** dejo. *The shirt? I'll leave it.*
them	*(m. pl.)*	**los**	Los zapatos – ¿me **los** puedo probar? *The shoes – can I try them on?*
	(f. pl.)	**las**	Las sandalias – ¿me **las** puedo probar? *The sandals – can I try them on?*

C1.3 Disjunctive pronouns

- After certain prepositions like *para* (for) and *sin* (without), you need a disjunctive pronoun. You will see that they are the same as the subject pronouns (see C1.1 on this page), except for the first two. Note that you need an accent on **mí** to differentiate it from *mi* (my).

mí	*me*
ti	*you (informal, singular)*
él, ella, usted	*him, her, you (formal, singular)*
nosotros/as	*us*
vosotros/as	*you (informal, plural)*
ellos/as, ustedes	*them, you (formal, plural)*

  ¿Es para **mí**? ¡Gracias! *Is it for me? Thank you!*

  ¿Y para **ti**? ¿Un té? *And for you? Tea?*

  Para **nosotros**, café. *For us, coffee.*

C2 Negative sentences

- To make a sentence negative in Spanish, put the word *no* in front of the verb.

  No quiero café, gracias. *I don't want coffee, thanks.*

  No voy a ir al cine. *I'm not going to go to the cinema.*

  ¿**No** puedes venir mañana? *Can't you come tomorrow?*

- The following common negatives are wrapped around the verb:

  no... nada *nothing, not... anything*
  no... nadie *no-one*
  no... ni... ni... *not either... or.../ neither... nor...*

  No quiero **nada**. *I don't want anything.*

  No viene **nadie** a la fiesta. *No-one is coming to the party.*

  No tengo **ni** boli **ni** lápiz. *I have neither a biro nor a pencil.*

  No como **nunca** pescado. *I never eat fish.*

C3 Questions

- You can turn statements into questions by putting an upside down question mark at the beginning (¿) and one the right way up at the end (?) and making your voice go higher at the end of the sentence.

  Puedo ir al patio. *I can go to the playground.*

  ¿Puedo ir al patio? *Can I go to the playground?*

  Notice that the word order changes in English but not in Spanish.

- Many questions contain special question words like these:

cómo	*how*	¿Cómo vas al colegio?	*How do you go to school?*
cuándo	*when*	¿Cuándo nos encontramos?	*When shall we meet?*
cuánto	*how much*	¿Cuánto dinero recibes?	*How much money do you get?*
dónde	*where*	¿Dónde vives?	*Where do you live?*
por qué	*why*	¿Por qué no te gusta el inglés?	*Why don't you like English?*
qué	*what*	¿Qué vas a hacer?	*What are you going to do?*
quién	*who*	¿Quién te da el dinero?	*Who gives you the money?*

- When question words are not used in questions, they don't have an accent.

  No salgo **cuando** llueve. *I don't go out when it rains.*

- *Por qué* (why) becomes one word (*porque*) when it means 'because'.

  ¿**Por qué** no te gusta este libro? **Porque** es aburrido.
  Why don't you like this book? Because it's boring.

C4 Prepositions

C4.1 a: al, a la

- **a** means 'to':

  Voy **a** Madrid. *I'm going to Madrid.*

  ¿Vas **a** la discoteca? *Are you going to the disco?*

- ***a + el > al***

  To make it easier to say, when *a* is followed by *el* it becomes *al*.

  Me gusta ir **al** cine. *I like going to the cinema.*

- **a** + distance and time

  To say that something is so many kilometres or minutes away, use *a*.

  Vivo **a** cinco minutos del centro.
  I live five minutes away from the centre.

  Mi casa está **a** quince kilómetros.
  My house is fifteen kilometres away.

C4.2 de: del, de la

- ***de*** means 'of':

  In English you say 'my parents' bedroom' and 'the Spanish teacher', but in Spanish you say, *el dormitorio* ***de*** *mis padres* (literally: the bedroom **of** my parents) and *el profesor* ***de*** *español* (literally: the teacher **of** Spanish).

- ***de + el > del***

  As with *al*, to make it easier to say, when *de* is followed by *el* it becomes *del*.

  Vivo cerca **del** polideportivo. *I live near the sports centre.*

C4.3 More prepositions

- Some prepositions are followed by *de* in Spanish:

al lado **de**	*next to*	detrás **de**	*behind*
delante **de**	*in front of*	debajo **de**	*underneath*
encima **de**	*on top of*	cerca **de**	*near*
lejos **de**	*far from*	enfrente **de**	*opposite*

  El pueblo está cerca **de** la costa. *The town is near the coast.*

  La lámpara está encima **del** armario.
  The lamp is on top of the cupboard.

- ***En*** means 'in' and is used in a lot of different expressions:

  en el norte *in the north*

  en Madrid *in Madrid*

  en clase *in class*

  en primavera *in spring*

- Use ***para*** (in order to) + infinitive to say the reason for doing something (see **B17**).

  Trabajo **para** ahorrar dinero.
  I work (in order) to save money.

C5 Adverbs

- Adverbs describe verbs, adjectives or other adverbs.
  Adverbs are often words that end in –ly in English.
  To form an adverb, add *–mente* to the feminine singular form of the adjective.

masculine singular	feminine singular	adverb
aproximado	aproximada	aproximadamente
difícil	difícil	difícilmente
exacto	exacta	exactamente

  ¿A qué hora llega el tren **aproximadamente**?
  What time does the train arrive approximately?

  ¿A qué hora llega el tren **exactamente**?
  What time does the train arrive exactly?

- Some common adverbs do not follow the pattern above:

bastante	*quite*	muy	*very*
demasiado	*too*	nunca	*never*
mal	*badly*	poco	*little*
mucho	*a lot*	siempre	*always*

C6 Linking sentences

- Use the following words to link shorter sentences and make longer ones:

y *and*	Los sábados voy al cine **y** los domingos juego al baloncesto. *On Saturdays I go to the cinema* ***and*** *on Sundays I play basketball.*
pero *but*	Me gustan las matemáticas **pero** prefiero la geografía. *I like Maths* ***but*** *I prefer Geography.*
y luego *and then*	Los viernes por la tarde tenemos inglés **y luego** tenemos física. *On Friday afternoons we have English* ***and then*** *we have Physics.*
o *or*	¿Prefieres la Coca-Cola **o** el té? *Do you prefer Coke* ***or*** *tea?*
porque *because*	Odio la ciudad **porque** es ruidosa y sucia. *I hate the city* ***because*** *it's noisy and dirty.*

D Numbers, time, frequency

D1 Numbers

1 un	30 treinta
2 dos	40 cuarenta
3 tres	50 cincuenta
4 cuatro	60 sesenta
5 cinco	70 setenta
6 seis	80 ochenta
7 siete	90 noventa
8 ocho	
9 nueve	31 treinta y uno
10 diez	32 treinta y dos
11 once	41 cuarenta y uno
12 doce	42 cuarenta y dos
13 trece	
14 catorce	100 cien (ciento)
15 quince	200 doscientos
16 dieciséis	300 trescientos
17 diecisiete	400 cuatrocientos
18 dieciocho	500 **quinientos**
19 diecinueve	
20 veinte	600 seiscientos
21 veintiuno	700 **setecientos**
22 veintidós	800 ochocientos
23 veintitrés	900 **novecientos**
24 veinticuatro	1000 mil
25 veinticinco	2000 dos mil

- Use ***cien*** to talk about exactly a hundred:

  Hay **cien** alumnos. *There are a hundred pupils.*

- Use ***ciento*** when 100 is followed by another number:

  Ciento cuarenta y dos profesores.
  A hundred and forty-two teachers.

- Numbers are normally formed in the hundreds by adding ***cientos*** to the number: tres**cientos**

  BUT the following are exceptions: **quinientos**, **sete**cientos, **nove**cientos

- Numbers ending in ***–cientos/as*** are adjectives and must agree with the noun they describe:

  setecientos libros
  seven hundred books

  ochocientas veinte profesoras
  eight hundred and twenty female teachers

- In Spanish, the word 'and' is placed between the tens and units but **NOT** after the hundred words:

  trescientos cuarenta **y** dos *three hundred* ***and*** *forty-two*

- In Spanish, you don't need to add 'a' or 'one' before hundreds and thousands:

  cien = *a or one hundred*
  mil = *a or one thousand*

D1.1 Ordinal numbers

1st	primero/a	6th	sexto/a
2nd	segundo/a	7th	séptimo/a
3rd	tercero/a	8th	octavo/a
4th	cuarto/a	9th	noveno/a
5th	quinto/a	10th	décimo/a

- Ordinal numbers are adjectives so they agree with the noun they describe:

  la **primera** calle a la derecha *the first street on the right*
  Vivo en el **segundo** piso. *I live on the second floor.*

- When they come before a masculine noun, *primero* and *tercero* lose their final *–o*:

  Está en el **primer** piso. *It's on the first floor.*

D2 Time

The 12-hour clock is written as follows:

Es la una	Son las dos menos veinticinco
Es la una y cinco	Son las dos menos veinte
Es la una y diez	Son las dos menos cuarto
Es la una y cuarto	Son las dos menos diez
Es la una y veinte	Son las dos menos cinco
Es la una y veinticinco	Son las dos
Es la una y media	

- To talk about time past the hour use **y**:

  las dos **y** cuarto
  a quarter past two (literally the two ***and*** *quarter)*

- to talk about time to the hour use ***menos***:

  las dos **menos** cuarto
  a quarter to two (literally the two ***minus*** *quarter)*

- to say at a certain time, use **a**:
  a las dos *at two o'clock*

- use **es** for any time related to one o'clock *(la una)* and **son** with all other hours:

  es la una *it's one o'clock* **son** las tres *it's three o'clock*

D3 Days and dates

- Use the usual numbers in dates:

  Mi cumpleaños es el treinta y uno de diciembre.

  My birthday is on the 31st of December.

- Days and months don't have capitals in Spanish:

  lunes 5 de junio *Monday the 5th of June*

- When talking about what is happening on a specific day of the week, put ***el*** in front of the day:

  El lunes, voy al polideportivo.
  On Monday I'm going to the sports centre.

- When talking about what happens regularly on a certain day of the week, use ***los***:

  Los domingos, salgo con mi familia.
  On Sundays I go out with my family.

D4 Expressions of quantity

- Expressions of quantity are followed by **de**:

  Un kilo de…

  Un paquete de…

  100 gramos de…

D5 When and how often

- Use the following phrases to say how often you do something:

  una vez a la semana *once a week*
  dos veces al mes *twice a month*
  todos los días *every day*
  el fin de semana *at weekends*
  por la mañana/tarde *in the morning/afternoon*
  temprano/tarde *early/late*
  entresemana *during the week*

E Stress and accentuation

- There are relatively simple rules about where the stress falls on a Spanish word. Remember this simple rhyme:

  Vowel, *n* or *s* penultimate stress

  All other words last vowel stress.

  h**a**blo, h**a**blas, h**a**blan – stress on penultimate (next to last) syllable

  habl**a**r, habl**a**d – stress on last syllable

  Madr**i**d – ends in a consonant (other than *n* or *s*)

  Barcel**o**na – ends in a vowel

- If the stress is to be put on a different syllable, an accent will be in place. For example: *jamón, cóctel, kilómetros, estación, televisión, teléfono, está, ¡Así!*

- In some cases, the accent over the vowel does not change the stress. It is there to remove any confusion that there might be between two words that are spelt the same. We write *para* ***mí*** and *para* ***él*** but in *para* ***ti***, the word *ti* does not need an accent because there is not another word that could be confused with it.

Para **mí**, el gazpacho.	**Mi** gazpacho está bueno.
Para **él**, el salmón.	Creo que **el** pollo es delicioso.
¿Quieres **té**?	¿**Te** gusta el chocolate?
Vamos a tomar **esta** mesa.	Prefiero **ésta**.
Pregunta a tu mamá **si** quiere café.	**Sí**, papá.

- Exclamations, like questions, have the same word order as statements in Spanish. The intonation has to show you are pronouncing an exclamation.

Vocabulario Español – Inglés

¡Así se hace! *Using the glossary*

Words are in alphabetical order. To find a word, look up its first letter, then find it according to the alphabetical order of its 2nd and 3rd letters:

e.g. **amigo** comes before **azul** because **am-** comes before **az-**.

A

la **abogada f** *lawyer*
el **abogado m** *lawyer*
abril *April*
abrir *to open*
la **abuela f** *grandmother*
el **abuelo m** *grandfather*
aburrido/a *boring*
aburrirse *to be bored*
el **aceite de oliva m** *olive oil*
acostarse *to go to bed*
de **acuerdo** *agreed, OK*
¿adónde? *where to?*
afectar *to affect*
las **afueras fpl** *outskirts*
agosto *August*
el **agua f** *water*
el agua con gas *sparkling water*
no **aguanto** *I can't bear*
ahora *now*
el **aire acondicionado m** *air conditioning*
al **aire libre** *outdoors*
el **ajo m** *garlic*
el **alemán m** *German (language)*
alemán/alemana *German*
algo *something*
de **algodón** *(made of) cotton*
allí *there*
la **almendra f** *almond*
la **almohada f** *pillow*
el **almuerzo m** *lunch*
alojarse *to stay*
alto/a *high, tall*
la **alumna f** *pupil*
el **alumno m** *pupil*
amable *kind*
amar *to love*
amarillo/a *yellow*
la **ambición f** *ambition*
el **ambiente m** *atmosphere*
la **amiga f** *friend*
el **amigo m** *friend*
el **andén m** *platform*
el **anillo m** *ring*
añadir *to add*
el **año m** *year*
el año nuevo *new year*
el año pasado *last year*
el **antibiótico m** *antibiotic*
antes *before*
anticuado/a *old-fashioned*
antipático/a *unpleasant*
el **anuncio m** *advert*
apagar *to switch off*
aparecer *to appear*
el **apartamento m** *apartment, flat*
me **apasiona** *I love*
¿te **apetece...?** *do you fancy...?*
aquí *here*
el **árbol de Navidad m** *Christmas tree*
el **argumento m** *plot (of story)*
el **armario m** *wardrobe*
el **arquitecto m** *architect*
la **arquitecta f** *architect*
arreglar *to tidy*
el **arroz m** *rice*
el **artista m** *artist*
la **artista f** *artist*
el **asado m** *roast*
la **asignatura f** *school subject*
la **aspirina f** *aspirin*
atractivo/a *attractive*
el **atún m** *tuna*
el **autobús m** *bus*
el **autocar m** coach
el **avión m** aeroplane
ayer yesterday
ayudar to help
¿En qué puedo ayudarle? *How can I help you?*
el **azúcar m** *sugar*
azul *blue*
azul celeste *light blue*
azul marino *navy blue*

B

el **bacalao m** *cod*
la **bahía f** *bay*
bailar *to dance*
bajo/a *short*
la **ballena f** *whale*
el **baloncesto m** *basketball*
el **baño m** *bath*
barato/a *cheap*
la **barbacoa f** *barbecue*
el **barco m** *boat*
la **barra f** *loaf*
el **barrio m** *neighbourhood*
bastante *quite*
la **basura f** *rubbish*
la **batalla f** *battle*
batir *to beat*
el **bebé m** *baby*
beber *to drink*
la **bebida f** *drink*
el **belén m** *nativity scene; crib*
el **beso m** *kiss*
la **bicicleta f** *bicycle*
bien *good, well*
el **billete m** *ticket*
un billete de ida y vuelta *a return ticket*
un billete sencillo *a single ticket*
la **biología f** *biology*
el **bistec m** *steak*
blanco/a *white*
blando/a *soft*
el **bocadillo m** *sandwich*
bonito/a *pretty*
la **botella f** *bottle*
el **brazo m** *arm*
el **brujo m** **la bruja f** *wizard/witch*
bueno/a *good*
¡buenísimo/a! *really good!*
buenos días *good morning*
el **bungalow m** *bungalow*
buscar *to look for*

C

la **cabaña f** *cabin*
la **cabeza f** *head*
cada *each*
el **café m** *coffee*
la **caja f** *box, packet*
los **calamares mpl** *squid*
los **calcetines mpl** *socks*
callado/a *quiet*
la **calle f** *street*
el **calor m** *heat*
hace calor *it is hot*
tengo calor *I'm hot*
la **cama f** *bed*
la **cámara f** *camera*
el **camarero m** *waiter*
la **camarera f** *waitress*
cambiar *to change*
la **camisa f** *shirt*
la **camiseta f** *T-shirt*
la **campanada f** *chime*
el **camping m** *campsite*
el **campo m** *countryside*
el **canal m** *TV channel*
cansado/a *tired*
el **caramelo m** *sweet*
cariñoso/a *affectionate*
la **carne f** *meat*
la **carnicería f** *butcher's*
caro/a *expensive*
las **carreras fpl de toros** *bull-running*
la **carretera f** *road*
el **cartón m** *cardboard*
la **casa f** *house*
casado/a *married*
casi *almost*
el **castillo m** *castle*
la **cebolla f** *onion*
celebrar *to celebrate*
se celebra *is celebrated*
celoso/a *jealous*
la **cena f** *evening meal*
cenar *to have dinner*
la **central nuclear f** *nuclear power station*
el **centro m** *centre*
cerca (de) *near*
los **cereales mpl** *cereal*
cerrar *to close*
el **champú m** *shampoo*
la **chaqueta f** *jacket*
el **chicle m** *chewing gum*
la **chica f** *girl*
el **chico m** *boy*
el **ciclismo m** *cycling*

las **ciencias fpl** *sciences*
la **científica f** *scientist*
el **científico m** *scientist*
el **cine m** *cinema*
la **cita f** *appointment, date*
la **ciudad f** *town, city*
claro/a *light*
la **clase f** *class; lesson*
el **clima m** *climate*
el **coche m** *car*
la **cocina f** *kitchen*
cocinar *to cook*
el **cóctel de gambas m** *prawn cocktail*
coger el autobús *to catch the bus*
el **colegio m** *school*
la **comedia f** *comedy*
el **comedor m** *dining room*
comer *to eat, have lunch*
el **cómic m** *comic*
la **comida f** *meal*
la **comida rápida f** *fast food*
¿cómo? *how?*
cómodo/a *comfortable*
compartir *to share*
comprar *to buy*
con *with*
¿con quién? *who with?*
conmigo *with me*
el **concurso m** *quiz show*
conocer *to meet, get to know*
consiste en *(it) consists of*
la **contaminación atmosférica f** *air pollution*
contaminar *to contaminate*
conveniente *convenient*
el **corazón m** *heart*
la **corbata f** *tie*
la **cortina f** *curtain*
cortar *to cut*
la **cosa f** *thing*
la **costa f** *the coast*
costar *to cost*
¿Cuánto cuesta? *How much does it cost?*
creer *to believe, think*
la **crema f (antiséptica)** *(antiseptic) cream*
la **criatura f** *creature*
el **cuaderno m** *exercise book*
el **cuadro m** *square*
de cuadros *checked*
¿cuál? *which?*
¿Cuál prefieres? *Which do you prefer?*
¿cuándo? *when?*
¿cuánto? *how much?*
cuidar *to look after*
el **cumpleaños m** *birthday*

D

dañar *to damage*
dar to *give*
dar una vuelta/un paseo *to go for a walk*
debajo de *beneath, below*
el **debate m** *debate*
deber *to have to*
debes *you should*
los **deberes mpl** *homework*
decir *to say*
dejar *to leave*
delante (de) *in front of*
delgado/a *thin*
demasiado *too (much)*
dentro (de) *inside*
la **dependienta f** *shop assistant*
el **dependiente m** *shop assistant*
el **deporte m** *sport*
deportista *sporty*
a la **derecha** *on the right*
desaparecer *to disappear*
el **desastre m** *disaster*
el **desayuno m** *breakfast*
descansar *to rest*
desde hace *for (a period of time)*
desde… hasta *from… until*
los **desechos domésticos mpl** *domestic waste*
desobediente *disobedient*
desorganizado/a *disorganised*
despedirse *to say goodbye*
el **despertador m** *alarm clock*
despertarse *to wake up*
después *after(wards)*
con destino *going to*
detestar *to detest*
detrás (de) *behind*
el **día m** *day*
el **día del Padre m/de la Madre f** *Father's/Mother's Day*
Buenos días *Good morning*
diciembre *December*
la **dieta sana f** *healthy diet*
difícil *difficult*
la **dificultad f** *difficulty*
el **dinero m** *money*
el **director m** *manager*
la **directora f** *manager*
la **discoteca f** *disco*
el **diseño m** *drawing, art*
disfrutar *to enjoy*
divertido/a *good fun*
divertirse *to have a good time*
divorciado/a *divorced*
la **docena f** *dozen*
el **documental m** *documentary*
doler *to hurt*
Me duele la garganta *My throat hurts*
el **dolor m** *pain*
el **domingo m** *Sunday*
Domingo de Ramos *Palm Sunday*
¿dónde? *where?*
dormir *to sleep*
el **dormitorio m** *bedroom*
mi propio dormitorio *my own bedroom*
la **droga f** *drug*
la **droguería f** *hardware shop*
ducharse *to have a shower*
el **dulce m** *sweet*
durar *to last*

E

ecológico/a *ecological*
educativo/a *educational*
egoísta *selfish*
el **ejercicio m** *exercise*
él *he, it*
elegante *elegant*
elegir *to choose*
ella *she, it*
emocionante *exciting*
empezar *to begin*
la **empleada de banco/oficina f** *bank/office worker*
el **empleado m** *bank/office worker*
me **encanta(n)** *I love*
encantado/a *pleased to meet you*
encontrarse *to meet*
¿Dónde nos encontramos? *Where shall we meet?*
enero *January*
la enfermera f *nurse*
el enfermero m *nurse*
enfrente (de) *opposite*
la **ensalada f** *salad*
la ensalada de fruta *fruit salad*
la ensalada mixta *mixed salad*
la ensalada verde *green salad*
entenderse *to get on*
entonces *then*
entre *between*
entretenido/a *entertaining*
la **entrevista f** *interview*
equilibrado/a *balanced*
el **equipo de música m** *hifi equipment*
escribir *to write*
la **escritora f** *writer*
el **escritor m** *writer*
el **escudo m** *badge*
el **espacio m** *space*
la **espalda f** *back*
el **español m** *Spanish (language)*
español/española *Spanish*
el **espejo m** *mirror*
esperar *to wait; to hope*
la **estación f** *station*
la estación del año *season*
la **estancia f** *estate, farm*
el **estante m** *shelf*
estar *to be*
estar de acuerdo *to be in agreement*
el **este m** *east*
el **estómago m** *stomach*
Tengo dolor de estómago *I have a stomach ache*
estresado/a *stressed*
No estés estresado/a *Don't be stressed*
estricto/a *strict*
el **estudiante m** *student*
la **estudiante f** *student*
estudiar *to study*
estúpido/a *stupid*
el **examen m** *exam*
el **éxito m** *success*
explotar *to explode*
extrovertido/a *extroverted*

F

la **fábrica f** *factory*
fabuloso/a *great!*
fácil *easy*
la **falda de tablas f** *pleated skirt*
la **familia f** *family*
fantástico/a *fantastic*
la **farmacia f** *chemist's*
febrero *February*
feo/a *ugly*
la **feria f** *fair*
el **ferrocarril m** *railway*
la **fiebre f** *temperature*
Tengo fiebre *I have a temperature*
la **fiesta f** *holiday, festivity*
el filete m *fillet*
el **fin m** *end*
el fin de semana *weekend*
al **final de** *at the end of*
finalmente *finally*

la **física f** *physics*
el **flan m** *egg custard*
la **flor f** *flower*
la **flota f** *fleet*
el **folleto m** *leaflet*
formal *formal*
fregar los platos *to wash up*
freír *to fry*
fresco/a *fresh*
frío/a *cold*
Tengo frío *I am cold*
la **fruta f** *fruit*
a **fuego lento** *on a low heat*
el **fuego artificial m** *firework*
fuera *outside*
la **fumadora f** *smoker*
el **fumador m** *smoker*
fumar *to smoke*
el **fútbol m** *football*

G

las **gafas de sol fpl** *sunglasses*
la **gamba f** *prawn*
ganar *to win*
la **garganta f** *throat*
el **gas m** *gas*
la **gasolina f** *petrol*
gastar *to spend*
el **gazpacho m** *cold tomato soup*
en **general** *in general*
generoso/a *generous*
genial *great, fabulous*
la **gente f** *people*
la **geografía f** *geography*
gordo/a *fat*
la **gorra f** *cap*
unas **gotas para los ojos fpl** *eye drops*
grande *big*
los **grandes almacenes mpl** *department store*
la **grasa f** *grease/fat*
grave *serious*
el **gripe m** *flu*
Tengo gripe *I have flu*
gris *grey*
guapo/a *good-looking*
la **guerra f** *war*
me **gusta(n)** *I like*

H

la **habitación f** *room*
hablador(a) *talkative*
hablar *to speak*
habrá *there will be*
hacer *to make, do*
hace falta *is lacking*
me hace falta una almohada *I need a pillow*
se hace con… *it's made of…*
hacer alpinismo *to go climbing*
hacer la cama *to make the bed*
hacer esquí (acuático) *to go (water-skiing)*
hacer excursiones *to go on trips*
hacer los deberes *to do your homework*
hacer trekking *to go trekking*
hacer la vela *to sail*
hacer windsurf *to go windsurfing*
hizo sol *it was sunny*
la **hamburguesa f** *hamburger*
hasta *until*
hay *there is, there are*
hay que *it is necessary to*
el **helado m** *ice cream*
helar *to be icy*
la **hermana f** *sister*
la **hermanastra f** *stepsister*
el **hermanastro m** *stepbrother*
el **hermano m** *brother*
el **hielo m** *ice*
la **hija f** *daughter*
el **hijo m** *son*
la **historia f** *history*
hola *hello*
honesto/a *honest*
la **hora f** *hour*
una **hora de retraso f** *an hour's delay*
el **horario m** *timetable*
el **hotel m** *hotel*
el **huevo m** *egg*
el **humo m** *smoke*

I

el **idioma m** *language*
la **iglesia f** *church*
la **imagen f** *statue, image*
impaciente *impatient*
incómodo/a *uncomfortable*
infantil *childish*
la **informática f** *IT*
la **ingeniera f** *engineer*
el **ingeniero m** *engineer*
el **inglés m** *English (language)*
inglés/inglesa *English*
la **insolación f** *sunstroke*
Tengo una insolación *I have sunstroke*
insoportable *unbearable*
el **instituto m** *school*
inteligente *intelligent*
el **intercambio m** *exchange*
interesante *interesting*
(el) **Internet m** *internet*
el **invierno m** *winter*
ir *to go*
ir de compras *to go shopping*
ir en bicicleta *to go by bike*
ir andando *to walk*
a la **izquierda** *on the left*

J

el **jabón m** *soap*
el **jamón m** *ham*
el **jarabe m** *cough medicine*
el **jefe m** *head, leader*
el **jersey m** *jumper*
el/la joven *young person*
jubilado/a *retired*
las **judías verdes fpl** *green beans*
el **jueves m** *Thursday*
el **juego m** *game*
jugar *to play*
jugar a las cartas *to play cards*
julio *July*
junio *June*
justo/a *fair*

K

el **kilo m** *kilo*

L

al **lado de** *next to*
la **lámpara f** *lamp*
de **lana** *woollen*
largo/a *long*
la **lata f** *tin*
la **lavadora f** *washing machine*
lavar el coche *to wash the car*
lavar(se) *to wash (oneself)*
la **leche f** *milk*
la **lechuga f** *lettuce*
la **lectura f** *reading*
leer *to read*
el **legumbre m** *vegetable*
lejos *far away*
lento/a *slow*
levantarse *to get up*
libre *free*
la **librería f** *bookcase*
el **libro m** *book*
el **limón m** *lemon*
limpiar *to clean*
limpio/a *clean*
luego *next*
el **lugar m** *place*
el **lunes m** *Monday*
la **luz f** *light*

LL

llamarse *to be called*
la **llegada f** *arrival*
llegar *to arrive*
llevar *to wear, to carry*
Lleva una hora de retraso *It's an hour late*
Se llevan trajes de flamenco *Flamenco dresses are worn*
llover *to rain*

M

la **madrastra f** *stepmother*
la **madre f** *mother*
malo/a *bad*
la **mañana f** *morning; tomorrow*
esta mañana *this morning*
mañana por la mañana *tomorrow morning*
la **mano f** *hand*
el **manto m** *cape; coat*
la **manzana f** *apple*
el **mar m** *sea*
la **marea negra f** *oil slick*
mareado/a *sick, dizzy*
Estoy mareado/a *I feel sick/dizzy*
el **marido m** *husband*
el **marisco m** *shellfish*
marrón *brown*
el **martes m** *Tuesday*
marzo *March*
más *more*
más… que *more… than*
las **matemáticas fpl** *maths*
mayo *May*
la **mecánico f** *mechanic*
el **mecánico m** *mechanic*
el **médico m** *doctor*
la **médico f** *doctor*
medio/a *half*
el **medio ambiente m** *environment*
mejor *better*
el mejor *the best*
lo mejor es… *the best thing is…*
menos *less*
menos… que *less… than*
al **menos** *at least*
el **mensaje m** *message*
el **mercado m** *market*

la **merluza f** *hake*
el **mes m** *month*
la **mesa f** *table*
poner la mesa *to lay the table*
quitar la mesa *to clear the table*
la **mesita de noche f** *bedside table*
el **metro m** *underground*
mezclar *to mix*
la **miel f** *honey*
mientras *while*
el **miércoles m** *Wednesday*
el **mil m** *thousand*
mirar *to look at*
la **Misa de Gallo f** *Midnight Mass*
la **montaña f** *mountain*
montar a caballo *to go horseriding*
el **monumento m** *monument*
morado/a *purple*
morir *to die*
mucho/a *a lot*
mucho gusto *pleased to meet you*
los **muebles mpl** *furniture*
muerto/a *dead*
la **mujer f** *woman, wife*
el **mundo m** *world*
muy *very*
muy bien *very well*

N

nacer *to be born*
nada *nothing*
nadar *to swim*
nadie *nobody*
la **naranja f** *orange*
naranja *orange (colour)*
la **nariz f** *nose*
la **naturaleza f** *nature*
la **Navidad f** *Christmas*
negro/a *black*
nervioso/a *nervous*
nevar *to snow*
la **niebla f** *fog*
la **niña f** *child*
el **niño m** *child*
la **noche f** *night*
La Nochebuena *Christmas Eve*
La Nochevieja *New Year's Eve*
normalmente *normally*
el **norte m** *north*
las **noticias fpl** *news (programme)*
la **novela f** *novel*
la **novia f** *girlfriend*
noviembre *November*
el **novio m** *boyfriend*
nuevo/a *new*
nunca *never*

O

o *or*
obediente *obedient*
octubre *October*
odiar *to hate*
el **oeste m** *west*
el **oído m** *ear*
el **ojo m** *eye*
olvidar *to forget*
la **opinión f** *opinion*
¿Cuál es tu opinión?
What is your opinion?
En mi opinión *In my opinion*
ordenado/a *tidy*
el **ordenador m** *computer*
el ordenador portátil *laptop*
organizado/a *organised*
orgulloso/a *proud*
el **oso m** *bear*
el **otoño m** *autumn*
otro/a *other*
otra vez *again*

P

paciente *patient*
el **padrastro m** *stepfather*
el **padre m** *father*
la **paella f** *paella*
el **país m** *country*
el **pájaro m** *bird*
la **pampa f** *prairie*
el **pan m** *bread*
la **panadería f** *baker's*
los **pantalones mpl** *trousers*
el **papel m** *paper*
el **paquete m** *packet*
¿para qué? *what for?*
la **parada f** *stop*
parecer *to seem*
Me parece que... *It seems to me that...*
la **pared f** *wall*
el **parque infantil m** *children's playground*
pasar *to happen; to spend (time)*
pasarlo bien *to have a good time*
¡Lo pasé fatal! *I had an awful time!*
¡Lo pasé genial/bomba!
I had a great time!
¿Qué te pasa? *What's the matter?*
pasar la aspiradora *to vacuum*
la **pasta f** *pasta*
la **pasta de dientes f** *toothpaste*
el **pastel m** *cake*
la **pastilla f** *tablet, pill*
la **patata f** *potato*
las patatas fritas *chips; crisps*
patinar *to skate*
el **patio m** *playground*
el **pavo m** *turkey*
pelearse *to fight*
la **película f** *film*
película de acción *action film*
película de aventuras *adventure film*
película de ciencia ficción *sci fi film*
película de dibujos animados
animated film/cartoon
película romántica *romantic film*
película de suspense *thriller*
el **peligro m** *danger*
el **pelo m** *hair*
pensar *to think*
Pienso que... *I think that...*
peor *worse*
pequeño/a *small*
la **pera f** *pear*
perder *to lose*
perezoso/a *lazy*
el **periódico m** *newspaper*
permitir *to allow*
pero *but*
el **perrito caliente m** *hotdog*
la **persiana f** *blind*
el **personaje m** *character*
la **pesca f** *fishing*
la **pescadería f** *fishmonger's*
el **pescado m** *fish*
picar *to snack*
el **pie m** *foot*
la **pierna f** *leg*
la **pieza f** *piece*
el **pimiento m** *pepper*
la **piscina f** *swimming pool*
la **pizza f** *pizza*
planchar *to iron*
el **plato m** *dish, course*
el primer plato *first course*
el segundo plato *second/main course*
Mi plato favorito es...
My favourite dish is...
la **playa f** *beach*
un **poco** *a little*
poder *to be able*
la **policía f** *policewoman*
el **policía m** *policeman*
el **polideportivo m** *sports centre*
el **pollo m** *chicken*
la **polución f** *pollution*
el **polvo m** *dust*
quitar el polvo *to dust*
poner *to put*
poner la mesa *to lay the table*
¿Qué ponen? *What's on?*
por *through, around*
¿por qué? *why?*
porque *because*
la **postal f** *postcard*
el **póster m** *poster*
el **postre m** *dessert*
practicar *to practise*
practicar la equitación
to go horseriding
practicar el golf *to play golf*
practicar la natación *to go swimming*
el **precio m** *price*
preferir *to prefer*
¿Qué prefieres? *What do you prefer?*
preguntar *to ask*
preocuparse *to worry*
preparar las comidas *to prepare meals*
presentar *to introduce*
la **prima f** *female cousin*
la **primavera f** *spring*
primero/a *first*
el **primo m** *male cousin*
el **problema m** *problem*
procedente de *coming from*
la **procesión f** *procession*
producir *to produce*
el **profesor m** *teacher*
la **profesora f** *teacher*
el **programa m** *programme*
protestar *to protest*
próximo/a *next*
la **psicóloga f** *psychologist*
el **psicólogo m** *psychologist*
el **pueblo m** *village, town*
la **puerta f** *door*
la **pulsera f** *bracelet*

Q

¿qué? *what?*
quedarse *to stay*
quemar *to burn*
querer *to want*
el **queso m** *cheese*
¿quién? *who?*
químico/a *chemical*
quince *fifteen*
quince días *a fortnight*
el **quiosco m** *newsagent's*
quitar la mesa *to clear the table*
quitar el polvo *to dust*
quitarse *to take off*

R

la **radio f** *radio*
rápido/a *fast*
de **rayas** *striped*
la **receta f** *prescription; recipe*
recibir *to receive*
reciclar *to recycle*
recomendar *to recommend*
¿Qué recomienda? *What do you recommend?*
recordarse de *to remember*
el **recreo m** *break time*
el **regalo m** *present*
regañar *to tell off*
la **regla f** *rule*
reír *to laugh*
relajado/a *relaxed*
el **reloj m** *clock, watch*
el **resfriado m** *cold*
Tengo un resfriado *I have a cold*
los **residuos químicos mpl** *chemical waste*
la **revista f** *magazine*
los **Reyes Magos mpl** *the Three Wise Men/Kings*
rico/a *tasty*
riquísimo/a *very tasty*
el **riesgo m** *risk*
el **río m** *river*
rojo/a *red*
un **rollo m** *a pain, a bore*
¡Fue un rollo! *It was boring!*
romántico/a *romantic*
romperse *to break*
la **ropa f** *clothes*
rosa *pink*
rubio *blond*
el **ruido m** *noise*
ruidoso/a *noisy*

S

el **sábado m** *Saturday*
la **sábana f** *sheet*
saber *to know*
No sé *I don't know*
sacar *to take out*
sacar fotos *to take photos*
la **sal f** *salt*
la **sala de juegos f** *games room*
la **salchicha f** *sausage*
la **salida f** *departure*
salir *to leave, go out*
el **salmón m** *salmon*
la **salud f** *health*
salvar *to save*
sano/a *healthy*
la **sartén f** *frying pan*
el **secador de pelo m** *hairdryer*
la **secretaria f** *secretary*
el **secretario m** *secretary*
segundo/a *second*
seguir *to follow*
la **selva f** *forest*
la **semana f** *week*
la semana pasada *last week*
la semana próxima *next week*
la semana que viene *next week*
La Semana Santa *Easter*
sensible *sensitive*
el **sentido de humor m** *sense of humour*
sentirse *to feel*
No me siento bien *I don't feel well*
separado/a *separated*
septiembre *September*
ser *to be*
la **serie f** *series*
serio/a *serious*
sí *yes*
siempre *always*
el **siglo m** *century*
la **silla f** *chair*
simpático/a *nice*
sin embargo *however*
el **sitio m** *place*
situado/a *situated*
sobre *on*
sobre todo *above all*
el **sol m** *sun*
el **soldado m** *soldier*
solo/a *alone*
la **sombra f** *shade*
el **sondeo m** *survey*
la **sopa de pescado f** *fish soup*
no **soporto...** *I can't stand...*
sorprendente *surprising*
subir *to go up, ascend*
suelo coger el tren *I usually catch the train*
la **suerte f** *luck*
súper guapo/a *very good-looking*
el **supermercado m** *supermarket*
el **sur m** *south*

T

también *as well, also*
tan... como... *as... as...*
la **taquilla f** *ticket office*
la **tarde f** *afternoon*
esta tarde *this afternoon*
por la tarde *in the afternoon*
tarde *late*
la **tarea f** *chore*
el **taxi m** *taxi*
el **té m** *tea*
la **telenovela f** *soap opera*
la **televisión f** *television*
temprano *early*
tener *to have*
tengo calor *I'm hot*
tengo hambre *I'm hungry*
tengo miedo *I'm frightened*
tengo prisa *I'm in a hurry*
tener lugar *to take place*
tener que *to have to (do something)*
el **tenis m** *tennis*
la **terraza f** *terrace*
la **tía f** *aunt*
el **tiempo m** *time; weather*
¿Qué tiempo hizo? *What was the weather like?*
Hizo buen tiempo *The weather was good*
Hizo mal tiempo *The weather was bad*
la **tienda f** *tent; shop*
la **tienda de ropa f** *clothes shop*
el **tigre m** *tiger*
tímido/a *shy*
el **tío m** *uncle*
tirar *to throw*
la **tirita f** *plaster*
la **toalla f** *towel*
todo/a *every*
tomar *to take*
tomar el sol *to sunbathe*
el **tomate m** *tomato*
tonto/a *silly*
la **tormenta f** *storm*
la **tortilla española f** *Spanish omelette*
la **tos f** *cough*
Tengo tos *I have a cough*
trabajar *to work*
trabajador(a) *hard-working*
tranquilo/a *peaceful, quiet*
el **tranvía m** *tram*
el **tren m** *train*
triste *sad*
el **trono m** *throne*
el **trozo m** *piece*
el **tubo m** *tube*

U

último/a *last*
la **universidad f** *university*
el **uniforme m** *uniform*
usar *to use*
útil *useful*
la **uva f** *grape*

V

las **vacaciones fpl** *holidays*
vale *OK*
los **vaqueros mpl** *jeans*
el **vaso m** *glass*
la **velocidad f** *speed*
la **ventana f** *window*
ver *to see*
el **verano m** *summer*
¿verdad? *really?/isn't it?*
verde *green*
ver *to see/watch*
la **verdura f** *green vegetables*
el **vestido m** *dress*
vestirse *to get dressed*
la **vez f** *time*
a veces *sometimes*
dos veces al día *twice a day*
de vez en cuando *occasionally*
una vez *once*
el **vía m** *(railway) track*
viajar *to travel*
el **viaje m** *journey*
la **viajera f** *traveller*
el **viajero m** *traveller*
la **vida f** *life*
el **vidrio m** *glass*
viejo/a *old*
el **viento m** *wind*
el **viernes m** *Friday*
el **vino blanco m** *white wine*
el **vino tinto m** *red wine*
la **viuda f** *widow*
el **viudo m** *widower*
vivir *to live*
el **voleibol m** *volleyball*
volver *to return*
el **vuelo m** *flight*

Z

la **zapatería f** *shoe shop*
las **zapatillas de deporte fpl** *trainers*
los **zapatos mpl** *shoes*
los zapatos planos *flat shoes*
los zapatos de tacón *high-heeled shoes*
el **zumo m** *juice*
el zumo de naranja *orange juice*

Vocabulario Inglés - Español

¡Así se hace! *Using the glossary*

Some words will need to be changed when you use them in a sentence, e.g.

- nouns: are they singular or plural?

Do you need the word for 'a' (*un* m, ***una* f**) instead of 'the' (*el* m, ***la* f**)?

- adjectives: masculine or feminine? singular or plural?
- verbs: check the grammar section for the endings you need.

A

a, an ***un/una***
to be able ***poder***
advert ***el anuncio m***
aeroplane ***el avión m***
affectionate ***cariñoso/a***
afternoon ***la tarde f***
after(wards) ***después***
again ***otra vez***
almost ***casi***
also ***también***
always ***siempre***
and ***y***
anything: anything else? ***¿algo más?***
appointment ***la cita f***
April ***abril***
arm ***el brazo m***
to arrive ***llegar***
to ask ***preguntar***
August ***agosto***
aunt ***la tía f***
autumn ***el otoño m***

B

back ***la espalda f***
baker's ***la panadería f***
basketball ***el baloncesto m***
bath ***el baño m***
to be ***ser; estar***
beach ***la playa f***
because ***porque***
bed ***la cama f***
  to go to bed ***acostarse***
bedroom ***el dormitorio m***
before ***antes***
to begin ***empezar***
behind ***detrás (de)***
to believe ***creer***
better ***mejor***
between ***entre***
bicycle ***la bicicleta f***
big ***grande***
biology ***la biología f***
birthday ***el cumpleaños m***
  When is your birthday?
  ¿Cuándo es tu cumpleaños?
  My birthday is on 15th June
  Mi cumpleaños es el quince de junio
black ***negro/a***
blue ***azul***
boat ***el barco m***
book ***el libro m***
bookcase ***la librería f***
boring ***aburrido/a***
bottle ***la botella f***
box ***la caja f***
boy ***el chico m***
boyfriend ***el novio m***
bread ***el pan m***
break time ***el recreo m***
breakfast ***el desayuno m***
  I have breakfast ***desayuno***
brother ***el hermano***
brown ***marrón***
but ***pero***
to buy ***comprar***

C

cake ***el pastel m***
cap ***la gorra f***
car ***el coche m***
cat ***el gato m***
chair ***la silla f***
cheap ***barato/a***
cheese ***el queso m***
chemist's ***la farmacia f***
chewing gum ***el chicle m***
chicken ***el pollo m***
child ***el niño m la niña f***
chore ***la tarea f***
Christmas ***la Navidad f***
church ***la iglesia f***
cinema ***el cine m***
class, lesson ***la clase f***
clean ***limpio/a***
to clean ***limpiar***
clock ***el reloj m***
to close ***cerrar***
clothes ***la ropa f***
coach ***el autocar m***
coast ***la costa f***
cold ***el resfriado m***
cold ***frío/a***
  it is cold ***hace frío***
comfortable ***cómodo/a***
computer ***el ordenador m***
to cost ***costar***
  how much does it cost?
  ¿cuánto cuesta?
cough ***la tos f***
country ***el país m***
countryside ***el campo m***
cousin ***el primo m la prima f***

D

to dance ***bailar***
daughter ***la hija f***
day ***el día m***
December ***diciembre***
departure ***la salida f***
dessert ***el postre***
diet ***la dieta f***
difficult ***difícil***
dining room ***el comedor m***
dinner ***la cena f***
disaster ***el desastre m***
to do ***hacer***
  What do you do? ***¿Qué haces?***
doctor ***el médico m la médico f***
dog ***el perro m***
door ***la puerta f***
dozen ***la docena f***
drawing ***el diseño m***
dress ***el vestido m***
  to get dressed ***vestirse***
drink ***la bebida f***
to drink ***beber***
dust ***el polvo m***
  to dust ***quitar el polvo***

E

each ***cada***
ear ***el oído m***
early ***temprano***
easy ***fácil***
to eat ***comer***
egg ***el huevo m***
end ***el final m***
  at the end of ***al final de***
English ***el inglés m***
to enjoy ***disfrutar***
environment ***el medio ambiente m***
every ***todo/a***
  every day ***todos los días***
exciting ***emocionante***

exchange *el intercambio m*
exercise book *el cuaderno m*
expensive ***caro/a***
eye *el ojo m*

F

fancy: do you fancy: ***¿te apetece?***
far from ***lejos de***
fast ***rápido/a***
father *el padre m*
February ***febrero***
to feel ***sentirse***
film ***la película f***
firework *el fuego artificial m*
fish *el pescado m*
fishmonger's ***la pescadería f***
to follow ***seguir***
flat *el apartamento m; el piso m*
flight *el vuelo m*
flu *el gripe m*
foot *el pie m*
football el *fútbol m*
to play football ***jugar al fútbol***
for, in order to ***para***
forest ***la selva f***
to forget ***olvidar***
fortnight ***quince días***
Friday *el viernes m*
friend *el amigo m* ***la amiga f***
in front of... ***delante de...***
fruit ***la fruta f***
fun ***divertido/a***
furniture *los muebles mpl*

G

game *el juego m*
girl ***la chica f***
girlfriend ***la novia f***
to get up ***levantarse***
to give ***dar***
glass *el vaso m*
glasses ***las gafas fpl***
to go ***ir***
to go shopping ***ir de compras***
good ***bueno/a***
I'm (not) good at...
(no) se me da(n) bien...
Good afternoon ***Buenas tardes***
Good morning ***Buenos días***
good-looking ***guapo/a***
grandfather *abuelo m*
grandmother ***abuela f***
great! ***¡genial!***
green ***verde***
grey ***gris***

H

hair *el pelo m*
half ***medio/a***
ham *el jamón m*
hand ***la mano f***
to happen ***pasar***
What's happening? ***¿Qué pasa?***
to hate ***odiar***
to have ***tener***
he/it ***él***
head ***la cabeza f***
health ***la salud f***
healthy ***sano/a***
heat *el calor m*
hello ***hola***
to help ***ayudar***
here ***aquí***
here you are ***aquí tiene***
his/her ***su/sus***
holidays ***las vacaciones fpl***
homework *los deberes mpl*
to do homework ***hacer los deberes***
to hope ***esperar***
horse *el caballo m*
to go horseriding ***montar a caballo***
hot: I'm hot ***tengo calor;***
it is hot ***hace calor***
house ***la casa f***
at my house ***en mi casa***
how? ***¿cómo?***
How are you? ***¿Qué tal?***
how many? ***¿cuántos?***
How old are you?
¿Cuántos años tienes?
how much? ***¿cuánto?***
how much is it? ***¿cuánto es?***
however ***sin embargo***
hungry: I'm hungry ***tengo hambre***
husband *el marido m*

I

I ***yo***
ice cream *el helado m*
in ***en***
inside ***dentro (de)***
interesting ***interesante***
to introduce ***presentar***
to iron ***planchar***

J

jacket ***la chaqueta f***
January ***enero***
jeans *los vaqueros mpl*
journey *el viaje m*
July ***julio***
jumper *el jersey m*
June ***junio***

K

kitchen ***la cocina f***
know: I don't know ***No sé***

L

lamp ***la lámpara f***
language *el idioma m*
laptop *el portátil m*
large ***grande***
lawyer *el abogado m* ***la abogada f***
last ***último/a***
to last ***durar***
late ***tarde***
lazy ***perezoso/a***
to leave, go out ***salir***
to leave behind ***dejar***
left: on the left ***a la izquierda***
leg ***la pierna f***
less ***menos***
library ***la biblioteca f***
life ***la vida f***
light ***la luz f***
like: I like ***me gusta(n)***
a little ***un poco***
to live ***vivir***
loaf ***la barra f***
to look at, to watch ***mirar***
to look for ***buscar***
a lot ***mucho/a***
love: I love ***me encanta(n)***
luck ***la suerte f***
lunch *el almuerzo m*

M

to make ***hacer***
March ***marzo***
market *el mercado m*
married ***casado/a***
May ***mayo***
meal ***la comida f***
meat ***la carne f***
to meet: Where shall we meet?
¿Dónde nos encontramos?
milk ***la leche f***
(on) Monday *el lunes m*
money *el dinero m*
month *el mes m*
more ***más***
morning ***la mañana f***
in the morning ***por la mañana***
mother ***la madre f***
mountain ***la montaña f***
my ***mi/mis***

N

name: What is your name?
¿Cómo te llamas?
near to ***cerca de***
neighbourhood *el barrio m*
new ***nuevo/a***
news ***las noticias fpl***
newsagent's *el quiosco m*
next (place) ***próximo/a***
next (time) ***luego***
next to ***al lado de***
nice ***simpático/a***
night ***la noche f***
no, not ***no***
nobody ***nadie***
noise *el ruido m*
nose ***la nariz f***
nothing ***nada***
November ***noviembre***
now ***ahora***
number *el número m*
nunca ***never***

O

October **octubre**
OK **vale**
on **sobre**
once **una vez**
onion **la cebolla f**
to open **abrir**
opposite **enfrente (de)**
outside **fuera**
outskirts **las afueras fpl**
or **o**
orange juice **el zumo de naranja m**

P

packet **el paquete m**
pain **el dolor m**
What a pain! **¡Qué rollo!**
peaceful **tranquilo/a**
pencil **el lápiz m**
people **la gente f**
petrol **la gasolina f**
place **el lugar m**
plaster **la tirita f**
platform **el andén m**
to play **jugar**
to play golf **practicar el golf**
pleased to meet you
encantado/a; mucho gusto
pollution **la contaminación f**
poster **el póster m**
to prefer **preferir**
present **el regalo m**
pretty **bonito/a**
price **el precio m**
proud **orgulloso/a**
pupil **el alumno m**, **la alumna f**
to put **poner**

Q

quite **bastante**

R

to rain **llover**
to read **leer**
really? **¿verdad?**
to receive **recibir**
to recycle **reciclar**
red **rojo/a**
retired **jubilado/a**
to return **volver**
rice **el arroz m**
right: on the right **a la derecha**
river **el río m**
room **la habitación f**
rubbish **la basura f**

S

sad **triste**
salad **la ensalada**
sandwich **el bocadillo m**
Saturday **el sábado m**
sausage **la salchicha f**
to say **decir**
school **el colegio m**; **el instituto m**
sciences **las ciencias fpl**
to see **ver**
to seem **parecer**
September **septiembre**
she/it **ella**
shelf **el estante m**
shellfish **el marisco m**
shirt **la camisa f**
shoe **el zapato m**
shoe shop **la zapatería f**
shop **la tienda f**
short **bajo/a**
shower **la ducha f**
to have a shower **ducharse**
shy **tímido/a**
sister **la hermana f**
skirt **la falda f**
to sleep **dormir**
slow **lento/a**
small **pequeño/a**
socks **los calcetines mpl**
some **unos/unas**
something **algo**
sometimes **a veces**
son **el hijo m**
soup **la sopa f**
Spanish **español/española**
Spanish (language) **el español m**
to speak **hablar**
I speak English, French and Italian.
Hablo inglés, francés e italiano.
to spend **gastar**
sport **el deporte m**
sports centre **el polideportivo m**
spring **la primavera f**
station **la estación f**
to stay **alojarse; quedarse**
step/half brother **el hermanastro m**
step/half sister **la hermanastra f**
stepfather **el padrastro m**
stepmother **la madrastra f**
stomach **el estómago m**
street **la calle f**
stressed **estresado/a**
student **el estudiante m**,
la estudiante f
to study **estudiar**
(school) subjects **las asignaturas fpl**
summer **el verano m**
sun **el sol m**
to sunbathe **tomar el sol**
supermarket **el supermercado m**
surprising **sorprendente**
to swim **nadar**
swimming pool **la piscina f**
to switch off **apagar**

T

table **la mesa f**
to take **tomar**
to take (something) off **quitarse**
tall **alto/a**
tea **el té m**
teacher **el profesor m** **la profesora f**
TV **la televisión f**
to watch TV **ver la tele**
temperature **la fiebre f**
then **entonces**
there **allí**
there is, there are **hay**
thing **la cosa f**
to think **pensar**
throat **la garganta f**
through/by **por**
Thursday **el jueves m**
ticket **el billete m**
ticket office **la taquilla f**
to tidy **arreglar**
tie **la corbata f**
time: At what time? **¿A qué hora?**
timetable **el horario m**
tin **la lata f**
tired **cansado/a**
toilet **el baño m, el aseo m**
too (much) **demasiado**
toothpaste **la pasta de dientes f**
towel **la toalla f**
town **la ciudad f**; **el pueblo m**
train **el tren m**
trainers **las zapatillas de deporte fpl**
tram **el tranvía m**
to travel **viajar**
tree **el árbol m**
Christmas tree **el árbol de Navidad**
trousers **los pantalones mpl**
tube **el tubo m**
Tuesday **el martes m**
tuna **el atún m**
twice **dos veces**

U

unbearable **insoportable**
uncle **el tío m**
under **debajo de**
uniform **el uniforme m**
university **la universidad f**
unpleasant **antipático/a**
until **hasta**
to use **usar**
useful **útil**
usually: I usually walk **suelo ir a pie**

V

vegetable **el legumbre m**
green vegetables **la verdura f**
very **muy**
volleyball **el voleibol m**

W

to wait ***esperar***
waiter ***el camarero m***
waitress ***la camarera f***
walk: to go for a walk ***dar un paseo/una vuelta***
to want ***querer***
Do you want to go to the cinema?
¿Quieres ir al cine?
wardrobe ***el armario m***
to wash ***lavar***
to wash up ***fregar los platos***
water ***el agua f***
weather ***el tiempo m***
What's the weather like
¿Qué tiempo hace?
Wednesday ***el miércoles m***
to wear ***llevar***
week ***la semana f***
weekend ***el fin de semana m***
what? ***¿qué?***
when? ***¿cuándo?***
where? ***¿dónde?***
while ***mientras***
white ***blanco/a***
who? ***¿quién?***
why? ***¿por qué?***
widow ***la viuda f***
widower ***el viudo m***
wife ***la mujer f***
wind ***el viento m***
window ***la ventana f***
wine ***el vino m***
winter ***el invierno m***
with ***con***
to work ***trabajar***
world ***el mundo m***
to write ***escribir***

Y

year ***el año m***
I am 12 years old ***tengo doce años***
yellow ***amarillo/a***
yes ***sí***
yesterday ***ayer***
you ***tú, usted***
young ***joven***
your ***tu/tus***

Common instructions in *¡Así!*

Phrases

Busca las palabras en el texto	*Find the words in the text*
Cambia las palabras	*Change the words*
Contesta al correo electrónico/a las preguntas	*Respond to the email/questions*
Contesta a la carta	*Respond to the letter*
Copia y rellena	*Copy and fill in*
Corrige las frases mentirosas	*Correct the false sentences*
¿Cuántas frases puedes escribir en 5 minutos?	*How many sentences can you write in 5 minutes?*
Elige/Escoge la respuesta correcta	*Choose the correct answer*
Empareja las descripciones y los dibujos	*Pair up the descriptions and the pictures*
Entrevista a tu pareja	*Interview your partner*
Escribe el número (correcto)/la letra (correcta)	*Write the (correct) number/letter*
Escribe en inglés/español	*Write in English/Spanish*
Escribe una lista	*Write a list*
Escucha y lee	*Listen and read*
Escucha otra vez	*Listen again*
Habla con tu pareja	*Speak with your partner*
Haz diálogos con tu pareja	*Carry out conversations with your partner*
Haz preguntas a tu pareja	*Ask your partner questions*
Haz una encuesta en tu clase	*Carry out/do a survey in your class*
Lee las conversaciones/descripciones/frases	*Read the conversations/descriptions/sentences*
Lee las frases a tu pareja	*Read the sentences to your partner*
Mira el mapa/plano/texto/los dibujos	*Look at the map/plan/text/pictures*
Pon ... en orden/en el orden correcto	*Put ... in order/in the correct order*
¿Quién habla?	*Who is talking?*
Practica los diálogos con tu pareja	*Practise the dialogues with your partner*
¿Qué significa la palabra ...?	*What does the word... mean?*
Rellena el cuadro/los blancos/los espacios	*Fill in the table/blanks/spaces*
Trabaja con tu pareja	*Work with your partner*
Une las frases (con los dibujos)	*Match the sentences (with the pictures)*
Une las preguntas y las respuestas	*Match the questions and answers*
Usa ... del cuadro	*Use ... from the box*
Verdad o mentira	*True or false*

Single words

Adivina	*Guess*
Añade	*Add*
Apunta	*Note*
cada	*each*
con	*with*
Di	*Say*
Dibuja	*Draw*
Diseña	*Design*
juego	*game*
mencionado/a	*mentioned*
Repite	*Repeat*
según	*according to*
sin	*without*
sobre (ti)	*about (you)*
sondeo	*survey*
Traduce	*Translate*
¿Y tú?	*And you?*

Acknowledgements

The authors and publisher would like to thank the following people, without whose support they could not have created ¡Así! 2:

Ian Blair and Carlos Diaz for their detailed advice throughout the writing.

Kathryn Tate and Michelle Armstrong for editing the materials.

Models shot by Martin Sookias courtesy of d'Overbroecks School, Oxford: Sam King, Andy Styles and Peter Warme.

Recorded by Nordqvist Productions España SL, Alicante in Spain with Chema Bazán, David Garzón, Vanessa Reyes, Inés Iborra, Andres Jesús Gil, María Santos, Lorena Martín, Omar Sanchos, Ángela Díaz, Diego Ramos, Mariana Ramos, Juan Penalva, Bielka A. Villagómez, Timothy P. Curtis, Clara Suñer.

Photo credits
Front cover photograph: Spanish Horse Riding School, Jerez, Spain by Carl Pederson/Alamy;

David Simson/B-6940 Septon (DASPHOTOGB@aol.com): pp6 (D, E, H), 8, 27 (1), 30, 43, 51 (1, 2), 55 (2, 3), 64, 65 (1), 68 (B, F), 69 (1A, 2A), 72 (1), 77 (1), 83 (1), 84, 89, 101, 126 (B, D), 129; Martyn Chillmaid: pp35 (2), 55 (bottom); Martin Sookias: pp14, 55 (4), 83 (2), 98-9 (A-J); CORBIS: (RF) tortilla p41, Richard Gross p6 (F), Randy Faris p6 (G), Jose Luis Pelaez, Inc. p44, Images.com p47, Kristi J.Black p69 (1), Vittoriano Rastelli p69 (2), Inge Yspeert p72 (2) and 126, Tim Graham pp6 (E), 29, Jose Fuste Raga p94 (1), Zuma p94 (2), Claudio Edinger p104 (C), (RF) p104 (B), Richard Clune p26 (2); Karl Weatherly p6 (B), Owen Franklen p25, Torleif Svensson p12 (1), Michelle Chaplow p12 (2), Bettmann p74 (D), Marco Cristofori p130 (E), Felix Ordonez/Reuters p130 (F); TOPFOTO.CO.UK: The Image Works Rob Crandall/The Image works/Topfoto p55 (1), David Frazier/The Image works/Topfoto p55 (6), Jeff Greenberg/The Image works/Topfoto p3 (bottom), Bob Daemmrich/The Image works/Topfoto pp32, 20; ALAMY: Ace Stock Limited p41 (b/g), ImageState p26 (1), Jacky Chapman/Janine Wiedel p53, Visual Arts Library p74 (E), Brian Seed p74 (B), TNT Magazine pp87, 130 (A), Malcolm Freeman p105 (F), Doifel Videla p110 (2), Janine Wiedel Photolibrary.p115 (2), MeaCreations p91 (2), Brand X pictures p91 (1), John Stark p77 (b/g), Foodfolio p38, Michelle Chaplow p37, Stock Image p130 (D), Motoring Picture Library pp 68 (H), 126 (E), Stockbyte Silver pp68 (E), 126 (C); EMPICS: p104 (A); World pictures p3 (Guggenheim museum); BUBBLES Photo Library: Loisjoy Thurstun p99; Spanish National Tourist Office: p130 (B);

Elizabeth Murphy: p40; Travel-shotspictures: p68 (1); Michael Calvert: pp68 (A, C, G, I), 76 (2), 126 (A, G, H, I); akg-images London: p82 (all); Ronald Grant Archive: p80; Bilderbox.com: p110 (1); Stock image/Pixland: p116; Ditta U. Krebs/Fotostock Mallorca/Photographers Direct: p12 (3); Tomeu Ozonas/Photographers Direct: p34 (1).

Photodisk 31 (NT) p105 (E); Photodisk 67 (NT) pp20 and 115 (1); Photodisk 83 (NT) p65 (b/g); Ryan McVay/Photodisk 76 (NT) p130 (C); Digital Vision TT (NT) p48; Digital Vision 7 (NT) p105 (D); Corel 377 (NT) p59 (b/g); Corel 436 (NT) pp68 (D), 126 (F); Corel 578 (NT) p6 (C); Corel 540 (NT) p23 (1); Corel 562 (NT) p95 (b/g); Corel 564 (NT) p27 (2); Corel 786 (NT) p23 (b/g); Corel 799 (NT) p95 (1); Corel 411 (NT) p74 (C); Corel 564 (NT) p74 (A); Corel 596 (NT) p79; Image 100 EE (NT) p51 (3).